T0323067

Probably Nothing

Also by Lauren Bravo

Preloved

Lauren Bravo

Probably Nothing

SIMON &
SCHUSTER

London · New York · Sydney · Toronto · New Delhi

First published in Great Britain by Simon & Schuster UK Ltd, 2024

1 3 5 7 9 10 8 6 4 2

Simon & Schuster UK Ltd
1st Floor
222 Gray's Inn Road
London WC1X 8HB

Simon & Schuster: Celebrating 100 Years of Publishing in 2024

Simon & Schuster Australia, Sydney
Simon & Schuster India, New Delhi

www.simonandschuster.co.uk
www.simonandschuster.com.au
www.simonandschuster.co.in

A CIP catalogue record for this book is available from the British Library

Hardback ISBN: 978-1-3985-1069-2
eBook ISBN: 978-1-3985-1071-5
Audio ISBN: 978-1-3985-2510-8

Lyrics on p.292 from 'Stop the Cavalry' by Jona Lewie.
© Universal Music Publishing Group.

Typeset in Bembo by M Rules
Printed and Bound in the UK using 100% Renewable
Electricity at CPI Group (UK) Ltd

For Cora,
who is definitely something

'She is a poor Honey – the sort of woman who gives me the idea of being determined never to be well – & who likes her spasms & nervousness & the consequence they give her, better than anything else.'

JANE AUSTEN,
Letters

PART ONE

1

A pleasant human male

Bryony knew it wasn't going anywhere with Ed the minute she arrived for their fifth date to find him drinking a protein shake.

'Have you just been to the gym?' she asked as he moved in to greet her.

'No?' he replied. He looked down reflexively, to see if perhaps there were surprise abs showing through his t-shirt.

'I meant the Whey-to-Gain?' She nudged it with her knuckle, as though it might be contagious.

'Oh.' Ed laughed, without any hint of embarrassment. 'Nope, just hungry.'

'So you bought a protein shake? And drank it in a bar?'

He shrugged, smiling, as though wanting to be included in a joke he didn't quite understand. 'Nice and filling, isn't it?'

She chastely kissed the cheek she knew would be pressed against hers and panting in less than two hours. It smelled of not-quite salted caramel.

'Funny,' she replied, 'they say the same about food.'

'Date' was a generous term for it. A quaint attempt to rebrand their series of lacklustre rendezvous and sporadic hook-ups as something more promising, less vague than what it really was: a thing. Not even quite a fling.

A thing she hadn't bothered to tell anyone about, beyond her flat-mate Marco, who liked to know her whereabouts for safety purposes and acted wounded if she so much as neglected to fill him in on a smear test. Marco called Ed 'The Egg Man', 'because he looks like John Lennon without the hair'.

Bryony called Ed only when drunk.

She had been 'seeing' Ed for three and a half months, technically. But they'd only met four times before tonight. Four drinks dates – early evening, increasingly perfunctory – during which he'd mainly recounted the plots of prestige TV shows on streaming platforms she didn't have, without offering to lend her his logins. She'd mainly told him long anecdotes about friends he hadn't met, which were never as funny in the retelling. Bryony would often script-edit these interactions later in her head.

Four late-night meals – bar snacks, burgers, pizza, burritos, each a reward for making it far enough into a drinks date that they could pretend dinner, as a concept, had only just occurred to them. Food! Hunger! Sustenance! Of course!

Four kisses, initiated coyly then consummated hungrily, relishing the adolescent thrill of snogging a near-stranger in public in your thirties, letting them cup your arse against the illuminated KFC poster at the bus stop while a gaggle of teens look on.

Four decent shags. Actually, six (and a half), which had been impressive given the burritos.

Four mildly awkward doorstep goodbyes – two in darkness, two in daylight – and four polite, postcoital deployments of the winky-face emoji.

But in between: dead air. They'd had conflicting holidays, then clashing plans. A slightly-too-long reply lag on both sides. A few too many ambiguous message exchanges, which held flashes of heat and promise but never quite got off the ground.

She suspected the main problem was not lack of commitment to each other, but rather to the noble art of flinging itself. Neither of them was enamoured enough to bother turning this into real romance, nor were they bold, or cynical, or self-assured enough to ditch all pretence of dating and call it what it was: no-strings sex. So, they were going through the motions. Gamely performing the dance of twenty-first century courtship, just slightly out of step with each other. Hoping sooner or later that things would click into place and suddenly – maybe? – boom! Fireworks.

It wasn't the way it happened in films. But, Bryony reasoned, it was the way it often did in real life. Wasn't it? Relationships started off lukewarm and heated up slowly, like soup.

You heard about it all the time; it was the realists' favourite fairytale. Couples who had little in common would roll over one morning and suddenly see the universe in each other's sleep-crusted eyes. Couples who barely *liked* each other at first would joke about it in their wedding speeches. There were rewards for perseverance, for sticking with it, for jollying along and putting the work in. For being a grounded modern woman who didn't expect a Disney prince with a perfect vinyl collection, but could instead learn to love a pleasant human male who said 'expresso' and clapped when the aeroplane landed.

And Ed *was* a pleasant human male, was the thing. 'Choose someone kind!' yelled the discourse. The discourse was obsessed with kind – people called their one-year-olds 'kind' in Instagram posts – and he'd passed the preliminary tests. He was nice to hospitality staff. He wore a condom without being asked. He spoke warmly of his late grandmother, said 'bless you' when Bryony sneezed. Curious in conversation, generous in bed. He was the kind of person who said, 'sorry, you go on,' any time your speech even slightly overlapped, which, personally, Bryony hated because it made the chat so stilted and formal – but she supposed it was a good mark against his character in society's great ledger. Pleasant. *Kind.*

She might not have slept with him at all, except that on their first date, he had quoted *Seinfeld* with an easy familiarity not commonly found in men with bare ankles. She'd quoted it back, and they had laughed. He had toyed with a strand of her hair and told her she had 'an Elaine Benes energy' – and after that it had seemed impossible not to sleep with him.

Nostalgia had become their most comfortable footing, which was enjoyable but didn't seem right for a brand-new relationship. One time they had made up a game to fill the fourteen-minute wait for an overground train, naming nineties kids' TV shows for every letter of the alphabet. *Animorphs, Bodger & Badger, Chucklevision* and so on. It had been almost adorable, until the awareness that they were doing an adorable thing – like a couple in a film! – hit her and killed it dead before they reached *Live & Kicking*. One time he got panicky when a wasp flew near them, which she found deeply unattractive but tried to reframe as cute.

Much of the time she'd spent with Ed had been like this; reaching a little too hard for things to be attracted to, straining to see a spark before it fizzled out or revealed itself to be a trick of the light. Grasping for potential between them was like trying to catch a bar of soap in the bath.

They had met on a dating app, naturally. It was called Alloi, and its overkeen graduate marketing team had run so far with the metallurgy theme that Bryony had found herself awarded 'copper' status within weeks and felt compelled to keep swiping and messaging until she turned gold. Bryony was a perfectionist overachiever – one of her greatest sources of shame.

Ed, as far as she could tell, was not a perfectionist nor an overachiever. For one thing, he lived in Acton. She struggled to reframe *this* as anything but poor life choices. For another, his favourite crisps were ready salted.

'Remarkable,' said Marco, when she announced this, the two of them breakfasting amid the pigeon shit on the balcony of their Walthamstow ex-council.

'That's just it,' she told him. 'He is *un*remarkable. There is so very little to remark upon.'

The protein shake was, at least, noteworthy, but it had finally nudged Bryony's ick-o-meter into the red zone. On the great ledger there were now one too many points in the 'cons' column.

Her mind was made up as she sat down opposite Ed. As she drank two glasses of wine and pushed herself, smiling like a pageant queen, through the motions of flirty conversation. As she kissed him across the sticky table, and again on the street, as she allowed his hand to wander up her skirt in the Uber back to his, and as she – may as well, fuck it, decent wasn't nothing – gasped her appreciation into his pillow one last time.

As she gathered up her things, made excuses about an early morning meeting and left him looking puppyish and proud in his doorway, she was resolved. No more Ed. No more waiting around for the lukewarm soup to heat up. She would be the grown-up who had the guts to end it – which, as a perfectionist overachiever, was a conversation Bryony knew she would perform well but find agonising.

Things were made significantly easier on this score the next day, when she received a phone call telling her that Ed had died.

2

A toast

Kelly has established a new ritual. Every time her period arrives, she gets drunk.

It isn't a *sophisticated* ritual, but she does it with style. She does it with old fashioneds. Has been to the fancy deli near work and bought a bottle of Angostura bitters specially, asking for it over the counter, its crinkled paper wrapping making her feel like a flapper girl buying something illicit from the drugstore.

She begins dreaming about that first sip from the moment the cramps set in, but only when the blood appears does she walk to the mahogany dresser in the dining room (ugly – it had been Leo's grandmother's, dumped rather than bestowed on them by his mother, who made no attempt to hide her distaste for Kelly's thick grey carpet and tonal scatter cushions), slide back the glass doors and take out the crystal tumblers that had been a wedding present from an obnoxious aunt (his, always his). The aunt had groped her at the reception, praising her childbearing hips.

She mixes the cocktail with precision – the first one, anyway. Whisky. Sugar. A few dashes of the bitters, their scarlet ink staining the liquid in a way that feels brutally apt. And orange peel, which she will smell on her fingers all of the following day.

As she takes her first sip she thinks about that aunt and forces herself to laugh about the fact her gift is being used to toast Kelly's still-empty womb. Then she swigs, purposefully, enjoying the sweet sting in her throat in lieu of tears. Perhaps next month she will go the whole hog and crack out a soft blue cheese, take a bath so hot it turns her skin raw and mottled. Light a secret cigarette in the garden and let it swirl through her body, leaving her nauseous in precisely the wrong kind of way.

Leo doesn't join in with this ritual. But he will walk past from time to time as she nurses her glass at the table, or on the sofa, or on the bedroom floor, and he will sweep the hair away from her temple, and kiss it and mutter, 'I'm sorry.'

3

A remarkable man

'I'm sorry, he's passed what?'

'Away,' repeated the voice on the other end of the phone. 'He's passed away.'

The voice sounded uncertain itself. Hesitant, as though reading from a script it had never seen before. Bryony hesitated too. Nobody had given her lines.

'He's left us,' the voice (male) tried again. Then, because she still hadn't spoken: 'Passed on. Um, deceased?'

'Y-yes, thank you—' she replied, before he launched into the full Monty Python parrot sketch. 'I— ... wow. Oh god. Oh my god. I'm sorry ... I can't quite ...'

She was standing in the queue at Sheifale, a new restaurant attracting rave reviews for its tahini-drenched sharing plates, and contempt for its stubborn no-booking policy. Bryony was always the person who volunteered to stake out a table.

She didn't have a big social group, but rather a galaxy of individual friends who didn't know, or didn't particularly like, each other. She was required to have brunch or dinner with each of them separately on a regular basis, which was fine, but exhausting. Any attempts to combine her friends for efficiency's sake had always failed, leaving Bryony feeling like a six-year-old trying to smoosh her Barbies together to make them kiss.

Tonight she was meeting Noémie, a Parisian in pharmaceutical PR and one of her most exacting friends. Soho thrummed around her, the noise of a thousand work weeks being washed down with pavement beers. And on the other end of her phone, a voice was telling her that Ed was dead.

Bryony's first thought was, should she leave the queue?

It seemed disrespectful not to. Sociopathic, even. To hold out for sesame-crusted Brussels sprouts while there was death on the table.

But then, what was there to be achieved by leaving it? Really? She'd been here twenty-five minutes already, was only another – she glanced up to check – twenty minutes away from the front, at most. And she would need to eat dinner anyway, wouldn't she? Her stomach growled in the affirmative.

So what difference did it make if she ate it here or in the Five Guys by the station? If anything, Sheifale, with all its dim lighting and charred vegetables, had the more funereal air. Yes, she reasoned, this made sense. This was fine. Probably? Fine. She could weep discreetly in a corner, while Noémie patted her hand and paid for the wine.

'I'm so sorry, I know this must be a massive shock,' the voice said now.

Bryony stammered out another thanks. Ahead of her, she could see a server handing out pillowy flatbread and little paper pots of hummus to the waiting hordes.

'Take your time,' said the voice.

But there is only so much time a person can reasonably take on a phone call with a stranger, especially under the imminent threat of free dip. So after a pause of a few seconds – *was that enough? How long was she supposed to need?* – she asked the question she always needed answered when somebody died, whether it was a long-forgotten celebrity or a man who had been inside her less than twenty-four hours earlier.

'How did it happen? I mean, if it's okay to ask.'

Bryony's mind leapt immediately to the bar snacks they'd both eaten the night before. Buffalo wings, padron peppers and pallid halloumi fries. Salmonella usually took about eight hours to present itself, but Listeriosis could take days, even weeks to kick in. What about Campylobacter? She mentally scrolled the NHS webpage from memory, sweat pricking at her temples. Was that definitely hunger gurgling in her gut just now, or—?

'Wasp sting,' came the reply. 'Anaph-phylax-tic shock.' He stumbled over the word, then added clarification. 'He was really fucking allergic.'

Bryony relaxed a little as the voice went on.

'But you probably knew that, right? Always was ... few bad reactions when we were kids, swelled up like the red Teletubby ... supposed to take an epi-pen everywhere ... still is – was – well, I'm, sure you know – but didn't have it on him today, the stupid pillock ...'

She concluded that the voice was not an undertaker, nor a medical professional.

'S'pose he'd got relaxed about it in recent years, it'd been so long since it had happened ... and nobody expects wasps on the first of October, do they?' The voice caught a little on this last part. 'Fucking climate change,' it said, on a shaky exhale.

'Terrible,' she murmured in assent.

The server had reached her in the queue now. She took a piece of flatbread but wordlessly waved on the hummus. The least she could do in the circumstances.

'Happened this morning on his run – dog walker found him collapsed and wheezing in the park but by the time they got him to the hospital it was ... y'know. Too late. Just like that.' The voice coughed gruffly. 'Gone.'

'I'm so sorr—' she began, but the voice cut across her with a more forceful wave of emotion.

'Bryony, I am *so* sorry. I can't even imagine ... I mean, I loved him too, 'course I did. But – well, please just let me say: I know what you guys had was special. He talked about you all the time.'

This was confusing. If the voice hadn't just used her name she might have trilled, 'Whoops! Wrong number!'

Instead she said, 'Did he?'

'Course. Absolutely smitten. I'm just gutted we never got those drinks in the diary while we had the chance. Never saw him as happy as he has been since meeting you, honest to god.'

Bryony's stomach lurched as though she'd missed a step on the stairs, or several. Her head felt swimmy. She made a few noises; noises that she hoped sounded like strong, but unspecified, sentiment.

Absolutely smitten?

'I told his mum I'd be the one to break it to you, Bryony, I hope that's okay – she would have called herself of course, but she's in a right state truth be told, I think they've had to give her a sedative or something ... well, you know Ann!'

She did not know Ann.

'And his family are all in total shock, of course ...'

'Of course,' she said.

The queue had moved up considerably in the past five minutes. Bryony panicked a little, wondering what would happen if she got to the front of the line before getting to the end of the phone call. She nibbled, silently, on a corner of flatbread. It was good. Smoky. Her appetite returned.

'... but they wanted me to apologize that it's taken all day to let you know. Everyone feels bad about it – you should never have been left in the dark for this long, obviously, it's just the hospital took a while to trace them and get him identified, they're so understaffed, sounded like total chaos to be honest – not that it's their fault obviously, NHS cuts, fucking Tories . . .'

'Fucking Tories,' she echoed.

'. . . and then we had to go pick up his phone and find your number, and it's all been . . . well, you can imagine. Obviously they'll be reaching out to you themselves, really soon – Ann said you should go straight to their house if you don't want to be alone tonight, Leo can pick you up from the station. But then Annie thought that might be too overwhelming for you, and you'll have Marco for company tonight, won't you?'

This must be how it felt to wake up from a coma and find out there was a new Prime Minister.

Leo . . . Annie . . . was Annie different to Ann or were they the same person? Bryony racked her brain frantically for details on Ed's family. Siblings? Two, she recalled dimly. Where did they live? Norfolk, was it – or Northumberland? He must have mentioned during one of those perfunctory drinks or polite, post-coital breakfasts. And *Marco*. The familiar name sounded alien in the context. How did this man know who Marco was?

'Yes, I'll have Marco,' she replied firmly, determined to grasp what little control she could of the conversation. 'I think it probably would be, ah . . . a little overwhelming – not tonight – but thank you, thank you so much to . . . um, Ann, and of course please send her my—'

'Oh, you'll have plenty of time to tell her. Obviously they want you to be involved, really involved, take a big role in planning the funeral and everything. Don't you worry.'

Bryony worried. A rogue crumb of flatbread went down the wrong way and she began spluttering into the phone, eyes streaming.

'It's okay Bryony, let it all out,' the voice said gently, interpreting her gasping and retching as an outpouring of grief. 'I'm so very sorry for your loss. He'll be really, really missed. By me and, well, everyone who ever knew him. Ed was,' the voice was thick with tears again, searching for the perfect word, 'a remarkable man.'

'Yes,' she rasped in agreement. 'He was.'

Noémie's halo of soft curls appeared in the distance, then Noémie beneath it, waving and looking cheerful – as well she might, for Bryony was now at the front of the queue. The scent of burnt spices crept out of the restaurant door, enwreathing her head like incense.

'Bryony, I'm so sorry to do this but I'd better go, I've offered to phone a load more people as I'm the only one who seems to be able to hold it together. Just!' The voice cracked again. 'But look, do you have someone with you right now?' he asked. 'Will you be okay?'

Noémie was at her side now, quizzical, widening her eyes and eating the rest of the flatbread. Bryony grimaced at her and motioned an apology.

'Yes, I have a friend with me,' she replied. Her voice was still hoarse from the choking, which sounded appropriate. 'I'll be okay. I mean, not *okay*,' she added hurriedly. 'Obviously I'm absolutely . . . you know . . .' she grasped for something poetic, romantic, profound, and landed instead on the truth. 'I just don't know what to say.'

'Of course, mate. Of course, you poor thing, it's been a big shock. I can't believe it myself, honestly can't believe it's true. Fucking surreal. I'll let you go for now, but you've got my number so just call me any time, any time at all. I mean it. We're all here for you.'

'I really appreciate it,' she replied, and in the moment she really did appreciate it. Just before the voice hung up, she asked: 'Who are you, by the way?'

'Oh! Sorry, just assumed you knew. Didn't I say? It's Steve.'

'Steve,' she repeated. There was an expectant pause.

'Ed's best mate? From school?' said the voice. '*Steve*-Steve.' As though this cleared it up.

'Ah, of course. Steve!' she said, because it seemed rude not to.

'Just two?' asked the hostess on the door, far louder than was necessary.

'What's that?' said Steve, as Noémie charged in hungrily ahead of her.

'Just too, too awful,' Bryony replied, hiccupping softly.

'Look after yourself,' he told her.

'I will,' she said. 'And you.'

4

A moot point

'You were not into him though, were you?' shrugged Noémie, chewing on an olive stone. So far there had been minimal hand patting. 'You do not seem sad.'

Bryony, who had a drama A-level, felt mildly insulted.

'I mean . . . I suppose I'm in shock? I must be,' she told her. 'It's terrible, terrible news.' Noémie frowned. Bryony added a third for good measure. 'Terrible.'

'You have never even mentioned this "Ed". I never saw him on your socials.'

'Well,' she paused and scooped up a dollop of garlicky yoghurt. Her earlier wooziness was beginning to subside now she was eating. 'We were . . . low-key.'

'So it was just sex?'

'No! No.'

'So you actually liked him?'

'Sure!'

'Sure?'

Bryony shoved a confit potato in her mouth, whole. Noémie watched her chew, one eyebrow arched in Gallic incredulity.

'Well, it's a moot point now,' she said once she'd eventually swallowed. 'He's dead.'

Back at home, Bryony tried to cry.

She whimpered, screwing her eyes up tight and gurning in approximation of heartbreak. Nothing. She relaxed her facial muscles, let her mouth hang open, willing her tear ducts to fill and spill elegantly down her cheeks. She faced herself in the mirror and affected a shudder, letting out great big noisy gulps of grief. But after a few minutes of this, all that happened was that she'd swallowed so much air, she belched. It tasted of garlic.

Bryony was usually a slutty crier. She cried at adverts and at radio dedications, at nostalgic playlists and elderly men fumbling for change in the supermarket. She cried any time she thought about the 2012 Olympics. She regularly cried reading about the deaths of strangers on the internet, their ages inversely proportional to the volume of her sobs.

But not now. For Ed, perfectly pleasant Ed, who had made her come and made her a cup of tea afterwards, she couldn't muster so much as one tear.

Perhaps if she put on a song that reminded her of him? But the only songs that reminded her of Ed were 'I Am The Walrus' – naturally – and 'Freed From Desire', because it had been playing on Kiss FM during one of their taxi rides home and he had sung along, believing the lyrics to be 'he's got his trombone knees'. If she played that now, would it be moving? Or deranged?

She opened her phone and read their last message exchange.

Ed: 'That was fun ☺'

Bryony: 'Yes! Great times.'

Ed: 'Get home safe x'

Bryony: 'Will do x'

Ed, an hour later: 'did you by any chance take my Airpods by mistake?'

Bryony: 'Um no, soz! Didn't see them.'

Ed: 'Ah ok no worries must have left them somewhere.'

Bryony: 👍

This achieved nothing, except to make a small and sinister part of her wish she had, in fact, taken his Airpods.

She scrolled back further, through weeks of stilted contact, telling herself, *He is dead. He is dead now. He cannot 'do it again sometime x', because he is dead.*

After a while she gave up, reached for her laptop instead and googled 'anaphylaxis'. She scrolled and clicked for twenty minutes, taking in the same information, phrased slightly differently each time, via the NHS and WebMD and Healthline.com and the Cleveland Clinic. Why did the Cleveland Clinic always rank so highly? What was happening in Cleveland that gave them such SEO clout? As a rule, Bryony trusted the NHS most implicitly, but preferred the American pages for colour, drama and lurid detail.

She googled 'can you become allergic wasps later life'. The answers were inconclusive but erred towards 'yes'. She read about venom immunotherapy, and googled 'can you have immunotherapy as precaution'. This mainly returned results about cancer treatment, so she spent a further twenty minutes reading about cancer.

Bryony had been like this for decades. Every flu-like symptom had been suspected Toxic Shock Syndrome, since the first time she read the leaflet in a tampon box.

Visits to the doctor invariably brought normal test results and all the usual questions about whether she ate breakfast, or whether she might be stressed at work. Was she sleeping well? Drinking enough water? Bryony always drank enough water; chugging back gallons of it from a series of increasingly hi-tech vessels. Her urine was always nearly colourless, like the palest vinho verde, and of this she was inordinately proud.

Eventually, she heard Marco come home. She walked into the kitchen to find him wearing his scrubs with a knitted tank top over them, whistling to himself while putting potato waffles in the toaster.

'The Egg Man is dead,' she told him.

'*What?* Seriously?'

'Wasp sting. This morning. He was allergic. And now he's dead.'

'Oh my god.'

'I know.'

'How old was he?'

'Thirty-three,' she told him.

'The same as Jesus.'

And just like that, Marco began to cry.

5

The present time

Kelly's job sometimes makes her feel like the most powerful woman in the postcode. Or the most useless, depending on the day.

It's true that being a receptionist in a GP's surgery isn't as glamourous as being a Mayfair members' club hostess or clipboard bitch on the VIP area at The Ideal Home Show – both jobs she has held in her time – but while the clientele are without doubt more depressing, they're also more grateful. Doling out a last-minute appointment to some limping, wincing hopeful can feel like handing them the keys to the sun.

Then there are the other times. The times when they lean over the counter towards her, spittle flying and sour breath steaming up the perspex screen, demanding that there must be something she can do – *must be* – and Kelly is forced to repeat her rote scripted apologies and nod towards the sign taped to the counter, reminding them that staff are working extremely hard 'at the present time' and that abuse will not be tolerated.

'The present time' is a helpfully vague phrase, suggesting a mere temporary blip, while the curling corners and yellowing tape at the edges of the sign reveal that the temporary blip has been going on for at least half a decade. The present time probably won't be ending any time soon. Kelly sometimes thinks they should etch it in brass.

Mostly, her job is a cross between nightclub bouncer and riddling sphinx. She's obliged to send people off into a labyrinth of 'alternative treatment routes', via centralized call centres, pharmacy visits, patronizing webpages and online questionnaires with the nuance of a Cosmo quiz; the whole process designed in the hope that people will either get bored or get better before reaching the end.

Only the truly strong of nerve and gammy of leg make it to a face-to-face doctor's appointment. By this point, Kelly has become so familiar with the trajectory of their symptoms that she almost wants to cheer as they shuffle out of plastic-chaired purgatory and through the waiting room doors. Her brave contenders. Her champs.

Then there are the chancers, who believe that if they turn up and sit there for long enough, Kelly will take pity and make an exception. The ones who say 'I'll wait,' with a wink, believing it to be some kind of secret passcode that will slide back a false wall to reveal a bonus doctor. These regulars are generally more pleasant than they were at the Mayfair members' club (some even try to slip her cash tips), but they are not without their quirks.

Kelly gives them private nicknames. There's Phlegmma Thompson, a well-spoken retiree who treats her recurring bronchitis like public performance art. Dave the Grave, who responds to every offered appointment date with 'I'll be dead by then,' and has done for the past seven years. Captain Beefheart, who has angina and smells of Bovril. Alfred Itch Cock; self-explanatory. And Monica Munchausen, worst of the local hypochondriacs, who pops in or calls the appointment line once a fortnight on average and peppers her conversation with, 'I read this thing on healthline dot com'. Monica has cried at the counter more than once, so sure is she that she must be on the brink of imminent demise. Her only diagnosis to date has been a UTI.

Usually Kelly feels defensive, even fond, of this motley crew. They feel as much like her colleagues as the coffee-breathed GPs and conveyor belt of wan, overworked nurses. But not today – today, she is resentful. Today she finds their ailments trivial, their ruddy noses and hacking coughs an obnoxious display of vitality.

When one woman implies that Kelly isn't being as helpful as she might be ('Fucking state of this fucking country, serve you right if I die right here on your piss-stained floor'), Kelly glances pointedly down at the sign, hoping it will communicate on her behalf that at the present time her brother-in-law has just died and it feels absurd to be here, helping strangers with their diverticulitis instead of at home with her husband's weeping head in her lap.

At the present time, she is worried she might be a psychopath because her thoughts keep returning not to how upset she is to lose Ed, who was a sweet guy, a lovely guy, but how she will prop up a grief-stricken husband for the next however long. Time is tight and this wasn't in her plans.

'I'm afraid the first appointment we have is two weeks on Wednesday,' she says, and the woman kicks a chair, which goes skidding halfway across the waiting room and collides with somebody's wheelie shopping bag, and Kelly says thank you, next please, how can I help.

The most powerful woman in the postcode. Or the most useless, depending on the day.

6

Personal reasons

'So, the oddest thing,' Bryony began over breakfast with Marco the next morning, 'they – his family, his friends – all seem to be under the impression that me and Ed—'

'Egg Man was called Ed? Ed the Egg Man?'

'Yes.'

'Go on.'

'. . . that we were madly in love. Or at least, *involved*. Seriously. In a relationship.'

'Why would they think that?' Marco asked, spraying pastry flakes across the table. He had got up early to go out and buy croissants, which never usually happened unless it was her birthday or the day after a general election. Bryony would have been touched if the gesture were born more out of sympathy than out of Marco's need to turn every trauma into an excuse for festive brunching.

'I don't know! Because he told them we were, I assume?'

She thought back to what *Steve*-Steve had said last night.

'He said Ed was the happiest he'd ever seen him since he'd been with me.'

'Well,' said Marco, 'that could just be coincidence.'

'He said they want me to be "heavily involved" in the funeral.'

'Oh. Oh no.'

They stared at each other, visions manifesting between them – of Bryony in a black veil and lace gloves, demurely thanking mourners for coming. Bryony delivering a clumsy eulogy; Bryony dropping the coffin.

'What the fuck do I do? I can't turn up to meet his devastated family and say, "Sorry for your loss but just to clarify, your son was a casual shag and I was about to ghost him."'

'And now he's beaten you to it. The ghosting.'

'That isn't funny.'

'It wasn't meant to be funny. It was meant to be respectfully acerbic,' said Marco, reaching for his tomato juice. Bryony had drawn the line at full Bloody Marys, out of respect.

'Look, calm down. We don't know he actually told anyone anything. His friend might just have been laying it on thick out of politeness. You know what it's like when someone dies; everyone gets a relationship upgrade. People you did shots with once in a club eight years ago become treasured friends, "wiv the angles now" etcetera.'

Bryony considered this.

'I once told his grieving widow that my Great Uncle Ron was "one of my greatest role models", when I'd only met the man once and he had mustard on his crotch,' Marco added.

'Maybe you're right.'

'Of course I'm right,' he said. 'I bet none of his family even know who you are.'

'Bryony! Oh it's surreal to finally get to speak to you. I feel like I'm talking to a celebrity.'

It wasn't the kind of phone call she usually received at her desk on a Monday morning, though she preferred it purely for not being about budget projections. After five years in local government, any illusions Bryony had once held about jobs 'in politics' being sexy or adrenalized had long been put to bed.

She stammered out some gracious thanks, not unlike a celebrity.

'It's Annie. Oh god, Bryony, I don't even know what to say. Isn't all just complete shit? I'm a mess.'

The woman on the phone sounded young, or younger than her anyway, with a flutey, sing-song voice better suited to kid's TV than bereavement admin.

It was complete shit, Bryony agreed, trying to sound as messy as possible herself. She gave a long, filibustering sigh, then felt she should add: 'I've heard so much about you too.'

'Oh have you? Oh that's so sweet. All good I hope!' said Annie. 'Of course he's such a family boy, is Ed – *was* Ed, oh god I keep doing that ... oh god!' her voice swelled with emotion. 'It's so awful. But that's why it's so weird we never got to meet you, before! We kept begging him to bring you up for one of Ann's Sunday salons –a stupid name for a bog standard roast, except she does always try to stir up a philosophical debate along with the gravy – but I know you're often busy Sundays aren't you, with your classes ...'

Annie spoke fast, on the in-breaths as well as the out ones. Conviviality kept bursting through her grief, then she would catch herself and attempt to slow her voice to a solemn whisper.

'God, I wish I had your discipline, I'm lucky if I put trousers on most weekends. Ed always calls me Stig of the Dump. Called. Oh god. Oh Ed! Sorry, I'm off again.'

Bryony made her best comforting noises, telling Annie to let it all out, that she didn't need to apologize. *Classes?* She dimly recalled making up an early spin class as an excuse to get Ed out of the flat one Sunday morning, when she'd wanted to go back to bed with a mixing bowl of Coco Pops and a new season of *Below Deck*.

'Anyway, shut up, Annie,' Annie scolded herself. 'I didn't want to bombard you when I know you must be in bits as well, I can't even imagine ... so cruel. Fuck this universe. But anyway, Ann – *Mum* – wanted me to ask you to come up to the house tomorrow, so we can finally meet you and talk through all the plans for the- the- well, you know.' She coughed the word out like a fur ball. 'Funeral. And whatever.'

'Oh, how nice!' Bryony said, then hastily corrected herself. 'I mean, not *nice*. But thank you, that would be ... good. I've been, ah, so keen to meet you all. Did you say tomorrow?'

'I mean, if you're free? Don't worry if you have plans or anything, obviously.'

There was a hint of challenge in Annie's voice. What kind of ice-hearted monster would keep plans three days after their boyfriend's death? On a Tuesday?

'No, no, of course I don't!' she insisted, making a mental note to cancel a post-work threading appointment. 'I'd love to come. I mean, not *love*, obviously, but—'

'Good.' Annie sounded relieved to have completed her mission. 'We'll see you at noon-ish, ok?'

Bryony had assumed she meant the evening – but of course, only an ice-hearted monster would be going to work under these circumstances.

'Noon sounds great,' she said. She should probably send herself home sick this afternoon in that case, lay the ground work. *Personal reasons.* She could get into bed, watch a film, have some soup. 'I don't know if I have the *exact* address, could you send it to me?'

'Will do. Wait! You can't drive, can you?'

Annie said this tenderly, as though it must be due to a medical condition. Bryony confirmed that she couldn't.

'In that case just text me your train and someone will pick you up from the station,' she said.

'Lovely. Thanks so much. I mean, not lovel—'

'We'll see you tomorrow then. I'm sorry in advance if it's awful. It will probably be awful,' said Annie, sounding almost cheerful again.

'I'm so looking forward to meeting you,' said Bryony, because she wasn't sure what else to say. Then, realizing with a yelp, just as Annie was about to end the call:

'Sorry, remind me – which station?'

7

Powering through
and soldiering on

Everyone is pregnant. Absolutely everyone. Five expectant mums have waddled through the waiting room this morning alone. Friends are pregnant, colleagues are pregnant, cats are pregnant – even the autumn hedgerows are heavy with fruit, the trees lousy with conkers. All around her, swollen bellies bob up like lurid sea buoys in their stretchy yoga tops. At the supermarket, at the pub. Hovering level with her eye line in the hairdresser's chair.

Kelly hasn't noticed before now that they live in a place peopled exclusively by procreators; where coffee shops are no-go zones without an infant as visa, either somersaulting inside you, wailing in arms, or grizzling over a babyccino.

Is it bad, she wonders, for a person who wants a child so badly to feel irritated by every single one that she sees? What does it mean that last week she had a dream that she was running up and down Orford Road with a giant pin, bursting pregnant bellies like balloons – *pop! pop! pop!* – like something off a nineties late-night gameshow?

She never tells Leo any of this. Although the fact of their trying is well established – ten months, now, which puts them in an awkward holding pen, not being long enough to qualify as 'issues' but long enough to start getting worried – she prefers to maintain the illusion that she's going to be fine about it either way. *Que será será.* Leo has always been proud of his wife for her straightforward nature, her unflappability, her chill, and she isn't about to ruin her reputation in the lads' group by becoming a baby-mad mess.

Besides, Leo is the mess now and a couple can only have one at a time. He has been in sweatpants for two weeks, watching all the most depressing televised sports with the curtains shut. Formula One, snooker, horse racing.

Kelly had ideas about the kind of wife she would be in the face of family tragedy and has only discovered what they are by falling short of them. She thought she'd be unfailingly patient, she realizes as she snaps at Leo for forgetting to put the bins out. She thought her empathy would override all pre-existing arguments. She assumed she would draw on a bottomless well of love and self-sacrifice, strengthening their bond as they work through the pain. But now that the initial shock and tears have subsided, all of their interactions have taken on the tone of tight-jawed actors in a retro sitcom. Would you like tea darling? Yes thank you darling. I say, the sun is out, shall we go for a walk? No thank you darling, perhaps later. Yes of course darling, whatever you like. Shall we shower today? No thank you darling, perhaps later.

Sometimes she sits and watches the TV with him, holding his hand and staring at the screen until the cars or balls or horses all blur into an ambient mush. Is this supportive? Is this what he needs? Sometimes she invents a spurious reason to pop out – they need milk, they need petrol, they need badger traps, he isn't listening – just to sit somewhere on her own for an hour and let her facial muscles drop into a neutral arrangement.

It is on one of these especially low days, scrolling the Outnet sale while trying not to notice she is the only woman in the room not cradling a bump or disinfecting a Sophie the Giraffe, that Kelly gets a notification. Her sister-in-law has tagged her in an Instagram post.

'Are you well?', it reads in flouncy cursive, bright green on a dusky pink background.

They're innocuous words. Almost invisible words; just the ambient white noise of social convention. Who would ever answer anything but yes? You're not really meant to answer at all, she has learned this.

Kelly looks at the words again, blinking on her phone. Annie's post is a video for something called 'Gel Lyfe'. It seems to be a kind of health supplement, though it could as easily be a religious sect or a Center Parcs advert – lots of clear-skinned women laughing at nothing, running through tall trees, hugging. The post is captioned with green heart emojis and sits on a thick thatch of hashtags. *#gelibility #mentalhealth #smallbusinessowner #adaptogenius #womensupporting-women #aloealoe #success.*

Is she well?

Kelly rarely takes a sick day. She grew up with the kind of mother who thought anything less than viral meningitis was a pisstake, who believed nobody in the world had ever actually had flu. She would pack them off to school on a paracetamol even as they were still rolling the glass down their arm. To Kelly's mother, illness had been an embarrassment; a sign of mental weakness, poor personal hygiene and probably hanging around with the 'wrong sort of lads'. Even as she was dying of cancer a decade earlier, she had seemed less sad about leaving the world behind, more aggrieved at it ruining her holiday plans.

As a result, Kelly has spent her life powering through and soldiering on. Clubbing with streaming colds, date nights with diarrhoea. Taking every winter virus to work with her, covering up a chapped nose with industrial strength concealer. The fact she now works as a GP's receptionist isn't ironic so much as appropriate.

She books in with her own clinic for smears only. 'They do my fanny, everything else looks after itself,' she has said on more than one occasion. And generally, her body got the memo. Until now.

Is she *well*? The hollowed-out shape of that word. It's an empty vessel you can pour anything into and draw anything out of. 'You look well!' is a dreaded phrase because everyone knows it's code for 'you've filled out around the face!'. Clients at the cosmetology clinic a few doors down pay thousands to have their buccal fat sucked out to avoid the compliment. They're jostling for space on a waiting list to look less well.

Is she well *in herself*? She feels well out of herself most of the time at the moment, did even before Ed died. Tracking the monthly machinations of her body like a trainspotter or an astronomy buff, writing it all down in a nerdy little notebook. Waiting for the star that never falls.

Is she well? She must be, she owns five pairs of Sweaty Betty leggings. Her hair shines. She knows how to call a solitary salmon fillet and a logpile of asparagus 'dinner'. There is a rose quartz face roller in her fridge. Of course she's well.

Well. She's fine – and that's all anyone can really aspire to.

Kelly likes the post, to be polite.

8

Just the best bloke

Bryony had no idea who was coming to pick her up.

Thanks to a lengthy consultation at the ticket office she had some idea of where she was – Little Buckton, Northamptonshire, and crucially *not* Long Buckton, Northumberland – but Annie had only replied with a thumbs-up emoji when she'd texted her ETA, and it seemed crass to demand a name or reg plate as though waiting for an Uber driver. Leaving the tiny station, pruning a bouquet of M&S flowers that had got crushed on the journey, she prayed it would be Annie herself. Less painful to make small talk with someone she'd already done Big Talk with.

It had still felt like summer back in London, but a thick autumnal fog had descended somewhere just north of Milton Keynes, and for a few moments she couldn't see anyone or anything beyond the suggestion of distant fields and the glowing logo of a nearby Aldi. Then, out of the mist, a tiny red Fiat Punto appeared and screeched to a halt a few feet away.

Out of it climbed a tall, broad man – a giant bear of a man, in fact, in comical contrast to his car. He was dressed in tracksuit bottoms, trainers and a baggy fisherman's sweater, with a rumpled hair and beard situation that brought to mind those old iron filing pictures made by dragging a magnet across plastic.

'Bryony? Steve,' he said, smiling wanly – and now the voice had a face.

Steve gave her a little salute as she approached, which Bryony took to mean they were not required to hug. Then he jogged round to gallantly open the passenger door for her. She wondered if this were part of some extended rich-widow-and-devoted-chauffeur roleplay, or if Steve was merely nice.

'I'm so sorry,' she said, as they pulled out of the station car park. She'd been determined to get the words in before him this time, to make sure his (actual) loss took precedence over her own (largely fictional).

'Thanks Bryony,' he said, gruffly. 'Still can't quite get my head round it, y'know? I know it's the biggest cliché in the book, but it's like – one minute he's there like always, sending memes, hosting his curry nights and smashing it with his fantasy team, and the next he's . . . he's . . . up in the sky and he doesn't even know that Salah scored as his captain on Saturday.'

Steve slammed a hand against the dashboard, and let out a small hiccupping noise.

'Five-two,' he added, softly.

She reassured him that it wasn't a cliché at all, and that she understood. She tried not to feel slighted by the fact Ed had never made her a curry.

'Anyway, Bryony, sorry, the last thing you need is me wanging on about him when you're struggling just as much as I am, Bryony,' he said, clearing his throat. Steve seemed to be a heavy namer, one of those people who slips your name into every couple of sentences to make you feel special. Bryony usually enjoyed this. But every time Steve did it, she felt like a fraud.

'Not at all,' she told him. 'I mean, it's really nice hearing about him.' *Feel free to tell me much, much more about him,* she wanted to add. *I'll make notes.* 'I know you guys had been friends for . . .' she took a wild punt here '. . . ages.'

'Ever since Buckton Juniors. Ethel always knocked for me in the mornings. Ann used to pack him an extra Gold bar for me because she knew they were my favourite and my mum only gave me tangerines. But Ethel usually gave me his as well. Just the best bloke.'

Something twisted itself in her stomach at this detail. He had, she recalled, always let her eat the last halloumi fry.

'I love Gold bars,' she said. 'I haven't thought about them in ages.'

He nodded in solemn approval. 'An underrated classic.'

Her stomach lurched again, this time as he took a sharp bend in one of the country lanes, and Bryony wished she'd remembered her travel sickness bands for the journey. A hot wave of nausea rose in her throat.

'You alright?'

Steve glanced over at her, watched her trying to thumb her own pressure point.

'I'm fine! Totally fine, I just get a bit . . ah, queasy on car journeys.'

'Shall I put the air con on, would that help?'

She shook her head, gingerly. 'Thanks but that aggravates my sinuses.'

'Right.' Steve slowed the car to a speed just above mockery. Bryony tried to deflect.

'Why do you call him Ethel?'

She hoped the answer might be more nuanced than nineties playground homophobia. But Steve looked bemused, as though perhaps she was stupid.

'It's short for his name, isn't it?'

'Edward?' she asked, trying to make the connection. Maybe she *was* stupid.

'Ha!' Steve blasted out a single, trumpeting laugh, and the car stalled. 'He never told you? I can't believe he never told you.'

She bristled a little, embarrassed on behalf of the devoted partner she was supposed to be. 'Clearly he didn't.'

'Ed wasn't short for Edward, mate. His name was *Ethelred*.'

'No!' she slapped her own hand on the dashboard, forgetting herself for a moment. '*Ethelred*?'

'You heard. Ethelred Slingsby.'

'Ethelred, as in . . . *the Unready*?'

Steve nodded, eyes back on the road. After a few seconds he said, softly again: 'Ironic, when you think about it.'

They both fell silent, watching grey mackerel clouds knitting together over the fields beyond. Yes, she agreed, after another pause. Painfully ironic.

Finally they pulled up outside a house – or what seemed to be two and a half houses, held together by optimism and cement.

The central kernel was a chocolate box cottage, with leaded windows and ivy climbing up its ancient stone facade, but the majority of the building looked like it had been added sometime during the eighties, with boxy pebble dashed extensions built at odd, jutting angles. Overall, the impression was that one house had eaten and half-digested the other.

A much newer extension in glass and black steel was also visible beyond one of the gable ends, but this had a series of blue tarpaulins thrown over it in a way that suggested not so much a temporary pause in construction, as abandonment dating back years. A hanging basket swung from the tarpaulin. A jack-o-lantern grinned gruesomely within.

'Here we are. The Burrow,' said Steve, unfolding himself from the tiny car and stretching his neck with an audible crack.

Bryony took a deep breath and started towards the front door, which had a sign next to it that read, somewhat improbably for a landlocked county, 'Harbour House'. Steve was already disappearing through a side gate. She hurried after him and found him at another door with a wooden porch over it and a heap of wellies, Crocs, Dr. Martens and battered trainers in front of it.

'They never use their front one,' he told her, in a tone that suggested nobody normal ever would. Then he opened the door without knocking – apparently they didn't lock it either – and with no further warning, Bryony was launched into the middle of Ed's family's kitchen.

It was a large, low-ceilinged room with a vast scrubbed-pine table in the centre of it. The interiors were as muddled as the exterior, with a blanket-strewn sofa and armchair, chequerboard linoleum on the floor, tiles in varying shades of seventies fawn and mustard, and brightly-painted MDF cupboards giving the whole place the municipal feel of a church hall. In one corner was a fridge laden with magnets holding photos, holiday postcards, newspaper clippings, coupons, leaflets and letters from the council. A fat, elderly-looking black spaniel held court on the sofa.

On the table were boxes and boxes of Mr Kipling cakes, a milk bottle, a gin bottle, a colony of mismatched mugs, a toolbox, a stack of newspapers, numerous bunches of flowers displayed mostly in pint glasses, a large box of tissues and a ceramic fruit bowl filled with rubber bands, blister packs of pills and one solitary, withered satsuma. And around the table were people – hundreds of them, it felt like, though it couldn't be more than a dozen – who had all just stopped talking and turned to stare at the newcomer in their midst.

Bryony opened her mouth to say something. What would she say? God knew.

But before she could get a word out, a voice yelped 'Bryony!' and suddenly she was blinded by a hedge of grey curls, her breath being squeezed resolutely out of her by a woman several inches shorter but many times stronger than she was.

Bryony hugged back as best she could. After half a minute or so, she became aware of a dampness seeping through her sweater. Tears, she assumed and hoped. She closed her eyes because it felt rude to start looking around the room during this tender moment, but the effect was disorientating. She half-opened one eye and it landed on Steve, who was helping himself to a cherry Bakewell. He saw her and winked.

Finally, the woman released her and stepped back. She was wearing a quilted gilet and a long purple skirt that seemed to be both knitted and tie-dyed at the same time. Holding Bryony at arm's length by the shoulders, she gulped and wailed: 'My daughter-in-law that never will be.'

Then, after an appraising glance, 'You're prettier than your pictures. I'm glad you grew the fringe out.'

So this was Ann.

9

In the cloud

It was odd that Ed had never told her about his family. Or perhaps he'd tried and she'd steered the conversation in a different direction, as she tended to do. But if asked to put money on it, she would have guessed that the Ed she'd known had grown up in a neat suburban semi-detached with a neat suburban family; probably an only child or the younger of two interchangeable brothers, with a proud mother who went to Zumba and a monosyllabic father who wouldn't let people eat in his car. She would never have imagined this casual, sprawling chaos – even in the depths of grief, the room had the air of a Boxing Day knees-up – and certainly not the woman at the centre of it all.

Ann introduced everybody as though Bryony ought already to know who they were. She was still weeping and so the roll call was punctuated by noisy nose-blowing and loud, rattling sniffs.

'This is Lynn and over there is Susan – wave, Susan! – oh, and of course that's Susan's Bob, underneath Twinkle.'

Bryony was at least fairly confident that Twinkle was the spaniel.

'And there's Steve, but of course you know Steve, and cousin Chloe is just in the loo, and her Bob is the one vaping out of the window there . . .'

It was hard to tell whether this was simply Ann's style or if she really did expect Bryony to have memorized the family tree.

'. . . and that's Annie, my youngest.'

Ann gestured towards a birdlike girl in a miniskirt and a giant, hairy cardigan, sitting with her legs slung over the side of an arm-chair. 'Oh Bryony!' the girl cried, leaping up to hug her too. On closer inspection, she didn't look much younger than Bryony after all, though she did have what Bryony privately thought of as 'Gen Z hair'.

'Here's Leo – Leo, darling, look, it's the famous Bryony.'

Leo, presumably the brother, was tall and stubbled and – she felt treacherous thinking it, but the fact was undeniable – a more attractive version of Ed. He pulled her wordlessly into a fierce hug, warm and solid, like being swaddled in a weighted blanket. He held her there for a fraction too long, but the famous Bryony struggled to mind.

'And this is Emmett, my second husband.'

Ann said it as though perhaps a third and fourth husband might materialize any minute from the pantry. Emmett was extremely tall, a rangy scarecrow in a sweater vest, with small wire-rimmed glasses and a thatch of wild grey hair that complemented his wife's. He loped over when prompted and shook Bryony firmly by the hand.

'Dreadful, dreadful,' he muttered, then loped off again.

Everyone else in the room continued looking at her, the dog included, and for a terrible moment she thought they might expect her to make a speech.

She and Marco had rehearsed scenarios the night before. They had practised facial expressions, workshopped the most sensitive and appropriate lines of dialogue, discussed at precisely which point – if any – she ought to try to cry. He'd relished the chance to inhabit the grief-stricken mother, his performance becoming hammier with each take until Bryony felt compelled to remind him that it wasn't a regional Chekov. Somebody's son had actually died.

'It's part of my process,' Marco had sulked. 'We take it big, so we can strip it back again.'

'You're a vet,' she'd reminded him.

'We're all just animals, Brian.' Marco said this a lot.

But now that she was here, standing in the midst of Ed's family's grief, with its mess and noise and dog hair and ambiguous relations, it didn't look anything like the way she'd scripted it.

Ann ordered her to sit down and accept a cup of tea, which she did. She offered snacks, water, wine, ice; a cushion for the back of her chair; a cardigan in case she was cold. Bryony refused everything instinctively and Ann replied each time with 'Are you sure, ducks?'. This aggressive hospitality threw her for a loop. Surely everyone should be fetching water and cushions for Ann? Finally Bryony managed to hand over her own flowers, which Ann received with the grace of a minor royal on a walkabout.

'Dahlias! How unusual! We heard you had fabulous taste.'

Bryony smiled and said nothing. It would be crass, in the circumstances, to disagree.

Then, as if somebody had pressed 'play' on a paused film, the room re-animated around her. Multiple conversational threads were picked back up at once, and she caught snatches from different corners of the room. All seemed related to Ed's death, though most more logistical than emotional. 'Same ones we used for Nana, but the prices have rocketed.' 'These London parks, you get all sorts.' 'Remember the time he . . . ?' 'If there's one thing I've always said about him . . .'

The dog tip-tapped back and forth between them all like an invigilator.

'. . . organ donations.' 'At the hospital?' 'No at the church, the pipes have rust.'

For a few blessed minutes it seemed as though no one expected Bryony to say anything at all. But then, just as she'd helped herself to an especially gooey French fancy, Ann suddenly leaned forward and clasped Bryony's hand in hers. She could feel the icing becoming adhesive between their fingers.

'Bryony, love. We were hoping you might choose something to read. At the funeral. It'll be two weeks on Wednesday.'

'At the . . .? Oh, wow. Yes. Of course. I mean – I'm really not a very good public speaker . . .' She tried to protest, but Ann only gripped tighter.

'Nobody's going to be scoring you, love.'

'No, no. Of course.' Bryony felt instantly sick. She gulped down a bite of cake, which threatened to reappear. 'I'd be honoured. I'll look for something that really does him justice.' She reached for one of her pre-prepared lines. 'I just wanted to say, Ann, Ed was a wonderful, wond—'

'Unless you'd rather write something yourself, of course?' said Ann. She had large, round, amber-ringed eyes which gave her the look of a bush baby. 'We know how creative you are, Ethy told us all about your many projects.'

Bryony racked her brain for evidence of her many projects, or indeed any projects. All she could come up with was the time she'd cancelled a drink with Ed because she needed to make a papier-mâché aubergine for a hen weekend. There was a dirty limerick she'd written for Marco's birthday on their fridge, maybe he'd interpreted that as a poetic bent?

'It's entirely up to you! I know it's a lot of pressure when your mind is in pieces – you might prefer to stick with something safe, one of the classics.' Ann squeezed her hand in reassurance, then added: 'But of course it is so hard to really do a person justice with some stuffy old dead poet's words from hundreds of years ago, isn't it? And grief can unlock such wonderful reservoirs of creativity – so if you felt *able* to come up with something that really immortalizes our Ethelred, really captures his spirit . . .'

She trailed off and reached for a tissue with her free hand, though her eyes looked dry and it seemed more out of habit than anything. Ann held it to her nose and closed her eyes for a few seconds. 'Whatever you choose, my love, I know it will be what he would have wanted. You've seen sides of him that the rest of us can only imagine.'

Bryony cleared her throat, desperately trying to shift the mental image of a side of Ed that his family definitely wouldn't – she hoped to God – have seen. She grasped desperately for more respectful memories. Sweet memories. Fully-clothed memories.

'I'd be honoured, Ann,' she told her. 'I'll certainly do my best to find the right words.'

Ann smiled bravely, released Bryony's sticky hand and wiped her own discreetly on the tissue. 'Whatever you feel moved to contribute. Now, have another cake, they won't keep.'

'Have you asked her about the photos?' said Annie, as Bryony obliged.

'Oh yes,' replied Ann. 'We're hoping to put together a slideshow of photos of Ethelred, for the funeral—'

'Like in *Love Actually*,' added Annie.

Susan piped up. 'Brian Gleeson's dead wife.'

'*Brendan* Gleeson,' corrected Ann.

'Liam Neeson,' corrected Annie.

'We thought you must have some nice ones, Bryony? Nice recent ones.' They all looked at her expectantly. Her phone was in front of her on the table, as it usually was. She wished it had a pin, so she could pull it out and hurl it through the window like a grenade.

'Of course!' she said, brightly, forcing down a mouthful of fondant. 'What a lovely idea.'

Bryony had no nice recent photos of Ed. They'd never taken a selfie together, never felt compelled to snap pictures across the table in a bar. The only photo she possessed of him, she knew without even checking, was a photo of his back retreating into the bathroom in a towel, sent to Marco with the caption, 'so I found out where all his hair went.'

Ann was still looking towards her phone, and Bryony realized they were expecting to see photos now. *Here's Ed at the zoo. Here's Ed at the beach. Here's Ed on date night, wearing a shirt and smiling at a steak.*

She stammered. 'I don't actually have any photos on my phone anymore, they're all in ... the cloud. You know, for security. But I'll send you a nice selection.'

As she'd hoped, Ann and Susan glazed over at the mention of the cloud and asked no further questions. Even Annie nodded respectfully. *For security.* It was almost funny, when you thought about it, Ed being stored in the cloud(s). Should she make that joke? Probably not.

Instead, she said, 'I wanted to tell you, Ann – well, all of you – what a kind, considerate and wonderful man he was. You should be very proud, I know he'll be greatly missed.'

She held off on speculating about his proximity to the 'angles'.

'Thank you, pet. That means a lot,' said Ann. 'We've had so many lovely messages already, it's been quite overwhelming. And I'm sure you must be in the same boat, I know how fond he was of your friends and vice versa.'

'Uhhh yes, completely,' she busked, remembering Marco's tears. 'All of my friends who knew him are just devastated.'

'And what about your family, dear?' Ann's tone was casual but her expression territorial. 'Had Ethy spent much time with your parents?'

'No, he never met them,' she told Ann, and Ann looked pleased. 'I mean, he hadn't *yet*. Of course they wanted to. And he was hoping to, very ... ah, soon.'

'And are you all very close?'

Back to the lies, then.

'Yes.'

Bryony thought of her family in much the same way she thought of her appendix – which is to say, she was glad she had one, albeit useless, knew roughly where it could be located in case of emergency, and considered every year that passed without it rupturing a success.

Her mother had died when she was ten and a stepmother ushered in to fill the vacancy three years later. Whether Kath and her father had ever been madly, or even reasonably, in love was a question lost in the mists of childhood grief and teen self-absorption, but these days she considered them divorced in all but paperwork and postcode. They had separate bedrooms, separate routines and almost entirely separate channels of contact with Bryony – save for the handful of times a year she was obliged to journey down to the South London/Kent borders to sit stiffly around the too-large dining table, forking a too-small portion of salmon en croute into her mouth and fending off pointed questions about her love life, her living arrangements, her underwhelming career. They never came to visit her.

Her father phoned semi-regularly, usually on Sunday nights, which gave their relationship the flavour of unfinished homework and reluctant goings-over with the nit comb. And her stepmother occasionally texted, in messages formatted like letters, with line breaks . . .

Hi Bryony,

How are you? Weather down here disappointing but had nice trip to McArthurGlen with Linda.

Roadworks on high street finally finished thank god.

Hope that presentation went okay.

Kath

She could never remember the presentation she was referring to, or who Linda was, but the attention to detail felt just warm enough to pass for parental love.

There was also Tim, Kath's son, who was two years her senior and had come along at a time – she thirteen, he fifteen – when they were too old to do any real growing up together but too young to forge a friendly adult bond. Tim now lived in Brussels for work, had a disproportionately beautiful fiancé called Clementine and conducted their entire sibling relationship through emoji reactions to Bryony's Instagram posts. Tim was fine. They were all fine.

But Ann didn't seem like a woman for whom a fine family would be good enough. And given the circumstances, she didn't want to look ungrateful. Tim might never remember her birthday, but at least he was still alive.

'We're pretty close,' she told her. 'At least, ah . . . geographically. But I know you have such a tight-knit family. Ed told me so much about you all, I feel like I know you already.' This was a stretch. 'It must be a real comfort at a time like this.'

Ann nodded as though the family's tight-knitted-ness was a widely acknowledged fact. To demonstrate, she reached out behind her and grabbed the nearest limb, which belonged to her daughter walking past. Annie stopped, draped her arms around her mother's neck and sweetly kissed her temple. Ann stroked her hair and gave a watery smile.

'You're right, Bryony,' she said, as Susan's Bob announced that the dog had just been sick in the downstairs loo ('Mainly pink icing'). 'We must never take family for granted.'

10

A tributary

'And can I ask what this is regarding?'

It has been policy to ask this question for years, but people still invariably look scandalized, as though Kelly has asked them to drop their trousers in the waiting room and cough.

She tries to ask it as casually as possible. She's careful to keep her voice even and disinterested, her eyes focused on her computer screen rather than scanning them for unsightly growths. She used to attempt a jolly, matronly tone, the kind of 'I've seen it all before!' attitude beloved of bra-fitters the world over – but from Kelly, it always came across as oddly flirtatious. Alfred Itch Cock had looked mildly alarmed; Dave the Grave far too pleased. So she switched back to dully bureaucratic. When in doubt, no frills. That's what people want from the National Health Service.

'Um,' says the man in front of her. His eyes shift from side to side and he stalls for time with a symphony of noisy throat-clearing. He's middle-aged and wearing a wedding ring, which means this visit is probably the result of months – even years – of gentle nagging.

'That's sexist,' Leo had said when she'd made this observation over dinner one night. Kelly had protested. It wasn't sexist, it was *statistics*. Married men have longer life expectancies than single ones, and this was why. Someone to police their vitals and book their colonoscopies, to pay attention to their ageing bodies beyond receding hairlines and erectile dysfunction. She'd be doing it for Leo before long.

'Is it your throat?' she asks the man. He shakes his head. 'Ahem. No. Ahegghm. It's about my . . . pee—'

'Nis?' she finishes for him, helpfully.

Kelly has always struggled with her directness. Or rather, others have. 'You're quite a straight-talker, aren't you Kelly?' has been a line used in more than one performance review, and never as praise. She resents the way the phrase itself is a coded way to say 'stop being a gobby mare, we don't like it.' Talking, apparently, is not supposed to be straight, but full of twists and kinks and deception, everyone dancing around the point like a Regency ballroom. She has never understood this, and finds it tiring. Life is too short not to say what you mean, not to ask the question you want answered. Life is too short, full stop.

'No! Christ no! My *pee*,' the man repeats, angrily, then pauses. 'Well, I suppose technically you *could* say . . . I mean, that's the, ah, vessel, isn't it. But it's more about my . . . my *bladder*.' He looks pleased to be back on firm, anatomical ground. Kelly nods, encouragingly.

'It's just taking a while to, y'know . . .'

'No?'

'Get going.'

'Ah.' Kelly types 'Instagram.com' into her search bar, scrolls a little through her feed. The man shifts nervously from foot to foot, clearly assuming she is about to hand him a pamphlet with the words 'So You Have Cancer' on the front. She smiles reassuringly at him, and checks her notifications.

Forty-six new likes, eighteen comments on the tribute to Ed; a photo of him at their wedding, looking happy and relaxed and relatively handsome in a suit and boutonnière. It was one of the main purposes of professional wedding photos, really – to give you a stash of flattering images of loved ones to share on future birthdays and Father's Days and if they happened to suddenly die.

'Not that I *can't*, ah, get going, eventually – it's just a bit of a . . . well, not so much a *stream* as a . . .'

'Dribble?' asks Kelly.

She moves on to Facebook, which she has barely used for years but keeps ticking over in the way everyone does for events such as this. Condolences are pouring in, mainly because she has tagged Leo – who doesn't use his social media at all, but whose passwords she has saved on all devices – and, in her new role of grief secretary, approved it for him. Most are pretty generic; sorrys and sending loves and ribbons of heart emojis, with the odd proprietary comment ('I was so sad to hear this yesterday when Ann told me personally'), weird agenda ('if the lefties weren't feeding all the wasps because of so-called climate change it might not have happened xxx') or confusing punctuation choice from an older family friend ('Such sad news! I'm heartbroken!!').

'I wouldn't say a *dribble*,' the man replies, seriously. 'What's a word for somewhere between a stream and a trickle?

Kelly thinks back to GCSE Geography. 'A tributary?'

He nods, satisfied with this. 'Yes. Ok. It's a *tributary* of pee. Is that . . . enough?'

'Enough pee?'

'Enough to see the doctor.'

'Oh.' She clicks back onto the appointment programme and checks available slots. 'Two weeks on Thursday, at noon?'

The man looks as though he's about to protest but then appears to think better of it. Perhaps he's just delighted to have the conversation over with.

'Thank you. That will be fine.'

11

Ed's favourite

On the drive back to the station, the sun was making a watery retreat below the trees and everything looked different to the way it had several hours earlier. Annie did the honours this time, driving with the confidence of one who grew up charging down country lanes in the dark from the age of about fifteen. Again, Bryony cursed the forgotten travel bands. She could feel fondant pulsing around her body like amphetamine. Her mouth was dry. Her eyelid twitched. Annie jiggled one knee as she drove, which didn't help.

'It's so lovely to finally meet you, Bryony,' she said, repeating the party line of the afternoon. 'I just wish it didn't have to be like this.' Her voice became thick and she mopped at her face with the sleeve of her hairy cardigan.

'Of course. Me too. It's such a terrible, terrible tragedy.'

She had said this so many times now that it had started sounding less like sincerity and more like the meaningless call of an animal. The lesser-titted hedgerow warbler. The unfeeling imposter bird.

And yet, even as most of her wanted nothing more than to be safely on the train and speeding back towards normality, a part of Bryony had struggled to wrench her away from the Slingsby clan. Even in the grips of grief, they were more fun than her family on

their best days. She'd left with a carrier bag of biscuits 'for the journey', a crocheted blanket she'd idly admired ('take it, take it! I will
be furious if you don't!') and the disorientating sense that in having
casual sex, she'd somehow picked up a new parent.

'Your mum, is she . . . coping ok?' she asked Annie. 'I mean, only
as well as could be expected, of course, I can't imagine how awful
it must be. It's just that she seems . . .'

'Bizarrely fucking fine?' asked Annie. She rolled her eyes as she
checked her rearview mirror and pulled out onto a roundabout.
'That's Ann! She doesn't really do, like, sadness? Not in an ordinary
way. It's either a massive, wailing fit of hysteria or she's making a
whole performance of jollying on and showing everyone how brave
and stoical she is.'

Bryony mentally replayed examples of both, which she'd
witnessed that afternoon. Ann breaking down to the point of hyperventilating over a Simply Red track on the radio that had been 'Ed's
favourite' when he was twelve. Ann asking Steve, who evidently
worked in some kind of ladder-having profession, to take a look at
her blocked guttering 'while you're here'.

'I mean, I'm sure you know what she's like,' added Annie. 'He
must have told you.'

This had been the other party line of the afternoon. *He must have
told you!* From childhood memories to his LinkedIn password ('He
had so many headhunters interested in him,' Ann had said. 'It seems
only polite to let them know'), the unanimous assumption across
the family was that Bryony was familiar with every detail of Ed's
life, and theirs by extension.

Bryony had mostly responded to these comments with a noise
that she hoped communicated 'yes, we told each other everything,'
but also, 'our love transcended details, please don't ask.' It was a kind
of weary half-grunt, half-bleat. She made it again now.

'In the nineties she was one of the Samaritans volunteers who had to work the helpline when Robbie left Take That,' said Annie, swinging the car suddenly and violently around a lycra-clad cyclist. 'She used to play them the Grateful Dead down the phone. Tell them to pull themselves together and go discover some musical heroes that understood the true nature of mortality.'

'Oh my god.'

'Yeah. Parents of weeping eleven-year-olds started phoning to complain. Dad said they'd have to start a second helpline for people who'd been affected by Ann answering the first.'

This felt like as good a prompt as any for Bryony to ask, 'Your dad, is he . . . around?'

'Oh yes,' said Annie. 'I mean, no, not technically – he lives in Wales. On a farm. Has done ever since they split up in 2002. Family legend is that he needed to get away from Ann so badly that he just started walking west and didn't stop until he reached sea. But he's always there, hasn't had a holiday in twenty years, so in that sense I suppose he *feels* around?'

The car lurched as Annie swerved to avoid a ditch. Bryony's stomach lurched as Annie added: 'Didn't you know about the farm? I'm surprised he didn't whisk you off down there. Leo always took his girlfriends there to grope them in a barn full of hay bales.'

Bryony didn't know what to say to this. So she said: 'Emmett, he seems nice though?'

'He thinks antihistamines are an example of woke culture.'

'Ah.'

They fell silent for a few seconds, the knee still jiggling. Bryony fiddled with her hair and looked out of the window, trying to focus on one still object in the glowering sky to calm her stomach. She hoped this would come across as wistful, rather than rude.

It was much harder, she reflected, trying to make 'normal' conversation with Ed's family than it was delivering generic, one-note sympathy. Conversation felt a little like the country road; full of unseen potholes. One wrong move and she could plunge them both into darkness.

'So, how's your . . . work?' she asked vaguely. Annie brightened at this.

'You mean my business?'

'Sure. Yes! How's business? I've heard so much about it.'

'It's actually *great*, thanks for asking, Bryony. Going really well so far. Obviously it's all early days and of course I'm hardly thinking about it right now, not with everything . . .' Annie trailed off, her voice waterlogged again. She coughed. 'But actually, I think he would *want* me to throw myself into building my vision. Don't you?'

Bryony quickly agreed that he would. Annie seemed relieved to hear it.

'I've been reading this amazing e-book,' Annie went on, 'all about taking our struggles in life and harnessing their potential power for, like, professional motivation. It's called *From Rock Bottom to Bottom Line: How to turn your pain into profit*.'

Bryony made the noise.

'Oh, have you read it?' asked Annie.

'No. No, but . . . ah, it rings a bell,' she replied.

'It's incredible. My team leader recommended it and I'd started reading it the day Ed . . . the day it happened, which feels like it was meant to be, I think?'

'Definitely,' said Bryony. She wanted to know what the business was, but couldn't ask because she was already supposed to know. It was probably craft-based, she decided. Annie looked like someone who might sell swearing cross-stitch kits on Etsy.

'So, he told you about Gel Lyfe, did he? Bless him,' Annie said.

'Gel . . . ? Yes, totally. All about the gel,' she busked. 'All about its special . . . properties.'

'Seventy-two all-whole, nature-inspired minerals and adaptogens!' said Annie. 'I never knew he'd been paying so much attention.'

'Oh yes.' She may as well double down, offer a little comfort where she could. 'Ed was very proud of you.' She stumbled, remembering his mother's commitment to his given name. 'I mean, ah, *Ethelred*.'

Annie gave a little snort. 'He didn't make you call him his full name did he? Like, in bed or anything?'

Another wave of nausea broke over Bryony. 'No! God no. Actually, I only found out today that that *was* his full name.'

'Stupid names are the family trademark,' Annie explained. 'She always said it was on account of having such a boring name herself. Ann with no e. Felt it held her back in life.'

'Aren't you named after her, though?' asked Bryony, curiosity overcoming her queasiness.

Annie squeaked with delight. 'Guess.'

'An . . . tonia? Annabel?'

'*Antigone.*'

'Oh. Oh, wow.'

'Yup.' Annie enjoyed this reveal, Bryony could tell. At some point in her life she'd clearly forgiven her mother for the curse of a weird name, grateful for the gift of an easy comedy routine.

'And Leo?'

Annie performed a little drumroll on the steering wheel.

'Galileo.'

Bryony spluttered, then caught herself and adjusted to her grief laugh: a soft, appropriate, nasal chuckle. But Annie was cackling herself and didn't seem to care.

'Kelly only found out when they went to get the marriage license. She was fuming, almost called the whole thing off. Then the ushers sang "Bohemian Rhapsody" at the reception and she nearly had to be sedated. It was a whole thing.'

'Christ.'

Leo and his wife lived near her, it had transpired. This wasn't

surprising to Bryony, because you could travel to the depths of
the Amazonian rainforest and still bump into thirty-somethings
in chore jackets who had recently been priced out of Clapton. But
Ann seemed enchanted by the coincidence. 'Such a shame the four
of you never got together, they're practically round the corner!'
she had said, with a hint of accusation, as though if they'd spent
an evening drinking low-intervention wines in a railway arch, Ed
might still be alive.

Bryony and Leo had agreed what a shame it was, a terrible shame.
Then he'd sat and made small talk about local takeaways while his
mother ruffled his hair and scrubbed at a mark on his sweatshirt with
a damp j-cloth 'before it sets'. She wondered what Kelly was like.

'I can't believe Ed never told you about the names!' Annie went
on, dragging on the joke like it was an oxygen mask. 'What did he
think, that he could hide his driving licence from you *for the rest of
his life?*'

She said it casually, but the implication of these words seemed
to strike them both in different ways. Annie gave another little
whimper and fell quiet.

'I know, it is . . . surprising,' was all Bryony could manage.

They were only a quarter mile from the station now; she'd just
seen a road sign. If she could make it out of the car and back to
London before Annie probed any further, or she vomited fondant
over the dashboard, maybe it would all be fine. She could write a
long, tactful letter explaining the miscommunication, make a big
donation to a wasp sting charity and move on with her life.

Finally Annie spoke again. 'I think . . .' she said, slowly, as though
piecing together something revelatory. Bryony held her breath. 'I
think . . . he must *really* have loved you, Bryony. I mean, to try and
keep you away from us all for as long as possible. In case we scared
you off.'

Bryony made her final noise, somewhere between agreement and asphyxiation, as Annie screeched to a halt in front of the station. She turned to face the passenger seat, red eyes brimming again, and grasped Bryony hard by both arms.

'But now you've met us, you aren't going to be scared off – are you?' said Annie, tightening her grip just a little. Bryony wondered if Annie's tragic namesake wasn't such a bad fit after all.

No, she promised. Of course she wasn't going to be scared off. And as she walked shakily into the station, to discover the waiting room locked and the next London-bound train delayed by twenty-six minutes, Annie's headlights illuminated her every step.

12

Negative energy

'So you don't know if he was actually in love with you? Bite please.'

Bryony bit. 'Nfflghghhumnaffflurg,' she replied through a mouthful of silicone.

'Or if he'd just told everyone he had a girlfriend, when actually he had no feelings for you at all? Leg please.'

She raised a leg, breathing hard through her nose to dull the pain. 'Gnggndthefffigh,' she replied, as her sartorius muscle took a pummelling.

'And you cannot find out, because he is dead? Relax please.'

She spat out the bite guard. 'No, that's the thing,' she said, 'short of finding and reading his diary, I don't know how I'll ever find out. And he definitely wasn't the kind of guy who kept a diary.'

'*Aich*,' said Ewa. 'You carry lots of tension and worry, I can feel.'

'I do,' whimpered Bryony, while Ewa sunk her thumbs into the flesh of her left hip as though it were focaccia dough. 'So much tension and worry. And it's everyone! Not just his mum, which you could understand, especially if you met her – but it's his friends, his sister, the man in the local chip shop – they all know about me. It's so weird. I'm like this legendary figure to them.'

'Be careful Bryony, it is hard to live up to a legend,' said Ewa, sagely. 'Even if the legend is you.'

Ewa was a complementary therapist who had somehow become a friend. This was partly because she had no studio to keep her overheads down and, therefore, worked out of her clients' homes, which fast-tracked intimacy because Bryony felt obliged to keep offering her food and beverages – and partly because, if she was honest, Bryony liked the idea of having a personal healer in her rolodex, the way celebrities did. She occasionally daydreamed about she and Ewa being pictured together on the society pages.

What particular type of therapy Ewa practised was hard to say, because it changed depending on which retreats she'd been on, which books she'd been reading and which ancient practices were deemed 'emerging' that month. The result was an exciting, if erratic, treatment plan that could feature anything from deep tissue massage and acupuncture to cupping, oxygen therapy and once, memorably, a mugwort enema. Today it was the biting.

'Bite harder, to release more negative energy from the jaw,' Ewa instructed, popping what appeared to be a silicone dog toy back between Bryony's teeth. Bryony obliged. It felt good to vent her frustration in a way that didn't require words.

'Complementary to what, exactly? The doctor's hold music?' asked Marco after one especially loud session. 'Or is it compl-*i*-mentary? Does she just tell you your hair looks nice and then whip out her card reader?'

'Ewa would never tell me my hair looks nice,' said Bryony. 'She believes in hard truths, it's part of her approach.'

The hard truth was that she was sceptical about Ewa's talents too, but it would be far too awkward to stop seeing her now. At the end of every session, once she'd finished her complementary refreshments, Ewa would ask when Bryony would like to schedule their next appointment and Bryony had never found a way to not do this.

'I'll check my diary and let you know!' would have worked in the days before iCal, but how was a person with a phone supposed to pretend they needed to circle back? How was a person with a phone supposed to escape anything?

Besides, she did always feel better after their sessions, if only in vague, unquantifiable ways. It was impossible to sort the placebo effect from the genuine improvement, so why bother? Sometimes she wondered if what she needed wasn't alternative therapy, just a lie-down on a special padded table.

'So you will never know if this guy might have been your soul-mate,' Ewa went on, not phrasing it as a question. She placed her elbow squarely in the middle of Bryony's back and left it there, like a threat.

'I'm fairly sure he wasn't. I'd have noticed, wouldn't I?' said Bryony, clenching in anticipation.

'Sometimes we don't notice what is right under our noses,' said Ewa. 'I have this one client who lived for years without noticing she has a wheat intolerance. Years! Just puffed up like a haemorrhoid cushion every time she eat a bagel. Is amazing how people can be so determined to live in denial. In the end we did spelt enema, released all toxins and she is like a whole new woman.'

'I don't know if that's quite the same thing,' said Bryony, who had always suspected she was wheat intolerant but preferred not to know for sure. 'But thank you, I'll give it some thought.'

'All part of the service,' said Ewa. 'I'm going to workshop on bee-venom therapy next week, would you be interested in a trial session? It helps reduce inflammation.'

'Inflammation of what?'

'Whatever is inflamed,' replied Ewa. 'The knee, the liver, the ego. The bees find it. I can give you a discount.'

'I'll pass thank you, but it sounds lovely,' said Bryony, thinking of poor Ed and wondering if bee-venom therapy was disrespectful to the allergy community.

'If you're sure,' said Ewa, suddenly bringing her elbow down with an audible crunch. Bryony screeched on impact, then laughed hysterically as the shock subsided with the pain. 'You see? These muscles prefer to stay in denial, I show them the truth. How does that feel?'

'Much better,' lied Bryony. 'Thank you.'

In truth, she felt as though she'd been drunk for four months, then had woken up and discovered that instead of falling into a skip or something, she'd accidentally slipped, semi-conscious, into a relationship.

During moments alone she'd started mentally retracing her footsteps, combing over every date and interaction with Ed, as far as she could remember them. Searching for clues. At first she looked for clues that he had been more into her than she'd realized (the time he picked a glob of sleep out of her eye and wiped it on his duvet, was that love?). Then, once she'd drained that particular reservoir dry, she started looking for clues that he had been, after all, her soulmate (choosing sex with Ed over a night spent at Noémie's new boyfriend's spoken word show in Deptford, was *that* love?). But she was coming up with nothing.

'What are you thinking about?' Ed had asked one night, the third time, during the postcoital lull. Had actually said those words, like a line from a bad film and Bryony had laughed, assuming he was being ironic. But when she'd looked at his face, sweetly open and expectant, it seemed he genuinely wanted to know. So she had told him.

'Do you ever get railway stations stuck in your head?'

'As in . . . the buildings?'

'No, the names.'

'The names of railway stations?'

'Yes. But a particular one, stuck in your head like an ear worm.'

Ed had thought about this for a second and then said, 'Hayes and Harlington.'

'Mm,' she'd said, approvingly. 'Satisfying. Where is that?'

'I haven't a clue. What's your one?'

'Carshalton Beeches.'

He had nodded and repeated it a few times under his breath until it began to feel like ASMR. '*Carshalton Beeches*. Good one.'

Then they had gone to sleep, because it was two a.m. and Ed had better pillows than her, and for all her cynicism Bryony was still a human woman who believed in the possibility of brunch. But had Ed gone to sleep falling in love with her? Because she got railway stations stuck in her head? Was it really that easy to be a loveable woman, when all evidence in her life thus far suggested otherwise? And if he had, then why hadn't they gone for brunch?

She compared their star signs (Virgo, Pisces – a celestial disaster) and pored over his photos on Alloi (still live – was it her job to get them taken down?), waiting to see if the sight of his face sparked any kind of alchemy in her stomach (no). At one desperate point she looked up an online compatibility test based on their names, the kind she remembered from magazines in her youth. But typing in 'Ethelred' felt so absurd that she wasn't as alarmed by their 87% passion score as she might have been. Bryony and Ethelred 4eva. Madness.

'Did I love him?' she asked Marco one evening. They were eating takeaway in front of a new streaming show, where drag queens gave makeovers to Amish women and then they all went on a cruise.

'Who?'

'Egg Man.'

Marco paused, thought, chewed, swallowed.

'Not as far as I noticed.'

13

Two blue lines

Kelly is wondering how best to seduce her grieving husband.

There are no guides for this – she knows, she's looked it up. No established etiquette as far as she can find. No *Refinery29* round-up of cutest underwear for the recently bereaved. Would it be better if she pretended to actually be in the mood, or just sent him a calendar invite; all business?

It would be better if she didn't also have Covid. An occupational hazard – it's her sixth bout – the virus less novel and more tedious with each snotty comeback.

'Blast from the past!' replies her friend Tariq when she texts to cancel drinks. 'I swear I didn't know it was still a thing.'

She has lost her sense of taste, which she can't help seeing as karmic punishment for how unsympathetic she was when Leo had had it two months ago and his mother had driven over in a hazmat suit to deliver soup that looked like punishment and pond slime, trilling, 'It's time you learned to make this, Kelly – it gets rid of everything!'

'Except mother-in-laws?' Kelly had muttered. The universe had heard her and now, as punishment, it has robbed her of the thing that brings her most pleasure in the world.

Well. One of the things.

The other thing has to be enforced. Because ovulation stops for no virus, and no grief, and nobody's getting any younger. Kelly turned thirty-seven in the small hours of Tuesday, watching two blue lines form on two little sticks; one for swabbing, one for pissing on. She carries the latter to Leo, upright like a birthday candle. A suggestion. He looks at it for a moment, brow furrowed, then says, 'Oh. Right. Yeah, okay.' And so commences the least sexy sex in history.

Is it bad to conceive a baby through such joyless, dutiful coitus? Will it affect the child, psychologically?

Maybe it's better, she thinks. Maybe one day they will tell the kid: Hey, we wanted you so much we had sex while your mum had Covid! She couldn't breathe through her nose! Your dad had to stop in the middle to cry! We didn't enjoy it, but we did it for you. For the pleasure of being your parents.

And if not, at least she can enjoy food again in the less-distant future. Though not, she vows, Ann's soup.

14

Funeral blues

Bryony was having a meltdown. Ten pages deep into a Google search for 'funeral poems obscure short'. Nothing seemed good enough. Nothing seemed fitting.

Or perhaps it was just hard to gauge 'fitting' for a man she'd barely known, except biblically. Even the conversations they'd had – and they *had* had some, she knew that – seemed to have evaporated from her mind.

For her own integrity she vetoed anything that involved grand declarations of everlasting love, warm bodies or the word 'doth'.

For terror's sake she vetoed anything more than twelve lines long and for obvious reasons anything with mention of wasps, wings or 'death's cruel sting'. The collected works of Auden, Larkin, Wordsworth, Dickinson, Donne, Wendy Cope and Rupi Kaur had all been thoroughly ransacked and rejected, as had several dozen speeches from *Doctor Who* and *Grey's Anatomy*, and the poem Miranda read at Mr Big's funeral. She had no idea if Ed had any personal connection to *Charlotte's Web*, *The Velveteen Rabbit*, *Harry Potter* or *Winnie the Pooh*, and didn't feel able to ask. Song lyrics? Was Ed a song lyrics kind of guy? Could she stand up there and slowly recite 'Freed from Desire' and just hope that nobody noticed?

'You'll have to write it yourself, cherub,' declared Marco, appearing in her doorway. 'There was a young fella from Northants / Who made frequent visits to my pants—'

'Shut up! You're not helping!' she shrieked, throwing *The Little Penguin Book Of Sombre Verse* at his head. 'I have to take this seriously. His poor family, Marco – his *Mum*. Everyone is expecting me to be the devastated grieving girlfriend and I can't let them down. I can't let their overriding memory of their beloved son's and brother's and best friend's funeral be some presumptuous bint in a pleather mini reciting the lyrics of the *Birds of a Feather* theme tune. I cannot.'

'Shhh.' Marco pulled her into a hug and stroked her hair gently, a technique she suspected he used for calming skittish animals at work. 'It's going to be fine, Brian. It's all going to be fine.'

'Am I a terrible person?' she muttered into his sweatshirt.

'No.'

'I really think I might be a terrible person.'

'Of course you're not, you're an angel on earth.'

'What if Ann thinks I'm a terrible person?'

'You'd never even heard of Ann a week ago.'

'That's not the point!'

Marco released her and gave her a look. 'With all due respect, Brian, her son just dropped dead. I'm sure she has more important stuff on her plate than your character assessment.'

'So you think I'm being self-absorbed. I *am* a terrible person.'

'Well, so what if you are?' shrugged Marco. 'Terrible people have more fun.'

'That's blondes.'

'God no,' he winced, 'the memory of your egg yolk highlights will never leave me.'

'Stop joking!' she yelped. 'I'm struggling to breathe. My chest has been tight and weird all week. I think maybe *I* might be dying?'

'Self-absorbed, she asks? Never!'

Bryony flopped headfirst into her pillows.

'Look,' he said. 'You are not a terrible person. A terrible person would have said: "Who? Oh, that guy? I'm not his girlfriend, he must have been delusional or a compulsive liar, RIP, byeeee." But you – you're going to tea with his poor grieving mother to keep the whole charade up, at great personal sacrifice ...'

Bryony nodded. 'I did miss Taco Tuesday at work.'

'Because you are a *good* person.'

She nodded again. 'Okay,' she said slowly. 'Okay, I believe you.'

'A good person who is going to read a stale, clichéd poem at a funeral, because that's what everybody does,' said Marco. 'You can be a good fake grieving girlfriend without having to also be a professional poet, Brian. Unless Egg Man told his nearest and dearest you were one of those as well?'

For all she knew, perhaps he had. Bryony cringed at the memory of her *creative projects*.

'But ... maybe I should at least try to write something? Ann did seem to expect it.'

'Have you ever written a poem before? Besides filthy limericks?'

Bryony nodded. 'An acrostic in my Tudor topic book.'

Marco looked doubtful. 'What did T stand for?'

'The ... Tudors.'

'Oh god save us.'

But Bryony was already flipping to a blank page in her work notepad, biro between her teeth. 'I have to try! It's the least I can do.'

'No, the least you can do is turn up.'

She ignored him. 'I just need to find a way of feeling more connected to Ed. I need to find a way of remembering stuff – *anything* – about him from the times we were ... together.'

'Well,' Marco shrugged, 'What made you feel connected to him when he was alive?'

Bryony thought about this. 'Alcohol.'

'There's your answer then.' He was already walking back in the direction of the kitchen, calling over his shoulder as he went. 'Frankly it's absurd you even tried to do this sober.'

He returned a few moments later with a bottle of Absolut and a tumbler.

'Here you go, Hemingway.' Marco placed them in front of her. 'I need my sleep. I'll mark your work in the morning.'

'Oh, and Brian?' he shouted back along the hallway. 'Whatever you do, don't rhyme "Ed" with "bed".'

'Write honestly about how you feel,' said the internet, and so Bryony wrote down: *nauseous*.

After some further bodily interrogation she added: *but also, hungry? Lethargic. Light-headed. Tight chest. Heavy leg. Weird taste in mouth. Heart palpitations, maybe?*

It wasn't the best start, but maybe it could be a high-concept poem. One of her ear canals itched, as they often did – a side effect, self-diagnosed, of chronic sinusitis. She added that to the list.

This wasn't the first time Bryony had made this kind of list; indeed, it was the only signature poetry in her repertoire. Various self-help books over the years had encouraged her to write down the things that ailed her, presumably with the idea she would feel calmer seeing all her worries on a page and realize things weren't that bad after all. But it never worked, because all it did was give Bryony visual evidence, measurable in centimetres, of how soon she would likely be dead.

Sometimes she would go back and cross a symptom off the list – when she realized that the tingling arm was no longer tingling, for example, or the tapeworm had turned out to be undigested spaghetti – but while she was there she would think up at least three new symptoms to add, and so the list never got any shorter.

Persistent pain under rib cage, she wrote now. *Possible gallstones?*

She took another swig of vodka, and winced. There were mixers in the kitchen, but carbonated drinks and fruit juice tended to give her heartburn.

Overactive bladder. She crossed her legs to quell the urge. *Pressure around eyes. Swollen glands. Twitching upper lip.* Then, because un-flinching candour was surely the mark of a true poet: *suspected fungal nail infection (big toe left foot).*

Ed hadn't noticed the toenail, or if he had he'd been too polite to mention. That was Ed, she thought morosely; a polite man, if not a passionate one. Although, she thought about everything his family had said about him; their stories and Steve's stories and the effusive – apparently – way he'd told them all about *her*. Perhaps he had been a passionate man all along and she'd just never noticed?

Bryony read their text exchange again.

No.

But then, was it wrong to write someone off because they weren't a dazzling verbal communicator? Was she being . . . *wordist*? Didn't the uneloquent (ineloquent?) also deserve love?

Besides, who was she to judge? She couldn't even write a poem.

Bryony lifted her glass in another toast to poor dead Ed, drained it, then balled up her list of symptoms with a flourish. She considered burning this, but smoke inhalation was one of her primary cause-of-death fears and she was just sober enough to realize that her breath was probably a fire risk.

She threw the wad of paper into the bin instead, which proved a harder target than expected. Then she stared down a new blank page and began to write.

It wasn't until after she had staggered out of bed the next morning, downed two pints of water and one of Berocca, taken a fistful of supplements, eaten a restorative fried egg sandwich (with kimchi, for the probiotics) and put her bedding in the wash as a displacement exercise, that Bryony found the poem.

She read it once, then again.

She woke up Marco, and they both looked at it for some time.

Eventually he said, 'Well. It's no *Stop All the Clocks*, but you might just get away with it.'

15

Susan's bureau

Kelly is struggling to focus at work, having been added to a WhatsApp group for something called 'Savannah's Sprinkle'. She doesn't know what a sprinkle is but the context clues are a baby emoji, several gift emojis and an emoji of clinking champagne glasses.

'Sav is insisting she only wants a sprinkle instead of a shower this time round, but let's sprinkle her like nobody's ever been sprinkled before!', reads the top message, which is from an unknown number, a photo of a smiling woman with a twisty up-do cut out of a bridesmaid lineup. There follows a link to a gift registry ('only wooden toys in neutral colours please'), a £45 afternoon tea menu at a cafe called Divas Drink Loose Leaf and instructions for a party game involving nappies and jars of korma sauce ('Child-free girlies, get practising, lol!').

Savannah is a friend from drama school who Kelly hasn't seen since her last baby shower, where guests were obliged to pin the umbilical cord on a life-size cutout of a naked infant. Kelly leaves the group.

The first round of babies had been exciting and disorientating in equal measure; as though someone had one day fired a starting gun without warning, when Kelly hadn't finished warming up. She had watched, almost in awe, as their social circle began to swell and multiply, the business of reproduction never seeming less like a magic trick for witnessing it at close range. *That could be us,* she had said to herself each time another tiny, swirly head made its social media debut. *This could be ours,* she had thought each time another brand new shrimp was placed in her arms, weighing both everything and nothing at all.

But the second round of babies simply feels like showing off. Wouldn't it be polite to wait for everyone to have their first turn before joining the queue again? The longer she waits, the more this kind of logic makes sense in Kelly's mind. *Stop being greedy. I only want one.*

Actually this isn't true. Hypothetically, she has always wanted two; Leo, three. Leo believes a family is only a proper family if kids outnumber the grown-ups. If every lasagne must be hacked into uneven portions and every holiday feels like a trip in a clown car. Once he even made noises about having four, just to best his own parents. 'Imagine, Kels! Imagine the noise at Christmas. We'd have to borrow Susan's bureau for extra seating.'

Susan's bureau. Apparently no volume of offspring is enough to move Leo's visions of family life out of his mother's house.

Ann makes no secret of her desire for grandchildren. They are dropped into conversation at virtually every family occasion, these phantom infants, so that Kelly has almost begun to think of them as smug competitive cousins, rather than the children she herself is supposed to be having.

Ann uses the grandchildren as a cover story for her hoarding problem (Kelly considers it a 'hoarding problem', Leo and the others think of it as a charming quirk, or else don't notice it at all. They apparently find it completely normal to go for a pee, watched over by a framed certificate for a one-day first aid course and a dust-covered assortment of Happy Meal toys), proudly hanging onto crap from her own children's youths 'for the future littlies' and frequently coming back from local charity shops with dog-eared board books, matted teddy bears and, once, a highchair. 'I saw it and thought "may as well! I'll need one sooner or later",' she'd announced, scratching some dried-on gloop off the side with her fingernail. Kelly had said nothing, but helped herself to a large slug of Emmett's gooseberry wine.

'She's just excited,' had been Leo's defence later. Every sentence about his mother starts with 'She's just . . .'

She's just protective.

She's just interested.

She's just enthusiastic.

She's just been cautioned for letting the dog piss in Aldi again.

Kelly has often wondered privately whether she would be devastated if Ed or Annie beat them to the punch and had a baby first, or whether in fact it would be a relief to take the pressure off. Maybe she would feel both at once? Kelly used to think of herself as a straightforward person with rational emotions, but she has been feeling a lot more 'both at once' lately. Like the patients at the surgery who, when asked if they've been sleeping too much or too little, simply answer 'yes'.

'Yes,' says the woman at the counter now, and Kelly can't remember the question. 'Five,' the woman adds.

Five . . . fingers? Haemorrhoids? Gold rings? Five will make you get down now?

Kelly types 'five' uselessly into the 'extra information' box on the appointment form.

'Tuesday thirtieth at five-forty p.m.,' she tells the woman, and the woman shuffles off again.

Next up is Desmond, an elderly widower, who is always immaculately dressed year-round in a suit, sweater, tie and fedora. Desmond's wife used to bring him to the surgery regularly 'for a checkin'' and since she died (the irony of nagging wives dying first), he tends to pop in more from habit than ailment. As though the surgery is his pub.

'Alright Desmond?' she greets him, as he steps up and tips his hat gallantly to her.

'Hello my darlin',' he says. 'You keeping well?'

'I have to, Desmond,' she tells him. 'It's in my contract. I'm the advert for good health.'

Desmond chuckles. 'That you are, sweetheart.'

Kelly enjoys a PG flirtation with men old enough to be her grandfather; always has. She likes being told to 'keep out of trouble now,' by the kind of sandpapery old geezer who smells of extra strong mints. She was more than a little disappointed when Leo introduced her to Emmett and he appeared to be made entirely from straw. A psychologist might conclude that Kelly has daddy issues, but that isn't it. She just likes to feel vital, in the other sense of the word.

'What can we do for you today, Desmond?' she asks, and Desmond leans against the counter and clicks his tongue as though deciding which of his many problems to dust off and present her with. Kelly ignores the queue growing twitchy behind him and indulges this skit, cocking her head to one side in rapt anticipation.

'Well . . . let me see. The hip's been botherin' me again since the weather set in . . . but I take my walks and I take my oils and they keep me limber, see?' He mimes pointing an oil can at the offending joint, the way Dorothy revives the Tin Man. 'And I won't be having no replacement, I tell the doctor, no, no, no – because if I needed a replacement, could I still do this?'

Desmond dances, a creaky approximation of The Twist. Kelly applauds. The queue huffs.

'Now, my daughter, she tells me she thinks I'm goin' deaf – get your ears checked, Daddy, she tells me, you can't hear the phone – but I says, maybe it's your mumbling, have you thought of that? The older she gets, the more she mumbles! Don't have children, I tell you lovely girl, nothing but trouble,' he twinkles, clearly not meaning a word. 'But you're far too young for all that anyway, far, far too young. You're still enjoying your life as you should.'

Kelly nods in agreement, happy to buy into this lie for a moment. *Far too young.*

'And then I says to her,' Desmond leans over the counter, building up to his punchline. 'I says to her, anyway, only people who ever call in this day and age are the scam artists, I see it on the news – do you want me to give them all my money before you can get it?'

He wheezes heartily at his own joke, then produces a silk handkerchief from his pocket and wheezes into that for a while longer.

'How's the chest, Desmond?' Kelly asks. He flaps the hanky at his ear for her to repeat herself.

'YOUR CHEST?' she shouts through the screen. Behind him, a toddler screams.

'I'll see the doctor please, darlin',' Desmond rasps when he finally gets his breath back. 'If it's not too much trouble. It's my chest.'

Kelly's heart sinks when Desmond departs and reveals Monica Munchausen behind him in the queue.

Monica begins the interaction the way she always does: sweetly, faux-chummily, asking Kelly how she is without waiting for an answer, peppering their exchange with 'thanks *so* much' and 'amazing, amazing'. Kelly is pretty sure she wouldn't be able to pick her or any of the other surgery staff out of a lineup.

'How can I help?' Kelly cuts across her.

'I wondered if you had anything for . . . today?'

Kelly has to stop herself snorting. It is twelve-fifteen. Monica knows the rules: fastest finger first. Urgent appointments are released at 8am on the dot, radio station-style, to whichever lucky callers manage to dial in first. Statistically you have a better chance of Beyoncé tickets.

'Not today I'm afraid. If you want to gohomeandfillintheon-lineformadoctorwilltakealookandgetintouch with the best course of action for your condition okay?' She says it the way she has perfected over the years, running the words together into one impenetrable exhale – so that only the most determined or desperate will even attempt to cross the barricade. Unfortunately Monica is both of these.

'Please,' she bleats, poshly. 'I always fill in the form and nobody ever gets back to me. I'd really like to see someone today if at all possible.'

'It isn't at all possible, sorry about that,' says Kelly.

Monica pouts and sighs deeply. She has the kind of head-girl energy that tends to make Kelly feel as though she is being scolded for wearing her tie too short. Not *angry,* just *disappointed.*

'I ... well, I'm just ... not quite sure what you want me to do,' she is saying now, still at the counter, a queue of spluttering and whimpering people forming behind her. Monica sighs again, her big hazel eyes beginning to brim. 'It's really *quite* urgent, is the thing. I can't quite believe there's *nothing* you can do for me. Really?'

Kelly sighs too. She isn't a monster.

'Can I ask what it's regarding?'

Monica drags a hand across her temple. 'I just feel *awful,*' she replies, then seeing Kelly's face, quickly elaborates. 'I've been very lightheaded and nauseous. I'm having difficulty sleeping but I also feel really fatigued? My chest feels tight all the time, like I'm not getting enough oxygen in. And there's a sort of lump in my throat that won't,' she gulps twice to illustrate the point, 'go down.'

Kelly opens her mouth but before she can speak, Monica goes on, 'I know what you're going to say, that it sounds like anxiety,' she adopts a gormless voice for the word *anxiety,* as though such a trope couldn't possibly be true, 'but the doctor said last time that if the symptoms got worse, I should come back for tests.'

Kelly can see the queue growing ever longer behind her, several necks craning to find out why they're being delayed. There is a digital check-in screen on the waiting room wall but it hasn't worked since 2019.

'And they *have* got worse, so I really think I ought to have those tests. To be on the safe side.'

She steadies herself on the counter, as if the exertion has left her in danger of toppling over. Which, who knows, maybe it has.

Kelly struggles with those words, 'to be on the safe side.' For all her professional pragmatism, she is still a little scared of the unsafe side. Massive unknowns hover like rainclouds over the waiting room, and she is forever worried that someone might sue her for malpractice, even though her only 'practice' is maintaining the appointment system and sticking the 'COULD IT BE SEPSIS?' poster back up each time it falls down. Mostly she tries to forget the role she plays in people's lives; it is too huge to think about how many times a day she might be the conduit for a just-in-time diagnosis – or not.

Anyway, it isn't the people in her waiting room who are cause for concern, but the people who *aren't*. Those who let their funky moles and embarrassing toilet trips languish at the bottom of their to-do list, or are too busy and stressed to even notice. Her own mother treated screening letters and reminder texts like they were trying to sign her up for a timeshare in Fuengirola. At least the world's Monica Munchausens are trying to get ahead of the game.

'Look, I'll make a note on your file,' Kelly tells her. 'We'll get a doctor to call you as soon as possible for a phone assessment, okay?'

Monica nods, eyes still brimming but now, presumably, with gratitude. 'Thank you, thanks so much.'

'You're welcome, take care,' says Kelly, as Monica finally turns and leaves and the screaming toddler is wheeled up to the counter in her place.

She pulls up Monica's file and adds a new line to the 'Notes' section.

'Patient has seen condition (hypochrondria) worsen; request phone call asap.'

16

That's intense

Bryony met Agnes, her artiest friend, at a film screening in Deptford. Agnes entered her orbit roughly once every three months, when she would message to ask if Bryony was free the next day for some kind of cultural event; a new exhibition or a lecture by someone she'd never heard of on a topic she wasn't aware was even a problem. Bryony would inevitably say yes because she had never worked out how to lie about these things.

The evening would always be fine, the chat pleasant but stilted. Agnes would seem a little bored and distant throughout, but then she would suggest getting a drink as soon as it was over and Bryony would say yes to that too.

'So, are you seeing anyone?'

Bryony always ended up asking this, like a terrible uncle, once the conversational reservoir had run dry. Agnes was usually seeing about five people but rarely did anything as square as label it. She sipped at her Paloma and shrugged.

'There's someone at work I've been hanging out with. They're cute – but, like, a bit low-energy?'

Bryony agreed that this must be a drag.

'I just think I really need to be with another extrovert, you know?' said Agnes, picking up her phone and starting to scroll.

'Mm,' said Bryony. She waited for the question in return but it never came, so she volunteered the information herself. 'I was seeing someone. Super casually. Like, not really a thing at all. But he's turned out to be pretty low-energy too, as it happens.'

'Ugh, such a pain,' said Agnes.

'Yeah. Well, I mean, he's dead.'

A beat passed before Agnes looked up, her eyes wide beneath their blue graphic liner. 'Shit, what? Like, fully dead?'

'Well they're cremating him tomorrow, so I assume so.'

'Wow, fuck. That's intense.'

'It is, quite.'

'What did he die of?'

'Wasp sting.'

'Huh.' Agnes nodded slowly, as though forming an opinion of Ed based on his choice of exit. 'That's wild.'

'Thank you,' said Bryony. 'So yeah, anyway – I've got to go to the funeral, in Northamptonshire. His family think we were in love.'

'You and him?'

'Yeah.'

'Why do they think that?'

'Well, he told them we were. It seems.'

'Oh my god.' Agnes blinked at her. 'So you've been, like, coerced into a relationship by a guy who isn't even alive to participate?'

Bryony considered this fresh new take on the situation. 'I guess so?'

Agnes drained the rest of her drink and shook her head in disbelief. 'Men.'

17

The unconvincing girlfriend

Bryony had managed only through strenuous politeness to avoid riding with the family in the funeral cortège ('I think I'd find it too upsetting,' she insisted, which was entirely true) but no amount of arguing could convince Annie to let her take a taxi from the station on the day.

'There are no taxis,' she kept saying.

'There *must* be taxis,' said Bryony, who tended to believe that if one critiqued the world outside London sternly enough, it would magically change its ways. 'And I can't let you do that, you need to be with your family.'

'I might want the excuse to escape,' said Annie, darkly.

But in the end it was Steve who was waiting outside the station that morning, face baked into the expression of one who is hoping to conquer his own feelings by being of service. He looked sombre and crumpled in a dark suit and skinny tie, the kind suggestive of a youth soundtracked by landfill indie. She could see weary half-moons beneath his eyes. There was a brief, agonising shuffle over whether or not they would hug.

'The roadworks on the high road have ended now, so that makes things easier,' he said, once they had finished patting each other on the forearms.

Bryony remembered, dimly, these kinds of comments from the day of her mother's funeral. People congratulating each other on the weather forecast, the parking facilities, the acoustics in the room – as though they'd been off hosting a village fête while she was babysat by a neighbour. Useless proclamations, that were actually anything but.

'That's great news,' she told him.

The village church was everything one would hope. A dinky grey chapel with stained glass and towering spire, tombstones protruding like wonky teeth from the bumpy churchyard and a lychgate draped prettily in ivy. Bryony could sense the centuries of love and loss, faith, hope and ancestry that must fill its cool stone chambers. Which made it something of a surprise when Steve drove straight past it and on up the hill, eventually pulling into the car park of a squat, seventies-built crematorium that looked a like a leisure centre.

'Oh,' said Bryony. She mentally re-jigged her image of herself as the grieving girlfriend against a backdrop of hessian noticeboards and greige carpet tiles. 'Not the church then?'

'Ann has beef with the vicar,' said Steve. 'Something to do with a Harvest Festival tin mix-up a few years ago. Don't ask me the details but she's boycotted it ever since. And the whole family are raving atheists of course, but it's not like that means anything in the countryside.'

Bryony hadn't been to many funerals. Only one out of four grandparents, two having died before she was deemed old enough, the other still alive and obnoxious in a care home in Eastbourne. There had been a distant great-aunt, an elderly neighbour and a legendary teacher, whose memorial had been treated as a kind of quirky high school reunion, bottles stashed in their handbags for afterwards.

This, she realized, as they climbed out of Steve's car and straightened their clothes like a pair of goth prom dates, would be the first truly *sad* funeral she'd ever been to. The first unequivocal tragedy.

Nobody would be able to use phrases like 'a good age' or 'a peace-ful end', or reflect on Ed's life as though it were a complete story and not a brutally truncated novella. She'd rejected Marco's offer to come along as moral support, in case he made her laugh during proceedings. But she regretted it now.

The messages she'd received on the Slingsby grapevine had been confusingly mixed re: vibe. 'It should be a celebration of life!' Ann had declared at their tea last Tuesday. 'Bright colours, joy, something that really captures his essence.'

Three days later, Annie had texted, 'Mum wants to know if you have any black lace gloves she can borrow to go with her veil?'

Bryony privately reflected that the best dress code to capture Ed's essence would be top-to-toe Superdry. But she'd played it safe with subdued polka dots and a dark pea coat. There was a black beret in her bag that she'd deemed too try-hard on the way here, although, seeing several giant, frothing hats in the distance, perhaps she needn't have worried.

A clutch of guests was already milling around the entrance as they approached; most in black, some in the claret polyester of Northampton Town FC. Only one had gone the whole hog and worn the silky shorts too.

'Right, here we go,' muttered Steve as they approached. 'Will you be okay?' But before she had a chance to reply he'd been swallowed up in a flurry of hugs, handshakes and back-slaps by mourners, sev-eral of whom were already crying.

Bryony hovered behind, her face set in a stiff, blank approximation of grief. She felt similar to the way she had the time Marco took her to an immersive theatre piece, the poster of which said only 'brace yourself!' – except this time, she was the one expected to perform. It was a relief when Annie appeared in the doorway of the chapel, wearing an improbable combination of black leather pencil skirt, black Doc Martens and a handknitted, rainbow patchwork poncho.

'Thank God you're here,' she said, as though she'd been half expecting Bryony to do a bunk. Had that been an option, Bryony wondered? Could she just have said, 'whoops, soz, forgot!'?

But then Annie threw her arms around her and suddenly this felt like the only place in the world she could possibly be.

The anonymous brick room had been decked out with an abundance of houseplants, rather than flowers. It was strangely beautiful. Her throat grew tight.

'Ann's idea,' said Emmett — tweed jacket, baggy corduroys, wellies — nodding to the jungle. 'Rather a horticulturist in his, ah, youth — earned a scout badge for keeping a spider plant alive or some such ... um ...'

'We're going to give them out at the end, like wedding favours,' added Annie. 'Nice right?'

'Very nice,' she croaked. The music playing could only be intentional, because surely there was no way any funeral director would have 'Gangsta's Paradise' on their playlist. Still, it felt oddly moving.

'Here's Leo and Kelly,' said Annie as the couple emerged from behind a huge monstera. Leo was in a well-cut dark suit, crisp shirt and no tie. He pulled her into another embrace, and Bryony didn't mind this one either. Every second she spent being hugged by people was a second that she wasn't baldly exposed in the chill of the chapel, waiting to mess up her part.

Turning to Leo's wife, Bryony was startled to find that she recognised her.

Kelly was beautiful in an Instagrammy kind of way, with eyelash extensions and laminated brows and hair that had been coaxed against nature into bouncing, tubular waves. She was wearing a midi dress with a little pillbox fascinator, the kind of politicians-wife-attends-royal-wedding ensemble that Marco liked to call 'Karen Millinery'. And her face. Her face was eerily familiar, but didn't feel like a former colleague or a friend-of-a-friend's. Bryony found she knew, too, exactly how Kelly's voice, rich and wry with an Essex twang, was going to sound before she heard it.

Was she a minor celebrity? An influencer, maybe? She had the sheeny, plump-cheeked look of a person enjoying many comped 'tweakments'. But no, because Kelly was also – was she imagining it? – looking at Bryony in recognition. And – no, she wasn't imagining it – mild alarm.

'So nice to meet you,' the two women said in unison. They hugged, a little stiffly, because that is what nice women do.

She remembered that Leo and Kelly lived near her, and thought she must recognize her from 'around'. Maybe Kelly was her barista, glammed up outside of work hours? Though that wouldn't explain why Kelly looked so startled by Bryony's presence, except that sometimes Bryony could be quite exacting about the temperature of her foam.

Anyway, it was too late now. There is only a very narrow window in which you can say 'hang on, don't I know you from somewhere?' before it becomes too awkward because you're already invested in the mutual charade of being strangers. Bryony felt the words retreat past her soft palate. She had missed her chance.

But she was saved from any funeral-flavoured small talk by Leo looking at his phone and announcing, 'Right, she's summoned us.' Presently there came a Slingsby exodus, as Ed's siblings, Kelly, Emmett and a few familial hangers-on all left the crematorium to drive back down to the village, climb into the hearses alongside Ann and drive back up again. What Ann had been doing until this point, or why the family hadn't been doing it with her, was unclear. Bryony seized the opportunity to find the toilets and spend a few moments breathing deeply with her face against the cubicle door.

'I just can't get my head around it, can you?' murmured a voice outside by the sinks.

'Dreadful. It isn't right. Poor Ed deserved so much better,' replied another.

For a moment she was convinced they must be talking about her. The unconvincing girlfriend. Until she remembered for the twelve hundredth time that day, that her unconvinced boyfriend was dead.

Ann arrived after everyone else was seated. Flanked by Annie and Emmett, one on each arm, she walked in to hushed whispers and craned necks, her floor-sweeping black skirt and birdcage veil making it feel not unlike the entrance of a bride. Ann nodded graciously at the mourners as she glided down the aisle and settled in her spot on the front pew, the layers of her skirt puffing up around the small woman like a bird taking to its nest. Beneath them, Bryony noticed she was wearing hiking boots.

Then came the coffin.

No amount of knowing you're going to see a coffin at a funeral can prepare you for the moment you actually do. Bryony felt the great riptide of emotion swell through the room before she finally saw it, hoving into her peripheral vision. And then, it was all she could see. Just the coffin, surrounded by fuzzy brown shapes as her eyes began to cloud at the edges. Bryony bit down hard on the insides of her cheeks and sucked a few shallow breaths through her nose. If she were sick right now, into her appropriate black leather handbag, would it be the worst thing in the world? Or would nobody even care, because the worst thing in the world had already happened?

Nobody had told her the running order, and she'd forgotten to pick up one of the orders of service that everyone else was clutching. A photo of Ed in a cagoule, grinning, on a windswept beach. As a result, every new moment of the service brought with it the possibility of her public mortification. Each time the celebrant drew breath, her sphincter tightened.

Opening remarks were made. Ed's verve for life, his compassion for others, his dedication to his family, friends and community. Then a hymn followed by a rendition of 'The Long and Winding Road' accompanied by a bassoonist called Roger, who apparently needed no further context and a kind of prayer that wasn't a prayer because instead of 'Dear Lord' it began 'O, Universe' and nobody said *Amen* at the end. Bryony had never been religious, but she found herself longing for the familiar C of E set menu. You knew where you were with *Amen*.

Before she could dwell on this further, she was summoned.

'Ethelred's loving partner Bryony' – *dear Lord, O Universe* – 'will now read a poem she has written in his honour. Thank you, Bryony.'

Making her way to the front of the chapel, she had the curious sensation of walking on quicksand. Her throat was dry and she clutched her bottle of water to her chest – unchic, yet necessary to stop herself gagging. Bryony reached the lectern and clung gratefully to its sides for support.

Only from here could she fully take in how crowded the room was. Mourners were packed in tightly on the wooden benches, many standing at the back and down the sides of the chapel. There was a wide spectrum of ages, from a pair of solemn-faced primary schoolers in black bow ties and waistcoats, to numerous watery-eyed pensioners, heads nodding in silence, as though to some invisible force more commanding than Bryony. And there were rows and rows of people her own age. Surely far more than would attend Bryony's own funeral, if she were to die tomorrow. Even with all her diligent brunching.

Looking around the room, she felt the truth of the matter pressing down on her shoulders and up against her pounding chest. Ed had been loved.

Not by her, maybe, but by all these people who were waiting for her – and it had been a weirdly long pause, now – to speak on their behalf. Bryony took a swig of water, coughed twice, and began.

'*Who was this man?*
I wish I knew.'

She stopped. Her voice had come out oddly unlike her voice. She sounded like somebody on the BBC teaching wartime housewives to dye their hair with carrots. She took another swig and continued.

'*I wish I knew*
The fullness of this person who
In only months has made my world
Brand new
I have few words
No detailed histories
Mainly just the unsolved mysteries
Of a life so rich it contained
All of you'

Here she looked up and gestured, limply, to the room – Marco's stage direction. A few people smiled, kindly. One man near the back was filming her on his phone.

'*Who was this man?*
I wish I could say
Compare him to a summer's day
Or count the ways
That he is missed today'

It was odd, she noted, as yet more verses swum on the page in front of her, that despite being so determined to keep it short and sweet, she seemed to have written one of the longest poems in the English language.

'*He wasn't one*
but infinite men
A son, a brother, a colleague, friend
A yet-to-be-defined but cherished
"Hey"'

Also one of the worst poems in the English language.

'Who are we now
That he is gone?
And life so cruelly stumbles on
Darkening
Before we reach the dawn'

It began as a tremor somewhere in her diaphragm, before re-verberating up her oesophagus. Not vomit, but something else. Standing here before so many trusting pairs of eyes, the bare, brutal sadness of the situation had finally cut through all the farce and confusion. Ed was dead and the rest was just detail.

Her voice wavered perilously.

'One thing I know: he's gone too soon
He had so much more to give
But whether we got months or years
Funny stories or bitter tears'

The reservoir that had been dry for three weeks was suddenly brimming and Bryony knew she had only seconds to croak out the final words.

'Before he left'

Although, she thought, as her eyes pricked and her sinuses filled up like a pressure hose, this really was the best and most convincing way to end.

'He showed us
How to live'

Then, in front of a room full of strangers, Bryony cried.

18

Who's who and whathaveyou

She wasn't sure how she ended up in the receiving line at the wake, any more than she knew how she ended up being namechecked as 'Ethelred's loving partner', or holding a collecting bucket for Allergy UK in the car park. All Bryony knew was that whenever she sensed a gap in proceedings through which she might slip out and run into the woods, there would be Annie or one of the myriad aunts and cousins, sweetly ushering her in the opposite direction, or a black-blazered member of staff sombrely holding the door open for her, or Ann's small but insistent hand on her lower back, steering her back into the throng.

The rest of the ceremony had been a blur.

Bryony continued crying after she had stumbled back to her seat, a hundred pairs of eyes pressed against her in pity. Annie handed her a tissue, mouthing 'Thank you,' with such sincerity that it launched a new flood.

She had cried throughout a pained performance by 'Ed's former bandmates' of a song Ed had 'helped to write' and which consisted mainly of the line 'She's easy, breezy, beautiful / She's my cover girl' over a synthesizer melody. She had cried as the non-vicar gave a non-sermon about life's purpose being to seek truth and forge honest human connections and she cried extra hard when he looked straight at her while saying it. She had cried as the little velvet curtain began its stately chug around the coffin to the theme from Jurassic Park.

She had fished globs of mascara from the corners of her eyes and sunk low in her chair as the mourners began gathering coats and bags, wondering if it was rude to leave their orders of service behind on their chair rather than take them home like miserable theatre programmes. She had scrubbed at the sooty trails on her face with a tissue, listening to Ann insisting that everyone take a plant – 'We have to have the whole place cleared out for the next one! Barbara, you'll have a Begonia, won't you?' – until the gulping stopped and she could breathe normally again.

And now here she stood, in the line next to Ed's family at the entrance to the local scout hut, shaking hands with everyone who deemed her important enough to do so. Which, it turned out, was everybody.

To be fair, some people – and Bryony respected these people more – looked at her with mild confusion. A few said 'lovely poem' in a way that didn't sound exactly like praise. But others were so deferential it was actively embarrassing. One, a quivering bundle of a woman in a black feather fascinator, actually *curtseyed*. Bryony found herself bobbing her head graciously in recognition, clasping the woman's hand and saying 'thank you so much, it means the world.'

At one point a familiar-looking man approached the line and she realized with some alarm that she recognised him from the dating apps. She was sure they'd messaged, borderline salaciously, not that long ago. Frozen with horror, she waited for the awkward moment of recognition when he reached her in the line – but none came, he just muttered 'so sorry for your loss, great guy,' and moved smoothly on. She felt mildly offended.

Bryony had deleted Alloi, along with Hinge, Bumble and several other more niche applications, the day before the funeral. She told

herself this was out of respect, though it was really fear that notifications would pop up during a crucial interaction with Ed's family,
or somehow beam themselves onto the crematorium wall during the
service. But even as her brain told her it was a good thing, a healthy
thing, to take a break for a little while, get back in touch with herself
and reflect on what she'd learned from her dating life so far (mostly to
have the 'so, what *are* we?' chat before one of you dies), her fingers were
still itching for the swipe. Curiosity gnawed at her like heartburn. She
couldn't help imagining the nameless, faceless crop of new men who
might at any moment be released like limited-edition crisp flavours
into the hungry market. Even as a sensible person who had read all the
think pieces about dating fatigue and dopamine addiction, it was hard
to shake the fear that her real soulmate might be out there, meeting
someone else while she wasted time at her pretend soulmate's funeral.

'You look miles away, said Steve, appearing at the end of the line
and giving her arm a matey squeeze. 'How you holding up?'

'Oh,' Bryony hauled her mind back into the room. 'Just thinking
about . . . missed opportunities.'

Steve nodded. 'I get that. I was thinking earlier about how Ethel
and I always said one day we'd take a weekend to watch all the *Fasts
and Furiouses* back-to-back, make a proper marathon of it, but we
never got round to it. It kills me to think now we never will.'

She squeezed his arm back. 'I'm so sorry.'

'Great poem, by the way,' he said.

Bryony studied his face for traces of mockery but found none.
His eyes were bloodshot and there were a few pilled scraps of tissue
clinging to his lapels, but his expression was entirely sincere.

'Was it actually?'

''Course! It was perfect. Pure Ed. I was just saying to Emmett –
really showed how well you understood him.'

She murmured some thanks, then admitted, 'I worried maybe it
was too– ah, vague.'

Steve shook his head.

'That's what made it so good – it was the way you said it was hard to sum him up in words. He was never really about the chat, was he? Not a showman, our Ethel. His thing was being reliable, and easy-going, and just always ... well, *there*. You really captured all the different things that he was to so many different people. All those memories and experiences that Ed was somehow at the centre of, just quietly, making things better.'

Bryony nodded dumbly. She was struck by a vision of Ed as a kind of Forrest Gump figure, his lopsided smile and ambient presence superimposed across history. Would she look back and realize that he had been there, quietly completing her, all summer? Had she mistaken his essential Ed-ness for ambivalence, while she could have been falling in love? Was she, in fact, a fucking idiot?

Steve looked embarrassed by her silence.

'And the rhyming,' he added. 'He'd have liked that. Nice and neat.'

It was one of the more eclectically catered wakes she'd attended. Alongside the traditional ham sandwiches and gritty-looking scones were several large chafing dishes of shepherd's pie, beef stew and dumplings and what appeared to be slightly sweaty paella. Next to these was a platter of fried chicken that looked to have been decanted straight from a KFC bucket, and beyond that, a tagine of couscous. All around the room, mourners attempted to eat stew off dainty side plates, battered drumsticks balanced precariously on top.

'Ann's idea,' explained Annie, appearing at Bryony's side as she weighed up the optics of helping herself to a boneless zinger fillet. 'She thought it would be nice for the food to reflect all of Ed's travelling.'

'Ed's ... travelling,' she said. 'Of course.'

But she could only remember that he'd been to Málaga, Camp

America and the summer he did the Three Peaks Challenge. 'So . . .' she gestured to the table.

'That makes sense,' said Bryony.

'I'm sure you two would have travelled together, wouldn't you?' said Annie, turning to look at her with warmth and pity wrought across her dainty features. 'Did you have any trips planned?' Her eyes seemed to genuinely 'soften', something Bryony always assumed only happened in trashy books – and yet here they were, gooey with sympathy.

'Absolutely,' said Bryony. 'I mean, nothing concrete, but I'm sure we talked about places we'd like to . . . well, maybe a long weekend in Porto, to start with . . .'

'Oh you should go!' Annie urged her. 'Go anyway! Honour his memory. I'm sure it's what he would have wanted.'

Bryony pictured herself eating custard tarts and sipping port at a pavement cafe. Maybe that wasn't a bad idea. *For Ed*. Nobody could argue. She could go to the loo right now and look up flights on her phone.

'You could take some of his ashes, to scatter there,' Annie added, and Bryony's winter sun fantasy was suddenly engulfed in a cloud of charred human remains. They settled like cinnamon on top of her imaginary *pasteis de nata*.

'Oh I'm not sure it would be my place to . . . I mean, I'm sure Ann has plans for the . . . the scattering.'

From somewhere behind her, Kelly let out a soft snort.

'Ann has a lot of plans.'

She needn't have worried about having nobody to talk to. An hour later, she was still rooted in the same spot, being besieged by a seemingly endless parade of Ed's friends and relatives, former colleagues and childhood teachers. No sooner had she rounded off her polite, hushed-volume small talk with one than another would seamlessly take their place. Her jaw had begun to ache from looking appropriately sombre.

'I'm his Auntie Merle,' the latest one announced, taking Bryony's hand with the one that wasn't holding a plate of mash, mince and a tuna sandwich. 'Well, only a fake auntie – but you know how it is. Lots of us are frauds!'

'I can fully imagine,' said Bryony.

'And what do you *do*, Bryony?' asked Auntie Merle.

She told her, 'I work for the council.'

'Oh! *Well.*' The small woman suddenly became animated and clutched Bryony sharply by the wrist. 'Do you have any say over the bins? Because I'm sorry but this new system with the different weeks for the tins and the tubs is ridiculous, I'd only just grasped it before when it was Tuesdays for the green and Wednesdays for the blue – but now they've switched to *Thursdays* it's thrown my whole week off. Because Denise, my cleaning lady, she comes on a Wednesday, and—'

'No, I'm afraid it's Waltham Forest council,' Bryony interrupted.

'I didn't know they had a separate council just for the forest! Trees is it? You must *know* someone in bins though, surely?'

'. . . in London . . .' She tried to explain, but Merle still had her by the arm and was blinking up at her determinedly through eyes ringed thickly with bright blue shadow. 'I'll have a word,' said Bryony, weakly. 'See what I can do.'

'Good girl,' the aunt sniffed, then released her and wandered off towards the buffet. Bryony saw her chance for escape. But before she could wriggle her way towards the door, a man caught her eye.

Short, sixty-odd, bald and wiry in a slightly wrinkled black suit, he was entirely unremarkable – but next to the striking eclecticism of the Slingsbys, this was remarkable in itself. His face, she realized as he made his way across the room towards her, was a careworn version of Ed's.

'Hullo,' the man said shyly, offering his hand. 'I'm David. I understand you were in love with my son.'

Bryony shook it, though even doing so felt dishonest. 'It's good to meet you, David. I'm so very sorry for your loss.'

'Thank you,' he said, softly. 'It's a horrid business, to bury your own child. The very worst. I wouldn't wish it on my greatest enemy.'

She nodded, feeling with some relief that for the first time today she was not expected to contribute. Only to repeat: 'I'm so sorry.' The comfortable safety of that phrase.

David accepted her condolences, then looked apologetic. 'How long exactly had you and Ed been an item? I'm sorry, I'm sure I ought to know these things – I always try to keep up with who's who and whathaveyou, but clearly news takes a while to reach the old man in the valley.'

'Oh, it really wasn't all that long,' she stalled, trying to decide how far she ought to lie to protect her cover, but spare his feelings. 'Only a few months. But a very, ah, *special* few months, of course,' she added.

'Well, I suppose it's not all about time, is it?' he said kindly. 'It's about what you meant to each other.'

'Absolutely.'

Over his shoulder, she could see Annie and her mother locked in a tense-looking exchange beside a photo of Ed propped up on an easel. He was wearing wraparound sunglasses – something else, Bryony realized with a twinge, she would have added to the ick list had she ever witnessed them.

Following her eyeline for a moment, David asked, 'Are they looking after you well, the family?'

'Oh yes – absolutely,' she said. 'Everyone has been so welcoming and really made me, um, a part of things.'

'I'm sure,' said David, smiling wanly. He glanced over his shoulder and lowered his voice further. 'I hope they're not being *too* welcoming? My ex-wife means well but she can be something of a . . . force.'

She was scared to agree with this verbally in case it was a trick, in case he was perhaps wearing a wire that fed directly back to a control room in Ann's cellar. But she pressed her lips together and gave a tiny nod.

'Ah,' said David. 'Yes.'

He looked as though he was about to say something else, perhaps share some helpful nugget from the Slingsby handbook, but just then a small commotion broke out across the room and they both turned to look. The place was so crowded that it took a while to establish the source – an upturned tray of scones, a tearful Annie, a belligerent Ann, an unidentified auntie calling for a hoover to nobody in particular – and when Bryony turned back around, David had been swept away in the throng. In his place, a woman of around her own age was stood beside her, looking at Bryony. She had long, wavy red hair and an unreadable expression.

'Lovely poem,' she said.

'Thank you, thanks so much.'

'So, you and Ed . . . it was serious then, was it?' asked the woman, in the same breezy tone with which one might ask if a chair was free.

'Um,' Bryony gulped. 'Yes? Sure! Absolutely.'

The woman narrowed her eyes. 'You don't sound so sure.'

Bryony felt defensive. Who the fuck was this person?

'I mean, we hadn't been together very *long* – but it's not all about time, is it? It's . . . it's what we meant to each other.' She was shocked to find tears spring easily to her eyes. Apparently now the seal was broken, she would cry all the time, at anything.

'Of course, totally,' replied the woman, chastised. 'It's just . . . no, of course, you're right. I'm sorry for your loss.'

'Thank you,' Bryony did her gracious head-bob, willing her to leave. She didn't.

'Ed was a really good guy,' the woman went on. 'He'll be so missed.'

'Yes,' agreed Bryony, firmly. 'He was. And he will.'

'I was actually saying to Laurie, just before we heard the news – you must know Laurie, right?'

'Sure,' Bryony said without thinking, then panicked inwardly in case Laurie was also a test. 'Or at least, I know *of* her.'

'Him,' corrected the woman, and Bryony's back started sweating. 'Laurie, short for Lawrence? One of the Cromwell High lads? The Brixworth Sixworth?'

'Oh! Yes, of course, *that* Laurie. Sorry, my head's all over the place today,' she replied, dabbing delicately at her eyes with a tissue and hoping this was enough to absolve her. The throb in her jaw had begun to feel glandular.

'Ed *must* have introduced you to the Brixworth Sixworth, surely? And the So-Corby Crew? Wasn't it the twentieth annual Brigstock-stock a couple of months ago?'

The woman was surely just making noises now. Bryony nodded her aching head like the Churchill dog, trying to decide whether to come clean or spin a few new layers into her big web of lies. It was stifling in the scout hut, she hadn't been able to find water anywhere and now the combined effect of excessive crying and salt from the buffet was making her feel dangerously dehydrated.

'Anyway,' the girl eyed her curiously. 'I was just saying to Laurie, how much I always hoped Ed would meet someone. Someone who was, you know, *right* for him.'

She flipped her hair over one shoulder and placed a hand on Bryony's arm. 'And it's so nice, Bridie, to know that he did.'

'Mmmhmm,' said Bryony. 'If you'll excuse me, I actually just have to . . .' she wafted a hand in the direction of the door, turned and fled.

19

Be prepared

Squatting in the tiny toilet of the scout hut, Kelly inserts the test mid-stream with the skill and precision of one who has been pissing on sticks for almost a year. Not a single droplet ends up on her hand. It is a shame, she thinks, that there is no way of turning this into a marketable skill.

Admittedly doing it here, now, at her brother-in-law's funeral, feels perverse – but then that is all part of her new set of superstitions. The more casual she is about the tests, the more likely they are to go in her favour. No more making an occasion of it, the way she had in the early months. No more reciting affirmations on the drive home from work, wondering about the phantom warmth she feels beneath her bellybutton. No more ceremonial setting of the phone timer, making Leo hold her close for the full three minutes in a silent, hopeful slow dance.

These days she is careless and unromantic about it, doing the deed alone and whenever first opportunity strikes. The more inauspicious the setting, the better. Work loos. Cinema loos. The loos on the first floor of Westfield, watching the one solitary line creep into view while a clutch of tweens eat cookie dough and discuss BTS conspiracy theories outside the cubicle. The less she appears to want it, she tells herself, the more chance the universe will finally deliver.

Unlike his wife, Leo has a healthy respect for woo – probably genetic – and has always accepted the superstitions around the tests unquestioningly, even while Kelly thinks she is losing her mind. But then the superstition extended to include not doing the tests with Leo, then to not telling Leo about the tests at all – and now she isn't sure when he stopped asking, whether it was out of deference or disinterest.

She dries her hands on a crispy peach hand towel and reaches for the stick, glancing briefly at it en route to the bin.

Once again, the universe has failed to get the memo. Her mouth begins to water for whisky and bitters, her consolatory curl of orange peel, as Kelly makes her way back out into the throng.

20

Bereavement white noise

Having finally made it to the foyer without being waylaid by any more riddling mourners, Bryony was having a discreet panic attack – tight chest, lump in throat, fuzzy head, the classic jazz trio – when she bumped into Kelly coming out of the loos. Kelly looked about as uncomfortable as she felt. Her eye makeup was a little smeared and she was hastily shoving something into her handbag.

'You okay?' Bryony asked her. 'Was it the stew?'

It was funny, she noted, the way someone else's distress could stop one's own anxiety cold, like a game of nervous system top trumps. If only she could carry somebody who was a bigger wreck around with her, for emergencies. Pull a rip cord and *whoomp*, activate their panic and instantly quell her own.

'What?' said Kelly, turning towards her with a glazed look in her eyes. 'No, no – I'm fine.' She tugged at her immaculate black body-con. 'I mean, you know, not *fine* – very, very, um, sad . . . but fine.'

'You don't look fine,' pressed Bryony. She felt a strong urge to win over this frosty, unplaceable Kelly. Partly because she might be a useful ally when it came to placating, and ultimately escaping, the Slingsbys – but mainly because Bryony was physically incapable of living with the knowledge, even the suspicion, that someone, somewhere didn't like her.

She put her hand on Kelly's forearm and smiled her special funeral smile; a brave, tight-lipped little grimace. 'How are you holding up?'

Kelly flinched a little at the hand on the arm, looking down at it almost as though she expected to see a rash spreading.

'Oh, you know,' she replied mildly. 'I'm alright.'

'As alright as you can be, I guess,' offered Bryony. 'It's so awful. I can't even imagine.'

This was a lazy stock phrase, straight from some Bereavement White Noise compilation, and only as the words left her mouth did it occur to Bryony that they made no sense; she didn't need to imagine how sad a person could be about losing Ed when she was supposed to be that sad herself.

'I mean!' A frantic back peddle. 'I can't imagine how Leo must be feeling, losing a brother. And for you too, your brother-in-law . . . it must be devastating.'

'Yeah, it's a lot,' said Kelly, matter-of-factly. 'Everyone's a mess. But how are *you*?'

It felt loaded. Kelly was looking at her in the same way she had earlier, that odd mix of confusion, wariness and disdain.

'Oh, you know. Just taking each day as it comes,' Bryony replied. Bereavement White Noise, vol.2.

'But how are you feeling? In yourself?' Kelly pushed.

Bryony performed a quick body scan. Head: woolly. Stomach: acidic. A rising tide filled her chest, crashing waves roared in her ears and a dull throb in her lower calf suggested either sitting with her legs crossed for too long in the crematorium, or a blood clot about to start the upstream journey towards her brain.

Conflict raged so readily on the battlefield of her body that explaining how she 'was' to people often felt like being the correspondent for a long, confusing and far-away war that ultimately had no bearing on them.

'Oh, I'm fine,' she told Kelly. 'I'll live!'

Kelly raised her eyebrows at the expression – unfortunate – but said nothing. Bryony channelled Fake Auntie Merle, determined to steer them onto more neutral terrain.

'So, what do you do, Kelly?'

Kelly held her gaze steady, unsmiling. 'I'm a GP's receptionist,' she replied.

Then, 'I'm your GP's receptionist, actually.'

And suddenly Bryony saw her clear as day, as though a smeary perspex screen had fallen between them. That voice, with its Estuary vowels, flatly apologetic on so many phone calls. That face, with its immovable brows, deflecting her panic and shame.

She stammered something witless; *of course, I thought you looked familiar, how funny, how lovely to see you, how are you, oh hang on we covered that* – but they were interrupted by a middle-aged couple exiting the scout hut, faces sombre, clutching chicken legs wrapped in floral serviettes.

'Lovely poem,' said one of the guests, patting Bryony on the shoulder as they passed.

'Thank you so much,' she said. And when she turned back round, Kelly had walked away.

21

How lovely

It was two days after the funeral and Bryony was back at her desk, finishing her own portion of leftover shepherd's pie – not bad, in a school dinnerish way – when her phone rang. An unknown number.

Like every normal member of her generation, Bryony feared spontaneous phone calls more than nuclear war. But of course she could never ignore them either, in case it was a mystery doctor calling about some tests she didn't remember having done, or some other mystery doctor calling to make her an orphan. The confidence to ignore unknown numbers and voicemails at leisure was a privilege not enough people talked about.

'Hello?'

At first all she heard was a honking noise, followed by a rustle. Perhaps she was being pranked by a malevolent goose.

'*Hello?*'

'Bryony? It's Ann. How are you doing love? Just wanted to check in.'

She was touched by this, and felt briefly wounded that none of her friends had called to check in on her yet. Until she remembered that they didn't know.

'Thank you, I'm actually at wor—' she began, but Ann was still talking.

'Oh Bryony,' she gasped, 'I saw a single magpie on my walk this morning and it nearly destroyed me. One for sorrow! Landed right in my path, as if it was trying to *tell* me something – I went cold all over and then all of a sudden I just *sensed* Ethy's presence there with me, you know? It had the same little twitch in its eye.'

Bryony pictured a magpie blinking the way Ed had, twice, hard, as soon as he'd finished speaking.

'And then two more came to join it – three for a girl, you know – and I thought, well there's my prompt from the universe to phone poor Bryony and check. You're not, are you?'

'Not . . . what?'

'Pregnant.'

A rogue blob of mince made a reappearance at the back of her throat, and she choked it back down.

'No, I'm afraid not.'

Ann sighed, audibly disappointed. 'Are you sure pet? I'd half convinced myself that you must be, I got so worked up on the way back. And then the sun came out, and I thought . . . Definitely not a chance? What were the two of you—'

'Definitely not,' she interrupted. The answer was condoms, Bryony having sworn off hormonal contraception after spending the whole of her twenties having violent physical and emotional reactions to every pill, patch and implant the NHS would put in her. Eventually she'd decided no sex was worth the side effects – and so far none had been.

But she wasn't about to tell Ann that. Not in the office.

'Well, that's a pity. It would have been so poetic, don't you think?' said Ann.

'Mmm,' said Bryony. She hoped Ann wasn't planning any post-humous fertility experiments. Was there still a used Durex in Ed's bedroom bin? She shuddered.

'But look, will you come up for tea on Sunday? Steve can fetch you, he won't mind.'

She hesitated, briefly mourning her weekend plans. The lie-in, the hypothetical yoga class, the leisurely wank. The time she'd allocated for what she and Marco called Luxury Sunday™ or 'the mighty bouge' – swanning around the neighbourhood buying bread and bunches of organic radishes, smelling overpriced candles, getting a coffee, looking at her phone while cradling a book she was never going to finish. Bringing home flowers that she would then leave for weeks to wither and die in their vases, their stems turning slimy and the water taking on the stench of death. Taking a selfie in a woolly hat with the sun on her face. Breathing deeply.

'We'd so love to see you, and there are a few plans afoot that I wanted your help with,' Ann went on. 'Everyone has been falling over themselves suggesting lovely things to commemorate Ethy, really establish his legacy you know – and of course you must be central to it all, Bryony. I don't want you to think for a second that we're going to leave you all alone now the funeral is over.'

'Of course,' she told her, faintly. 'How lovely.'

'You're not,' said Marco. 'Again? The whole schlep to Northumberland, *again*?'

'Northamptonshire.'

'Potarto.'

'I have to!' she wailed. 'There doesn't seem to be a way of physically getting out of these invites. It's like the words "no thank you" freeze in my mouth and instead I hear some other idiot saying "yes, of course, how lovely".'

'Just say you're busy.'

'Busy doing what? They think that I'm grieving, like they are. No brunch plans trump death.'

Marco conceded this was true.

'It's like you're trapped in a game of bad luck musical chairs. Just because you happened to have been boning the guy right before he died, you're the one who has to assume the role of grieving widow for ever after.'

'Ever after?!' yelped Bryony.

'Well.' He paused. 'A year? Maybe ten months with good behaviour? Moving on too quickly might look crass and insensitive. As though you didn't value your love.'

'I *didn't* value our love! There was no love!'

'Shhhh.' Marco put a finger against her lips. 'He could be listening.'

'I hope you've washed those hands. And I hope he *is* listening! I hope he can hear how fucking . . . fucking *inconvenient* it is for me to have to pretend to have been in love with him.'

'Not as inconvenient as being dead though.'

'SHUT UP.'

Bryony's chest was tight again, each in-breath a conscious effort against the steel cage of her ribs, the creaking bellows of her lungs. *Ten months. A year.* She knew Marco was joking, but suppose he wasn't?

A thought broke free and drifted to the front of her mind, from the murky part she usually kept suppressed with sturdy feminist rhetoric. *I don't have a year. I can't spare a year.*

At thirty-four she'd been mostly single, save for a handful of relationships that never made it to an anniversary, for the past ten years. She'd been mostly happy, save for a handful of tearful meltdowns on the way home from people's weddings, for the same length of time. And yet, even on her staunchest, most empowered, most blithely optimistic days, the days where she would write off a date because he smelled like car upholstery or thought Elon Musk 'deserved the benefit of the doubt', it was hard to completely shake the sense of impending deadline. Hard not to picture the guillotine fall on her fortieth birthday, the 'time's up' music from Super Mario playing as her eyes turned to crosses and she slid off the screen.

'Bollocks! Social conditioning! Toxic heteronormative bullshit!' Marco would roar whenever she mentioned these feelings. He was also single and two years older than she was.

'Nope, I refuse. I'm getting out of this,' she said, play-acting assertiveness and slamming a hand down on the kitchen table. 'And you're going to help.'

'How will I do that?' he asked. 'Do I even want to know?'

'Because you're coming with me.'

'Oh, Brian, no,' he said. 'I'm busy.'

'You don't work on Sundays.'

'That's because I *live* on Sundays.'

'Please? I need you Marco, I'm weak. You know I am. Without you there to stop me I'll probably agree to dress in mourning garb for the rest of my life or paint all the Little Buckton railings black like Queen Victoria.'

'I don't think she painted them herself.'

'Please? I need a witness. I need you to be my appropriate adult.'

'We're inside friends, Brian, you know that. Our relationship doesn't travel well.'

This was true, she and Marco rarely went out together. Their relationship thrived in isolation, blooming like hothouse flowers – or mould – within the walls of the flat. Sometimes in her darker moments, she worried she had hallucinated him.

'Pleeeeease?' she whined, pawing his arm. 'I'll pay for your train ticket. I'll buy you a panini.'

'I don't want a panini! I just want my Luxury Sunday, is that too much to ask? I want to go out and get my silly little coffee and a silly little pastry and maybe a silly little piercing. Can't I milk a little *happiness* from the withered teat we call *life*? I could drop down dead tomorrow like whassisface!'

He waved a theatrical fist at the sky. To both of their surprise, Bryony burst into tears.

Marco looked horrified. 'Brian! Shit! I'm sorry, I was just being . . .'

She gasped for breath between sobs, hot salty tears sliding into her open mouth.

'It's . . . *hugghgghh* . . . fine, I'm . . . *hegggghh* . . . fine,' she insisted, fishing a moulting tissue out of her sleeve. 'It's just a weird thing that keeps happening.'

'Crying is a weird thing that keeps happening?' said Marco, as she leaked snot all over his shoulder.

'Yeah. I dunno . . . *heggggh* . . . why.'

Marco pulled away from the hug and looked at her quizzically.

'Do you think it might be because you're . . . sad? About the man you were dating who recently died?'

She dabbed at her streaming mascara and hiccupped. 'I wouldn't have thought so.'

22

Sunday in the Midlands with Ann

'Shit, that's awkward,' said Marco, as he drained his silly little coffee somewhere just beyond Leighton Buzzard. 'So every time *you* go to the doctor, she's—'

'There, yes.'

'And every time you phone them?'

'Yes.'

Marco knew about the frequency of her dealings with the NHS, but, as far as she knew, not their intensity. She was unnerved that he looked so unnerved for her.

'But they have patient confidentiality, right?' She tried to sound breezier than she felt. 'They have to take an oath.'

'I don't think the receptionists take an oath, Brian.'

'Surely the oath is implied!'

'I'm not sure they're paid enough for an implied oath.'

'Stop it,' she pleaded. 'I'm freaking out enough as it is.'

'What are you scared of?' asked Marco. 'That she's going to tell his mum about the time you thought you'd caught legionnaires' disease on a spa day?'

'I can't have them thinking I'm a lunatic. I need to give the poor guy a nice, normal girlfriend.'

'I'm sorry, are you worried you're not eligible enough to date a dead man? Is that the conversation we're having? Because all the dead guys would be *lucky* to have you, duchess.'

'I just don't want to disappoint his family,' she said, primly. 'It's the least I can do.'

'I think we passed the least you could do back when you started writing poetry.'

Her lower intestine contorted at the memory of her Vogon turn.

'I just need to get through today, and then I can start the gentle withdrawal,' she said. 'And they can always remember me fondly, as the lovely girl who made Ed so happy in his final months.'

'Final hours, even,' countered Marco. 'Wasn't "the Gentle Withdrawal" his other nickname?'

Bryony yelped and threw a wadded-up napkin at him. 'I've changed my mind, you shouldn't come after all. Get off here and have a lovely day in ...' she squinted through the window '... Bletchley.'

'No chance Brian, I'm invested now. This is my cryptic code to crack.'

'Just make me seem healthy and normal, I beg of you.'

Marco sighed. 'Fine. But everyone knows it's better to just be yourself.'

To her relief, there was no sign of Kelly. Today's supporting artists were Annie, who was folded into the huge sagging armchair with her knees up beneath her chin, Leo and Emmett, watching the cricket in silence on an ancient TV, a wizened old man in overalls who might have been a family friend or hired handyman – this remained unclear, as he performed the job of neither – and Susan, who was holding an iPad at arm's length and squinting. She looked up as they walked in behind Steve, squinted at them too, and then waved cheerily across the kitchen.

'Cooee, Bryony! And this must be the gay flatmate. I'm Susan.'

Bryony winced. Marco bowed. 'Actually Susan, I prefer Queer Musketeer.'

Then he turned to Ann and before she had a chance to say anything, Marco had pulled her into a fierce hug.

'Ann. Ann, Ann, Ann.'

He clasped her by the shoulders and looked deep into her eyes.

'Ann, you have been in my thoughts. What a truly special person he was.'

Bryony winced some more, but Ann was already falling under this spell, smiling tearily and pulling out a handkerchief. 'Thank you, Marco, that means so much.'

'Let it all out, Ann,' he told her, while Bryony sank onto one of the melamine chairs and prayed that she wouldn't. Ann made a visible show of gathering herself, blowing her nose and clapping her hands together. 'Tea! Tea? Tea.'

Today the refreshments looked like a trolley dash in the lunchbox aisle. Ritz crackers, Scotch eggs, a little net of mini cheeses, a stack of salt and vinegar Snack-a-Jacks and – she looked again, to be sure – a packet of Peperami. Bryony hadn't known until now that she held views on bereavement food. It was supposed to be lasagnes, surely? Vast, beautiful, burnished lasagnes, dropped off by a conveyor belt of kind neighbours. Perhaps a whole roast chicken, or something soothing and nourishing with nursery-school texture, like daal. It was confusing – Ann looked like a woman who knew her way around a lentil, and yet . . .

'But of course,' said Ann, sitting down and passing them both a Capri Sun, 'knowing he'd found Bryony in his final months has brought me so much comfort.' She placed a hand over her heart and sighed: 'I only wish we could have seen them together!'

Marco placed his hand over his heart too. 'Ann, they made a beautiful couple,' he told her. 'Love's young dream!'

Ann beamed, which only encouraged him. 'Absolutely mad for each other,' he continued. 'More than once I made the mistake of entering a room without knocking, only to find them—'

'*Agh!*' he yelped as Bryony issued a swift kick to his ankle. But Ann just chuckled fondly, as though the image of her late son getting his end away on a Walthamstow kitchen table was truly a source of peace.

'Ann,' Bryony tried to change the subject. Or at least the sub-subject, being as it was hard to escape the main subject: death. 'You mentioned some kind of tribute you wanted help with?'

'Yes what's the plan, Ann?' asked Marco, reaching for a Babybel. Bryony glared at him.

Ann looked puzzled for a moment. 'Oh! Yes, so I did. Well, I was talking to Mr Duggan in Morrisons—'

'Junior or Senior?' asked Annie.

'Senior,' said Ann, then clarified for Bryony and Marco. 'Mr Duggan Senior is head of the junior school, and Mr Duggan Junior is head of the senior school.'

'How confusing!' replied Marco, brightly. 'Both played by Dick Van Dyke in a beard?'

Ann nodded, ignoring the joke.

'Mr Duggan Senior must be due his bus pass, but then I suppose he has something to prove ever since the scandal with one of the governors and all that sugar paper—'

'Mum,' interjected Annie. 'Irrelevant.'

'Well, anyway, he was saying it might be nice to instate some kind of prize in Ethelred's memory, seeing as he was such a shining star at the school and is still so fondly remembered by some of the caretakers. We're going to have a memorial ceremony on his birth-day, in March, and we thought perhaps you, Bryony, might want to get involved and help with – well, I'm not sure exactly. Perhaps naming the prize—'

'The Ed Slingsby Memorial Prize. Done,' muttered Leo, without taking his eyes off the cricket. Leo seemed especially gloomy today. He hadn't hugged her hello this time, Bryony had noted with disappointment.

'... or designing the trophy or the posters, that kind of thing?' Ann went on.

'Well, um, I can't say my strengths lie in design,' said Bryony, 'but of course I'd be happy to help however I can. I could ... ah, present the prize, maybe?'

She envisaged herself in a cream skirt suit, looking like the Princess of Wales, shaking hands with a gummy eight-year-old who had picked the most litter.

'Well, I think actually they might quite like *me* to take on *that* duty,' replied Ann, who was clearly envisaging herself in a turquoise skirt suit, looking like Camilla.

'Of course! Of course,' said Bryony.

'Quite right,' chipped in Marco.

'There's the quiz as well,' piped up Steve, tearing into a bag of Frazzles and offering them around with the air of a canapé waiter. 'To raise some funds for the prize – we're gonna do an Ed-themed pub quiz, all contribute a round.'

'A quiz! About Ed! Fun!' said Marco. Steve grinned.

'Just let me know what you want to do your round on, Bryony.'

Bryony ignored this in the hope it would go away. Instead she turned to Ann. 'I have to say, it's lovely he stayed in touch with so many people,' she said. 'I barely kept up with anyone from back home once I moved to London – and I only moved in from the suburbs.'

'Well, that's the advantage of him staying at home,' replied Ann. 'I always said to him, so much nicer to stay part of the community here than throwing all that money away on rent having a lonely old time of it in London.'

Bryony smiled and replied, 'Yes, absolutely,' before she'd had time to process what Ann had said.

'Sorry, staying at home?'

Ann nodded. 'His room is still exactly as he left it, I haven't felt up to moving anything. And of course you'd be welcome to stay over, any time! I thought perhaps you'd like to help go through his things, when the time feels right.'

'Sorry, his room ... here?' She wondered if Ann was suffering from some kind of psychological grief response, or perhaps early onset dementia.

'I always told him you'd be very welcome to spend the night – I'm not old fashioned! Don't want you thinking I'm a prude, Bryony! And our room's in the other annex so you could have got up to whatever you liked.'

It seemed unusual, for a mother to take so much comfort in imagining her dead son's sex life, but Bryony had more pressing mysteries to solve. She laid a hand gently on Ann's forearm.

'But Ann, Ed lived in Acton.'

Ann looked as confused as Bryony felt. 'Only Monday to Friday,' she said, as though this wasn't the bulk of the week. 'It was such a convenient arrangement, what with that chap only wanting the room at weekends, so much better than spending all that money on a whole flat to himself. He never felt at home in London anyway, did he? Couldn't wait to get back here on a Friday. He used to ring me from Newport Pagnell services and tell me to get the dinner on,' she clucked, fondly. 'He was a real homebody, was Ethy. And he was so excited about bringing you up for the weekend – such a shame your courses always got in the way.'

'Yes,' said Bryony, faintly. 'Such a shame.'

*

'What courses? Your menstrual courses?' asked Marco on the train home.

'For all I know!' she shrieked. 'It's killing me, I want to know what I was fake-qualified in. Coding? Glass blowing? Tantric massage?'

Bryony craned her neck to check the seats around them were empty, before she added:

'Did you hear what Ann said while you were showing Susan how to update her iOS? He still lived at home.'

'What? Who?

'Ed.'

'No he didn't.'

'He did! He did one of those deals, sub–let a flat for the weekdays while the guy who owned it was working away in Zurich or Ipswich or somewhere, then went back to his mum's every Friday.'

'That can't be right.'

'I thought about it, and it's true – I never saw him at the weekend. It was always Wednesdays or Thursdays, except that one time he'd been at that festival on Clapham Common and he came and stayed at ours.'

'But did he tell you it was his flat?'

'Yes? No? I don't know, I never asked to see a tenancy agreement. It's not like there were photos of other people's kids on the walls.'

There hadn't been any photos anywhere, come to think of it, but that was hardly unusual for a man living alone in his mid-thirties. Bryony had once slept with a guy who still had the stock images in his picture frames. She'd encountered Stanley Kubrick posters still held up with Blu-Tack, Camden Market throws disguising blood stained sofa cushions, bedroom weed farms, entire colonies of silverfish, and a man who shared one cereal bowl ('the bowl') with three other housemates. Compared to all this, Ed's grey-carpeted show suite of a home had been bland enough to actually count as a point in his favour.

'Well, really what's the issue?'

Marco loved to play devil's advocate; he fancied himself in an imaginary barrister's wig. 'In this economy, loads of people are forced into less-than-ideal living arrangements. A weekday sublet is nothing, some people are sharing literal beds.'

'That's true I suppose.'

'And *some* people live with people who make them go to the Midlands for tea with Ann.'

'You adored Ann.'

'I did, it's true,' he sighed. 'She's like an off-brand Tracey Ullman.'

'Then maybe you should live with her.'

'Hey,' said Marco. 'He might have just been saving up to buy somewhere.'

'I don't get the impression he was though? I think he just loved having his mum wash his pants and cut the crusts off his toast. It's so deeply unsexy.'

'I'm sorry, was being dead not the red flag?' said Marco. 'Are you annoyed that your dead fake boyfriend has become *less of a catch*?'

'No!' said Bryony, although she was. She was annoyed that everyone thought she'd been in a serious relationship with a man who still lived with his mother, like a kind of half-baked Buster Bluth. But she was even more annoyed that she'd spent three-and-a-half months of her life entertaining the notion, however vaguely, that Ed could turn into a serious relationship. Three-and-a-half months of keeping him on the mental shelf marked 'potential?'. Drafting messages first in her Notes app. Waxing things.

Then there was the guilt that accompanied being so judgemental, so shallow – in this economy! – and that annoyed her most of all.

Bryony tended to experience guilt as a physical complaint, and always had. The first time she was cruel to another girl at school (Christine Marks, for failure to master a Billie Piper dance routine), she had felt so genuinely sick with remorse that she'd been sent home early, pleading a tummy bug but privately believing it to be a curse from God. Decades later it still took her longer than it should to correctly identify that sickly sense of unease. She felt it to a lesser or greater degree pretty much any time she'd socialized with anyone – the deep-pitted churning, which no amount of Gaviscon would banish, of personal details she'd got wrong, questions she'd forgotten to ask, the eternal fear that she'd talked too much about herself and now everyone hated her. This, she rationalized, was the reason she always slept so badly after nights out. Not the wine.

'If anything,' Marco went on, 'I'd have thought you'd be relieved. It's another ick to add to the pile. Less to be upset about.'

This was a good point. A comforting point.

'That's a terrible thing to say,' she told him.

They watched the darkening sky whoosh past the train window for a few minutes, making her feel melancholy and sentimental in a way only train windows can. Then she asked Marco: 'What if he was actually The One and I never noticed because he wore a dated cut of jean?'

'I think if he'd been The One, the jeans wouldn't have mattered,' he replied.

'Alright Barney the dinosaur, that sounds nice but you don't actually mean it. Tell me the truth. Life is short. Apparently even shorter than I realized; should I just fall in love with one of the Egg Men so I can settle down and be happy and call it a day?'

She expected him to dismiss this with another blast about toxic heteronormative bullshit, but instead Marco crossed his hands like Yoda and said:

'It's the deathbed paradox.'

'What's the deathbed paradox?'

'It's something I just made up, but listen: imagine you go to visit your grandfather on his deathbed.'

'Both my grandfathers died in the nineties.'

'Shh, that's not the point. Imagine you go to visit *a* grandfather on his deathbed; anybody's grandfather. You go to see him and you look into his wise, crinkly eyes, and you say, "Grandfather, tell me the secret to love." And he takes you by the hand and says in a raspy, trembling voice, "Son . . . "'

'Son?'

'This is happening in a folksy American film set in the nineteen-fifties.'

'Oh. Okay.'

'"Son," he says, "Life is short." And then he dies.'

Marco paused for effect, his eyes glossy. He was moved by his own little scene.

'I don't get it.'

'Right, okay, so . . . does he mean: Son, life is short. Stop over-thinking it! Just go and find someone nice to love. Settle down. If you want, you can marry.'

'Are you quoting Cat Stevens?'

'Boyzone. But that isn't the point – the point is, does he mean that, *or* does he mean: "Life is short. Don't settle! Find that one person who makes you feel alive with the fire of a thousand suns. Keep searching until you find *The One!*"'

'I don't know, which does he mean?'

'I don't know either,' shrugged Marco. 'None of us do.'

'That's the deathbed paradox?'

'That's the deathbed paradox. Do you run out of there deter-mined to date every guy on every app until that lightning bolt finally strikes, or do you run out of there determined to just pick the next decent-hearted person you meet and make a ruddy good go of things? Because either way, life is short.'

Bryony was surprised to find tears in her own eyes now. If Ed's death held a lesson for her, which was it? Stop wasting time with men you have only lukewarm feelings for, or stop wasting time looking for red flags and reasons not to give someone a chance? Satisficers were happier than maximisers in life. Everyone had seen that TED talk.

She turned to Marco. 'Is there a third scenario where he means: "Life is short. Just give up on dating and accept yourself as a whole, complete person who doesn't need a romantic relationship to validate her existence?"'

Marco shook his head. 'Honestly Brian, he's a folksy old man from the fifties. So probably not.'

23

See something, say something

Kelly has tried hard to resist acquiring any medical knowledge. She would prefer not to be burdened with information that might make her responsible, liable, *obliged* to offer advice to old ladies on buses or diagnose people at dinner parties. 'I'm just the receptionist!' has proved useful on more than one occasion, when Ann presents a friend with a Dickensian cough or a conspicuous growth and demands Kelly prescribe them something.

Sometimes they're not even a friend, they're just someone she met in Aldi. Sometimes Kelly thinks she's doing it purely to hear her daughter-in-law say, 'I'm just the receptionist!', as though the reminder might jog her into becoming a barrister or the head of Channel 4.

But for all her attempts to remain blissfully medically illiterate, she still knows more than most people. When you stare at enough awareness posters, when you listen to people's pick-n-mix ailments, when you must effectively triage the results of the online symptom quiz into 'urgent attention needed' and 'better luck next time – try Reddit', things are bound to seep in.

So, when Kelly sees the woman with the mole, or rather the mole with the woman, she can't help running a mental checklist.

Larger than end of pencil? Check. Uneven shape? Check. Colour variation? Check. Swollen, itchy, crusty? She squints. Check, by the looks of it. This is a big, scabby Bran Flake of a mole on her upper back, right where a person wouldn't necessarily see it themselves. It's only visible to Kelly because the woman is bending down to tend a baby in a pram right next to the counter, her hoodie slipping off her shoulder. Kelly is looking at it for so long that the patient she's currently serving turns to follow her eye line.

'Sorry! Take this slip to phlebotomy at the hospital and we'll see you on the seventeenth. Thanks. Next?'

The mole woman steps up. 'I've got an appointment at eleven,' she says. 'It's for—', the baby squeals and she pauses to look down. Kelly interjects.

'Your mole?'

'My . . . what? No. It's for him. For his reflux.'

'Oh. Right, of course – take a seat and we'll call you when the doctor's ready.'

The woman does so with an affronted air, as though perhaps the mole was a decorative feature or a misjudged tattoo.

She zips up the hoodie, but not before twisting awkwardly to sneak a look at her left shoulder.

24

Everything is death-adjacent

Ed had started appearing in Bryony's dreams now, as though her subconscious was trying to retrofit an infatuation.

The dreams tend to fall into two camps: mundane domesticity or erotic and absurd. She and Ed assembling flatpack furniture; she and Ed bickering over the correct way to load a dishwasher; she and Ed having sex on the middle of a roundabout while the cars, all driven by Ann, honk their horns in appreciation.

Often the sex dreams devolved into lewd scenarios involving other Slingsbys and associates. Leo, naturally. Emmett, unnaturally. Chloe's Bob, who she hadn't exchanged two words with and who appeared in the dreams as a kind of blank-faced shuffling Christmas gonk. In these dreams, Ed would generally arrive at some point in proceedings and either burst into tears at her infidelity, or join in. Either way, she woke up sweating.

And all the while, Ann was calling.

Not texting, but regular phone calls. Or rather, irregular phone calls, their timing suggestive of the expansive schedule of a retiree and their content everything from the grandiose ('Should we all go and volunteer for Camp America next year, in his honour?') to absolute minutiae ('I found his collection of plastic toys from cereal packets, would you like them?').

One morning she rang at 7.32 a.m. to ask if Bryony could roll her tongue.

'Um. Yesss,' Bryony slurped, hanging out of the shower to take the call.

'He could too!' Ann had gasped, before talking for twenty-five minutes about the dog's arthritis.

The calls were a nuisance, but a novelty too. Given her social life usually involved so much typing that it had begun to feel like an out-of-hours temp job, there was something refreshing about speaking on the phone with someone who regarded this as normal. 'Just on my way to work, Ann!' she would say, and instead of taking the hint, Ann would ask Bryony if her desk chair had enough back support, and were they offering her enough opportunities for career development, and when did they last give her a raise?

Besides, if she didn't pick up, she was gifted a voicemail instead, which would inevitably cut off midway through with an 'oof' and a scrumping noise, leaving her obliged to call back and check Ann hadn't fallen into a ravine. It was easier just to answer.

Others phoned too – Susan, Cousin Chloe, Lynn, all 'checking in' – in a rotation that suggested they were passing her number round like a takeaway menu. She pictured it scribbled on a roadside A-board next to the sign calling Little Buckton 'The heel tip of Northamptonshire'. Annie sent her motivational TikToks. The town crier had followed her on Instagram. Somebody called Wendy had emailed to ask if she had any interest in helping to run the local Brownies chapter. 'You'd need all the relevant CRB checks etcetera but what with all your volunteering work I assume you might have them already.'

Bryony had thanked Wendy for her kind offer, but explained that Walthamstow was really quite far from Northamptonshire and therefore she probably wouldn't be able to make it by 5pm on a Tuesday.

Still, it was nice to be checked in on. There was a special tone of voice they all used; the hushed inflection, the gently drawn-out syllables, making her feel precious and cared for. It began to seem almost rude when her colleagues and baristas spoke to her at a normal volume. Didn't they know someone close to her had just died? Didn't they know she was special?

Then there were the invites. Little Buckton prided itself on a punishing calendar of collective merriment, in which barely a week went by without some kind of event, festival, fundraising drive or pagan ritual that all residents past and present were expected to rush out and join. All residents, and all new-but-very-serious widowed girlfriends. Having resisted a charity coffee morning, a HIIT class and a community clothes swap on the basis that she had a job and was actually expected to be at it sometimes, Bryony found herself agreeing to go up for the Halloween parade.

'But *surely* you're off the hook now,' insisted Marco. 'These aren't death-adjacent activities anymore. They're just ... activities.'

'Everything is death-adjacent, to them,' she protested. 'It's only been a few weeks – if I stop joining in now it'll look strange.'

'Sure,' said Marco, watching as she plaited her hair into a passable Wednesday Addams. 'Mustn't look strange.'

'It's Ed's favourite tradition!' Annie said in the car. 'He must have told you about it?'

Bryony did what she had learned to do every time, now – fake a noise of bright recognition and say: 'Ah yes, rings a bell!'

Ed's fear of woodlice? Rings a bell! Ed's imaginary childhood friend, Clarice? Rings a bell! Ed's unlikely campanology phase? Rings a bell!

'The village has been doing it since fourteen-hundred-and-something,' continued Annie. 'And Ann's been decorating the house for it since slightly before that.'

True enough, when they arrived at Harbour House, all the windows at the front were bedecked with crêpe paper silhouettes – witches cackling over cauldrons, vampires bearing down on victims, something that looked alarmingly like a human autopsy – and cobwebs. A heap of pumpkins and assorted gourds was piled up by the unused front door, including a butternut squash with the price sticker still on it.

They entered to find Ann drinking wine from a chipped mug and stirring a huge, bubbling pot of something soupy and unidentifiable. She was wearing a long purple crocheted dress beneath a black suede waistcoat, with a pair of Blundstones. Bryony opened her mouth to admire her 'costume', then thought better of it.

'Hello love,' said Ann, pulling her in one-handed for the usual too-long embrace. 'Happy Halloween.'

'Thank you! And, ah, to you,' replied Bryony. Ann sighed a weary sigh, and went back to her stirring. 'Honestly Bryony, my heart isn't in it this year. Every day feels like Halloween to me. But the show must go on – for the kids.'

It was unclear whether this meant her own adult children, or an unseen chorus of local trick-or-treaters. Ann was recently back from doing 'the Halloween run', which was a trip to Costco ('nobody knows how she got a card,' muttered Annie, 'and nobody asks') to stock up on great vats of off-brand sweets called things like 'Mallibo Fizztastics' and 'mini Nougat Neptune bars'.

'The village takes it all very seriously, then?' asked Bryony.

Ann turned to look at her, and only then did Bryony notice, with a jolt of alarm, that she was wearing novelty contact lenses that made her irises entirely white.

'I wouldn't say that, Bryony,' said Ann. 'It's just a bit of fun.'

The bit of fun looked like something straight out of a Scandinavian folk horror, albeit with a high number of cult members dressed as

Elsa from *Frozen*. A solemn procession of what felt like hundreds, even thousands of people snaked through the village to the sound of Mike Oldfield's 'Tubular Bells', played through invisible speakers; not just children and parents but adults of all ages, participating without any hint of embarrassment.

Some waved and snarled into the darkness as they went, hamming it up like Disneyland actors. This was unnecessary, seeing as nobody was actually watching the parade because everyone was *in* the parade. In fact, after about twenty minutes Bryony realized that there weren't hundreds or thousands of people at all – the parade was just going in an endless loop down the high street and around the churchyard, getting rowdier with every lap. At one point there was a punch-up, reportedly over some planning permission, between Freddy Krueger and a six-foot Minion.

It was too warm, unnervingly warm, for the end of October. Bryony dabbed at the sweat beading on her upper lip and regretted wearing velvet. Annie had arrived as one of the girls from *The Craft* in a mini kilt and slashed t-shirt – although in fairness this wasn't far off her usual style – while Ann had added a homemade wire headpiece to her outfit, which gave her, with her violet-bagged eyes and the beginnings of red wine mouth, the look of the witchy one from Shakespeares Sister's 'Stay' video. Steve, in his funeral suit, was a too-healthy-looking Lurch. Leo and Kelly arrived as someone and someone-or-other from *Game of Thrones*, she looking like the model from the costume packaging and avoiding Bryony's eye.

'A moment!' cried Ann, as the parade wound down and they found themselves lingering by the duck pond. 'For Ethelred. Our darling, darling boy. He always loved this night so much – and I can feel him here with us now. Can't you?'

She looked around at the assembled faces and they all murmured in assent. Ann closed her eyes then, which seemed reckless given the number of silly string blasters in the vicinity, but it would have been heartless not to do the same. So they did, one by one, closing their eyes while the crowd screeched and hummed and jostled around them. Bryony swayed slightly on the spot. She willed herself to feel something – anything – that might suggest she had, if not a spiritual connection to her dead fake boyfriend, then at least a human soul.

After a few seconds, she did feel something. A small, featherlight tickle began at her lower back, creeping around her hip and waist. She shivered, feeling a sudden chill despite the stagnant air, then gasped as something else brushed against her leg. *Ed?*

Bryony opened her eyes and looked down to find a small child dressed as Peppa Pig reaching for her plastic pumpkin of treats, eyes wide with gleeful terror.

'Here, take it all,' she whispered to the girl, who didn't look as grateful as she might have done.

Meanwhile, Ann was crying. She had pulled Leo and Annie into a sort of maternal headlock, while Kelly, Steve, Susan and Emmett all stood solemnly by, nodding and rubbing her on the arm and back where appropriate. It was a heartbreaking scene, made no less so by the hidden speakers beginning to pump out 'The Monster Mash'.

Bryony expected someone to suggest they all go home now; that perhaps it was too much, too overwhelming, too soon. But presently Ann stopped her crying with one final, gulping shudder, kissed her children sloppily on each of their heads and declared, 'Right! To the pub.'

25

It's nice to be an optimist about things

Two hours later there had been a remarkable transformation. Bryony watched as Ann and her children, along with Susan, Cousin Chloe, Chloe's Bob, Steve and various others including Mr Duggan from the senior school, danced the Time Warp in the middle of the patterned carpet at The Stag and Barrow.

Kelly sat beside her, just far away enough that they weren't obliged to chat. Bryony marvelled at the core strength she must have to look poised on a bar stool.

'Come on you two! No spectators!' cried Ann, waving a hand in their direction whenever she jumped to the left, or stepped to the right. Kelly would laugh and do an awkward little approximation of sitting-down dancing, then she'd go back to looking at her phone and Ann would be forced to give up and put her hands on her hips, bringing her knees in tight. The pelvic thrusts came as a special kind of shock each time.

After several rounds of this, and when she was sure the song was nearing the end, Bryony drained the rest of her wine and jumped up to join them. Annie whooped and threw her arms around her. Steve went to clap her on the back but mis-timed a jump and ended up slapping her arse instead, mortified. And Ann took her by the hand, fingers clasped tightly around her own, and squeezed it as if, of all the gestures Bryony had pulled out for the Slingsby family in their short acquaintance, this was the most meaningful one.

From her bar stool, Kelly looked on.

After the playlist had exhausted itself and started back on the Monster Mash (really there was a huge gap in the canon for contemporary Halloween pop), Bryony looked at the time and realized with horror that she only had half an hour until the last train left for London. She gathered her things and mimed large, effusive good-byes to everyone on the dancefloor.

'Stay the night!' cried Annie. 'You can have Ed's room!'

But the idea of Ed's room gave her the creeps at the best of times; she wasn't about to cross the threshold on Halloween.

'Another time!' she promised.

'How are you getting to the station?' asked Steve, breaking away from the crowd.

'Oh, I'll get a taxi,' she said.

'No you won't, I'll take you.'

'Don't be silly, I'll be fine!' she protested. Steve had definitely been drinking. She'd seen at least three different pints in his hand.

'Seriously, let me drive you.'

'Honestly!' Her voice was getting higher with each insistence. 'I'm absolutely fine to get a cab! You stay! Have fun!' She gave him a playful little shove, back towards where Susan and Susan's Bob were now demonstrating a surprisingly proficient Lindy Hop.

'If you're sure.' Steve frowned. 'And you say you've booked a taxi yeah? Because I'd be pretty surprised if . . .'

But Bryony was already marching into the frigid night air, pulling out her phone. She opened Uber – more from force of habit than anything, but also because it was nice, sometimes, to be an optimist about things. *I do, I do, I do believe in fairies.*

There were no Ubers. Obviously.

With twenty-four minutes until the train left, Bryony googled 'taxi firm Little Buckton' and waited an agonising further minute for the results to load. It would probably have been quicker to ask for a phone number in the pub, but that would have involved going back in after she'd said goodbye to everyone, which Bryony considered more uncomfortable than sleeping in a ditch.

She called the first number. Nobody answered.

She tried the second. An answerphone informed her that all drivers were busy and to please leave a message with details of her trip. The tone suggested this was more out of curiosity than any guarantee of a taxi.

With nineteen minutes until the train, she tried the third number and punched the air when somebody answered.

'I'm afraid Terry's out,' a woman told her. Bryony asked if there was anyone besides Terry.

'Not really,' said the woman, considering this. 'There's sometimes Ian but only when the post's on strike.'

Bryony asked if Terry was going to be long on his current job, and the woman told her that Terry wasn't on a job, he was at the pub. 'For Halloween.' Bryony thanked her very much for her help, and kicked a dry stone wall.

Fifteen minutes.

She was just looking up local accommodation options (one boutique shepherd's hut, booked until March) when Kelly appeared beside her with her coat on.

'Come on,' she said.

'Oh. Hello! How are y—'

'Get a move on, you'll miss your train.' Kelly was walking away from her, up the lane. She blipped her car keys and some headlights blinked in the darkness.

'Oh no honestly, I'm fine!' Bryony called after her.

'You're not fine,' she said. 'You're about to miss your train because there are no taxis in bumfucknowhereshire and your only other option is sharing Ann's kitchen sofa with Twinkle, who, I can tell you from experience, is a sleep-farter. Get in.'

Kelly's eyes shone with fierce authority in the darkness. Bryony got in.

26

Sand and treacle

Thankfully as well as looking like a Bond girl, Kelly drove like one. Bryony braced herself against the passenger seat as they sailed down foggy lanes, swung with ease around overgrown hairpin bends and at one point appeared to clear a small stream with the grace of a showjumper. Kelly didn't seem bothered about making conversation, but Bryony was pathologically intolerant to silence. She grasped for something to say, and landed on their common ground.

'How's everything at the surgery?'

'Fine thanks,' said Kelly. 'How's everything at the council?'

'Oh, fine. You know. Not enough money, understaffed, everyone furious at us all the time for things we can't control.'

'Sounds familiar,' said Kelly. Bryony laughed weakly. It was important she kept the conversation up or else risk her most uncomfortable verbal tic: scatting. It was a condition she had never managed to diagnose, the urge to freestyle like a jazz singer any time there was a lull in conversation.

'Have you lived in Walthamstow long?' she ventured.

'Actually we're in Chingford,' said Kelly.

'Oh, lovely,' said Bryony.

'Is it?' said Kelly, and Bryony was forced to admit that she didn't know, she'd never been.

'But it always sounds nice. I know it's becoming really popular with families.'

Kelly made a noise that could have meant anything. Bryony ploughed on.

'Well you're ahead of the game, moving there now! Snapping up the good property before it gets a decent deli that stocks Perello olives and all the prices rocket. Very smart.'

'Actually I was born there,' said Kelly. 'I've always lived in Chingford.'

'Oh,' said Bryony, faintly. 'Lovely.'

Kelly made the noise again. She swung the car violently around a shape in the road that could have been a lost jumper or a badger. 'Shoo-bop-be-do-bop,' muttered Bryony into the headrest.

She looked at her phone. Seven minutes. It was interesting, the way opposing forces were making time move simultaneously like sand and treacle.

'Still, it's a shame Ed never introduced us – before,' she said. 'I would have loved to have had dinner with you and Leo.'

'Mm,' said Kelly. 'But that wasn't really Ed's style, was it.'

Bryony laughed and agreed. More silence. *Scoo-bop-de-dum-bop-bah*. Five minutes.

'What wasn't Ed's style?' she asked, when agony and curiosity got the better of her.

'Well, bringing women he was dating round for dinner,' said Kelly. 'To be honest with you, Leo always thought he made them up. We were pretty surprised when you turned out to be real.'

'Ahahaha,' Bryony barked out a laugh. 'Well, I'm real! As real as . . . J.Lo.'

'I know, babe,' said Kelly. 'I've seen your medical records.'

'Ahahaha,' said Bryony again, because there seemed to be no other option. 'I'm sorry,' she added.

'What you sorry for?'

'Ah. Well, you know – darkening your waiting room doorway so often. I must be your worst patient!'

Kelly didn't laugh, or refute this.

'Not the very worst,' she said, evenly. 'You've never shat on the floor.'

'Well,' said Bryony, after a pause. 'You've always been brilliant, at the surgery – and all the doctors are great, really great . . . I mean, god bless the NHS, right?'

Kelly snorted.

Four minutes.

'Anyway, I promise to stay out of your hair for a few months at least.'

This was a rash promise. For Bryony nearly every week brought some new cause for panic. Mysterious twinges. Strange headaches. Hot legs.

'Yeah?' said Kelly, seeming interested. 'Are you feeling better then?'

'Oh, I think so! I mean, there's always something isn't there.'

An itchy tongue. A twitching eyelid. A shaving rash that could be cellulitis.

'Apparently,' said Kelly.

'But I guess I'm trying to keep things in perspective. After everything that's happened. Losing Ed.'

'So it was the real deal then was it, with you two? True love?'

It was startling to hear it asked so plainly, when everyone else seemed to have accepted this as fact. Bryony opened her mouth to reply but at that moment, the station emerged from the mist like a blessed desert oasis. With a cool three minutes to spare, Kelly pulled up smoothly at the entrance and Bryony began gushing as she climbed out.

'Thank you so, so much, you're an angel.'

'It's fine, don't worry about it.'

'No but really!' she insisted. 'You're an absolute lifesaver.'

'Nah,' said Kelly, dryly. 'I'm just the receptionist.'

27

A nice chat

The next day Bryony had lunch with her friend Noor, the only school friend she stayed in contact with beyond her twice-yearly Facebook logins and anyone she had the misfortune to bump into in Orpington big Tesco.

Noor maintained dutiful contact with at least half of their year group and so every meeting included a comprehensive rundown of who was getting divorced, who'd had bad fillers and who'd lost their life savings in crypto. A journalist who had started out writing listicles about forgotten reality stars, Noor had quietly moved up the ranks of the industry to a point where she now won awards for her investigations and sporadically appeared on the *Today* programme. When they saw each other they would generally talk about Bryony's life for about ninety seconds and Noor's for upwards of an hour, which always felt valid because Noor's career was interesting and Bryony's wasn't.

'So what's new with you?' asked Noor, putting her phone away after a lengthy dissection of Jessica Craig's botched Brazilian bum lift.

'Well, not much.'

Bryony carved into the £11 hummus on toast that had the nerve to call itself 'Mediterranean medley'.

'My boyfriend died.'

She chewed.

'I'm sorry, your what?' Noor's eyes widened.

'But I didn't know he was my boyfriend until afterwards.'

'After . . . ?'

'He was dead, yeah.'

Noor was visibly struggling to decide how to respond, and a part of Bryony relished this. It made such a change from their usual script; the 'met anyone nice – nope – hang on in there! – same for your marriage!' exchanges that had been seeing them through brunches and drinks for the past however many years.

'Oh my god,' said Noor. 'I'm so sorry! Can I tell people?'

'If you like,' said Bryony.

There was a lull as Noor pulled a face at her lunch and made to flag down a teenage waitress. Her eggs were overdone, her toast medium-rare and wasn't there supposed to be a drizzle? Bryony willed the moment to be over. Noor was one of the fussiest eaters she knew and yet she continued placing her faith in very obviously average establishments, the kind with laminated menus and photos of smoothies in the window. It was inspiring, in a way.

'I saw your Dad the other day in big Tesco,' said Noor, as though this information might cheer Bryony up. 'We had a nice chat. He didn't mention anything about a dead boyfriend?'

That Noor could have 'a nice chat' with her father was not surprising; her skills as a parent-charmer came from the same place as her skill for coaxing headlines out of reluctant politicians. That he'd been in big Tesco was more surprising. Perhaps he was having an affair.

'Oh, he doesn't know about Ed,' Bryony told her.

'That he's died?!'

'That he existed,' she clarified, and Noor tipped her head to the side and cooed.

'Aw. Poor Richard.'

'Poor me!' said Bryony. 'My dad hasn't been interested in my dating life since I stopped needing lifts back from the Megabowl. I'm the one with the dead boyfriend.'

'I thought he wasn't your boyfriend?'

She shrugged. 'I'm conducting investigations.'

'Anyway,' Noor went on, cutting and inspecting her replacement egg (gloopy) with a wounded little sigh. 'He was saying they're going to meet Tim in France next week, are you going too?'

'Going where?'

'Lille, to talk wedding plans?'

'I ... uh, no, no I can't go,' said Bryony, because it was easier than admitting she hadn't been asked and didn't in fact know it was happening. She barely knew the wedding was happening. 'Busy at work, you know.'

'And the grieving,' said Noor, generously.

'Sure,' nodded Bryony. 'And that.'

28

It's the other

'Oh my god, Kels Bells, I thought that was you!' trills the woman who has been avoiding her eye, clearly hoping to be called by the other receptionist. 'How are you? What are you up to these days? It's been so long!'

It has been so long that for a moment Kelly doesn't know who this woman is. She studies her – fashionably slick ponytail, lip fillers, designer bag – and finally a mental image clicks into focus, of the same face with a deflated mouth and a halo of glitter butterfly clips, howling with laughter after Kelly chipped a tooth on the netball court. Jenna McKenzie. Jenna McKenzie had never, to her memory, called her Kels Bells.

Having grown up in the area, seeing people she went to school with is an occupational hazard. The ones who betrayed their roots by living south of the river for a few years, before crawling back to the top end of the Victoria line for free childcare and better tube links. The ones who get off on being 'born and bred', who drop their ts and roll their eyes at anybody calling it 'the village' even while they're paying £6 for a long-fermentation rye.

Those people often go pink and awkward when they recognize

Kelly behind the surgery counter, as though they've walked in on her doing something embarrassing.

What are they up to these days, she'll ask, because you have to, and they'll tell her about their job as a creative director at an ambiguous startup, then out of habit they'll ask *her* what she's up to these days, and she'll remain completely straight-faced and say: 'I'm a receptionist at a doctor's surgery,' and they'll laugh and apologise and look mortified, or sometimes they won't. Either way, she'll quite enjoy it.

Then they'll say, 'any kids?' and the enjoyment will end.

Kelly has been bored and unfulfilled at the clinic for as long as she has worked at the clinic. A while ago she'd taken an eight-week virtual coaching course on 'How to hustle your way to happiness' and as a result had spent a long time embellishing her CV, curating her LinkedIn and inviting inspirational CEOs on coffee dates. None had accepted, but her course leader insisted it was the intention that really 'shifted vibrations in her favour'. Kelly had asked for her money back.

She'd applied for a raft of jobs and had a handful of promising but ultimately unsuccessful interviews, then she'd stopped applying when they started trying to get pregnant, reasoning that she couldn't rock up at a new job and immediately go on maternity leave. She knew that legally, of course, she could, but sensed this was only in the same way that legally you can pay for a latte with postage stamps.

Recently the trying has become a job in itself, beholden to schedules and cycles and swallowing pills, pissing on sticks and reading the backs of shampoo bottles for hidden nasties, scouring forums, burrowing deeper and deeper into Google in search of weird science and practical magic, doing Pilates and cutting out sugar and trying the whole time to stay calm, because stress is worse than poison, everyone says. And when the Jenna McKenzies of the world appear and ask her what she's up to these days, it takes a moment to remember that trying to get pregnant is not, in fact, her career.

'What can I help you with today?' she asks, looking pointedly at Jenna's hands, which are trying to cram a plastic-bagged item back into her quilted tote.

'Oh that can wait, how are *you* though?' Jenna stalls, visibly flustered.

'I'm great thanks. Are you here for an appointment, or ... ?'

'You got married, didn't you? What's his name?' asks Jenna.

'Leo,' supplies Kelly. 'Did you want to *make* an appointment?'

'Leo, that's it! I knew I'd seen him on your Insta. Fit one, isn't he!'

Kelly can't help smiling, knowing her husband's face is valuable currency, even if his clients and colleagues are enjoying more of his charm than she is right now. In the weeks since the funeral, Leo has started going out a surprising amount – work drinks and birthday drinks and [insert sport here] with the lads – while at home he remains crumpled and silent.

'Any kids?'

Her smile stiffens and she nods to the queue behind her. 'Can't really chat now, sorry Jenna. What is it you've come for?'

'Ahahahaha.' Jenna laughs maniacally at nothing at all. Kelly waits.

'It's ... oh, I mean, it's probably nothing but the doctor said to bring it in, so ... is there a box I can just stick it in, or?'

'Well that depends what it is,' says Kelly, and Jenna laughs again, her hand still clutched around the object inside her bag as though perhaps she is about to hold them at gunpoint.

'Is it a sample?' Kelly asks, leading her, the way one might a toddler.

Jenna looks relieved. 'Uh-huh, that's right ... a sample. Where do the samples go?'

'A urine sample? You can just give it to me.'

More laughter. More stalling. Eventually Jenna says, 'No, it's . . . the other,' and slowly draws out the specimen pot in its sealed bag, a turd like a prize conker just visible within. She places it gently on the counter.

Kelly thinks, as she directs Jenna to the specimen box at the end of the desk and spritzes a bottle of D10 in her wake, that maybe the course did shift vibrations in her favour after all.

29

A single beam of light

Bryony was still working through her Halloween hangover when she got the Bonfire Night invite from Annie. Was Bonfire Night always a week after Halloween? Had the calendar always been this relentless?

It was less an invite and more a directive.

Mum is insisting on doing her usual baked potato party, Ed's favourite! Saturday from 5, bring spare tupperware for the chilli or she'll make you take it in a freezer bag xxx.

Bryony squinted at it through dried-out raisin eyes, the week-end's sugar still pounding its way round her system. Was it possible for one big binge to tip a person into diabetes? She hadn't checked for a while; there might be new research out.

Another message from Annie.

Oh and there's going to be some kind of fireworks tribute to Ed, they might want you to push the button x

'No,' she said out loud to nobody. 'Absolutely not.'

But even as she was saying it, she knew she would go. Bryony had always loved Bonfire Night, or at least the idea of Bonfire Night – the cold-nose-warm-heartedness of it all, the childish purity of a holiday that wasn't about buying a load of stuff or getting off with anyone.

Just standing in a field for half an hour with a Thermos of soup, taking shit photos of fireworks against a too-cloudy sky while a local radio DJ played Katy Perry. Lots of the best London displays had fizzled out with Covid and never returned, but she could fully imagine the kind of affair Little Buckton might put on. Wholesome, charming, thrillingly untouched by modern health and safety regulations.

Plus, she'd been craving baked potatoes recently. She never had the patience to wait an hour for a proper one in the oven.

Bryony left Annie on read for the afternoon, then replied that she'd love to come.

Emmett was her chauffeur this time. It was a mercifully quiet journey.

'Chaffinch,' he said at one point, without indicating where.

'Yes,' Bryony agreed.

They arrived at the house to find about fifteen people in gilets and fleeces milling around the kitchen while Ann stirred three huge, catering-style vats of chilli, one with each hand and one with the wooden spoon in her mouth. The room was a mess. Industrial numbers of empty plastic mince packets were stacked up along the windowsill, leaking pinkish juice onto a copy of the local paper, which was open perilously close to the gas hob. The dog was trembling violently under the table.

'Poor thing! Is she scared of the fireworks?' asked Bryony, giving the creature a tentative pat. She wasn't a dog person, but experience had taught her it was safer to pretend.

'No. She ate half a tray of treacle toffee earlier.'

'Ah.'

During her first few visits, Bryony had assumed the state of the Slingsby house reflected the chaos of bereavement. The post and leaflets piled on every surface because nobody had the energy to sort and recycle them; the discarded mugs and half-eaten sandwiches reflecting the unreliable appetites of the grief-stricken and the attempts by kind visitors to feed them. But she was starting to realize that this was just how the house always looked.

She jumped as Emmett appeared at her elbow – despite being seven foot tall, the man had no audible footsteps – offering her a glass of something from a green bottle with no label. Bryony accepted, but her eyes began streaming in protest before the liquid touched her lips.

'Get stuck in before the rest of the hordes arrive,' said Ann, handing her a baked potato the size of a guinea pig. 'The end one is vegetarian, these two pots are normal.'

'Lovely! What's in the veggie one?'

'Everything except the meat,' said Ann.

'Lovely,' said Bryony.

When she turned, paper plate warm and sagging under the weight of the chilli, she found a smiling woman at her elbow.

'I liked your poem. At the . . .' the woman waved a hand to fill in the blank. It was odd how people were scared to say the word 'funeral', as though by not naming the thing, Ed would somehow be less dead.

'Oh! Thank you,' said Bryony. She was already used to this idea, that she was an established literary talent. On top of the idea that she was Ed's serious girlfriend, it didn't seem so much of stretch. Was this the con artist pipeline, she wondered? You start flexing your duplicity muscle and before you know it you're founding a cryptocurrency or masquerading as a German heiress.

'We've heard so much about you,' the woman said.

'All lies I hope!' said Bryony, and the woman chuckled obligingly. She had a kind, toothy face, like a critter from a picture book, with heavy-lidded eyes that seemed to blink at twice the normal rate.

'Actually, can I ask,' Bryony glanced around to check for lingering Slingsbys, then leaned a little closer, 'what have you heard?

About me, I mean? Or are you just saying that because it's the kind of thing people say and actually you never knew I existed? You can be honest, I won't mind.'

The woman blinked. 'Well,' she began, hesitantly, 'we heard you and Ed were ...' the hand wave again. Apparently if you flapped away sex it wouldn't be real either. '... a couple. And that your name is Bryony, and you work for the government.' The poor thing looked nervous now, as though recounting vital intelligence under threat of torture. Bryony put down her fork.

'And you live in London,' she added. Bryony nodded, encouragingly, 'And that he was absolutely barmy about you,' she finished, with a smile.

There it was, the barminess. Bryony smiled back, because how can you not smile at the idea that somebody, anybody, was barmy about you?

'Well, that's lovely,' she said and the woman looked relieved. But she wasn't dismissed yet.

'And can I ask ... sorry, what was your name?'

'Trish.'

'Can I ask, Trish, who told you all this? Ed himself?'

Was this mad, interrogating strangers through mouthfuls of mince? Bryony's grip on reality had been so shaken by recent events that she couldn't work out if this came off like spirited party chat or would mark her out as a figure of concern.

'Um. Nooo ...' the woman drew out the word as though playing for time. Perhaps she thought 'the government' meant MI6. 'I *think* it was Ann.'

Obviously it was Ann.

'That's right, I remember now! Ann told me all about you.'

They both looked over to where Ann was standing, ladling chilli one-handed with the air of a fairy godmother granting wishes. She waved.

*

Another pagan fervour had seized the village, only a week after the last.

Little Buckton's Bonfire Night proved to be a muddled celebration that involved burning effigies of loathed politicians and disgraced royals, casual anti-popery and setting off bangers at the feet of unsuspecting observers (mainly Bryony).

A huge bonfire blazed on the village green and a troupe of goth Morris dancers performed beside it, eliciting whoops and gasps every time their black hankies got too close to the flames. Children who couldn't have been older than about four waved flaming torches with gleeful abandon. And Ann appeared to be in her element, passing around a flask of hot booze and being hugged by a constant stream of friends and neighbours, all keen to tell her how strong she was, how amazingly she was doing. The words 'his favourite!' whistled on the wind.

The fireworks themselves were due to start at seven p.m., and Bryony was breathing a sigh of relief that no more had been mentioned about a tribute to Ed, or her 'doing' any 'honours'. But, just as the dancers took their final bows and people started milling towards the barriers, a familiar voice rang out over the tannoy. Not a local radio DJ, but Annie.

'Helloooo, Little Buckton!' She sounded slightly shaky. But then Annie always sounded slightly shaky.

'So the fireworks will kick off in a minute don't worry, but first we – my family, the Slingsbys, you know us, hiya – well, we just wanted to say a little something. Ahem. As many of you know, we tragically lost my brother Ed just over a month ago. It's been a really hard time, the worst time in the world. But everyone in the village has been so, so kind . . .'

The loudspeaker cracked, just as Annie's voice did. Bryony wanted to rush up and hug her, but in the darkness she couldn't make out where she was speaking from.

'. . . and we just wanted to say a massive thank you for all the support, and . . .'

A second voice was audible on the speakers then: Ann, who it seemed was no longer in the crowd next to Bryony and the family, but side of stage, hissing instructions to her daughter.

'. . . and because this was Ed . . . um, *Ethelred*'s favourite time of year, we hope everyone agrees that it would be nice to dedicate this year's Buckton Blaze to him. And now, to do the honours . . .'

Oh shit.

'. . . we have Ed's late – no, sorry, former – I mean not former but . . . Ed's, um, *partner*, Bryony, as our special guest to start proceedings. Please give her a big Little Bucks welcome.'

A round of applause began to swell through the crowd. Bryony thought she heard Steve whooping from somewhere behind her.

'Bryony, where are yooou? Up you come!' Bryony considered pretending to faint, or pulling her bobble hat down over her eyes until everybody gave up and went home. But even Kelly was smiling encouragement at her, or at least she was smiling about something, and Leo had placed his hands on her waist from behind, steering her firmly through the crowd towards the small, upturned crate next to the Bonfire – where Ann, Annie and a scowling man in a hi-vis vest were standing.

The Sugababes' 'Push the Button' began playing. Annie hugged her like a competition winner. Ann initiated a countdown, and the crowd joined in: 'TEN . . . NINE . . . EIGHT . . .', as the scowling man handed Bryony a red plastic knob that looked like an upside-down yoghurt pot glued to a piece of plywood.

'Should this be connected to anything?' Bryony asked him.

'Nah. S'just a prop,' he told her. 'We've not gone digital yet.'

Sure enough, when she squinted over his shoulder, she could see another man in another hi-vis walking towards the centre of the grass with a huge, lit splint.

'FIVE . . . FOUR . . . ,' screamed the crowd. Was she supposed to say anything? Should she read her funeral poem again?

'THREE . . . TWO . . .'

Bryony smiled in spite of herself, feeling like a Spice Girl switching on the Oxford Street lights.

'ONE!'

'This is for you, Ed!' she called to the crowd, and slammed her palm down on the red button. It immediately crumpled, because it was, it turned out, an upside-down yoghurt pot glued to a piece of plywood.

Next came an agonising pause, as the music cut out and nothing else happened. The crowd was silent, necks craned expectantly upwards. Finally, a single beam of light whooshed into the sky and sputtered into a golden spider's web. Everyone cheered, including Bryony.

'Thank you, darling girl.' Suddenly, Ann was hugging her from one side, Annie from the other. 'You really are doing amazingly.' Bryony thanked her. And in an odd way it felt like she was.

30

I'm afraid that was a test

Bryony was back on the apps.

Because life was short and the whole dead Ed situation had, if anything, upped her sense of urgency around dating in general. The musical-chairs-ness of 30-something romance was hard to ignore at the best of times, let alone when the nice ones had started dying.

Still though, all the admin ('Edmin, surely,' said Marco) had led to a long lag in her replies.

She returned to her Alloi inbox with the trepidation of a person opening up misted boxes in the back of the fridge, hoping to find something for dinner. Every conversation was either festering or long past its use-by date. She paused with a pang on her message history with Ed, but didn't click. Either because she knew that would be stale and unappetizing too, or perhaps because she was scared it wouldn't be.

Bryony swiped through the new arrivals – a sparse crop. They were heading into cuffing season after the last of the late-summer flings, but the annual spate of festive breakups hadn't happened yet. Still, after some fiddling with her search parameters, the result was two dates this week – one with Kyle, a twenty-something semi-pro footballer who played for Epping Athletic ('You know Ted Lasso was fictional?' warned Marco), the other with a newly divorced dad in his forties, Theo, who lived in Sydenham, wore Crocs and requested they meet 'out of catchment'.

Theo was on a spree, clearly. He had strenuously suggested they go somewhere near Bryony's flat, 'so it's convenient for you.'

'No honestly, happy to travel!' she'd replied, although she wasn't.

'Really, I insist! I'll come to you,' he'd messaged. '*near* you, I mean, ha ha ha,' he'd messaged again, with laugh-sweating emoji for good measure. Which was how they ended up in The Milk Churn, a pub that prided itself, revenue be damned, on being both child-free and 'cat-friendly'. In fairness, it was convenient for her.

'This must be a treat for you, not being surrounded by mewling kids,' Bryony said as they carried their drinks back from the bar. Theo looked affronted. Or perhaps he just didn't want to be sur-rounded by mewling cats, either.

Theo was into music. This had been established early on by his Alloi profile, which featured several photos of him straight-faced in front of an Ikea Kallax full of vinyl. He'd turned up wearing a faded *Marquee Moon* t-shirt and was now singing along to Bryan Ferry under his breath, in the manner of a person who really wants you to know that they are Into Music.

Bryony began singing too. 'Love this album,' she said. *Song* was too basic, to love an album showed depth. Besides, it was true. Roxy Music had been a shared passion of her parents. Their coffee-ringed records had soundtracked her early years, back when her father had soul. It was music that had always felt heavy with memories, even when she was a child hearing it for the first time; as though the adult world was lifting a velvet curtain and letting her in on a great secret.

Theo grinned at her, and nodded in respect.

'Absolute classic,' he confirmed. 'Can't beat Eno's production.'

He was wrong, Brian Eno wasn't on this album and she knew it. In later years, once the LPs had been packed away and Kath's

Michael Bublé CDs instated, Bryony had spent hours in her bed-room memorizing music trivia with which to make boys love her. But twenty years on it felt churlish to correct Theo, so she nodded enthusiastically.

'Yes! So good.'

Instantly his expression shifted to one of equal triumph and disappointment.

'Aha!' he said. 'I'm afraid that was a test. Eno actually didn't do this album, it was Rhett Davis – Eno's last with Roxy was For Your Pleasure back in seventy-three.'

Bryony gagged a little on her wine.

This wasn't an unusual interaction. She'd noticed that most of the men from the apps acted as though they were screening for reasons not to go out with her, or maybe with anyone. As though each date were a prime-time TV quiz format; just a string of in-creasingly difficult questions designed to leave her toppling into the metaphorical sea.

Ed hadn't acted this way, she realized now. If anything, Ed had seemed entirely unbothered by the question of whether they were compatible. He was just happy to be there.

'I actually knew that,' Bryony told Theo. 'I just didn't want to correct you.' It was impossible not to sound defensive.

'Sure,' Theo smirked. 'Ok.'

She dug a fist into her thigh in mute frustration. But whether she was about to be eliminated by Theo, or he by her, they never found out. Because it was at that moment that Bryony looked up to notice, with a jolt, Kelly and Annie sitting at a corner table.

It was half a moment later – not long enough to duck and hide, or conceal her face behind a passing tabby – that they saw her.

'Bryony? Bryony!'

Annie sounded delighted to see her. Kelly's eyes were narrowed in suspicion and fixed on Theo, as she stood up and followed her sister-in-law over to their table.

While Annie hugged her with the usual vigour, Bryony willed Theo to disappear. Perhaps fall backwards out of an open window, or transmogrify into a middle-aged colleague called June. But no, there he still was, looking at the women in turn. Probably assessing whether one of them was more attractive than Bryony, or knew more about early eighties synth-pop.

Annie looked at Theo. Kelly looked at Theo. Bryony looked at Theo, wondering if she could get away with pretending she didn't know him either. *Thank god you rescued me, he just sat down and started talking about Brian Eno.*

A friend, she decided, she would say he was a friend! My friend Theo. The perfect solution.

'Hi, I'm Theo,' he stuck out a hand to Kelly. 'I'm Bryony's date.'

31

Almost completely
100% low risk

'Date?'

Annie repeats the word with a quiver in her voice. 'You're on a date?'

'No!' Bryony says. The man raises an eyebrow. 'Yes,' she stammers. 'No. Yes, *but*—'

Annie is gone. The heavy wooden pub door swings in her wake and Kelly half expects to hear the doof-doof-doof of the *EastEnders* theme.

Kelly stands there for a few seconds longer, eyes still narrowed at the pair, before she walks back to the corner table, picks up both of their bags and leaves too.

She knows she ought to be furious in solidarity with Annie, and Ed, but actually she is grateful to Monica – *Bryony* – for the interruption.

Inviting Annie to stay had been Kelly's idea, hoping Leo would feel better with his sister beneath the same roof for a few days – and then better still when she had gone. Taking her to the cat pub had been Kelly's idea too, Annie being a person who loved a gimmick and wasn't fussy about hairs in her nachos. Taking her alone had *not* been Kelly's idea, but Leo had announced last-minute that he'd committed to a work meeting at a bar in the City that specialised in VR clay pigeon shooting, and Kelly hadn't felt able to protest. Because Leo was sad, and sometimes sad people need to blow simulated pretend birds to pieces with a plastic gun.

Before the drama, Kelly's evening with her sister-in-law had gone like this:

Annie: I have a wonderful business opportunity for you!

Kelly: I have a job, but thanks!

Annie: That's why this is such a great opportunity – it can fit around your nine to five!

Kelly: I work eight to six, but thanks!

Annie: Gel Lyfe is a perfect side hustle. I know you're really keen to find a more creative outlet, something a bit more stimulating than the surgery. You know, with more potential for growth.

Kelly: Do you? Am I?

Annie: Ann said.

Kelly: Oh.

Annie: And the great thing is, it's almost completely 100% low risk! I'd be your boss! Wouldn't that be cool?

[*Kelly considers a world in which Annie is her boss. Annie is chronically broke, forever begging loans off Leo for vague reasons and spurious purpose – a course she wants to do, a holiday she wants to take, her old banger needs a new exhaust, she's being evicted from another undocumented house share. Annie's also quit more jobs than she has had gel-based dinners.*]

Kelly: Yeah, very . . . cool.

Annie: So all you'd need to do initially is sign up for the Gelevation Starter Pack—

Kelly: The what?

Annie: Unless of course you wanted to just say fuck it and go for the Surprise and Gelight premium package, really maximize your potency potential from the start? Actually that could be a really good option for you – if we're talking price-per-gel it's—

Kelly: Annie, how much have you spent on this stuff?

Annie: Oh, not much. Hardly anything really! I got a really good discount because Maxine – she's my Diamond Team Queen – said I had so much potential. That's the great thing about Gel Lyfe, they really care about women and helping us achieve self-fulfilment. Like Tamara says, she's feminist first, capitalist seco—

Kelly: So do you think you'll be able to pay Leo back the money he lent you?

Annie: Sure, definitely, really soon! Although if you wanted, I guess you could see it as investment?

Kelly: An investment—

Annie: In my business? Or I guess if you'd rather be paid back in gel, that could work too.

Kelly: We'd rather be paid back in money.

Annie: Sure, that's fine, because I'm making loads of it now.

Kelly: Are you?

Annie: I mean, every business has start-up costs but—

Kelly: When you say 'business'—

Annie: Bryony? Bryony!

Now they are standing on a street corner and Annie is crying, and miraculously none of it is Kelly's fault for not being supportive about her business.

In the Slingsby family 'not being supportive' is a crime of the highest order, punishable by short hugs, barbed comments and being served the least edible parts of the roast. Once, her mother-in-law got wind that Kelly had discouraged Leo from applying for a job as a fintech CEO in Helsinki – partly because of her irrational childhood fear of The Moomins, but mostly because he had no relevant financial experience – and Kelly's Christmas present that year had been a book called *'Finnish What You Start: How to embrace life the New Nordic way'*. Ann has never met a grudge she can't bear.

Now Kelly is being incredibly supportive, stroking Annie's arms and calling Bryony every name she can think of – *bitch, sociopath, narcissist, ice-hearted monster*; it's cathartic to be honest – while Annie wails and sobs with the raw public abandon that only the recently bereaved can. Annie has never been one for inhibitions, but grief has rendered her somehow both skinless and completely invulnerable; as though the world and everyone in it are merely a painted backdrop to her pain.

'He's only been *gone* five weeks and she's *dating*? She's out there trying to get laid again while Ed . . . while Ed . . . *hegghhhhhh.*'

'I know,' says Kelly.

'What kind of *ice-hearted monster* does something . . . *heggghhhh* . . . like that?'

'I don't know,' says Kelly.

'And he was such a good guy! It's basically . . . *heggghhghh* . . . cheating?!'

'I know,' says Kelly.

'What was she planning to do, just keep *shagging around* while she helps us plan his memorial?'

'I don't know,' says Kelly.

'*Hegggghhhh.* Anyway. Fuck her.'

'Fuck her,' says Kelly.

'Have you decided . . . *heggghhh* . . . about the Surprise and Gelight package?'

'Um,' says Kelly.

32

If there's anything I can do

It took Bryony an hour of strenuous self-flagellation to bring Annie round.

'I don't understand why you care,' said Marco. 'If she never wants to see you again, that's your out.'

'But then she'd be out there in the world, hating me! Thinking I didn't care enough about her dead brother not to get straight back on the apps.'

'But that is the truth,' said Marco, slowly, as if to an idiot.

Bryony shook her head. She squirmed, as though Annie's anger were a physical irritant, crawling like nettle rash across her skin. 'I couldn't bear it.'

She arranged to see her the next day, with a threefold defence: 1. *It wasn't a date*. 2. *Did you see his shoes though*. 3. *I am a grieving mess and cannot be held responsible for my actions.*

Annie seemed to want to believe number one but in the end it was number three that resonated most. 'I suppose I'm not exactly myself just now either . . .' she began, and Bryony leapt on and rode the point home. Honestly, it was *because* she felt so strongly about Ed that she was compelled to go on the . . . well, *not* date, – because all those strong feelings have to find somewhere to go. In a *way*, if she had felt *less* devastated about Ed, she would have been *less* likely to go on the not date, definitely not a date, I Can't Believe It's Not Dating, do you see?

Astonishingly, Annie did see.

'I guess I understand,' she said eventually, once the crying and shouting portion of their meeting had concluded and she had promised, solemnly, not to tell her mother. 'I haven't been making good decisions lately either.'

'Do you want to talk about it?' asked Bryony, sensing a chance for redemption. She could feel her buttocks sweating.

'No. Well. So, you know my business?'

'Mmm?' said Bryony, hopefully. She thanked God that Annie had come to this realization by herself. It had been painful, hearing her talk as though she believed friendly gut bacteria were her path to financial security.

'Well, I had this great opportunity to level-up my gelibility rating and become a Team Queen in Training, which would have boosted me up from Flint level to Peridot, just like that. But I've been such a wreck these past few weeks that I missed the discount window. So stupid. And now I'm way behind on my targets.'

'Mmm,' said Bryony, her heart sinking again. 'What a shame.'

'I knew you'd understand, Bryony. You said it yourself, the first time we met – Ed would want me to pull myself together and focus on work.'

'*Is* that what I said?'

'You were so wise and comforting, like you really understood me. I could see exactly why Ed thought you were so great. I know it sounds stupid but having you around; it makes me feel connected to him? Like, if you had that connection with him then you must understand us too. Or I thought you did, anyway.'

Bryony shivered as the sweat turned cold on her skin.

'Honestly Annie, I feel awful for upsetting you. If there's anything I can do . . .'

Those words. How many times had she used those words in her life? Scattering them liberally like friendship confetti, knowing there wasn't a chance anyone was ever going to gather them up and piece them together into something meaningful. *If there's anything I can do* . . . a sentence so hollow it didn't even warrant finishing.

'Actually,' said Annie.

33

Theoretically nice
but materially pointless

Bryony's Gelevation Starter Pack arrived two days later by courier.

For a moment she got excited – *A present! For meee?* – before opening the box to reveal the notecard, printed to look handwritten in violent aloe-green, which read 'HEY GELIEVER! WELCOME TO THE FIRST DAY OF THE REST OF YOUR LYFE.'

Her heart sank. Even the Yodel man looked judgemental.

Below the text was a photo of 'Tamara Mucklethwaite, Gel Lyfe CEO and founder'. Tamara was of ambiguous age but unquestionable wellness, with the thick, glossy mane of a thoroughbred horse and the large, shining eyes of a nut-drunk squirrel. In the photo she was holding a mug and wearing muted athleisurewear, muted soft furnishings just visible behind. *This is not a hard-nosed businesswoman*, the picture seemed to scream. *This is not a person who spends the 9–6 shackled to her desk at someone else's beck and call. Her nose is soft, like yours! Her life is soft, like a cashmere hoodie! And yours could be too.*

Beneath the notecard and thick booklet titled 'Aloe, Aloe! Your Gel Lyfe Handbook (Flint level)' she found small, embossed pink and green boxes stacked five-deep. Bryony opened a box and took out a patented Gel Lyfe 'delivery pouch'. She tore it open, inhaled deeply and retched.

'I have delicate digestion,' she'd told Annie. 'I'm not sure it would agree with me.'

But Annie had been insistent. 'Gel Lyfe is great for gut health!' she'd said. Then, solemnly, as though quoting Maya Angelou, 'The gut is the heart of the lower abdomen.'

Bryony had long struggled with her gut; both physical and metaphorical. Just the words 'trust your gut' were enough to send her spiralling, because hers had been an unreliable narrator for as long as she could remember. If she genuinely followed her gut instinct she would spend every day in A&E, or M&S, cancelling plans, taking the long route home, throwing away perfectly fine food, or friends, or opportunities, and running from things – mostly in the direction of the nearest toilet.

Although she might also avoid ending up in situations like this.

She replayed the memory, trying to pinpoint all the parts of the conversation at which she could have saved herself and didn't.

'It's a hyper-potent blend of seventy-two all-whole, nature-inspired minerals and adaptogens that harness the power of science and the spirit of plants to supercharge your system and help you feel like your best self,' Annie had said. Then she had rummaged in her bag and produced a small bottle with a label on an aloe-green ribbon around its neck, designed to look like the 'drink me' potion from *Alice in Wonderland*. This homespun charm was offset by a list of ingredients and legal disclaimers too long to fit on the back of the bottle.

'Oh,' Bryony had said. Or maybe it had been 'ooh'? Ooh was a more encouraging 'oh'. Ooh was a dangerous noise.

But in spite of herself, there was a twang of curiosity. As a little girl, Bryony had been obsessed with mixing up potions. She would trawl the kitchen cupboards, the bathroom cabinet, the flower beds and garden shed in search of ingredients, indiscriminately mixing the botanical and the synthetic, the familiar and the alien, oats and avocados and rose petals and once (though never again) peanut butter, in her pursuit of transformative alchemy. What mostly happened was that her mother would sigh about the mess and her father would yell at her for leaving a yoghurt and cat litter face mask in the fridge where it could be mistaken for cheese and chive dip – but still she could remember the shiver of hope and excitement that inspired these endeavours. Because this time, just maybe, she would hit on the magical combination that actually worked.

'Basically, it makes you feel ah-mazing all day long. Even if you eat a load of shit and never sleep. There's evidence it can actually repair free radical damage and promote cell renewal by up to seventy-three percent.'

'*Up to* seventy-three percent?' Bryony had said.

'Yes! Amazing right?'

'Ooh,' Bryony had replied. She slowed down the memory like a televised magic trick, to see if she could spot the sleight of hand.

'And after the initial one-off investment you can start earning immediately.'

'Uhh.'

'Trust me, once people give it a go they'll be jonesing your door down for more!'

Annie never got an idiom right. It was highly endearing. In fact Annie was highly endearing in general, with her guileless face and kooky teen wardrobe; her overfamiliar habits, like snaking an arm around your waist or playing with your hair without asking, tapping into some deep-rooted *primal* – no, *primary school* – need to feel special, chosen, anointed. Maybe this, and not the guilt, was the real reason the words "sorry, no" had disappeared from Bryony's vocabulary, replaced with 'totally!' and 'sounds interesting'. And of course, her best friend, the ooh.

'Perhaps I could just buy a couple of packets off you instead?' she had tried, or thought she had. 'I really don't think I'm cut out to be a saleswoman! I'd be shit at it.'

This was a tactical error because Annie had then launched into a pep talk, wide-eyed and earnest in her cartoon mouse voice, about how Bryony must not do herself down. 'Women diminish their own abilities all the time and it holds us all back!' she had squeaked, until Bryony was forced to agree, chastised for her sins against the sisterhood. Would a white man think he couldn't run a business? Would a white man let himself be thwarted by self-doubt?

No, agreed Bryony, though perhaps quite a lot of them should?

But by that point, she was a lost cause. She felt it then and she saw it in hindsight; once 'Bryony taking a compliment' had become inextricable from 'Bryony buying, and ultimately selling, Gel Lyfe', the aloe-green dye had been cast.

'Do you promise me you'll have more faith in your potential, Bry?' Annie had asked, and Bryony had promised, meekly.

'Maybe you could send me over the details so I can take a look and—'

'I'm so excited for you! Shall we get you set up on the system right now, while you've got the momentum?'

'Sure, although I don't actually have my cards with me just n—'

'Ed would be so happy to know we're becoming business part-ners,' Annie had said, tearily. 'A Monzo transfer is fine.'

And thus, Bryony was a businesswoman. A direct-to-consumer dis-tributor of Gel Lyfe, which was alarmingly expensive for something Marco had already nicknamed 'wanker's Berocca'.

An hour after the starter pack arrived she was added to a group chat and strenuously welcomed by a series of enthusiastic avatars, all keen to share their tips for sales success. Their tips for sales suc-cess mostly focused on badgering friends and family ('using your extended network') to buy Gel Lyfe, then badgering *their* friends and family to badger their friends and family and so on, all while 'thinking positive'. Bryony had a flashback to a primary school charity project in which she had failed to sell enough friendship bracelets to send a child with cystic fibrosis to Florida; an experience so stressful she'd ended up in the nurse's office convinced she, too, had developed cystic fibrosis. But then, she probably hadn't been thinking positive.

It seemed unfair that the person in her extended network most likely to buy some gel from her was Ann, who would presumably have bought it already from her daughter.

Kath, could she be a target? There had been a short-lived Avon phase in the early aughts, brochures everywhere, packages of Pretty Peach piling up in the hallway. But though Kath was robustly healthy – obnoxiously so, Bryony had always felt, as though she did it on purpose to make a point – she was also stingy and highly suspicious of anything that could be called 'wellness'. She still used talc.

'What you need is one very rich, very stupid friend,' said Marco. 'You must have one. A lovely silly Tabitha with an *Apprentice* complex and a trust fund.'

Marco refused to mix with her other friends. 'Like oil and water,' he'd said once, without explaining which he was.

Bryony thought about it. 'I only have rich sensible ones and stupid skint ones.'

'That's unhelpful.'

'Maybe someone at work. A suggestible intern, would that be wrong?'

'Why do you need to sell it at all?' asked Marco. 'Can't you just write it off as a penalty for being a horny little fake widow and dump the lot on a charity shop?'

'Charity shops don't accept food and drink.'

'Or a food bank?'

'I asked, they said Gel Lyfe doesn't count as food. Or drink.'

'Next door has a skip for their kitchen reno?'

Bryony shook her head. 'Annie is expecting me to sell it. She thinks I've joined her business. I have to give her quarterly reports. I have had,' she checked her phone and whimpered, 'seventeen emails and forty-six WhatsApps since yesterday.'

'You know this isn't pre-school, don't you, Brian? You don't have to play pretend shops with her just to be nice. This isn't like when the lady in that empty boutique makes you spend seventy pounds on a soap dish. This is a pyramid scheme.'

'Technically it's a direct-to-consumer multi-level sales franchise,' she said. 'It's actually got a conical rewards structure.'

'An inverted cone? Bigger at the bottom, smaller at the top?'

She went quiet.

'Brian.' Marco took her face tenderly in his hands, which he always did when he was about to say something devastating. 'It's very sad that this girl's brother died and it's highly unfortunate that for some reason everyone thinks he was in love with you. But if you get yourself embroiled in a pyramid scheme *while knowing full well it is a pyramid scheme*, you deserve everything you get.'

'But I can't just—'

'It isn't politeness, it's stupidity.'

'Well don't sugar-coat it.'

'Look. *I* love you, but if I died and my sister tried to co-opt *you* into a wellness cult, I'd come back as a ghost just to tell you what a twat you were.'

'That wouldn't happen. Your sister breeds labradors in Hampshire.'

'Are you joking, Hampshire is ripe for dangerous cults.'

'She wears a gilet.'

'The point *is*,' Marco went on, 'the kinder thing would be to tell Annie the truth and help her get out before she loses any more money.'

Bryony flinched at this suggestion. It was funny how contorting herself into endless shapes to avoid confrontation was always more comfortable than simply using her backbone.

'I am being kind,' she said sulkily, though she knew she was defeated.

'No you're not, you're being nice,' said Marco. 'They aren't the same thing.'

'You're not nice at all,' said Bryony.

'Nope. And yet you love me all the same.'

She did, was the thing. Every hour Bryony spent with one of her satellite friends, niceing each other all over town, was an hour she'd rather be with Marco, listening to him explain in academic detail everything that was wrong with her personality. Was that masochism or was it true friendship? But then, Marco was made of different stuff to Annie. He thrived on brutal honesty and hilarious home truths, he wasn't sweet and earnest and wide-eyed and wounded.

'Her brother—'

'Died, yes! It's been mentioned. I wish I'd known that was the rule – when my dad had cancer, I could have forced you to buy that NFT off me.'

The cancer had been a mercifully brief period early on in their flat-share. Bryony would make notes in her diary to remind her to enquire about every scan and test result and treatment round, and Marco would tell her this was creepy and please could she stop. It had been an intensely bonding time. The NFT, meanwhile, was a relic of a crush Marco had had on a twenty-four-year-old conceptual artist called Mork, which had ended abruptly when it turned out, in his case, NFT stood for No Fucking, Thanks!

But at least it took up no space in the physical realm, where as the Gel Lyfe boxes were destined to end up stacked up down the side of Bryony's dressing table, in the tower where she kept all the crap she didn't want but was too guilty or lazy or superstitious to dispose of. Theoretically nice but materially pointless presents people had given her; promotional discount cards for meal kits and beauty subscription boxes and a lingerie brand she had shopped from once and probably never would (but might!) again; clothes that she had bought in full knowledge she wouldn't wear them, because the words 'actually I think I'll leave it, thanks' had frozen on her tongue as she watched her own hand tapping her debit card on the reader. Theoretically nice but materially pointless gifts *she* had bought for other people but ended up not giving them because she'd panicked and bought something better, nicer, more pointless, etc, etc, etc. The tower had long since grown higher than the dressing table itself, so she'd had to start a second one on the other side. A kind of hoarders' overflow car park of shame.

She told herself the things in the tower were aesthetic enough to look intentional. She dusted them about four times a year.

Marco appeared in the doorway as she was wedging the Gel Lyfe boxes into the gaps. One fell from the top of the tower and landed on her bedroom carpet, emitting a small cloud of green powder. Bryony rubbed at it forlornly with a toe, staining her sock green too.

'Hashtag business casual lyfe,' said Marco, and disappeared into the bathroom.

34

Thinking

The mole woman is back, and Kelly recognizes her as she pushes her pram up to the counter. She feels a private pang of satisfaction, glad to see her offhand comment made an impact. Sometimes straight-talking could pay off.

Mole woman greets her wearily and gives her a name and a date of birth. The date is this year.

'Oh,' says Kelly.

'Is something wrong?' asks the mole woman. 'I definitely booked for this morning, I've got the text—'

'No no, all fine,' says Kelly, checking the baby in for its appointment. 'Was there anything for yourself as well?'

The woman looks confused, as well she might because it sounds as though Kelly is trying to upsell her a chocolate bar in WHSmith.

'No,' she says. 'Just that please.'

It's a cold day and the woman is swaddled in a puffer coat, but Kelly can't help letting her eyes slide across to the shoulder where she saw the mole last time. The woman looks down, perhaps to see if there is baby sick on her coat, which in fairness there is, but not in the place Kelly is looking.

'All good. Take a seat please,' says Kelly.

Wednesdays at work are Kelly's worst days, for a number of reasons. Firstly, it's the day her least favourite locum GP tends to be in, which means she's obliged to have a conversation that begins 'Happy hump day!' in the morning and endure the smell of his microwaved gym bro lunch – dry chicken breast, brown rice, broccoli – all afternoon.

Wednesday is also the day she goes to a class called 'Body Smash' at a terrifying brutalist fitness studio in a railway arch. Or rather, Wednesday is the day she doesn't go to Body Smash; it is the day she pays £22 to carry her kit to work with her and then carry it home again, eating a Twix.

But mainly Kelly hates Wednesdays because it is the day the nurse works, which means it is the day all the babies come in for their vaccinations, which means it's the day Kelly must watch sweet, cooing infants arrive and leave purple-faced and screaming, having experienced their first great betrayal. Wednesday is the day the babies learn that life isn't fair.

She soothes herself on these days by judging other people's parenting. She tells herself she wouldn't use her phone in front of her baby (she would), that she wouldn't resort to plugging their whines with a dummy (she would), that her child wouldn't be quietly cooked in that too-warm pram suit or shivering in that flimsy romper (it almost certainly would; Kelly rarely lets weather get in the way of a good outfit). She treats the babies' names as though they are a sport she follows closely, noting which are becoming too popular or too tacky, occasionally writing down the maddest ones to tell Leo, so they can reassure each other they'd never choose something so pretentious themselves (they might).

But mostly, Wednesday is a day to be endured. Squawk by squawk, the parade of chubby exposed thighs and pouting, tear-stained faces, each one making it more and more likely she's going to sack off Body Smash and head home to smash a packet of Fox's half-dipped cookies instead. Traditionally Leo will find her when he gets home several hours later, prostrate on the living room floor, and she will remind him about Wednesdays. Then, because Leo is first and foremost a problem-solver, he will present the best solution he can think of.

So Kelly will do Body Smash, of a kind, after all. Happy hump day!

Afterwards they lie in bed, Kelly's legs propped up against the velvet headboard with two pillows under her hips – she does this just long enough to encourage the sperm on their big journey, but not long enough to give her a UTI – and Leo asks what she is thinking about.

It's a tradition that goes back to the early days of their relationship, when she'd made an offhand comment about him not being 'with her for her brain', and he had taken great care to ask for her thoughts every time they'd had sex, as though turning it into a joke proved anything at all. Still, it was cute, and over the course of their relationship the postcoital confabs have plumbed greater philosophical depths than Ann's Sunday Salons ever have.

There was a time when she'd prepared answers in advance, memorizing current affairs topics and *Guardian* headlines to impress him, or wrong foot him, or at least make him laugh. Then as their relationship had shifted gear, the answers had become more honest, exposing the most vulnerable parts of herself like a wound to the air. Then they'd become practical – extended symposiums on which holiday should they book, which flat should they buy, how should they do the table plan at their wedding to balance Leo's surfeit of parents with her lack, would Annie try to wear Doc Martens with her bridesmaid's dress and whose job was it to wrangle them off her. Finally, the existential; Kelly giving answers that aren't really answers at all but noises; a long, extravagant sigh that he will nod through as though it is Shakespeare. 'I know, babe. I know.'

Does he know, though? That motherhood is already consuming her, and she hasn't even got there yet? That she sees it daily, although it is usually easier to ignore – women continually deprioritizing their own health, sanity and personal hygiene in the name of nurture? They paper the lamp posts in their corner of London with posters for missing toys; ratty, spit-soaked bunnies whose wellbeing carries more weight than theirs. Ann was still washing her son's pants until two months ago, and would cheerfully have carried on forever. Kelly's own mother was so deeply intolerant of fuss that Kelly had to fight to be allowed to visit her in hospital, beg to pass her tissues and jellied fruits from the box on the nightstand. And yet here she is, hips raised to God in prayer for the chance to join their ranks. Does Leo know all that is contained in the sigh? Does he really?

'What are you thinking about?' he asks her tonight, and she tells him: 'The mole woman.'

'A mole woman?' he repeats. 'Like the people who live underground?'

'Not like that,' she says.

These exchanges have traditionally been one-sided. She never asked what Leo was thinking, and that was the real joke of it all, in the beginning. He didn't realize that she wasn't with him for his brain either.

Since Ed died, however, she has broken with convention.

'What are you thinking about?' she asks her husband, and he lets out a long sigh, a noise made only sadder by the sight of his rapidly deflating cock.

Kelly leans across the bed, dislodging the pillows and trying not to panic as she tips herself upright again (too soon!) to wrap her arms around him, wishing she knew how to reply. If she were a better wife wouldn't she have the right words? If she deserved to be a mother, wouldn't she be deprioritizing her own health, sanity and personal hygiene to deliver exactly the comfort he needs?

Leo doesn't seem to think this, at least. He only squeezes her arm gratefully as she holds him and tells him, 'I know, babe. I know.'

35

What are normal things?

By the end of November, Bryony had begun to feel like a victim of cyber-stalking. Messages from the Gelievers were piling up like Hogwarts letters in every inbox she owned, lighting up her phone day and night with their pleas for her to believe in herself, to dream bigger, to dare harder, and to take advantage of the special one-time offer to reach Gelibility Level four if she sold ten starter packs by next Tuesday. She tried muting the group, but within hours Annie had called to check she was okay.

'You're not reading any of the messages.'

Not for the first time, Bryony cursed the surveillance state of social media.

'I'm so sorry, I've just been busy. With work, and all the,' she caught herself just before the word 'Edmin' passed her lips, 'the events. To tell the truth it's slightly overwhelming, I'm not sure I can keep up.'

'Oh I felt the same at first, don't worry!' said Annie. 'Completely overwhelmed. But you know why that was? *Self-doubt*, Bryony. You have to stop holding yourself back. Promise me you'll try and get out of your own way? I know it's daunting, but you can do it! It's like Tamara says, we can do hard things!'

Bryony had told her Glennon Doyle said that too, but not about selling gut gel. Annie had asked who he was, and Bryony had sent her a TED talk and Annie had shared it with the group chat and before she knew it she had invites to four different 'gels night in' parties in four different counties and the beginnings of carpal tunnel in her wrist. The gel remained unsold.

It was jarring, amidst the motivational onslaught, to see her father's name appear on her phone one evening. The words *'Dad (ICE)'* felt, as they always did, a little too apt.

'Hullo, hullo,' he began. 'Kath wants to know if you're coming for Christmas this year?'

Bryony had never gone anywhere else for Christmas, and yet the question was posed like this every year – would she be attending? Could she kindly RSVP? – in a way that made her feel pathetic, at her advanced age, for not having alternative plans. She half expected one year to arrive home and find they'd gone on a cruise and forgotten to mention it.

'Yes,' she told him. 'Why wouldn't I be?'

'I don't know,' said her father. 'You might want a change.'

Christmas with her family hadn't been enjoyable for years. Sitting around in the too-big, jacquard-swagged dining room, politely sawing at Kath's desiccated turkey crown and making small talk with her elderly step-grandmother, each banal observation and pleasantry rendered ludicrous by the need to yell it three times down the length of a mahogany table.

Sometimes Tim and Clementine would come too, which made little to no difference to the atmosphere but did at least fill up the room. After a strained opening-of-presents she would be obliged to watch 'the afternoon film' with her father, whatever it was, even though this was rarely any longer a film he would enjoy such as a Bond or a bank heist, much more likely a progressive CGI about big-eyed bacteria learning to be their best selves. Inevitably it would feature a dead parent, which would leave them both belching with the effort of swallowing down tears. Then cheese, then at around nine p.m. he would bid her goodnight and Bryony would be left wondering if the early bedtime was because he'd run out of energy to interact with his daughter, or because Christmas Day was the one day a year he and Kath still had sex.

And yet, that *was* Christmas. Tension and resentment were baked in, like indigestion and the big *Radio Times*. Where else would she go? Would she hole up in a hotel like some fictional spinster? Take herself to Thailand and drink from a bucket with student backpackers in Santa hats? To go anywhere else for Christmas without a partner as an excuse would be too loud a statement, too big a break from convention. Too high a risk of eating an entire family-sized trifle on her own.

'No, no, I'm coming,' she said. 'I mean, if I'm invited that is?'

'Of course you're invited!' said her father. 'Why wouldn't you be?'

She shrugged, childishly, which he couldn't see down the phone.

'Sorry, what was that?'

'Nothing, Dad. I didn't say anything.'

'Good, well, that's sorted then. And Kath wants to know if you're eating normal things these days?'

'What are normal things?'

'Well, I don't know,' he blustered. 'Turkey. Cheese. Brandy butter. Or does she need to put some Quorn on the Ocado? She wasn't sure if you were still vegan.'

Bryony had done Veganuary once, in 2016, and had been haunted by the legacy ever since.

'I'm not vegan Dad. And it's pronounced "Kworn", not Corn.'

'Does it matter?' he asked, and she struggled to think of a reason that it did.

Agenda items ticked off, they moved on to the 'Any other business' portion of their call.

'How's work?' he asked.

Work was Richard Carter's comfort zone. His safe space. Though retired for several years now, he still carried himself like a man forever on the verge of whipping out a business card. He liked to quiz Bryony on the intricacies of her job, as though simply asking was in itself a feminist act. My *daughter*, you know! With her *career*!

'Work is fine. Busy. Boring. Meetings and spreadsheets.'

It didn't help that she could never find a way to talk about her job without sounding like a six-year-old pretending to have one.

'Good, good, glad to hear it. Keep that nose to the grindstone,' he said, with forced jollity.

She pictured the Gel Lyfe boxes stacked up in her bedroom and the increasingly aggressive messages from Diamond Team Queen Maxine stacked up in her inbox, and wondered what would happen if she told him, 'Actually I've started a business!' It would be interesting to see if her father was savvy enough to spot the red flags, or would be blinded by parental pride the way Ann was.

Then she thought back to her conversation with Noor and wondered if she should tell him about Ed instead. But to explain the whole situation (fake version) would be to taunt him with a son-in-law who he would never be able to take for a cheeky nine holes, and to explain the situation (real version) would involve talking to him about her sex life, which wouldn't work as she and her father preferred to maintain the notion that Bryony was made of fabric from the waist down, like a rag doll. She had learned how to use tampons from the encyclopaedia Encarta.

'And how are you?' she asked, waiting for him to tell her about the trip to France.

'Yes, yes, fine,' said her father. 'I bumped into your friend the other week, the one with the nose thing. Ring.'

'Noor.'

'She's doing well for herself.'

'I know she is.'

'She's bought one of those big houses by the roundabout.'

'I know, Dad. I told you about that last year.'

'They've asked her back to your school to give a career talk to the girls.'

'I know, Dad,' she repeated, although she didn't know this. The idea of Noor being called up to inspire the next generation made her throat swell with various emotions, some purer than others. She coughed it back.

'Are you under the weather?' asked her father.

'No, no. Well, no more than normal,' she replied.

'Good, good. Well, I'll let you go then.' Richard called their meeting to a close the traditional way, as though they had trespassed on each other's time for long enough. 'I'll let Kath know about Christmas. Take care of yourself.'

'I will, Dad. And you.'

'Cheerio then.'

'Cheerio.'

36

No worse than oysters

If Halloween and Bonfire Night in Little Buckton had been community spirit on steroids, they were clearly nothing compared to the six-week endurance test that was Christmas. Ed's memorial quiz was scheduled for the last Saturday in November, squeezed in between a wreath-making workshop and something truly monstrous called *Elf On The Shelf: Live On Ice*.

Fortunately, Bryony was only expected to show her face for the quiz. Unfortunately she *was* expected to contribute a round, and the anxiety of this was almost as bad as the funeral poem.

'Flags of the world? Can I just do flags of the world and claim it's another tribute to Ed's travelling? Does Málaga have a flag, or—'

'Famous Eds,' suggested Marco. 'Ed Harris, Edwina Currie, Edd the Duck. Prince Edward.'

She considered this. She probably knew more about Prince Edward than she did about poor dead Egg Man. 'But he's not really an Ed, he's an Ethelred,' she reminded him. 'Famous Ethelreds,' said Marco. 'One question, very short round. They'll love it.'

'I'm supposed to demonstrate how well I know him! Knew him. If I don't put in some personal details it'll seem suspicious.'

'You're acting like these people are MI6, investigating you for fake girlfriending.'

'I'm just worried they might start to think I wasn't really madly in love with him.'

Marco produced a Peperami from his pocket and slowly unwrapped it. Ever since their trip to Ann's, he'd developed a taste.

'I'm going to ask a controversial question,' he said. 'Why?'

'Why what?'

'Why do you have to let them believe you were madly in love?'

Bryony looked at him in bewilderment. 'Because he's dead, Marco. He's dead and they're miserable and their only crumb of comfort is knowing he died with the love of a good woman, AKA me.'

'Alright, good woman.' He mimed tapping the ash-end off a cigar with his Peperami. 'Is it possible they might have other crumbs of comfort? You don't think that perhaps this nice family can focus on their thirty-something years of happy memories with their son and brother, rather than the fact he spent a few months boning some random girl they hadn't met?'

'Not boning,' she corrected him. *'Making love.'*

Marco let out the noise a steam kettle makes when it boils.

'You won't admit that you're quite enjoying playing the stricken widow here? I'm not judging. When my dad had his cancer I lived on "thinking of you" brownies for months. But the great withdrawal has to happen sooner or later, you know it does. Don't you think you could just tell Ann the truth ...' she opened her mouth to protest '... a *delicate* version of it, but say you don't feel it's appropriate for you to be quite so involved in everything, as really you didn't know him as well as you wish you had and you want to give his close friends and family the space they deserve to grieve?'

Bryony thought about this. She pictured herself saying these words to Ann. She pictured Ann crumpling in on herself like a time-lapse candle, mouth sagging in shock, molten with the pain of losing not just her son but now her almost-daughter-in-law too.

'Oh, piss off if you're not going to help.'

Steve was compering the quiz, and sweetly nervous about it. He'd taken to sending Bryony voice notes – long, leisurely and unpunctuated – explaining the running order, updating her on its contents so far, asking her opinion on dilemmas such as whether it would be funny to kick things off by saying *'Contenders, are you Ethelredy?'* in a *Gladiators* voice, or whether the prize for best team name should be a crate of the local IPA or a slab of sausages from Billingham's the butcher. 'You know what Ed was like with those sausages.'

'Of course! The sausages!' Bryony would say when she voice noted him back. You had to voice note them back, that was the unspoken curse of the voice note. Reverting to the written word just looked rude.

'I feel sick,' she told Marco on the day of the event.

'You always feel sick,' said Marco. This was true. Her stomach was a delicately calibrated machine, as easily tipped off balance by strong emotions as raw onions. 'Maybe you should stop drinking that pond slime.'

Bryony paused, her glass of Gel Lyfe halfway to her lips. This was an error; if you stopped while drinking it the sediment would settle.

'I need to do something with it! May as well sample the merchandise. Anyway, it can't hurt. Seventy-two gut-positive adaptogens. If anything this should be helping me feel less sick.'

'Sorry, is that Gel Lyfe or Kool-Aid?' said Marco. 'You do know that "Ponzi" isn't a Japanese citrus?'

'I just like the taste.'

She took another long swig. This wasn't entirely untrue. It was half grassy, half chemical; like how she imagined astroturf would taste. But once you got used to the slimy mouthfeel, it was almost pleasant. No worse than oysters. Not that Bryony ever ate oysters.

The quiz itself was surprisingly good fun. Mercifully she had managed to get herself onto a team with Annie, Leo and a few members of the Brixworth Sixworth, meaning the vast gaps in her Ed-based general knowledge weren't as obvious as they might otherwise have been. It turned out all she needed to do was the thing she did in most pub quizzes anyway – pause after each question, eyes narrowed, wry smile playing across her lips as if to suggest she knew the answer but wanted to give everyone else a chance to jump in and have their moment of glory. Everyone hates a biro hog.

'His left knee!' said Annie, and Bryony said 'Yes! Of course!'

'Biffy Clyro?' ventured Leo, and Bryony said, 'I think you're right, yeah.'

'Beethoven Two!' they all agreed, and Bryony smiled and nodded. Of course it was. Of course.

The hardest part was not looking surprised as each new titbit of information was revealed, filling out and colouring in the rudimentary sketch of the man she had known until a picture emerged that was affectionate, interesting, even compelling. Although her own round, a crudely Photoshopped series of him at UNESCO World Heritage Sites titled '*Where's Your Ed At?*', went down as well as could be hoped, she cringed quietly throughout at not offering something more personal, then cringed at this impulse too.

Marco's words rang in her ears. Maybe he was right. Maybe it was time to extract herself.

Steve drove her back to the station. Bryony had given up protesting by now and started accepting the lifts, leaning into her life as a cut-price Lady Penelope. She wondered if they had discussions about it beforehand, perhaps drawing straws or tossing a coin to decide who had the pleasure of staying sober to ferry her about. She hoped they stayed sober. It was hard to know.

Steve was visibly elated that the quiz had gone well. He radiated relief, and the natural high of one who has survived a public speaking engagement.

'One thousand and seventy-five quid for the charity, did I tell you?' He drummed on the steering wheel, bouncing a little in his seat. He had told her.

'So good!' she replied, again. 'We did him proud.' They rolled off the tongue easily now, these proclamations on Ed's behalf. It turned out you could say pretty much anything you liked about dead people as long as it was positive.

Steve beamed. 'Thanks so much for all your help, Bryony. It's been so good to have you involved. I know he'd be glad.'

'Thanks, Steve.'

'Oh, and I swiped you something from the snack table, before they all went.'

He dug around in his jacket pocket and pulled out a Gold bar. She gasped and squealed her thanks as though it were real bullion.

Steve shrugged. 'Don't get too excited, they've got smaller.'

Bryony already had a mouth full of biscuit and blonde chocolate, her nausea temporarily abated.

'Or maybe we just got bigger?'

'That's true,' he said. 'Nice to be an optimist about things.'

'Did Ed tell you I liked them?' At this point the line between true and false, real and inconceivable, was nothing but a blur.

'No,' he said. 'You did. That first time we met, when you got car sick.'

'Oh. Right.'

Steve was crawling at thirty-five miles per hour in a sixty zone, she only noticed now, and was touched. Bryony saw her chance.

'Can I ask a question?' she began tentatively. 'What *did* Ed tell you about me?'

He smiled indulgently at her. Or, perhaps, at Ed.

'Oh, you know . . .' he began.

I don't know! I really do not know!, she screamed internally.

'He said you were amazing.'

'Amazing? Ed said that himself?'

'Pretty sure that was the word, yeah. And clever, funny, interesting, all the good stuff. Beautiful, obviously.'

He blushed a little and cleared his throat as if to cough away the compliment.

'He said – and I remember this, because we were at the archery range for Jonno's stag and Perks had just got himself in the toe, blood everywhere – he said he'd never felt so comfortable with a woman, conversationally. Like he could relax and just be himself around you. Didn't have to put on a front, pretend to be the cool guy, you know?'

'Oh wow,' she exhaled, ignoring the part of her that felt mildly offended.

'I mean, you know Ed – not the most verbose guy, not a massive one with the communication skills. I think in the past he'd been written off by girls – women, sorry – for not having the smooth lines, not always bringing the chat, you know? But with you, he was so grateful to have found someone who was on his page, who accepted him for who he is. Was.'

Bryony was finding it difficult to speak, but she made an affirmative noise. Steve went on.

'He was always pretty cagey about dating, Ed. Never really wanted to tell us about anyone unless he felt like it was serious. Especially Ann – one whiff of a third date and she'd be buying a hat and booking the scout hut.'

'Mhm,' she said. 'I can imagine.'

'But that's how we knew it was serious with you. Every

conversation was all "Bryony" this and "Bryony" that – always dropping in little things you'd told him, little details from your life. The places you took him, the games you guys made up together. Your funny flatmate. Like I said when I first rang you, after . . . afterwards,' Steve cleared his throat again. 'I'd never seen him so happy.'

For a moment she was completely absorbed by this fantasy image, reflected back at her as if from a fun house mirror. Of herself as the dream girlfriend, of their relationship as a beautiful, blooming thing that could have been the real deal if only fate hadn't had other plans. It was so tempting to spin all of Steve's nice words into a comfort blanket for her ego. But no.

'The thing is,' she began, and was alarmed to hear her voice come out high and quivery, 'we really hadn't known each other for very long . . .'

Steve sighed. 'I know, mate. All part of the tragedy, isn't it? Can only imagine how painful it must be for you, thinking of everything that could have been.'

'Y-yes,' she stammered, urging herself to keep going. To make him understand. 'But I mean, we hadn't actually spent all that much, ah, time together. Not in . . .' was she saying this? Apparently she was '. . . daylight hours.'

Steve blushed again, and she prayed he wasn't going to recount Ed's reports of that too.

'But that's the beauty of love I guess, isn't it?' he said, suddenly solemn. 'It's not about ticking a load of boxes, or jumping through relationship hoops. When it's right, it's right.'

Bryony looked at Steve, at his earnest expression and the twinkle of festive craft glitter in his beard, and felt completely defeated. For now.

'That's right,' she said weakly.

37

Occasional chuckles

They sit around Ann's kitchen table, the way they have every week for years.

There is nothing as painful or stark as an empty chair where Ed should be, because Ann piles crap onto every surface that doesn't have a human in residence. But Kelly will admit her brother-in-law was better company than a stack of La Redoute catalogues.

She struggles with Leo's family's style of grieving, it being so fiercely at odds with the way they mourn in her own. Kelly's mother had stipulated very clearly that she wanted *no nonsense*, and they had followed this instruction to the letter, crying only in private but maintaining a steady air of sobriety with each other for what felt like the appropriate amount of time (six months) before they graduated to small, fond smiles and then occasional chuckles. By the one-year anniversary they were all behaving as normal again and repeated the process on a smaller scale – one week sad, two weeks smiling, then laughter after a month. It was this precision and order that Kelly had found most comforting, when she looked back on it. There is no such luck with the Slingsbys.

'Somebody tell me something funny!' demands Ann. 'We will not sit around with faces like slapped arses, I won't have it. It's not our way.'

What constitutes 'our' way has never been open to consultation. It is Ann's way or the A428.

'A girl I went to school with had to give me her stool sample the other day,' offers Kelly.

'Oh poor thing!' says Ann, who only finds things funny when she isn't supposed to, and never when she is. 'Is she alright? What are they checking her for?'

'I don't know,' says Kelly, chastened. 'I'm just the receptionist.'

A momentary hush falls over the Paxo, before Annie chirps up. 'Remember when Ed threw that shit out of the window?'

They all laugh then, determinedly. Relievedly.

It's relief both that they are the kind of family that has anecdotes about people throwing shits out of windows, and the kind of family strong enough to take comfort in them during their darkest hours. Would Kelly like to create this kind of family, she wonders? She supposes she doesn't have much choice.

She doesn't remember the shit out of the window, not having been there in the late nineties, but she may as well have been because the story has become so vivid in the retelling. She knows all the beats; can picture the famous turd sliding muddily down the slanted glass roof of Susan and Bob's new conservatory. How this has become a fond tale to remember Ed by she isn't sure, but Kelly laughs with them, because that is her duty.

Her own memories of her brother-in-law are not riotously funny but sweet, calm and solid. He had been the earthing wire of the family, absorbing their shock and diverting their chaos. The person who took the smallest piece of lasagne, or sat uncomplainingly at Susan's bureau come Christmas. What Kelly privately thought of as a background person, one of life's supporting artists. She worries she might be one too.

On her wedding day, instead of saying how stunning she looked, or how happy she must be, or had she seen the catering manager because the band were asking for their contractual lamb shanks, Ed had hugged her and asked earnestly if she needed anything.

'Water? Or . . .' he'd grasped for something else that might be helpful, as she shivered bare-armed through their less-than-golden hour photo shoot, 'a jumper?'

It became their catchphrase, that day and for a while afterwards, every time the two of them crossed paths at a family function or a Buckton knees-up. 'Water, Kel? Or a jumper?' Maybe he was quite funny, looking back. That's the thing about supporting artists. Their presence is subtle but their absence is loud.

She squeezes Leo's knee beneath the table now, trying to communicate all this to her husband without having to say anything. He grabs her hand and squeezes it back, slightly too hard, her rings digging into her fingers.

'Tigs, how is everything with your business?'

Annie sits up straight then and tells her mother: 'Great! Good, yeah, all really exciting. I'm feeling really, really positive.'

It's hard not to picture Ann and Annie as they must have been years ago, either side of a cardboard shopfront, one serving the other invisible 'tea.'

'So you're making money then?' asks Ann. 'You're selling these smoothies?'

'Adaptogen gels,' Annie corrects her. 'Yes, yep, all going really well! I mean, I'm mostly focusing on building my team at the moment because ultimately that's the best route to long-term success, you know? Strengthen your network.'

Ann nods, smiling proudly. Kelly frowns.

'So you're hiring, like, staff? Already?' she asks.

'No no, not exactly – more like . . . finding colleagues,' clarifies Annie. 'Sharing the potential. That's why Gel Lyfe is different to your usual capitalist business structures, right? It's all about community.'

'Right,' says Kelly, as Ann echoes the word along with her. 'Community.'

'Actually, I've just recruited Bryony.'

Nobody but Kelly seems surprised by this.

'Bryony? Ed's Bryony?'

'She's my new downline! Like, an assistant? She's been really enthusiastic about the product actually, turns out she's super into her wellness.'

Kelly feels her smile stiffen.

'And I get the impression she's looking for something, you know? To take her mind off her grief, turn her pain into something positive. I think it could be a really beautiful opportunity. I'm taking her to a sales workshop next weekend.'

'That's brilliant, ducks,' says Ann.

'Are they expensive, these, er, workshops?' asks Kelly. Leo squeezes her leg under the table now, only it isn't a squeeze of affection but one of warning.

'I mean, they're not cheap but they're worth it,' says Annie. 'People who do the workshops climb the Lyfe Ladder up to thirty percent faster, so. And I can afford it now I've got your investment!'

'My what?'

Like the window-turd of lore, Kelly only sees the mess coming just before it hits.

'Now that you and Leo have invested in my business,' says Annie. 'You won't regret it, I promise.'

Leo squeezes her leg again, this time a squeeze of beseechment. Ann beams.

38

A wasp sting, not my vagina

'Oh my god. Oh my god that's awful.'

'I know.'

'We're in our mid-thirties and they're dying off?'

'*Early* thirties. I know.'

Bryony was having coffee with Mairead, a former colleague. They had barely worked together for four months, but the friendship apparently had a tail ten times as long as its body.

Mairead had left London several years ago to buy a mock-Tudor semi in Aldershot with her then-fiancé, who had since become her ex-fiancé, leaving Mairead stranded in Aldershot because she was too stubborn to sell the house and move back. She liked to come all the way to Walthamstow and say 'take me to one of your *cool places*', then make comments about the price of the pastries. Mairead only drank hazelnut lattes, so once every few months Bryony had to endure the private agony of hearing a barista tell her they didn't 'do syrups'.

'You hadn't even soft-launched him!'

'What?'

'On the socials!' said Mairead, slurping her consolation cortado. 'You never even posted a cryptic of his hand or shoes or anything? Not that I saw, anyway.'

Bryony shook her head, sadly. It seemed easier than explaining the protein shake. Mairead wouldn't think a protein shake was a dealbreaker. Since her break-up she'd adopted an intensive approach to dating rarely seen outside of nineties sitcoms, aiming to go out with at least two new men a week. 'I take five days off for my period,' she'd told Bryony, as though that made it normal.

'But are you ok though? Are you getting some help?'

'He didn't die on top of me or anything. I'm fine.'

She took an extra-large bite of quiche to illustrate the point. The cafe was renowned for its quiche, which Bryony never usually ordered because it sat on the counter unrefrigerated and she had no way of knowing how long it had been there. ('You could ask them?' Marco had suggested once, and Bryony had stared at him as though he barely knew her at all.)

Today, however, she'd started thinking about the quiche on the walk here and become near-rabid with thoughts of eating it. All other foodstuffs were repulsive to her, suddenly. Quiche was the only thing she wanted in the world.

'But that's so traumatic! The day after you slept with him! Do you feel like Lady Mary?'

Bryony frowned. 'Like I'm going to be burned at the stake by Protestants?'

'No, from *Downton Abbey*. She had a killer vagina.'

'Did she?' Bryony remembered the show being mostly about scullery maids and increasingly small hats.

Mairead nodded. 'Every man she slept with died.'

'Oh. That's nice. Well my body count so far is one, but I'll keep you posted.'

'Don't worry – I'm sure it was only a fluke, you're probably not cursed.'

'I mean, he died of a wasp sting,' said Bryony. 'Not my vagina.'

'Exactly.' Mairead patted her arm. 'I'm sure that was it.'

'And he was in love with me!' said Bryony, after a pause.

She never planned to tell people this part, but it turned out she couldn't stop crowdsourcing opinions. She needed to focus-group this situation until it started to make some kind of sense. Was she the kind of woman people fell secretly in love with and told their whole family about? Part of her hoped her friends would listen to the story and chuckle in fond recognition. 'Of course,' they might say, 'that's the power you have over men. It's blatantly obvious to everyone except you, because you are so modest and consumed by insecurity.'

They never said this.

'Huh,' said Mairead, when she'd finished. They all said huh.

'Have you ever had anything like this? Is it a new dating trend?'

Mairead read all of those articles – *Here's The Latest Toxic Behaviour We've Given A Cutesy Name To!* – as though she were revising for an exam. She thought about it. 'No,' she concluded. 'I've never had anything like that.'

There was a hint of envy in Mairead's voice, as though Bryony had found a Pokémon so rare she hadn't even heard of it. 'But you know, some guys just really don't know how to communicate their feelings. It's still hard for them to make themselves vulnerable in case they get rejected. Maybe he was obsessed with you the whole time and just didn't know how to tell you.'

'So he told his entire family instead?'

'It's possible.'

Bryony glanced at her phone, and as if on cue there was a message from Annie.

'Are you free on Saturday? I want to take you somewhere!' it read, and her heart sank because she was free on Saturday.

'Oi, I'm still here,' said Mairead. Bryony turned her phone over on the table, then changed her mind and tucked it into her bag instead.

Mairead was a demanding person, socially. Once, about 18 months into their friendship, she had texted: 'Can I ask, have I done something to upset you?'

Bryony had been startled. She didn't think about Mairead enough to be upset by her. If their friendship ended overnight she couldn't honestly say she would mind or possibly even notice, apart from a few free lunches in her diary and one fewer birthday to remember.

'No! Omg of course not, don't be silly!' she'd replied with a placatory barrage of heart emojis. 'What would even make you think that?'

'Phew!' Mairead had messaged back immediately. 'I'm sure I'm being dramatic, I was just worried you were being off with me. I feel like it's always me messaging you to meet up?'

The question mark was unnecessary because this was true, it was always Mairead messaging Bryony to meet up. Not because Bryony didn't *want* to meet up, exactly – just because she wanted to do about fifty other things more. Because it was all she could do to keep her head above water in thirteen different group chats. Because she was tired.

'I'm so sorry, I've been useless!' she had replied. 'Please forgive me, I'm a heap of shit.'

And then of course she'd had to put more effort in, suggesting extra bonus coffee dates and hearting all of Mairead's Stories and occasionally sending her links to articles – *Bumbledashing is the new toxic dating trend you didn't even know you were a victim of!* – just to prove she wasn't a bad friend. This had been nearly three years ago and Bryony still wasn't sure if her penance had ended.

'It's his – Ed's – sister, she's dragged me into her side hustle. Wants me to help her sell this gel stuff.'

'Gel Lyfe?' asked Mairead. 'My hairdresser's on it. It gives you the shits but her skin looks fantastic.'

'Oh! Do you want some?'

Mairead shook her head and drained her coffee. 'My IBS is shocking right now, can't risk it.'

'Mine too,' said Bryony, dumping sriracha onto the remains of her quiche from a sticky communal bottle.

When Mairead went to the loos ('Filthy,' she would declare on her return), Bryony pulled her phone back out and re-read Annie's message. She tried to think of anything she could possibly be doing on Saturday. She imagined writing 'no, sorry!' and seeing what would happen. She wondered about a second slice of quiche.

'*I think so, potentially,*' she messaged back. '*Where did you want to take me?*'

'*Yay!*' replied Annie, followed by three words that sent Bryony's heart squelching into her shoes. '*It's a surprise.*'

When Mairead returned they started their traditional wind-down gush.

'Thank you SO much for the coffee.'

'Oh no, thank YOU for coming all the way up here.'

'Oh god it was a pleasure, so lovely to see you!'

'So lovely to see YOU!'

This went on for some time, batting their thanks back and forth like a shuttlecock until they eventually tired.

39

Family fortunes

'How much?'

'A bit. Enough to get her head above water.'

'Leo, how much?'

'She's family,' he says, as though this is an answer.

'But we *need* that money,' says Kelly, painfully aware that whichever way their luck goes re: baby making, things are going to get expensive.

They've never been the kind of couple who police each other's spending. When they met they were both broke; she an aspiring actress with a bar job, he a junior designer with an online poker habit. And while Leo has earned more than her for pretty much their whole relationship, the gap didn't feel so significant until eighteen months ago, when he was promoted in his branding agency to a position of unclear seniority with both 'director' and 'lead' in the title. The new role pays him handsomely to drift between projects and meeting rooms in his socks, telling junior staff to 'punch up' their creative, without explaining how, then drifting out again to take clients to lunch. Professionally, it is all he's ever wanted.

Personally, Leo also wants a lot of stuff. Plain grey t-shirts with £90 price tags. Designer wallets made from reclaimed ocean waste.

Headphones that change colour with his body temperature and cologne that changes scent with his chromosomes. A smart speaker on every surface of the flat, despite the fact he rarely listens to music outside the gym. Silver-white trainers with internal springs; these are a few of his favourite things.

At first, Kelly loved this rampant consumerist streak in her boyfriend. He's always bought her great presents, enviable presents – stuff so luxe and unapologetically frivolous that she hadn't known it existed to want it. They would shop together, wince at their credit card bills together, eat Sainsbury's Basics noodles together at the end of each month, cuddled on the sofa in their tonal cashmere co-ords. She knows, anyhow, without either of them ever putting it into so many words, that Leo's tastes and habits are a direct reaction to his upbringing; to the glower and gaffer-tape of the Little Buckton burrow. To a mother who hand-painted murals on the bathroom walls, made him wear a homemade Scout uniform and take off-brand crisps in his lunchbox. To a father who lives on a farm and will probably always have the faintest whiff of sheep placenta about him. Leo likes nice things, clean lines, new releases, aspirational design features and stuff that works properly without having to be kicked three times or switched on with a special 'knack'. Kelly understands this. They have always understood each other.

But now, since her bougie boyfriend became a spendthrift husband and the bills started to look less like evidence of their compatibility, more as a strike against them in a hypothetical parenting interview panel, she has started to feel differently. Kelly has cut back on her own extravagances – the lash lifts, the self-gifts, the woman she used to pay to roll tiny needles across her face every month – and has become tight-jawed every time Leo brings home a stiff cardboard carrier bag or appears in a new, plain cream sweatshirt almost identical to his existing plain cream sweatshirts, but with a tiny motif embossed in a slightly different shade of cream at the neck. Or whatever.

She hasn't said anything until now, because Leo is sad and sometimes sad people need to buy stuff. She can't deny him that. But
at the news of their 'investment' in Annie's 'business', Kelly snaps.

'She needs to sort her own life out.'

'She's my baby sister!'

'She's thirty-one, Leo.'

'She's had a rough ride, Kel. Her last place going into liquidation,
that wasn't her fault. And all the stuff with that tax rebate. But now
she's gone into business with Bryony she's feeling really positive
about everything, she just needs that little boost to get her going.'

'They haven't "gone into business", babe, it's a scam. I don't understand why we're all keeping up this bollocks.'

'Because she's hurting, Kel. We all are.'

She bites her lip and squeezes his arm. Nobody has explained
how long grief remains the ultimate get-out in all matrimonial
arguments.

'I think we should have some faith in her,' he says. 'Annie has
loads of potential.'

'You sound like her now. Please god don't tell me you've bought
any of that gel shit too.'

Leo shakes his head but she wouldn't put it past him. That family
has always been too willing to participate in mutual delusions for
each other. She used to think it was sweet, when it was Ed's amateur
photography or Ann's attempt to get a team together for *Eggheads*,
but now Kelly worries it has set a dangerous precedent.

'She's only going to lose more money. She's going to lose *our*
money.'

'*My* money,' he corrects, then hastily apologizes when he sees her
face cloud in fury. 'I didn't mean that.'

'You did. You think because you earn more that I don't get an
opinion.'

'I don't! I didn't . . . it was a stupid thing to say. But you know, if you wanted to help out *your* brother with *your* wages, I wouldn't object.'

'My brother's fine! My brother has a scaffolding firm and a four-bedroom house, he's not exactly begging for handouts.'

'And my brother's dead, so I suppose you win that round don't you,' he spits.

'What the fuck? That doesn't even make sense,' Kelly says shrilly, her top lip becoming clammy. 'We're not competing. We're trying to have a *baby*, Leo. *This* family has to be your priority. The three of us.'

He looks aghast, like someone seeing the small print in a contract they've already signed. She'd assumed the rules of marriage were universal. That the hierarchy of family was a series of concentric circles, in which the relatives you chose and created usurped the ones you were landed with at birth. But she can almost see the alternative model reflected in his eyes. One in which Ann is the sun and everything revolves around her. She feels sick.

'I'm not choosing between my sister and a hypothetical baby, Kelly.'

'I'm not asking you to!'

She screeches it like an animal. Next door, the neighbours' TV goes silent.

Kelly has broken the rule she made with herself: no yelling at Leo while he is sad. Kelly has always been a sulker rather than a crier, but now she drops to the carpet and sobs, and between sobs she tries to explain in a reasonable, rational manner.

'I just ... *hegghhh* ... need to know ... *hegghghhh* ... that you still ... *hegghhhh* ... want this as much ... *heggh* ... as I ... *heggh* ... as I ... *heggh* ... d–do.'

He gathers her in his arms and says of course, of course he does, why would she even think he didn't, and she smears sooty wet mascara all over his cream sweatshirt, and he lets her. And she says sorry, and he says sorry, and they both accept this natural end to the argument, although neither of them is entirely clear what the other thinks they're apologizing for.

'Do you promise not to lend her any more money?' she asks.

'I promise,' he says. 'Not without discussing it with you first.'

'Put that top in the wash with some Vanish before the stain sets,' she tells his retreating back.

'I will,' he says, but he doesn't.

40

Common symptoms

Two days after the quiche, the pain began.

It started low, somewhere in the no-man's-land between her front and back. A kind of twanging, pulsing – right of a cramp but left of an ache or throb. Not quite *stabbing*, but a nervy, staccato sort of pain, enough to set her teeth on edge and leave her wincing through a team meeting.

Bryony had an extensive vocabulary for pain. Years of trying to articulate her various twinges and prangs for medical professionals had turned her into the Susie Dent of discomfort. But this pain felt new and deserving of its own descriptor. There was a depth and complexity to it; not the superficial, surface pain of a sore muscle or hangover headache. This pain had roots. It was reverberating from somewhere murky and unplaceable; a sonic call from the bottom of the ocean.

'My belly hurts,' she told Marco.

'I told you that hummus had gone fizzy,' he said.

She googled 'lower left abdominal pain', the link coloured purple to indicate that she'd searched it before. She googled 'lower central abdominal pain', then 'throbbing pain deep groin', then 'throbbing feeling deep groin' and immediately wished she hadn't.

She refreshed herself on the location and personality traits of the gallbladder, appendix, pancreas and spleen. She learned that common symptoms of leaky gut syndrome include fatigue, bloating, brain fog and cravings for sugar and carbs. Common symptoms of pancreatic cancer include fatigue, nausea, itching and indigestion. Common symptoms of kidney failure include fatigue, nausea, itching, muscle cramp and peeing more than normal, which as far as Bryony was concerned were also common symptoms of being alive. It was astonishing, really, that anyone managed to get through the day.

After her relationship with Kelly had progressed beyond the screen, Bryony had promised herself that she wouldn't go back to the doctors for at least three months. It was an arbitrary time frame but it felt appropriate. Three months was reasonable, wasn't it? Three months was a quarter of a year. Surely if she rode out Q1 then she was allowed to have some all-new problems for Q2?

But that had been before the pain.

As always, she narrated the situation in her head for some future documentary crew. 'I didn't want to make a fuss,' she heard herself saying. 'I thought it would go away of its own accord. I didn't want to bother the doctor.'

White text would appear on the screen. *Three weeks after filming this interview, Bryony died.*

Maybe she'd get lucky and Kelly wouldn't answer the phone today. She rehearsed her dialogue over the gentle strains of Roxette played on panpipes, and considered what her answer might be if they asked her about the pain scale.

Bryony had never in her life answered more than a six-point-five out of ten – after all, she wasn't a drama queen – but she did wish they'd be clearer about the criteria. Did they want her to rate just the strength of the pain itself, or more like the *emotional impact* of the pain? The duration of the pain? What about the *unusualness* of the pain, did that count for anything? Could she add a point or two for time lost to googling? And what about averages? Was everyone assessed in isolation or were they graded on a curve? Because if everyone else was going around throwing out eights and nines willy-nilly for bad backs and migraines, she'd like to adjust for inflation.

Bryony was just deciding she would say seven today – fuck it, see what happened – when Kelly answered.

'Hello,' said Bryony. Should she pretend not to know her, to be an anonymous patient?

Her rehearsed dialogue had been: 'I was wondering if you had any appointments for this week please.'

Her mouth, instead, said, 'I have a pain'. Just that. *Hello, I have a pain.*

'Bryony is that you?'

'Ah . . . yes. Yes, it is. Hi Kelly.'

Was that a sigh?

'How are you doing, Bryony?'

'Oh, I'm fine!' she said, reflexively.

'I thought you had a pain?' said Kelly.

'Well, yes. I do have a pain. Sorry, I wouldn't be bothering you with it, it's just quite . . . well, painful. And unusual. I can't really concentrate on anything.'

That was definitely a sigh. 'Sorry to hear that, Bryony. I'm afraid we don't have any appointments for today, the best thing would probably be if you fill in—'

'Fill in the online form, I know. It's just, I always do and nobody ever gets back to me.'

'I'm afraid we're extremely busy at the p—'

'At the present time, I know. I know, I'm sorry. I'll do the form.'

There was a pause on the other end of the line, through which a distant rattling cough could be heard. Then Kelly said, more softly:

'I'm sorry, hun. Look, I might be able to get the doctor to phone you later. Leave it with me and I'll see what I can do.'

Bryony refrained from mentioning that a doctor was supposed to phone her weeks ago, on Kelly's promise. Or that numerous doctors had been supposed to phone her numerous times for a period going back years, and that she had long since stopped believing that they ever would. Sometimes she wondered if doctors even existed anymore, or if they'd all been wiped out secretly during the pandemic while an army of admin staff were forced to busk madly to stop anyone finding out.

'That would be amazing,' she told Kelly. 'Thank you.'

'Could you tell me a bit more about your symptoms?'

'Sure. Well, there's this pain. A sort of low, crampy, not quite a throb, but—'

'Pain, got it. Anything else?'

'Well, nausea. I feel sick, all the time, except a lot of the time I'm ravenously hungry too. I'm dizzy, lightheaded really. Itching. Fatigue. And peeing more than normal.'

Kelly went quiet again, for longer this time. When she returned, the soft voice had gone and her tone was back to clipped, curt, professional.

'Right. Got the picture. Someone will be in touch.'

She rang off without saying goodbye.

41

One weird trick

It probably should have been less of a surprise than it was to Bryony when she arrived at Annie's mystery address, a featureless grey box of a business hotel off an A-road in Barking, to find several large signs in the foyer.

Garden Office Con – Princess Suite

British Association of Cosmetic Needling Experts (BACNE) – Empress Room

Gel Lyfe 'Let's Go Gels' Sell Your Way To Success Workshop – Duchess Lounge

'You're here! You came!' cried Annie as they hugged, and once again Bryony felt annoyed at the suggestion that not coming had been an option. The pain was still there, dull but nagging at her, like the pulse of bad music from a neighbourhood house party. She wanted nothing more than to take her pain back home to bed where it belonged, but Annie was already leading her towards the Duchess Lounge, its entrance framed by a giant green balloon arch. Through it she could see a mass – a flock? an *ooze*? – of gelievers, all clutching plastic wine glasses full of green sludge and tote bags bearing the legend '*Trust my gut!*'.

The crowd was more diverse than she was expecting, at least in

age and attractiveness if not in any meaningful sense. Women barely
out of their teens mingled with women in late middle-age; Boohoo
dresses and combat pants rubbed up against Per Una and FitFlops.
She eyed them all, looking for some comforting sign of her own
clear un-belonging, but it was hard to find one.

'I know you've been lacking in confidence lately, so I thought
this might be the perfect way to help you find some self-belief,' said
Annie, slipping an arm through hers and steering her towards a tres-
tle table full of anemic-looking pastries. Were pastries gut-happy?
'Plus we actually get to hear Tamara speak!'

'Tamara Mucklethwaite, founder and CEO?' asked Bryony.

'Yes! I heard on one of the forums that if she takes a shine to
you on the day she sometimes gelevates you to diamond level, like,
instantly.'

'Wow,' said Bryony, faintly. 'Amazing.'

She took a swig of her drink, some kind of gel-based breakfast
cocktail, and immediately regretted it. Her stomach roiled, voicing
its objection via a series of small acidic burps.

'So,' said Annie, as they took their seats in front of the stage.
'How are you getting on with recruiting?'

'You mean . . . selling the stuff?' asked Bryony.

'That too! Of course. But obviously the quickest way to supercharge your sales potential is recruiting a new downline, so you
definitely want to get on that.'

'Obviously.' She nodded. 'Ah, I haven't sold a whole lot yet, to be
honest – I think most of my friends are already pretty loyal to their
supplement brands, you know? But I'm doing my best!'

A watertight phrase. Nobody could argue with you doing your best.

'I know you are,' said Annie, squeezing her arm. 'That's the
thing, Bryony, I knew from the moment I met you that you were
just one of those people – someone you can really rely on, you
know? Not a flake. You're such a good friend.'

'Oh, pfft,' she batted away the compliment with a little swat of her hand.

'No, you are. Probably my best friend right now, to be honest.'

Annie said it so casually she hoped she'd misheard. This was an unwelcome but not unfamiliar feeling for Bryony, who people often tried to make their best friend. She'd never been entirely sure why, except that she rarely said no and therefore all applicants were successful, or believed themselves to be. Ever since a politically volatile situation in Year Five involving two different split-heart necklaces, juggling the needs and desires of various 'best' friends had been a normal part of her life. She knew that other people lived differently, though it was hard to see how. She had once read a very long article on modern polyamory – mostly the scheduling logistics and heavy reliance on shared Google calendars – and found it highly relatable; remembering so many birthdays, siblings' names, job titles and relationship histories with the fervour of a best friend was no mean feat. It took *work*.

'Fuck them all, just be MY best friend,' Marco had said once, drunkenly, after Bryony had broken down over the impossibility of attending one best friend's baby shower at the same time as another best friend's boutique opening.

'Do you really mean that?' she had said, clasping him on either side of his head and squeezing it like a ripe melon. 'I'll do it! I'll tell them all! Soz, we're over, it's just me and Marco BFFs 4 Lyfe.'

Marco had grimaced and wriggled free of her grip. 'Actually on second thoughts, I think you've got more best friend in you to give than I have the capacity to take.'

'I don't!'

'You couldn't go cold turkey, it would be too big a shock to the system.'

'It wouldn't! I could!'

He had shaken his head, suddenly sober. 'Besides, I already have a best friend. Craig.'

'Who the hell is Craig? I've never met Craig. You've never mentioned a *Craig*.'

'Craig is my best friend,' Marco had repeated firmly, and kissed her on the forehead. 'But it's okay petal, you are my *nearest* friend.' Bryony had accepted this as the best she was going to get.

Now she turned to Annie – currently her *nearest* friend – and said: 'I wondered if maybe some of your friends . . . your other friends, I mean . . . would they not be up for doing the whole Gel Lyfe thing? They might have more time . . . and, ah, potential, than I do?'

Annie shrugged, looking suddenly exhausted. Perhaps this was highly insensitive. Perhaps she really did have no other friends.

'They might,' said Annie after a long exhale. 'I don't know. Some of them probably would to be honest, if I said it would cheer me up. They'll all do anything to cheer me up just now. They keep saying – "let me know what I can do to help!" – as though there's an official chore rota or something. But it's just knackering having to be so grateful all the time, letting them come round and make me cups of tea and run me bubble baths or whatever, all so they can feel supportive. So they could go home and feel happy, like: box ticked, they've *done something*. When actually nobody can do anything. It's all pointless isn't it?'

This nihilism from Annie was both unnerving and refreshing. Bryony wondered for the first time how much of her forced jollity over the past few weeks had been in service to her mother.

'Honestly I can't bear it,' she went on. 'The special voice everyone uses when they speak to me.' She mimicked the drawn-out syllables, that hushed inflection. The sympathetic head-tilt. '"Heyyy, how you doingggg?" Arggh! I just LONG for someone to talk to me normally, you know? Stop treating me like I'm special. I'm not fucking special.' Annie gulped, pulling the sleeves of her hairy cardigan down over clenched fists. In a smaller voice, she added, 'Ed was special.'

Bryony was never quite prepared for them, these moments of naked grief. So much of her time with the Slingsbys was spent in the realm of the absurd, and so much of her brain was occupied with pretending to have loved Ed that it was becoming almost easy to forget the reason for it all: that Ed was gone. Seeing Annie so upset made her long to connect on a deeper level and offer her something real. She wished she got it.

'I get it,' said Bryony. 'But you really shouldn't be worrying about making other people happy just now. You need to put yourself first. Set some boundaries. Do whatever makes you most comfortable.'

Annie sniffed and smiled a watery smile. 'That's why I love hanging out with you, Bryony. You *do* get it. And I don't have to pretend to be fine, or pretend to be a grieving mess, or any of it. Because you're going through it all too.'

'Mm,' said Bryony. The acid burps had been joined by a pulsing headache in her left temple. She saw an opportunity. 'Hey, we don't have to hang out here though do we? Why don't we go and find a pub, where we can really chat? You can let it all o—'

But at that moment the lights dimmed and a hush descended over the Duchess Lounge. Lizzo's 'Good as Hell' began playing over the speakers and Annie grabbed her arm with a squeak of anticipation. It looked like they were staying.

One of the green t-shirted acolytes tried to get a rhythmic clap going in time to the music, but before this gathered any momentum Tamara Mucklethwaite appeared, waving at the crowd like a congresswoman. She was wearing a pink velvet trouser suit, expensively cut, and platform heels that clonked audibly on the stage.

'Who here wants to be her own boss?' she cooed into the mic. There were some whoops, a few polite cheers. Tamara cupped a hand behind her ear.

'Not good enough! I said WHO HERE WANTS TO BE HER OWN BOSS?'

A roar erupted through the room.

Bryony had very little interest in being her own boss. Having line-managed a few junior employees during her time and finding the whole exercise intimidating and tedious in equal measure, she was under no illusion that managing herself would be any better. It would probably be worse. She couldn't motivate herself to wash her bedsheets most weeks, what would make her think she could run a business? Running a business looked like far too much stress for not enough money, and besides, she was allergic to hustle. Needy 'creators' bemoaning the injustice of the Instagram algorithm. Ew.

And yet, it was hard to deny there was part of her that liked the idea of a secret back passage to success. This wasn't specific to her but rather a generational weakness, the result of having grown up with the unshakeable belief that someone, somewhere, really *was* making a thousand dollars a day by posting links on Google. Bryony was part of the 'one weird trick' generation, who graduated into an economic landscape so unrecognizable from the lush pastures their parents had enjoyed that it seemed only logical to look for trapdoors and loopholes. A world in which she could have a good education, a good degree and a 'good' job without even the faintest hope of buying a flat anywhere south of Sunderland seemed at times less rational than the idea that she might become a millionaire by selling bacteria on the internet. It was a difficulty setting so hard that there had to be, by rights, a cheat code.

Tamara kicked things off by inviting the attendees to raise a hand and share their 'most intense' dreams.

Bryony had a recurring nightmare in which she looked down halfway through her wedding vows to realize she was still wearing a hair bobble around her wrist. The husbands in these dreams were faceless or interchangeable, but the bobble always stayed the same.

She was on the verge of putting her hand up, until the first woman said, 'I dream of having a pool!' and the second woman said,

'I dream of taking my kids to Disney World', and Bryony realized she was not asking about that kind of dream.

'My dream is to pay off my credit card debt,' said one woman, who was wearing her own, badly cut, trouser suit for the occasion. 'I'd love to own my own house one day, so I know that my kids and I will never have to move again.'

'I want to make enough money so my husband can come home and stop working away on oil rigs,' said another. 'His health isn't good, I just want him to be able to rest.'

For the most part the dreams were all like this – modest, even slightly depressing, not the lust for sports cars and luxury cruises she might have expected. Tamara answered all of them in the same way.

'You can get there! You have the potential! I believe you can make it happen.'

When one woman explained in a timid voice that she'd already been selling Gel Lyfe for three years and dreamed of finally making it beyond 'Flint level', Tamara praised her stamina. 'Sometimes, the scenic route is the most beautiful.'

She then launched into a thirty-five minute monologue on dreams and how to achieve them, which boiled down to three main actionables: 1) drinking Gel Lyfe, 2) selling Gel Lyfe and 3) roping in other people to sell Gel Lyfe, with a much heavier emphasis on the third. Tamara was a polished public speaker, fond of breathy affirmations and staccato sentence delivery, punctuating each word with a hand in an 'okay' formation, like a shadow puppet of a hare. Before she said anything self-deprecating she would pause and place a hooked finger on her lips, cutely, as though perhaps they were about to be denied this revelation (they were not!).

At some point in the recent past people had stopped making statements sound like questions, with an upward inflection on the end, and started saying questions like statements instead. 'Do. You. Want. To. Realize. Your. Potential.' Tamara asked (?), and it was physically impossible not to join in when the rest of the attendees chorused back, 'yes!'

Every so often, she would set them up, asking if they wanted something – 'A six-figure salary?'; 'A white Mercedes?' – then scolding them when they shouted back 'yes'.

'No!' she would yell. 'You want a *seven* figure salary! You want a white *Maserati*! Demand more for yourself!'

'Demand more for yourself!' was a favourite catchphrase, used variously to refer to money, 'opportunities' and friendly gut bacteria. Tamara painted an image of the world as a vast gifting suite that you only had to wink at a bouncer to access, or an all-you-can-eat buffet where men grazed freely, filling their plates, their pockets and their huge hiking rucksacks, while all the women waited patiently in a queue. 'If *they* can have it, *you* can too!'

Bryony glanced over at Annie, who was taking notes. 'Demand more for self,' was heavily underlined.

Finally Tamara finished speaking and opened up the floor to questions.

The first two were lengthy enquiries about glitches within the Gelievers app, to which she nodded vigorously, replied 'I hear you, I hear you', then told the inquirer to email somebody called Malcolm. The third was a woman on the same row as Bryony and Annie.

'Yes? You there, with the gorgeous hair!' said Tamara. The whole room swung around to look at the woman and/or her hair, which was just ordinary.

'Um. I was just wondering if the gel is safe for pregnancy?' the woman asked quietly. 'Because – well, I know it says so in the handbook, but I've read a few things on the message boards that have made me nervous. Have there been any . . . well, any studies?'

Tamara gasped, and clasped her hands to her chest cartoonishly. 'You're pregnant! How wonderful! Stand up, sweetie.' The woman stood up looking terrified, as Tamara walked through the audience to stand beside her, placing one aloe-green manicured hand on her slightly convex stomach. Bryony inhaled on instinct.

'Such a blessing! What's your name, Mama?'

'Heidi,' the woman told her and Tamara bid the entire crowd to congratulate her and her unborn child. 'Congratulations Heidi!' they chanted. 'Congratulations, Heidi's baby!'

The woman smiled stiffly, her eyes falling nowhere in particular. Bryony felt for her. It looked worse than being sung Happy Birthday to in an open plan office.

'So, um, has it been tested on—' Heidi attempted to ask again, but Tamara interrupted.

'Not only is Gel Lyfe perfectly safe for you and little one, but it's actually an amazing supplement for this magical time, when new energy is flowing through you and it's crucial to give your body some extra love and support when it's working so hard and performing all that magic,' she cooed.

'In fact, when you think about it, you're the ultimate entrepreneur right now, Mama! Look what you're creating!' She jiggled poor Heidi's belly a little. 'Look what you're building, all by yourself! You're a creative genius. Don't you feel it? Don't you feel all that productivity and potential just flowing through your body?'

'Mhmm,' murmured the woman. Bryony suppressed another burp. She wondered if there was anywhere nearby that sold quiche.

'In fact, I'm going to tell you all a story,' says Tamara, finally unhanding poor Heidi's stomach and making her way back through the audience, sashaying a little as she went. Her home counties accent slipped into the rhythm of a country and western singer. 'When I had my first baby – oh, a hundred years ago!' – Tamara's eldest child was eight, Bryony had read it in the gelebration newsletter – 'I decided something. I decided there was no way I was going to let society tell me what a mother had to look like. I was not about to let them tell me my power was diminished when I *knew* it was the most powerful I had ever been.'

A woman two rows behind them let out a solitary whoop, then looked embarrassed. Tamara waited a beat and continued.

'I was not about to let them tell me I should hide myself away and sit on my arse all day, when I *knew* that I was filled with something incredible, something magical . . . . ' by now she had adopted a cadence not unlike a Baptist preacher and Bryony half expected her to say: 'the Holy Spirit.'

'Potential,' said Tamara. 'I discovered the secret they don't want you to know, and which you're about to discover, Mama.'

She pointed in Heidi's direction.

'I discovered that now is the best time to start a new business and unleash all that potential. The BEST time!' Tamara jabbed a triumphant fist in the air, and a few acolytes near the front let out a smatter of applause. 'I filled those sleepless nights with *ambition*. I began building my business with a baby on my boob and a laptop on my knee. I took all that magical, incredible goddess power that my body had held for nine months and I said "Wow. What if I could make other women feel like goddesses too? What if I could pass on all that magic and build a *community* of amazing kick-ass women who all feel *empowered* to reach their true *potential*? What if we never let society define our roles or our ambition for us again?"'

She was building to a crescendo now, the tips of her blow dry quivering as she gripped the mic with force.

'The answer . . .' she half whispered, casting her gaze slowly around the room, as though daring someone to yell out and ruin the payoff, '. . . was this. Gel Lyfe. YOU are all the answer. You are your OWN answer.'

Applause broke out in earnest now. Cheers and whoops filled the conference hall. Bryony fished around in her bag for her water bottle, clapping one hand politely against her thigh as Annie stamped her feet and whistled through her fingers. Tamara smiled beatifically at the response, dipping her head in a small bow.

A green-t-shirted team member darted forward and grabbed the mic as Tamara was whisked off stage by her entourage.

'And that's lunch, everyone!'

42

Crying over spilt soup

'Hey girl! QUIT YOUR JOB.'

Annie had tagged her beneath a post, which happened at least three times a day now. Their day in the Duchess Lounge had done nothing to communicate Bryony's lack of interest in the Gel Lyfe world, mainly because Bryony had done nothing to communicate her lack of interest in the Gel Lyfe world. She had started sending the emails straight to spam.

The caption read: 'The only thing that can hold you back is YOU. PSA: Life is too short to spend your days filling someone else's pockets – so QUIT THAT JOB and start filling your own! Every day that you go to work for someone else is a day that you're choosing not to back yourself fully. You're holding back a whole ocean of potential. So stop cruising and start swimming in it, lady!'

Beneath the post, row upon row of green heart emojis were stacked up from other gelievers. Bryony liked it, to be polite.

It was interesting, the way Gel Lyfe equated physical health and wellness with financial success when to her, the two had always felt more like antagonists. Bryony often wondered what she could've achieved in her life if she wasn't tending to her physical needs all day long. How successful might she be now if she was the kind of person who could forget to eat lunch, who never drank water and therefore didn't have to get up every forty minutes to pee? How much money might she have in the bank if she didn't buy designer supplements or apple cider vinegar? If the soft animal of her body wasn't such a pampered Pomeranian, perhaps she'd be a department head by now.

She had, in fact, lost out on a promotion at the council last year, for reasons unclear but not definitely *un*related to her taking so many half days for doctor, osteopath and acupuncture appointments, and a brief flirtation with cupping. If she quit her job to sell Gel Lyfe, at least she could schedule swimming in her ocean of potential around reformer Pilates. Bryony had never actually done Pilates, but liked the idea of being reformed.

She was still staring at her phone when she collided with a man coming out of a cafe carrying a takeaway tub of soup.

The soup went somersaulting upwards. It landed in a monstrous puddle of steaming green slime, across the pavement and down the man's t-shirt, missing Bryony by inches. He howled.

'Fuck!'

'Oh my god! Oh my GOD. I'm so sorry, I'm so, so sorry.'

Bryony was mortified. She longed to explain that she wasn't actually the kind of person who walked around staring at their phone, not looking where they were going, even though she clearly was because he was wearing the evidence.

'Let me buy you another one! I'll buy you another one!' she bleated, producing tissues from her handbag to mop up the damage. Then, as though they were Americans in a romcom and he was wearing a Brooks Brothers suit rather than a Uniqlo sweatshirt, 'I'll pay for the cleaning!'

Finally, in desperation, because at least thirty damp seconds had passed now and he hadn't audibly forgiven her yet, she added, 'I always look where I'm going usually, I swear, I never scroll and walk – it's just, my . . . ah, my boyfriend recently died.'

The man stopped scrubbing at himself and looked up, startled.

'It's fine,' he said, eventually. 'Don't worry, accidents happen. No use crying over spilt soup.'

He had nice eyes, she noticed. A shade of blue enhanced by the swamp stain down his front. Bryony smiled gratefully at him and for a second she thought perhaps they were having a meet-cute.

'You can go,' said the man.

'But I want to buy you another soup!' she insisted.

'It's fine,' he said firmly, as if to a child. 'I don't want any soup now.'

As she walked on, her phone began to ring.

'*See?!*' she wanted to turn round and shout down the road, although she wasn't sure what this would prove.

'Hello, is that Bryony Carter?' asked an unfamiliar female voice. 'It's Doctor Obasi, from the Ashgrove Surgery.'

At first she thought she must have misheard. Maybe it was a prank, or some kind of radio competition.

'Doctor . . . ?'

'Obasi, yes. You requested a telephone consultation?'

Bryony felt flustered and unrehearsed. If only she'd had warning! She could have made notes in advance.

'Thank you so much for calling, Doctor.'

'What seems to be the problem?' asked Doctor Obasi. Bryony could already hear the urgency in her voice; the need to rush through this call and onto the next.

'Well,' she began. 'I've been feeling very unwell—'

'In what way?' Doctor Obasi cut across her. Bryony mentally shuffled through her symptoms and grasped for the one that felt the most worthy.

'Abdominal pains!' She almost shouted it down the phone. 'I've been having these pains. Sort of stabbing, burning, throbbing pains, not quite cramps but cramp-ish, sort of between my back and my front.'

'Are you having them right now?'

'No,' admitted Bryony. 'They come and go.'

'How long have you been experiencing them?'

Twenty-two years.

'A few days.'

'Any other symptoms?'

'Yes. Shortness of breath, any time I do anything active. Lightheadedness. Or sometimes more like *heavy*headedness? I feel dizzy a lot, for no reason. And nauseous. But hungry too? Except I only really want to eat quiche. It's like there's a kind of . . . *rottenness* in my stomach that won't go away.'

'Something is rotten in the heart of your stomach, as Hamlet would say?'

This wasn't doctor speak.

'Yes,' said Bryony. 'Even with Gaviscon.'

She expected the doctor to interrupt again, but she didn't this time. Bryony carried on.

'My back hurts quite a lot. And my neck, if I sleep on it wrong. When I can sleep, that is. My vision is getting worse I think, I notice my eyes blurring a lot more than they used to, and I get those little floaters in the morning – you know the eye worms? Those guys. I don't know if that's normal. Oh and I have recurrent IBS, or at least what I assume is IBS, it's never been officially diagnosed. I wonder quite a lot if I might have a gluten sensitivity but when I'm feeling nauseous bread is the only thing I want to eat, so then I think maybe it's lactose – but when I went vegan for a while I got these terrible headaches and the left side of my tongue went numb, so I stopped. Although in hindsight it was also hay fever season and that tends to affect me in odd ways, I don't sneeze but I wake up feeling like I've been hit by a truck in the night? Like, every limb hurts.'

'Do you think you have hay fever now?' asked Doctor Obasi.

'No,' said Bryony. 'It's December.'

A pause.

'What would you say is the main priority for us to be focusing on today?' the doctor asked. 'If you had to sum it up.'

'I feel like ... I feel like my body is turning on me,' Bryony replied in a lame, half whisper.

Another pause.

'Bryony, have you been through any stressful events recently?' asked the doctor. 'Any shocks or big life changes?'

'No,' she replied, after a moment. 'Nothing that springs to mind.'

43

Do what you want to do

Ann wanted her to come for Christmas.

'We'll have far too much food this year,' she said, as though the food shop had been ordered before Ed died – which maybe it had – and as though Ed had usually consumed most of it.

'If you come up on the twenty-third you can be here for the Christingle,' she went on without explaining what this was, 'then stay as long as you like. Until New Year? We usually have a party – I doubt I'll have the strength, although god knows what everyone will end up doing if I don't. But either way you'd be very welcome, Bryony! You're part of the family now.'

It was at once both a terrifying and tempting prospect. At Ann's, she sensed, there would be noise and colour and borrowed chairs and everybody in skew-whiff cracker crowns, playing parlour games (Ed's favourite!), working their way through vats of off-brand Quality Street and performing archaic family rituals like swimming naked in the duck pond on Boxing Day. The kind of Christmas she'd always wanted.

Even if it meant pausing every forty minutes to console a weeping Slingsby, even if it meant sleeping in Ed's mustering bedsheets next to adolescent posters of Lara Croft and Rachel Stevens, even if it meant braving perilously undercooked meats and flogging mulled

Gel Lyfe with Annie from a tinsel-covered stall in the village square, it might still be a better way to pass the festive season. More distractions. Fewer memories.

She told Ann she'd think about it.

'You should go! Fuck it! Why not?' said Blod.

Blod was a university friend who she saw every time a Greta Gerwig film came out, or a hip, sad author did a book talk. Blod had the kind of fearless optimism that could only come from going through life being called Blod.

'Give me a reason not to,' she said.

'I don't know, it feels weird?' said Bryony. It struck her that this would be a perfect title for her memoir. *I Don't Know, It Feels Weird* by Bryony Carter. 'Visceral' – *The New York Times*.

'Everything feels weird right now though, because you're grieving,' said Blod. 'It could be a way to solidify your relationship with his family.'

The problem was that Bryony had now stopped telling people the whole story, focusing mainly on the 'my boyfriend died' part and casually omitting the part where she hadn't realized she actually had a boyfriend. It seemed simpler.

'Maybe you're right,' she said out of the side of her mouth, as the hip sad author shuffled onto the stage in a pair of oversized glasses. 'I mean, I don't want to be rude.'

'Forget about being rude, do what *you want to do*,' hissed Blod.

'What *I want to do* is not be rude though,' Bryony whispered back. The talk began.

'You can't go for Christmas, that's insane,' said Marco.

'I know, I know. Obviously it's ridiculous,' said Bryony. She paused. 'But theoretically, out of interest – why not?'

'Because it's *Christmas*,' said Marco, as though that settled it. Marco could be oddly traditional about some things.

In fact, he'd invited her to spend Christmas with his family every year for the past four that they'd been living together. Bryony had always declined because she assumed he didn't really mean it. She wondered now if he had.

'Exactly, and Christmas is a time to welcome in waifs and strays,' she said. 'I think it would make Ann genuinely happy to have me there.'

'You're not a waif. And you're not making Ann genuinely happy, you're making Ann *fraudulently* happy.'

Bryony bristled at this. 'How dare you say I'm not a waif.' She brushed quiche crumbs off her jumper. 'I've been feeling terrible lately, you know that.'

'I'm sorry to shit all over your Dickensian invalid fantasies, but having a dicky tummy for a few weeks does not mean you qualify for the biggest turkey in the window of Buckton's butcher shop,' said Marco.

'It's more than a dicky tummy, Marco. I feel horrendous. Like my whole body is shutting down. I'm bone-tired – like, *abnormally* tired. The doctor referred me for a blood test but said it was probably just stress. They always say it's fucking stress. As though that solves anything.'

'There is one answer you don't seem to have considered,' he said.

'Therapy?' said Bryony.

'No. Well, yes, you should absolutely have therapy. But I was going to say, maybe you're pregnant.'

Time stopped. The word shuddered through her. Bryony punched him, hard, on the arm.

'Why the fuck would you say that?'

'Because you might be! It's not an insult, it's a genuine possibility. Isn't it?'

She shook her head. 'I haven't slept with anyone except Ed for months and we always used condoms. It was one of the things I liked about him, actually – that I never needed to ask. He never did the sulky thing, the "ugh, I suppose if I *must*" thing. He was always there, popping it on quite willingly, before I even had to say. Like he was just delighted to make a dent in his supply.'

'I bet Ann bought him a massive box of them from Costco.'

'Stop it!'

'Oh Ed,' sighed Marco. 'A moment of silence for your conscientiousness. For being a good egg ... man.'

They paused, heads bowed, presumably both grappling with the same mental image. When the moment had passed, Marco said, 'You could still be pregnant though. Condoms are famously not one-hundred percent effective.'

'Famously?'

'It's how Emma Geller-Green was conceived on *Friends*.'

'Oh. I thought maybe it was part of your veterinary knowledge,' she said, distractedly. She was running through a list as though it were a cursed memory game, eyes swivelling in a bad imitation of a soap opera epiphany. *Nausea. Fatigue. Lightheadedness.*

'Animals don't use contraception, Brian.'

'Aha. Right. Of course.' She swallowed down the bitter saliva that had pooled in her cheeks.

Nausea. Fatigue. Lightheadedness. Peeing all the time.

'Besides sterilization, obviously, but that feels like an extreme response before you've even done a test.'

Nausea. Fatigue. Lightheadedness. Peeing. Pain, was the pain one?

'You'd look terrible in the cone.'

'Thanks.'

She began some frantic mental maths. She'd had a period since Ed died, hadn't she? At least one. Yes! She was sure she'd emptied a Mooncup in Ann's downstairs toilet. She remembered being grateful the room still had terracotta stippling from the nineties. But hadn't it been lighter than usual, that period?

Nausea. Fatigue. Lightheadedness. Peeing. Pain. Vision changes.

Tales loomed up in her consciousness; friends–of–friends who'd carried on menstruating throughout pregnancy; of girls at school who'd been six months gone before they noticed the bulge over their low–rise jeans; of women on the front of lurid magazines who'd had no idea until they went to the loo one day and shat out a baby.

'I can't be pregnant,' she told Marco.

'Okay,' he said. 'If you're sure . . . I was just pointing out, it would explain a lot of your—'

'No I mean, I *cannot* be pregnant. With dead Ed's baby. Can you even imagine? Oh god. Oh god I can't breathe.'

'Shhh, it's fine. It's not like you'd have it.'

'No.'

She swallowed again, wiped a hand across her clammy upper lip. Marco looked at her, eyes narrowed.

'Brian,' he said slowly. 'Please tell me you wouldn't have it.'

'Shut up, of course I wouldn't.'

'Brian!' He sounded genuinely panicked.

'What?'

'You can't have a baby out of awkwardness.'

'I know!'

'I'm sorry, I won't let you.' He was suddenly pink-faced and pompous. This was not a version of Marco she recognised. 'You can read a poem at a funeral and you can go to a million weird family gatherings and you can join a fucking pyramid scheme if you really must, but I absolutely draw the line at allowing you to bring a CHILD into this WORLD just to be POLITE, I'm sorry, I will not stand for it.'

Bryony snorted.

'You will not stand for it? Who are you, my Victorian grand-father? What will you do, pack me off to a convent?'

'It isn't funny, Bryony. Tell me you understand you *do not have to have* this baby.'

'There is no baby! I'm not even pregnant!'

Nausea. Fatigue. Lightheadedness. Peeing. Pain. Vision changes. Backache. Headache. Weird taste in mouth.

'If you were though? Promise me you wouldn't have it.'

'I'm sorry, what the fuck is this? I will not promise you. If I am – was – *were* pregnant – it would be my choice. You have no more right than any other man to tell me what I can and can't do with my womb.' She was the one turning pompous now. 'How dare you.'

Mood swings.

'I'm just saying, we can't fit a baby down the side of your chest of drawers.'

'It isn't funny, Marco.'

'No, it fucking isn't.'

'Well then stop talking to me like I'm a moron who can't run her own life.'

'I mean ...'

The ellipsis hung between them for a devastating second.

They'd never had a fight before. The thing she loved most about Marco was his ability to deflect conflict. Criticism rolled off him like Teflon. In a long line of flatmates, Marco was the only one she'd ever had who she genuinely hoped would be home when she put her key in the lock. Not a single passive-aggressive Post-It had ever passed between them.

But now, they were fighting. Now Bryony was storming out and slamming the front door while Marco huffed and crashed utensils around behind her. She had no keys or bag with her, no coat on, and slippers instead of shoes. Thankfully her phone was in her hand, because her phone was always in her hand, and her slippers were of the felted clog variety that could pass as outdoor footwear in Walthamstow.

She knew Marco would be leaving for his shift in an hour, potentially locking Bryony out for the rest of the day, but instead of swallowing her pride and turning around, or at least swallowing half her pride and sitting on the doorstep until he left, she started walking. She walked fast towards the high street, gurning against the drizzle but not really feeling the cold. She continued walking past pharmacy after pharmacy, branches of Boots, Superdrug, Savers, each time believing she would go in and make the purchase, but each time entirely unsurprised when her feet carried her right on up the street.

Nausea. Fatigue. Lightheadedness. Peeing. Pain. Vision changes. Backache. Headache. Weird taste in mouth. Mood swings.

She opened up Alloi and messaged Theo, then typed 'Sydenham' into CityMapper for train times.

Irrational behaviour.

44

Trust your gut

Kelly finds out that Desmond has died in the usual way, through an automated system message from the hospital.

She wishes it were different this time. She wishes it were one of the times that a patient dies at home and a relative has to call to let the GP know instead – although they rarely remember to do this until letters are sent to the dead person reminding them about routine appointments or flu jabs, upon which the relative calls, angry and upset, and Kelly has to apologise profusely for not knowing what nobody has told her.

Still, she wishes Desmond's daughter had called, because then Kelly could have said something nice about him. 'I was very fond of your father,' something like that. 'He always lit up our waiting room.' 'He made me feel hot and young.'

As it is, she must pay her respects to an automated system message, which is not quite the same.

'Go well, Des,' she whispers as she clicks the button to 'Update records' and watches his file move to its new resting place. She tries to hold a personal minute's silence, but Phlegmma Thompson fills it with a chorus of hawking and spluttering.

'Idiots,' says one of the GPs, appearing in the office behind her and ruining the moment further.

'Who is?'

'Patient has stopped taking her script because she thinks some snake oil vitamin drink off the internet is going to cure her,' says Doctor Obasi, pouring herself a coffee from the tarry pot and slamming the fridge in frustration. 'Ludicrous. And dangerous, these stupid fads, scaring people off actual medicine to make money.'

'Which drink?' asks Kelly, though she fears she can already see the green flash in the doctor's eyes.

'Some Gel something or other, I don't know,' she replies. 'The company is telling people to stop taking their meds because it will "interrupt their vibrations", I simply cannot.'

And Doctor Obasi strides out again, leaving her own vibrations in her wake.

On her lunch break Kelly looks at her phone to find Annie has tagged her in another post. This time it's a photo of herself against an ivy-covered backdrop which Kelly recognizes as the back wall of The Stag and Barrow, eyes downcast, arms wrapped around herself in a tender embrace.

The caption reads:

'Vulnerability moment!! A year ago I thought I was fine, but looking back now I realize I was in a really low place. I felt sluggish and tired and lacking sparkle. My career was going nowhere and I was failing to harness my inner power and live up to my true potential. Now I feel so energized and I look around at everything I'm achieving as a small business owner and WOW, I'm so proud. So I'm asking u today to pause and actually think about this question. Are? You? Well? Be honest. Are you deprioritizing yourself? Looking for a community that will nourish your MIND as well as your BODY? Want a wellness solution that actually (literally) WORKS for YOU? Bored of all the bullsh*t that is holding you back from becoming your very best self? It's time to take charge of your gut health and launch

your new and improved lyfe. Drop me a line to start the best journey you'll ever go on and become a Geliever today!'

She does not like the post. Instead she looks up the contact page on a popular news outlet, opens up an email and begins to type.

PART TWO

45

December, eh

Bryony was in denial.

It made very little sense, she realized, for someone who spent so much of their time hunting for diagnoses to refuse to go out and spend £3.99 on the test that could provide one in three minutes flat, but there it was – she would rather stagnate in the uncertainty than deal with whatever came next. She closed her eyes every time she saw magpies outside, which was leading to a lot of precarious road-crossing.

And conveniently, it was Christmas. 'Twas the season for inexplicable pregnancies! A time when everyone felt nauseous all the time anyway! Bryony allowed herself to be swallowed up by it all, accepting every last request to 'get something in the diary before Christmas' like it was a legal requirement, or as though parties and pubs and the opportunity to drink a mid-price peppery red in someone's kitchen might cease to exist come the new year. In her case, it might.

She dragged herself to festive brunches and lunches, pre-drinks and post-drinks. She sang along at screenings of beloved Christmas movies and ate melted cheese in an inflatable pod on the South Bank. She went to see *The Nutcracker*, twice; classic and contemporary versions. She wore a flammable jumper to parties that turned out to be candlelit soirees, and she wore sequins and heels to parties that turned out to be five people sitting on a sofa next to a sweating wheel of brie. She had her annual chats with the friends she only ever saw at these occasions, and whose lives therefore always had the air of an advert for a national bank – fast-forwarding through engagements, weddings, mortgages, pregnancies and increasingly sensible haircuts.

And she felt like shit. Her physical symptoms continued – if anything they were worse, with the addition of a snotty cold that was doing the rounds – but she leaned into them as a kind of penance, martyring herself to the festive cause and medicating with breakfast stollen. Whenever her head started swimming, she would rest her forehead on the cool melamine of her desk and groan a little, and everyone in the office would think 'December, eh'.

At least, she assumed they were thinking that. She couldn't see them.

She was on three Gel Lyfe sachets a day now, chugging down the verdant gelixir first thing in the morning the way she used to have hot water with a squeeze of lemon. She had begun to drink it openly in the office kitchen, sipping slowly like a promo model, smacking her lips in an exaggerated fashion in the hope that someone might stop and ask her about it, then buy some. Nobody did. One anonymous colleague complained to HR, and a cryptic email was sent around the office warning about 'inappropriate solicitation in the workplace.'

But Bryony remained calm, stoic, positive, bolstered by the cheery buzz of gelievers in her pocket.

'You deserve happiness,' they told each other, between tips on using Gel to ice festive gingerbread. 'Let go of the guilt,' they told each other, and Bryony would squeeze and relax her pelvic floor muscles, for lack of another mechanism. Let go of guilt. Release guilt. It doesn't serve you.

She went to Little Buckton only twice – a moderate amount, she thought, very restrained. But on the nights she returned from Northamptonshire she snuck in like a teenage stop-out, shoes in hand, so as not to arouse Marco's disapproval.

Marco had picked up some extra shifts at work, and so the two of them were like ships, if not passing in the night, then scraping awkwardly against each other on the landing. Marco wasn't a grudge-bearer by nature, but the way he spoke to her now – politely, sweetly, tentatively, as though he might be about to go off and eviscerate her with someone else – felt worse. He no longer asked about the latest on Ann, or Annie, or Gel Lyfe or any of Ed's associates, giving Bryony a sense that it was all a playground game he had got bored of, leaving her alone in her make-believe world.

'You still going home for Christmas?' he asked one morning, as they waited for the kettle to boil.

'Yep,' she said, and he looked relieved.

'Good. Great,' he said.

'Should be nice!' she said, and they both went to eat breakfast alone in their bedrooms.

46

Not like here

It was odd that Bryony's family home could feel so grey and joyless, even by comparison with people whose son had just died.

The tone was set when she arrived on the morning of Christmas Eve to find her father heading out to the golf course, and her step-mother on her hands and knees, bleaching the kitchen skirting board. A cinnamon bun reed diffuser made its presence known from the hall table. This had been the scent of Christmas for as long as she could remember it: synthetic calories and Dettol.

'Merry Christmas!' said Bryony, aiming for jovial but landing on sarcastic. 'I thought you had a cleaner?'

'She wanted to go home for two weeks,' sighed Kath, pausing to stand up and bump a powdery cheek against Bryony's. 'Not exactly ideal but I could hardly say no, in the circumstances.'

'What are the circumstances?'

'She's from the Ukraine,' replied Kath, mouthing the word as though it were taboo. 'So *naturally* I assumed she meant back there – be careful, I said, stay safe! We want you back again! I gave her an extra tip and everything, for Christmas – then, *then,* it turns out her parents and brothers are all in Berkshire and she's just going to stay there! Well, I couldn't very well say anything could I, at that point! Ha!'

She clucked and laughed and rolled her eyes at the rotten luck.

Kath was once a person who used to get up at 5am on Boxing Day for the Next sale. Though she'd since graduated to online shopping, the general sense that she would clobber you for a wraparound cardigan still remained.

'No,' said Bryony. 'I guess you couldn't.'

The next twenty-four hours passed as it always did: quietly.

As was their tradition, the entire Waitrose No.1 Christmas range was served up on a series of cut-glass platters. Each dish was presented with slavish precision, right down to the suggested garnishes – a dollop of crème fraîche, a flurry of chopped chives – and its full name read verbatim from the packaging.

'Aged Cornish Cheddar Pinwheel with Sticky Chorizo Jam?' Kath would proffer. 'Feta Popcorn with Hot Honey Drizzle? Shimmering Salmon Celebration Pâté? Chocolate and Hazelnut Quenelle Studded with Honeycomb Pieces?'

Kath rarely ate any of it herself. Bryony ate everything, and seconds when pushed, because she couldn't bear to see the excesses looking depressing in the kitchen bin later.

She wondered what Ann was serving. She pictured burnt stuffing sandwiches, an abundance of squirty cream, nets of Babybel and that smoked cheese that looks like a sausage – and yearned for it all.

It was as they were silently sawing into their Jewelled Stuffed Norfolk Bronze Turkey Crown with Red Wine Jus that her father made the announcement. He began with a lot of ceremonial throat-clearing – the turkey, as ever, was dry – and for a moment she thought he might be about to raise a toast. To her? To his lowered golf handicap? To Heston?

'We wanted to talk to you about something,' he began. Her

stepmother pressed her lips together and toyed with her napkin. Kath's mother picked at a stuffing ball, oblivious.

'Kath and I have made a big decision . . .'

Divorce, she thought. Well, it's about time. If anything it would be a relief. Although no sooner had this feeling established itself than more feelings followed – worry, for her father, all alone, again, and worry for *herself* having to deal with an all-alone father, this time with legal obligations and a much higher likelihood of falls in the shower, forgetting who he was in the supermarket or having to wrangle his car keys off him after he started swerving into neighbourhood pets. She played out the next twenty years in her mind via a series of greyscale scenes directed by Ken Loach. Then he completed the sentence.

'. . . we're emigrating.'

'You're what?'

'To France. We're retiring to France,' he said, and mimed clinking his glass with Kath's across the table.

'You're already retired.'

'Fine, we're *moving* to France. To continue our retirement.'

'Both of you? Together?'

Kath laughed a tinkly laugh, which had always been her tactic when Bryony 'acted out'. Kath had tinkled her way through broken curfews, unsuitable boyfriends, failed exams, paralytic hospital trips and an undiagnosed eating disorder. In fairness, she treated both her child and stepchild equally in this regard. When Tim had been found letting his friend Rupert rifle through Bryony's underwear drawer, Kath had laughed at that too.

'We've found a lovely house,' said Kath in sing-song pitch, piling extra potatoes onto her mother's plate. 'Three bathrooms, would you believe! And very reasonable, in a lovely village. Well, a town really but the towns *feel* villagey out there don't they? And it has a real *community*. Not like here.'

'But you don't speak French,' said Bryony.

'*Ex-pat* community, she means,' said her father, as though this were obvious. 'Loads of Brits.'

'That's right,' smiled Kath. 'Not like here.'

Bryony grimaced. She was playing a different mental film now. One in which she festered forever in a Zone Three bedsit, black mould spores filling her lungs, while her only parent chose to live out the rest of his years on a different land mass, redirecting his *Telegraph* subscription and complaining that bouillabaisse was too fishy.

'Oh,' was all she could think of to say. 'Lovely.'

She looked up and met Kath's mother's rheumy gaze, and for a few seconds it felt as though they were sharing something. How it felt to be abandoned by your primary carer without consultation; to be such a footnote in someone else's life that they'd rather live near a cut-price hypermarché than you. But then Beryl smiled at her and wiped a glob of bread sauce from her chin, and the moment was over.

'And of course we'll be closer to Tim and Clementine,' Kath was saying now. 'Which makes sense because I'm sure we'll be hearing the pitter-patter of tiny feet before long, so it will be nice to all be closer. To ... well, to them.'

'Than me, sure. Got it,' said Bryony. Kath laughed again. Bryony considered pointing out that it was quicker to get to Brussels on the Eurostar from Ashford than it was to drive hundreds of miles across the Ardennes, but decided it was pointless. They didn't believe in trains.

Instead she asked, 'Are you selling the house?'

Her father became engrossed in a parsnip. 'That's the long-term plan,' he said, evenly. 'The place out there, it'll need some work doing – roof repairs, bit of structural stuff and decorating. And Kath wants a pool, naturally. But we thought we'd rent out this house at first, just while we settle in and go through the whole visa rigmarole. Lucky to have the option.'

'You can make serious money renting out at the moment,' added Kath brightly, as though this were news. 'Linda's son lets out his flat by the bingo to a family with four children. Four, can you imagine! In a two-bed? And he gets a courtesy apartment in Singapore, so it's all just going straight in the bank.'

'Marvellous,' said Bryony. 'Good for Linda's son.'

Her father shot her a look. It was a familiar look; one that meant, simply, 'don't start.'

But Bryony had already started. 'I'm well aware the rental market is a fucking hellscape, actually Kath,' she said.

'Language!' chirped Kath.

'Landlords of your generation exploiting vulnerable renters of *my* generation to feather your massive nest-eggs is one of the biggest problems facing our society today—'

'Tchuh, this isn't a very Christmassy topic.'

'You brought it up!'

'Well, would you rather we just sell the house then?' her father interrupted. 'Would that be better, get rid straight away? I suppose you're thinking there'll be a chunk in it for you, which of course there *will*, although with tax and the amount we'll need for the kitchen extension I'm afraid I can't prom—'

'No! That isn't what I was thinking at all. It's just a lot to process, okay? This was Mum's home,' she added, sounding more petulant than she felt.

She looked around the room as though seeing the house properly for the first time in years – the boxy, mock-Tudor semi, most of her happy memories long lacquered over by gloss paint and resentment. Her mother's preference for bright colours and bare floorboards, splashy ceramics and crocheted cushion covers – it was hard to know now whether they were symbolic of a warm, bohemian spirit or just the tail end of the nineties. If she lived here now instead of Kath, maybe everything would still be grey plush carpeting and mirrored coffee tables. Who knew?

'I'm well aware of that, Bryony,' said her father, and Kath directed her gaze towards her dinner plate, as though observing a minute's silence, the way she always did when her personal *Rebecca* was mentioned.

'Would you like us to live here for the rest of our days, is that it?' He didn't say it angrily, exactly, more like he was trying to reason with a toddler.

'No!' she said again. 'I really wouldn't.'

What Bryony would really like was for Kath and her father to live in a different house, perhaps up the road, and for this house to remain empty but restored precisely to the way it had looked in 1999, down to the last floral border.

Or, no, that wasn't right – what she wanted was to live in it herself, maybe? But no, not alone. With Marco? With a dog? With a husband and two phantom children? And not *here*, obviously – but in Walthamstow? No, that wasn't right either.

The flowchart of hypotheticals kept leading her back to the same place every time. *What I want is for her to still be alive.*

Bryony didn't say this. Bryony said, 'It's fine. Sounds great. You should go.'

'Well! There we go,' tinkled Kath, miming a 'phew' gesture by wiping her forehead. 'Thank you Bryony, you'll understand when you see the cornicing—'

'Is it really fine?' asked her father, quietly. This jolted her. It had been many years since he'd sought her permission or opinion on anything. The last time she could bring to memory was probably when he had sat her down and asked her if she'd like a new mum.

'Sure,' said Bryony, her voice becoming shrill with the effort. Her chin was wobbling in a way it hadn't since childhood.

'Of course it is,' laughed Kath. 'Bryony's a strong, independent woman! If she doesn't need a boyfriend, then she certainly doesn't need us hanging around. We know you like your privacy, Bryony.'

'Do I?' said Bryony, mildly.

'She's a woman of mystery!' Kath carried on. She was directing this little speech towards Beryl, the way some couples conduct passive-aggressive conversations through their baby. 'Never been one for filling us in on all the little details of her life. I know she doesn't expect us to stay here gathering dust for the next forty years, just in case one day she breaks the habit of a lifetime and decides to pop down and spend some more time with us! Do you, Bryony?'

'I ... uh ... no,' was all Bryony could manage to say, thrown by Kath's apparent belief that she was going to live to one hundred and two.

'She can always fill us in on her dating adventures over the phone, if she remembers how to use one! And you know, if you do change your ways and decide to settle down with *someone special*, well! We'll always have space in France for you, you can bring him to visit! Or her!'

Kath had long been disappointed by Bryony's humdrum heterosexuality. A lesbian stepdaughter would have been quite the coup at her book group.

'Thank you,' said Bryony through gritted teeth. 'Good to know.'

'Or you never know, we might find you a lovely Jean-Paul or Pierre! But I think they're more traditional over there – Catholic, of course.'

She said this as though it was a complete point and went back to shuffling turkey around her plate. They ate, for a few seconds, in silence.

'Actually I was seeing someone special,' said Bryony. 'He died, two months ago.'

There was a clatter as Bryony's father dropped his knife. Kath began to laugh again; she was mid-tinkle before she looked at Bryony and realized she was serious. Her eyes bugged, and she swallowed the laugh into a cough. Richard met Bryony's eye for the first time that meal.

'So,' she continued before they could ask questions. 'Do what you like! Go and live in fucking France, I don't care. Life is short! Have fun! Go hate each other on the continent instead, see if that solves all your problems.'

Before anyone could reply, Kath's mother began spluttering, and had to be calmed with slaps on the back and sips of water.

'Hope you're okay, Beryl,' said Bryony as she stood up from the table to leave. 'Very dry turkey, isn't it? Like eating a loofah.'

Kath didn't laugh at this.

47

High-contrast features

Bryony was halfway through packing her bag – she would take the presents she'd already opened, she decided, leaving them behind would be a cruelty too far – when she remembered there was no public transport on Christmas Day. Really this was poor civic planning, Christmas being such prime family argument time. It was probably the peak storming-out day of the year, statistically. But perhaps most people learned to drive before they started storming out of places. A sensible forethought.

The Uber surge pricing was eyewatering, but it was the only way to get home. This wasn't home anymore. It hadn't been for years. Although being in London over Christmas didn't feel right, either. Like being at school on the weekend.

She returned to be greeted by her unwashed bedding and a festering slice of quiche in the fridge. The slanted grey light giving the whole flat the feeling of living inside a washed-out Tupperware.

For five days, Bryony festered too.

She ate old packets of ramen, watched ancient episodes of problematic sitcoms and examined all of her moles, writing down her observations in her Notes app. She tended to herself like a crisping houseplant, cutting her nails and her split ends and squeezing her blackheads and plucking out ingrowing hairs and chugging down so much water that her urine turned completely clear and she was forced to google 'water intoxication'.

She ignored missed calls from her father and experimented with Gel Lyfe in a variety of serves: with gin, with amaretto, with Ambrosia custard from a tin. She took short, healthful walks around the neighbourhood, looking at everyone she passed and wondering why they weren't elsewhere for Christmas either. She remembered that for plenty of people this wasn't a sacred time at all, it was just Tuesday.

And the whole time she was doing it there was an odd kind of pressure inside herself, like an urge to retch and heave or cough up something bloodied and sinister. Finally she decided to give into it, and when she did it wasn't the urge to vomit at all. It was the urge to go under her bed, pull out a box and look at photos of her mother.

Bryony had precious few photos of her, and even fewer of them together. Her mother had died back when photographs were something to be treasured, before the age of the smartphone devalued them to the point where they'd become great digital fatbergs, clogging up everyone's devices and slowing down everyone's lives.

She kept the photos separate from most of the other junk she was too sentimental to throw away, in an old box that had once held a Body Shop gift set and still smelled faintly of white musk. Bryony opened the box and looked at the photos rarely – about once or twice a year – because it always made her cry for several hours. It had occurred to her that if she looked at them more often then they might make her cry less when she did, but this was more of a worry than an incentive.

Being mostly from the nineties, the photos had undergone the curious evolution: from looking modern to looking embarrassingly dated, to looking romantically dated, to looking like historical artefacts, to looking like every youthful Instagram grid – just a grainy riot of wonky angles and comically drab backdrops, oversized sweatshirts and cycling shorts, high-contrast features and dilated pupils. Bryony still wasn't sure if her mother really had had such luminous skin or if the camera flash was just doing her the favour.

As she cried, she thought about Ed's family and just how many more photos there must be of him, and wondered if that was a blessing or if it only made everything harder. You couldn't romanticize a hundred shit selfies from a stag weekend. Or maybe in twenty-five years' time, those would look glossy and interesting too.

Purge completed, she put the photos of her mother away again, opened up Alloi, and checked Ed's profile (still there – was this not gross negligence on somebody's part? What if new women were developing feelings for him as we spoke?) and looked at each photo of him until those made her cry as well.

On the sixth day, she looked up the next train to Little Buckton – December 31st, three changes including one rail replacement bus – and booked it.

48

Silent night

Christmas without Ed is as weird as Kelly feared it would be.

Not the quiet, stilted, tear-stained Christmas you might expect, but a chaotic one – too much noise and colour and crashing about just for the sake of it. They are trying to fill the void and overcompensating wildly, considering Ed was always the calmest of the bunch. Ann is borderline manic, trying to start a singsong or a game of charades or a sprout-eating competition any time anyone so much as stops to draw breath. Annie is overwrought, Leo bombastic, both of them alternately laughing and bellowing, quick to pick fights with each other; their mother; the ancient appliances that are never replaced; the broken lock on the downstairs loo.

The aunts and cousins and fake aunts and fake cousins arrive day and night in one long chorus line, and Kelly is obliged to have the same conversation with all of them. 'Awful, so strange, first Christmas always the hardest, such a trooper, isn't she just, so strong, yeah thank you all fine, no still at the surgery, yes gin and tonic thanks, haha no, not yet, we'll see.'

It already seems insane to her that despite everyone knowing how babies are made, people still bring it up in polite conversation, their probing tantamount to asking 'are you shagging enough?' over the gammon and coleslaw. But it is *doubly* insane to her that people still want to know if they're shagging enough when Leo's brother has just died, the way they want to know if they're all eating properly and getting enough fresh air. 'We've lost one person – quick, make another one!' the logic seems to go.

Few parts of this are fun and yet not going to Little Buckton for Christmas would have been unthinkable, the way that not answering the aunties would be unthinkable, not playing the games, not eating the sprouts, not putting her arms around her pink-cheeked husband and telling him that he and his sister are both twats and that they love each other really. She hears herself quoting her own mother – 'I'm sure it's six of one, and half a dozen of the other' – an idiom that used to boil her blood when she was a kid but which rolls off her tongue with fluency now. Each night she hits the pillow exhausted from the effort of it all, and sleeps dreamlessly until they all start thrashing about again the next morning.

Kelly finds herself with Emmett a surprising amount. The two of them sit silently in the back garden in twilight drizzle, listening to the three of them bouncing off the walls – and each other – inside.

'Well,' says Emmett, after about ten minutes.

'Yeah,' says Kelly.

49

Big on festive spirit

Unsurprisingly, New Year's Eve at the Slingsbys was the hottest ticket in town.

'It's so good of you to spend the night with us when I'm sure you must have so many invites to exciting parties back in London,' said Ann.

The truth was that Ann's party was already shaping up to be far more exciting than any of the offers that had trickled in over the past week. This was mainly because everyone seemed to have decided that making an effort for New Year was desperately uncool, although of course Bryony could hardly tell Ann that.

People agreed that going anywhere near central London on New Year's Eve was a bad idea to the point of embarrassing – *imagine*, if anyone *saw* you on the *news* – which meant that you were banking on somebody having a gathering; something chic and spontaneous, small enough to feel intimate but big enough not to be tragic. But because the intimate gathering was supposed to be spontaneous, nobody planned it, and thus the whole thing became a game of hosting chicken, no one volunteering because they were hoping somebody else would first, until before you knew it, it was the 31st December and things had been at a social stalemate for so long that the idea of leaving the house at all had started to feel exhausting. Which left Bryony and her friends, and thousands of others like them all across the capital –across the country, probably – separately watching Jools Holland with a takeaway, pretending that this was their dream New Year's all along.

'It's a pleasure!' she told Ann. 'Thank you for having me.'

'Bryony I swear to god, if you say that one more time I'll set Twinkle on you,' clucked Ann. 'We're not having you. You're family now! If anything, you're having us.'

Not so long ago these words would have sent a chill through her solar plexus, but now they felt warming. Fuck Marco, she thought. If the Slingsbys wanted to adopt a bilious thirty-four-year-old then that was their business, not his.

And if they wanted to adopt a surprise grandchild?

Well. She knocked back the rest of her Prosecco (one glass was fine, or two even. There was very little evidence that moderate drinking did any harm to an unborn foetus) and sidled up to the buffet, which was everything she might have hoped for and more. A desert landscape of beige stretched before her, featuring – her heart leapt – at least three different types of quiche.

'Did you have a good Christmas?' asked Kelly, watching Bryony shovel half a Boursin onto a Hovis biscuit.

'Oh, not really,' she replied. 'My family doesn't go big on festive spirit.'

'That's a shame,' said Kelly, dryly.

'I always go big on festive spirit!' called Ann from across the room. Her cheeks were flushed in confirmation.

It was interesting how alcohol plus grief for most people was a depressive, and yet for Ann it seemed to bring her alive. Bryony turned back to Kelly, a sudden urge to get her on side with the only remaining tool in her arsenal.

'It's partly because my mum died around Christmas,' she told her, and Kelly's expression shifted a little. 'Well, really mid-January, but I think that last Christmas with her was so lacking in joy that we've just kept up the tradition, the way other families have a curry every Boxing Day. Like a tribute.'

The film that year had been *Chicken Run*. Her father had been determined they would watch it together, 'as normal', and she remembered laughing extra loud at all the jokes so that he would feel she was worth spending time with; that being left with her and her alone wasn't going to be the worst consolation prize. The burden had sat heavily on both of them to practise enjoying each other's presence before they had no other choice. Aardman Animations had made her faintly queasy ever since.

There was a part of her that always felt if they'd only practised harder, if Bryony had been good enough company, he might have given himself more time and found another wife he actually liked.

Kelly was still looking at her, not warily for once. 'I'm in the club too,' she said, as though noticing they both had the same handbag.

'The club?'

'Dead Mum Club.'

She said it casually, before biting into a celery crudité.

'Oh. That club. I'm so sorry. When did yours—'

'Nine years ago. I know it's not the same as them dying when you're a kid, but . . .' she trailed off.

'Oh, no, that's still entirely shit,' said Bryony. 'Probably harder in some ways.'

'But easier in others,' said Kelly, and they shared a consolatory smile over the king prawn ring.

Kelly seemed to consider this the end of the conversation, turning back to her phone in a way that somehow didn't feel rude, only efficient. Bryony clocked Steve standing by the fridge, working his way through a wine glass filled with cocktail sausages, and began to make her way over. When he spotted her, he pointed in an exaggerated pantomime of delight, then wiped his fingers on his jeans before drawing her into a hug.

'Alright mate? Nice to see you, I thought Ann said you weren't coming.'

'I had a change of heart,' she told him, bolstered by the warmth of his greeting. 'Felt like this was where I ought to be tonight.'

He nodded approvingly. 'Ed loved New Year's Eve.'

'Is there anything Ed didn't love?'

She asked it flippantly, but Steve considered it seriously.

'Wasps,' he said.

She was trying to work out whether it was okay to laugh at this when a familiar figure loomed into view above the sea of bodies. She almost dropped her quiche in shock.

Marco was here.

Briefly she assumed he must be an apparition; the ghost of Christmas present, come to take her on a tour of all her mistakes. But no, it was definitely Marco, standing in a circle of laughing Little Bucktonites, telling an inaudible anecdote. He caught her eye from across the room and waved.

'Why are you here?' she yelled, as he made his way over, expression determinedly breezy. It took him so long to shimmy and weave and whoops-excuse-me-can-I-just his way through the revellers that by the time he got there she had to yell it again.

'Why are you *here*?'

'I was invited,' said Marco, coolly. 'You're not the only Northamptonshire socialite on the circuit.'

'But how did you know *I* was here?' She wondered if he could tell she was consciously withholding a hug.

'I have you on Find My Friends, remember. Because I'm concerned for your safety and welfare.' This was true. She found it reassuring to know that in the event of her kidnap, Marco would be able to find her and alert the authorities. Marco mainly used the privilege for checking if she was near Pret when he fancied a jambon buerre.

She dragged him away from a fast-advancing Susan and into the downstairs toilet, where there was a half-eaten sausage roll abandoned like a smoking cigar on the side of the sink.

'I've told you too many times Brian, this lady's not for turning,' he deadpanned as she pressed herself against him to get the door closed. 'Not that it isn't always flattering to reject your advances.'

'Shut up. You're the one who can't stay away from me,' she said, realizing as the word came out "shhtay" that the booze had soaked into her synapses faster than expected. 'I don't understand why you're even here. Are you checking up on me? Have you come to tell me off and drag me back to the convent?'

'You're so self-involved! Maybe I just wanted to spend New Year with my good friends Ann and Susan, and Annie, and the hot one, and the Wicker Man.'

'You don't even know his name.'

'Edwin.'

'Emmett.'

'That's what I said.'

'*Marco.* Why are you here?'

He sighed. 'I came on behalf of the Quiche Advisory Board to tell you you've surpassed your RDA. There are dangerously high levels of egg in your system.'

She put down her paper plate on the sink, midway through a slice of salmon and broccoli.

'Marco, I am a grown woman. I don't need rescuing, or babysitting or whatever the fuck this is. You don't need to police my life choices, however much you may disagree with them. I'm not hurting anybody. I am *allowed* new friends, I am allowed to explore new . . . new *counties*, I am allowed to eat as much quiche as I damn well—'

'It's my *dad*, okay?' he snapped. 'The cancer's back.'

He said it with such a furious air of defeat that for a moment she almost cheered in triumph. Then she registered what he had said.

'What? Fuck.'

'He told us on Boxing Day.'

'Shit.'

Marco shrugged.

'It might be fine, might not be, might live another twenty years or twenty minutes, nobody knows just now. He didn't want to talk about it so we just went through the Twixtmas motions – telly, jigsaw, leftovers, garden centre, repeat – until I felt like I was going to get the bends from all the pressure of not talking about it there. So I thought I'd come and not talk about it *here*, instead.'

She stopped withholding the hug now, breathing sympathy and salmon into his neck.

'How's that going for you?' she asked, and his lips twitched with the hint of a smile.

'Fine until now, you shit.'

Marco's dad was a slight, softly spoken man in beige slacks and brown hiking trainers; an odd counterpart to his large, acerbic son. Bryony had only met him once, when he'd been in London for something and had insisted on buying them both lunch at Ask Italian with his Clubcard points. But Fred and Gloria were firm fixtures in their conversations, the affectionate punchlines to so many of Marco's anecdotes, that they felt as integral to her home life as the sofas or microwave. It was galling to hear that one of them was on the fritz.

'Do you want to get out of here?' she asked. 'Find a haunted B&B on a farm or something? Hitchhike back to London and take something illegal?'

Marco shook his head. 'I actually want to be here. It feels oddly therapeutic to be surrounded by people who have stared down death and chosen to keep on partying.'

This was a poetic way of putting Ann's borderline pathological grief response, but she knew what he meant. There was something intensely relaxing about spending time in a world where the worst had already happened – like a pressure valve had been released in your brain.

'I get it,' she said.

'Besides,' Marco added, his tone returning to normal, 'if I leave you here unsupervised I might wake up to find out you're running for Mayor of Little Buckton. You and your unborn child.'

'Shhhhhh,' she hissed, as voices passed by in the hallway. 'Don't you *dare* mention that to anyone here, I will kill you. And keep on partying.'

'Still not done a test, I take it?'

'I'm working on it.'

'Brian, it's been *weeks*.'

'I've always been irregular, you know that.'

'Title of your memoir,' he sighed, and polished off the sausage roll.

50

No scrubs

Around eleven p.m. the party is reaching full swing and Kelly finds herself next to a tall, drunk man in a scarf who is reading Susan's tarot.

'The chariot!' he says. 'The doomed vehicle. You must give up your car and start cycling.'

'Are you sure that's what it means?' asks Susan, suspicious. 'I'd have thought it meant I was going on some kind of journey. A spiritual journey?'

'No, definitely the car thing.'

'But it's on a hire purchase,' she protests.

'It's for the planet, Susan.'

He catches Kelly's eye and winks, as Susan retreats towards the part of Ann's kitchen lino that is threatening to become a dance-floor. Kelly doesn't dance because she is bad at it, a secret she has kept hidden from the world ever since an early trauma at an under-sixteens disco. Everyone assumes people who look like Kelly must be good at dancing. She prefers to let them go on assuming.

'I'm Leo's wife,' she tells the man.

'I'm Bryony's flatmate,' he replies, and before long they are talking about cancer.

This is another occupational hazard – people ask her what she 'does' and she tells them and then they grope for their most recent dalliance with the NHS and it is usually a sick relative, or a recent malaise, or their inability to get an appointment for their recent malaise, all with the unspoken suggestion that this is somehow, tangentially, Kelly's fault. Long gone are the days when people would fawn over her, call her a 'hero', or occasionally applaud in her face. During the pandemic Ann had relished these bragging rights by proxy, even while she was cheerfully breaking the rules re: distancing, stockpiling and hugs. 'I've told all the neighbours we're clapping my daughter-in-law!' The first time they drove up for a doorstep visit, she'd been visibly annoyed Kelly wasn't wearing scrubs.

But talking about cancer with Bryony's flatmate is better than dancing to Hall and Oates with half the Buckton bellringing society, and he seems fine. Funny, actually, and grateful for an impartial ear to offload on about the various merits of radiotherapy, brachytherapy, cryotherapy and how to coax a stubborn parent to look at a pamphlet.

'I'm a veterinarrry nurse,' he slurs. 'So I'm used to stubborn old dogs.'

Kelly laughs.

'Still,' he adds, solemnly, 'when you've performed CPR on a gerbil you do have a peculiar respect for the sanctity of life.'

'It must be nice, being such a hero at work every day,' says Kelly. 'I just get people blaming me when their rash spreads.'

'Oh, darling,' he says. 'I didn't say the gerbil survived.'

It isn't clear why he's here – is Bryony so ingratiated with the family already that she's started issuing her own invites? – but Kelly is enjoying having someone to talk to from outside the Slingsby social universe, who hasn't been prepped by Ann to enquire about grandchildren.

'And let's remember the one crucial thing your job doesn't involve, despite all the shit it currently does,' he says, puffing out his chest a little in a speechifying way, although nobody else is listening.

'What's that?' she says.

'Presenting any poor bugger with a bill.'

They both pause to send up the customary prayer of thanks for the NHS.

'Meanwhile we have old ladies weeping in the waiting room because they can't afford Mr Tibbles' dialysis on the *daily*, it breaks my heart.'

'I don't recognize you from the surgery,' she says. 'Are you registered with the quacks up the road?'

'No I'm just stupidly healthy,' he sighs, bearing wine-stained teeth. 'Not like my poor consumptive sidekick.'

They look over to where Bryony is making small talk with a pair of elderly Bucktonites. The words 'grateful for the time we had together' drift over in a lull between songs.

'What is it this week? Suspected mercury poisoning? Spontaneous human combustion?' asks Kelly, and the man's eyes light up with the glee of finding someone new with which to gently bitch about a loved one.

'If only,' he says. 'At least that would have no repercussions for me. Whereas if she has a *baby*, I suppose *I'll* end up responsible for it, the way I did with her fiddle leaf fig.'

Kelly's heart thuds into her stomach.

'Bryony's pregnant?'

The flatmate shrugs, eyes wide and a telling smile playing about his lips. He is evidently a person who loves gossip.

'Displaying every symptom in the book but refuses to find out. I think she prefers the idea of having some glamorous mystery wasting disease. Or whatever the opposite of a wasting disease is. A *rounding* disease.'

He pauses here, clearly expecting a fun response – a gasp, a scream, an 'omg *no way*!' – and when none comes it seems to instantly sober him up.

'Oh shit, don't say anything,' he adds, hurriedly. 'She probably isn't. It might be an exotic parasite after all.'

51

Two for joy

'Why haven't you done a test?'

Kelly cornered her in the kitchen, where Bryony was resisting Ann's attempts to start a game of Two Truths and a Lie.

'Sorry what?'

For a stupid moment she thought Kelly was talking about a driving test, and prepared her usual speech about growing up in suburban London (truth) and preferring to use public transport for the good of the planet (lie) and being cripplingly scared of dying in a road accident (truth).

'Your friend just told me. Although to be honest, I guessed last time you phoned the surgery. The nausea. The fatigue. The quiche. Why are you refusing to find out?'

Bryony struggled with a claggy mouthful of pastry, eyes bugging as Kelly waited for an answer. Cool, calm, rational Kelly, who may also have a dead mum but seemed to have entirely avoided being fucked up by the fact. Bryony hoped a reasonable explanation would present itself before she swallowed.

'I don't know,' she told her, when it didn't. 'I . . . I guess I've been telling myself each day that I'll deal with it tomorrow, and so on and so on and suddenly it's been weeks. You know like how you put off throwing away an old yoghurt at the back of the fridge because you know it'll be scary when you eventually do, and so you just leave it longer and longer and the yoghurt gets scarier and scarier?'

'Not really,' said Kelly. Which wasn't surprising because she looked like the kind of person who kept a spotlessly clean fridge. Kelly probably did a Mrs Hinch routine every Saturday morning, for pleasure. 'But then I wouldn't be thinking of a baby like it was a mouldy yoghurt,' she added.

'I mean, me neither!' said Bryony, hastily course correcting and trying her hardest to sound sober. 'Obviously. It would be ... significant. It would be really ... yes, huge. Wow.'

'It would be Ed's, right?' asked Kelly.

Bryony nodded, relieved that on this score at least she could offer some certainty. 'One hundred percent Ed's.'

Kelly didn't look pleased by this, only more perturbed. 'Look,' she said, adopting the same tone she used with patients at the surgery. 'You need to do a test. Stop putting it off. You'll feel better once you know for sure.'

Bryony knew full well there was only one side of the coin-flip that could make her feel better. But Kelly was clearly trying to be kind, so she said, 'You're right, I know I'm being stupid. I promise I'll do one, the minute I get home after new year.'

'No,' said Kelly, 'now. I have two tests in my bag, I'll go get them.'

Bryony flinched, as though somebody had ripped a plaster off her arm without permission.

'You just ... carry them around with you? In case you meet stupid girls at parties who've got themselves in trouble?'

As the words left her mouth, fuzzed with alcohol, she looked at Kelly's face and realized she really was a stupid girl.

'We've been trying,' Kelly said, lightly. 'Me and Leo. For a while, actually, so I've got pretty casual about it.'

'Taking a pregnancy test on New Year's Eve feels like the opposite of casual,' said Bryony.

'I have a weird superstition,' said Kelly, looking embarrassed. 'The less I make a big deal about it, the more likely it is to be positive. Like I have to trick the universe into thinking I don't care, or something. It's stupid. It makes no sense.'

Bryony placed a hand on Kelly's bare forearm and found goosepimples despite the warmth of bodies and pastry filling the house. 'That makes a lot of sense to me. It's exactly the kind of thing I would do.'

Kelly didn't look comforted by this.

'And I'm sorry,' added Bryony. 'Sorry you're going through that, and sorry I didn't twig. I'm an idiot. I should have realized.'

'Why would you have realized?' asked Kelly, brusquely. 'Did Ed say anything? Has Ann?' Her eyes travelled across the crowded room to her mother-in-law, who was finishing a story about the time she found herself naked in a sauna with Lesley Joseph, to hoots and cheers from her guests.

'No, nothing,' Bryony assured her. She thought back to Ann's phone call about the magpies, and wondered how many of these Kelly had received in her time. 'Look, you're really kind to take an interest but the last thing you want to deal with tonight is me, so you keep your tests and I'll sort myself out tomorrow. It can be my new year's resolution!' she laughed hollowly.

But Kelly was the one who was resolute. She shook her head. 'Nope, you're doing it now. You need to know. I'll do mine too, if that helps. Get it over with, so we can start the new year knowing where we're at.'

Bryony looked around desperately for Marco, but he was nowhere to be seen as she followed Kelly meekly into the hallway, up the stairs and into one of the house's numerous bathrooms, this one boasting a sky-blue suite and knitted loo roll doll in the image of Dolly Parton. Her head swam and her eyes began to water. The quiche threatened to reappear.

'Don't waste one on me, they're expensive!' was her final protest, but Kelly had already unwrapped the plastic stick, handed it over and diplomatically averted her eyes.

It was funny, she thought, to be performing such an intimate bonding rite with one of the few women in her life just now who had zero interest in being her friend. With Kelly the whole process felt clinical; the shambles of Ann's second-floor bathroom merely an extension of the doctor's surgery. She felt she ought to be peeing into a plastic sample cup, not inelegantly hovering over a toilet with her sleeves rolled up, joking weakly about people going to the loo together at parties.

When she'd finished she wasn't sure what to do with the test, but Kelly took it from her, her hand wrapped in tissue, snapped the cap back on and placed it on the side of the bath, window-side down. 'No peeking,' she said, meaning the test, as she pulled down her tights and performed her own with the brisk efficiency of a seasoned regular.

Bryony felt suddenly that it was she who had invaded, she who had overstepped the boundary, she who was being let into this most sacred of rituals without really deserving that trust. She wondered how long 'a while' was; how much of Kelly's life had now been measured out in little plastic sticks. She realized she was gawping at her instead of delicately looking away.

'I usually charge for this show,' said Kelly, meeting her eye and grinning for the first time that evening.

Bryony apologized, flustered, but Kelly seemed nonplussed, almost blasé about the whole thing. She clicked the lid onto her own test as though it were a pen cap and lined it up carefully alongside Bryony's, face down on the side of the bath.

'Yours is right, mine is left,' she said.

Kelly pulled out her phone and set an alarm for three minutes' time.

'And now we wait.'

52

Which emotions?

Kelly is trembling and hopes that Bryony won't notice. Not in anticipation of her own result – she's trained her nervous system well by now, maintaining the pretence of nonchalance right down to her glands and sinew – but in fear of Bryony's. She is terrified it will be positive, and she is terrified of how much she will care.

Bullying her into taking the test here and now seemed extreme and to be honest she's surprised Bryony complied. But then Bryony is clearly pissed, and Kelly has always been the Pied Piper where emotional drunk girls are concerned. For some reason they follow her lead.

'How will you feel if you are?' she asks her.

Bryony inhales deeply, eyes fixed on the Artex ceiling. 'Pretty emotional,' she says eventually.

'Yeah but which emotions?' Kelly pushes.

'Um. Fear, I guess? It would be a lot to process. Without Ed and everything.'

'So you'd have it then?'

She sees Bryony flinch a little at this directness, but as far as Kelly can tell she needs somebody to ask the question outright or there's a serious danger she could end up thirty months pregnant and still pretending not to have noticed.

'Would you keep the baby?' she tries again, because Bryony is still stammering and blowing hot air out of her nostrils. She looks at Kelly as though perhaps Kelly holds the answer.

Kelly does not.

If Bryony does have the baby – and it has become 'the' baby in both their minds now, its existence a solid, squirming certainty – then this virtual stranger, this mad neurotic interloper will have beaten her to the punch and given Ann the grandchild she's always wanted. Kelly will have to play the fond auntie, taking the bundle into her arms at every family gathering, cooing over its features that are almost-not-quite Leo's, mentally pasting her own DNA into the mix. And while the rational part of her brain knows that it isn't a race, the less rational part of her believes that if Bryony has a baby, it means Kelly never will. It's the same part of her that believes doing a pregnancy test at a funeral, or new year's party, or in the loos at Hyde Park Winter Wonderland means it's more likely to give her the outcome she wants.

Then there's the other answer, the one Kelly isn't sure she wants to hear either.

In that rational part of her brain, she is staunchly pro-choice. Of course she is. She's seen too many wailing children and exhausted, hollow-eyed mothers pass through her waiting room to ever believe a person should be forced to sign up to parenthood unless they want it wholly, unequivocally, right down to their wrung-out core. She's watched for years as girls from school, friends and colleagues all had babies in the most precarious of circumstances, congratulating them outwardly but wondering inwardly whether they knew, really *knew*, that they didn't have to. The rational part of her brain wants to tell Bryony she doesn't have to either.

And yet her stomach is dissenting. Deep down, somewhere in the murky seabed of Kelly's body, a tiny, shameful placard waves alone.

Don't you dare toss away the thing I want most, it says. *How could you?*
Her muscles tighten around it as she asks the question a third time
and Bryony shakes her head, slowly, then bursts into noisy tears.
Two minutes.

53

Choice cuts

'I don't know why I'm crying!' Bryony sobbed, mopping at her streaming mascara with one of Ann's more aged towels.

'Because you might be pregnant with your dead boyfriend's baby and you don't want to be?' supplied Kelly. This only made her cry harder.

'I'm so sorry, you shouldn't be having to deal with this,' she wailed. 'It isn't fair on you! I just feel *awful*. Morally, I mean, as well as physically. Like, poor Ed isn't here and this baby would be a connection to him, you know? His *legacy*. Can you imagine if Ann knew about it? How excited she would be?'

Kelly laughed, and the two of them paused to picture it. The anointed princelet, swaddled in the finest silks. Fed off-brand Angel Delight with a silver spoon.

'You can't have a baby to make Ann happy, that's insane,' said Kelly.

Bryony smiled weakly. 'You sound like Marco.'

'Bryony, I've been in this family a lot longer than you have and I've been trying to please Ann for a lot longer too, so I'm telling you now, babe: it isn't worth it. You can't win. It's like climbing up the *Gladiators* travelator – you can never actually get to the top.'

'That's very wise. You're very wise, Kelly,' said Bryony and Kelly smiled graciously, as though this was obvious but bore repeating.

'Ed wouldn't want you to change the entire course of your life just for his sake, I'm sure he wouldn't. That's not the kind of guy he was, is it? And even if it *was* the kind of guy he was, it wouldn't make a difference because it's *your* choice, okay, nobody else's.'

Bryony nodded solemnly, because of course it was hard to argue with any of this. And yet there was something about hearing the words out loud that made them seem borderline theatrical, as though they were acting in a radio play or some kind of public awareness campaign. Obviously, *theoretically*, it was her choice, but like so many things in life she felt there were invisible forces steering her towards a foregone conclusion. Bryony found it hard to choose lunch, most days. She rarely made it to the end of her street in the morning without the overwhelming desire to run back home and change. Multiple times a week she convinced herself that the course of her whole life might hinge on something as banal as which queue she stood in, or which tube carriage she sat in; the idea that she could simply choose – or not – this monumental thing, in the vacuum of her own freewill, felt absurd.

'Absolutely,' she said, still nodding. 'You're completely right. I know you are.'

She looked back up at the ceiling and forced herself to breathe deeply, before adding, 'There's another reason too. Not to have it, I mean.'

'What's that?'

Bryony exhaled at length, tracing each Artex swirl with her eyes as though one of them might lead to an escape tunnel. Then she said it.

'He wasn't really my boyfriend.'

There was a beat of silence, in which Twinkle could be heard barking in time to The Mavericks' 'Dance The Night Away'.

'I'm sorry, what?' said Kelly.

'I mean – we were dating. Well, hardly dating. Sleeping together. Casually. But then Steve, and Ann, and Annie, and everyone seemed to have the idea that we were . . . more than that. Much more. They seemed to know so much about me, and they were so happy to meet me. And I didn't feel I could really correct them, because . . .'

'He's dead,' finished Kelly.

'Well, yeah.'

'Fucking hell,' Kelly breathed.

One minute.

54

Mummy issues

'I'll come with you. To the clinic.' says Kelly.

'No, don't be silly!' squeaks Bryony, sounding as though someone is trying to treat her to lunch.

'I'm not being silly,' Kelly tells her, 'I'm being sensible. You can't go on your own. I'm guessing you don't want to drag a whole load more people into this, and I know about it now. So I'd take you. I can probably get you referred via work, to the nicest place.'

'Are there nice places?'

'Nic*er*,' says Kelly. 'It's not like any of them are day spas. You don't get cucumber water.'

'That would be amazing,' Bryony says, gratefully. It's the same word she always used when Kelly would offer her some crumb of hope at the surgery – *amaaazing* – but now it sounds as though she genuinely means it. 'I appreciate it Kelly, all of this. You really don't have to. Especially not with,' she pauses, looking pained, 'everything you've been going through.'

'I know I don't have to,' Kelly shrugs. 'But it's fine. It's shit, but it's fine. Everyone's going through something.'

'But not everyone is potentially pregnant with their dead pretend boyfriend's baby,' quips Bryony, and Kelly snorts. Her image of

Bryony is reconfiguring itself at speed, in light of this new information. Monica Munchausen is proving far more unhinged than she ever thought before, and yet Kelly finds she makes more sense too.

'I can't believe you wrote a poem for his funeral. I can't believe you switched on the fireworks! I can't believe you let Ann put a paragraph about you in her Christmas round robin letter, Jesus *Christ*.'

Bryony groans and flinches with each new charge, as though she is taking a physical beating.

'I don't know how I end up in these situations, I honestly don't. It's like a sickness in itself.'

'Have you referred yourself for talking therapies?' asks Kelly, and Bryony rolls her eyes.

'About eight times. I do my six sessions of beginners' CBT and then they pat me on the head and say well done, all better and I say thank you and put myself back on the waiting list again. Never mind that. Why do we care so much about pleasing Ann, do you think?'

The answer arrives in her eyes before Kelly needs to say it.

'Mummy issues?'

'Has to be, doesn't it? More original than daddy issues, I suppose.'

'Oh, I have those too,' says Bryony.

Kelly smirks. 'Course you do.'

But Bryony accepts the tease, shrugging and laughing as she adds, 'Also attachment issues, food issues, several phobias, generalized anxiety disorder and burnout.'

'Burnout isn't a real thing,' Kelly tells her. 'It just means you need to put your phone down, go outside and look at a tree.'

Bryony shakes her head fervently. 'It's very real, I swear – it's the modern affliction of our times. It's because of our overstimulated, hyperconnected lives where work and play and downtime all bleed into one another and none of us know how to set proper boundaries and ringfence our time anymore. I read a really good book on it.'

'What's the cure then? According to this book?' asks Kelly.

'Intensive digital detox, scheduling quiet time and re-immersing yourself in nature,' replies Bryony.

'So ... putting your phone down and going outside to look at a tree.'

Bryony bursts out laughing then and Kelly joins in. Footsteps thunder by on the landing and the bass line of Mousse T's 'Horny' throbs through the floor.

'I forgot for a second there what we were doing,' says Bryony, glancing over at the plastic sticks lined up on the side of the bath like an ominous pause symbol. 'Ohhh god. This isn't happening. I can't have a baby. I can't have Ed's baby.'

'Forget "can't" for a second,' says Kelly. 'Do you *want* to have Ed's baby?'

Bryony blinks at her, eyes brimming again, and for a queasy moment Kelly worries she is about to say yes, yes she does, against all her better judgement, yes she does want to have Ed's baby.

'Fuck no,' she says, and the seabed settles in guilty relief.

A second later, her phone begins to bleep.

'Okay deep breaths,' says Kelly, adopting the tone of a bikini waxer. 'Are you ready?'

Bryony nods. Kelly reaches for the plastic sticks, adrenaline prickling at her skin and shivering up her spine.

Suddenly there is a pounding at the bathroom door, and both women jump as Marco's voice crashes into the silence.

'BRIAN ARE YOU IN THERE? I've been looking for you everywhere! Stop stewing and get the fuck out, you'll miss the countdown! If I can't kiss you at midnight then there's a serious risk that scoutmaster's going to be losing his woggle.'

'I'LL BE OUT IN A SEC,' Bryony yells back, and turns to look down at Kelly where she is kneeling on the floor, next to the tests she just dropped in alarm.

Bryony falls to her knees too, letting out a strangled yelp when she sees the results under the glare of Ann's strip light.

One test has a distinct cross in its little window. The other just a single, solid line.

'Which is which? Who's is who's?' she demands. Kelly swallows a rising tide of bile as the guests begin to chant below them.

'Ten! Nine! Eight!' and 'Seven!' all pass before she can answer.

'I have no idea.'

55

Conscious unlearning

The pallid rays of the year's first dawn crept across the valley, washing everything clean. It would be an exaggeration to say that Little Buckton 'sparkled' or 'shimmered', but there was a dewy lustre to Ann's cabbages that didn't feel *unhopeful*, even as Bryony was vomiting into them.

She spent some time watching an earthworm wend its way through the soil and envied it, wishing she could bury herself in cool wet earth, and eat only cool, wet earth, and calmly split herself in two and start again any time a fateful spade might fall.

'Come the fuck on, Brian!' yelled Marco from somewhere up near the house, silhouetted against the back wall like a movie poster. More shadowy figures fell into line alongside him, swollen and misshapen in quilted outerwear, swinging bottles. In her woozy state she had the feeling she was about to be part of a cult abduction, and was not wholly resistant to it.

'We're going up the mound to do our resolutions!' came Annie's voice.

'It's tradition!' added Marco's.

Bryony wiped her mouth and made her way back up the garden to join the dregs of the party, feeling every bit like the dregs of herself.

Annie handed her a large, nubbly fleece and Bryony pulled it on, sliding her hands into the pocket and finding a half-eaten tangerine of dubious vintage. She held her sticky fingers up to her face and inhaled deeply, enjoying the bite of the cold and the zest in her nostrils. Citrus was a thing, wasn't it? A curative. Smelling oranges and lemons to soothe morning sickness. Or was she thinking of the oranges at Shakespearean theatres that used to mask the smell of the peasants?

The assembled troupe began to trudge through the village towards 'the mound', Little Buckton's disgrace, always referred to in inverted commas lest locals from rival villages think they didn't know it wasn't a proper hill.

'The second largest man-made hillock in the county, commissioned by the second Viscount of Daventry in the late 1700s as a tribute to his dead mistress,' explained Emmett as they began the feeble 'climb' up its bank, feet slipping over damp grass in a variety of inappropriate footwear. Bryony scanned the group in search of Kelly and spotted her, clinging onto Leo in a pair of his-n-hers duvet coats. She looked pale and drawn, but then so did everyone.

Everyone except Marco, who Bryony noticed then was walking with his arm around the lithe hips of a man in a waxed Barbour jacket and a tartan hunting hat. She ambled up on his other side and pressed her mouth against his ear.

'Scout master?'

Marco shook his head. She felt his cheeks swell into a grin, as he hissed: 'Mr Duggan Jr.'

Annie caught up to her and slipped an arm through hers as they walked.

'So what is this?' Bryony asked.

'Tradition,' said Annie. 'We've been doing it since we were little. Ann used to get us out of bed and drag us up here at dawn, promise us eggy bread with golden syrup for breakfast, and then make us vow to keep our bedrooms tidy and feed the goldfish and learn British Sign Language and stuff. The year she and Dad got divorced, she made us all change our resolutions to "consciously unlearning our father's bad habits and supporting her on her single parenting journey". I still remember the wording. I was ten.'

'What were Ed's resolutions like?' Bryony asked. She found she was suddenly curious about him as a child.

'Oh, always something cute and unambitious. Complete his football stickers, keep his African land snail alive. Only drink one Pepsi Max a day, that sort of thing. Very Eddish. Except for last year, actually,' she added. Annie stopped in the middle of the path and clutched her by the arm, her face stricken and grey in the moonlight.

'What was last year's?'

'I'd completely forgotten, it just came back to me. Oh god, Bryony.'

'What was it?' asked Bryony.

Annie hugged her, almost violently, as though trying to cushion her from the impact of the answer.

'To find someone to love,' she said.

When they reached the top of 'the mound', Bryony was taken aback by how lovely the view was. A faded patchwork of fields stretched before them, the black glitter of a river visible along their periphery, stars blinking overhead in the gauzy mauve of the morning.

'Oh how gorgeous!' she sighed, in spite of herself. The locals shrugged and grunted with the casual smugness of those who see their sky illuminated by stars more often than chicken shop signage.

'It must be so nice for you to get out of London,' said Ann, charitably, and handed her a lit joint. Bryony's stomach contracted violently in protest at the smell. She passed it on to an eager, giggling Lynn and reached for her pocket tangerine again.

Everyone arranged themselves in a rough kind of circle on the grass, sitting on an assortment of bags for life. Steve plonked himself down beside her, looking even more bearish than usual in a lumberjack jacket and a pair of sheepskin gloves. Winter suited him.

'How you doing, mate?' he asked, and for once Bryony gave a straight answer.

'Terrible,' she said, without elaborating.

'Same.' He clapped her softly on the shoulder with one of his enormous padded hands. 'Absolute same.'

Side by side, they both looked up at the sky, as if a feature film were beginning.

Feeling whimsical, she asked: 'Do you know any of the constellations?'

'Yeah,' said Steve. 'Oh yeah. See that one, up there, where the stars are in a kind of V-shape? That's the stapler.'

'The stapler? I've never heard of that one.'

'And over there, that's the USB stick.'

'Are you bullshitting me?'

'Yes, Bryony,' grinned Steve, his eyes still cast upwards. 'I'm bullshitting you.'

She punched him on the arm and he yelped gamely as her fist bounced off his cushioned sleeve.

'Did Ethel make out like we were all backwater bumpkins, gazing at the stars and romping through wheat fields with our slingshots?'

'No!' she protested. 'Actually he never told me much about the village. I'd have come up sooner, if I knew how nice it was.' They slipped out easily now, statements like this, so frictionless that she barely felt the lie.

'He'd have loved having you here right now, I'm sure he would. Maybe he's getting a kick out of it as we speak.'

Another queasy wave rippled through Bryony at the thought of a celestial Ed, watching all this unfold. Particularly everything that had recently passed in his mother's bathroom.

'Do you miss him a lot, at times like this?' she asked Steve.

He shifted his gaze from the sky to look at her in the darkness.

'I miss him at all times, to be honest.'

'Right! Everybody!' said Ann, raising an arm and clinking a wristful of silver bangles to command their attention. A hush settled on the group.

'As dawn breaks on a brand new year, we leave the last behind us,' she intoned, and suddenly the air on the mound felt heavy with more than just impending hangovers.

'I, for one, am happy to see the back of the worst year of my life. But at the same time, the idea of a whole new year in which my darling boy, my piggy in the middle, my Ethy—' her voice caught and she took a deep, shuddering breath before continuing. 'The idea of a year in which he doesn't feature ... well. Frankly, I don't want it.' Emmett laid a hand silently and solemnly on his wife's knee. Annie, who was already crying, laid her head on Ann's shoulder and nuzzled into her coat like an infant.

Bryony pictured the squirming cluster of cells, buried earthworm-deep, which could mean Ed had a presence in this year after all. What would Ann say if she knew his tiny legacy was with them right now? She closed her eyes and performed a body scan, trying to work out if the gnawing inside her was quiche and Cava, or the flail of tiny limbs. She brought her orangey fingers to her face again – it was funny how fast safety behaviours were formed – and sniffed. She felt sober, now, but fully insane.

'Let's get on with it then,' said Ann, swigging from her silver hip-flask and pulling her wild hair back with a scrunchie in a way that suggested she might be about to cast a spell. 'Leo darling, you go first.'

Leo stood up and cast his eyes around the circle with the natural gravitas of the firstborn. 'Thanks for the lovely words, Mum,' he said, as though she had just introduced him as keynote speaker. He cleared his throat.

'My resolution is to live in the moment,' he said. 'Just, you know ... not waste time worrying about stuff that hasn't happened, and might not happen, getting all het up waiting to move onto the next stage of life or whatever. I'm just going to focus on the here and now and having fun, making the most of life's pleasures and be grateful every day to be here, surrounded by people and things that I love.'

He lifted Kelly's hand to his mouth and kissed it, making eye contact with his wife in a way that left Bryony feeling faintly grubby. Kelly looked uncomfortable too, but mimed a kiss back at him.

'Perfect,' said Ann approvingly, dabbing at her eyes. 'Kelly, your turn.'

'Um,' said Kelly. 'I mean, same as Leo really? I guess. This year I just want to count my blessings, whatever they might end up being. And I want to stop feeling jealous of people. I'm going to stop wishing away the present, and accept that life might not always go the way I thought it would, and that's okay. Because it's all a privilege isn't it? Just to be here, getting out of bed in the morning. I'm going to try and remind myself of that every single day.'

'Ambitious as ever, Kelly!' trilled Ann, as though her resolution hadn't been exactly the same as Leo's with different wording. 'But good luck to you, dear,' she added.

Bryony, realizing she was going to have to share a resolution of her own, had begun to sweat as though she were on a team away day. She tried to smile supportively at Kelly, but Kelly seemed to be avoiding her eye.

Annie went next.

'Up until now I've wasted so much of my potential,' she began. 'I was just treading water, letting life happen *to* me instead of me happening *to* it. So my resolution is to honour my brother by demanding more for myself. I'm going to work really hard to hit all my professional goals, harvesting as much positivity as I can to grow my business and unlock double-diamond level Gelibility before next Christmas. To make Ed proud.'

She winked at Bryony, and Bryony smiled weakly back.

The resolutions continued in this vein, each person announcing a vague but passionate intention to live more fully in a way tangentially linked to Ed's death.

Steve resolved to take bigger risks and step out of his comfort zone. Emmett gave a surprisingly stirring speech about playing chess with Ed at the weekends and beating him every single time. 'He was terrible, terrible, the boy was, absolutely no, ah, grasp of tactical play ... and yet, he was in it for the thrill of the game.' A wet-eyed Marco managed to raise a murmur of collective emotion with a soliloquy on 'never being afraid to be ordinary, for ordinary can be a superpower in itself'. Susan vowed to 'never let the bastards grind her down' (bastards unclear) and 'to kill every wasp I see'. There followed a brief debate over whether or not Ed would wish such a fate on all wasps, before Bryony was finally obliged to take her turn.

'Um,' she began. 'This has all been really inspiring. I think, like, ah, everyone, I feel really determined to make the most of this next year as a tribute to Ed.'

It would have been easy, perfectly easy, to trot off something palatable. Something about seizing opportunities with both hands, staying true to herself, nurturing new connections, etcetera – and yet she didn't. It was hard to say why she didn't, except that the squirming cluster of cells seemed to have hijacked her brain and suddenly she understood how it felt to experience gut instinct. Her gut was driving her mouth now. Driving it clean off the road.

'But really, my resolution is to stop living for everyone else before myself. I'm going to tell the truth a lot more, and not just say what I think people want to hear or, frankly, out and out lie to keep everyone happy. And I'm not going to go along with things just out of awkwardness or politeness anymore, because life is short,' she caught Marco's eye here, and he mimed eating popcorn in captivation, 'and fuck me if that doesn't just lead to a whole lot more awkwardness and pain in the long run.'

For the first time in a long time Bryony felt the good kind of giddy, not the kind that led to her googling Ménière's disease. As she spoke – *was she still speaking? Yes, apparently* – she became breathless with the exhilaration of it all. Where would this lead, she wondered? What would she do next, turn down a hen weekend? Regift a candle? Hang up on a cold caller? Tell her hairdresser that after she tips him she goes home and rinses out his strange, wiggy blow-dry, every single time? Programme a find + replace on the words 'You choose, I'm easy!' in all her messaging apps? Would she finally have the guts to break up with Ewa?

She saw, stretching before her, a potential lifetime of not voicenoting back, not hearting every photo in the group chat, of eating the last potato in every small plates restaurant, or, hell, not going to a small plates restaurant in the first place. She could demand more for herself too; she could demand big plates only. Perhaps she would make Marco switch bedrooms because actually she *did* want the bigger one, actually it *did* make a difference to her, and while we're at it could he please stop leaving old bits of pasta in the sink? Perhaps she'd go and live on Orkney in a shepherd's hut. Perhaps she'd never go to another panel talk again.

Looking back, she had sensed this coming for years – a moment when the switch flipped and the axe fell on a lifetime of contorting herself into increasingly odd positions to make everyone else's lives easier. She hadn't expected her emancipation to happen on a fake hilltop in Northamptonshire with a hypothetical abortion at the top of her to-do list, but here it was. It felt painful, in a chiropractic way. She was finally crunching herself free.

When she finished, a few people looked mildly taken aback but there wasn't the collective howl of horror she had expected. Ann looked almost approving.

'Well, good for you Bryony,' she said. 'Nobody likes a pushover.'

Bryony remembered something she had heard a novelist say once – at a panel talk, as it happened – about people never recognizing themselves in books because they were blinded by their ego. She wondered if something similar was happening here.

She had pictured herself flouncing off down the hill at the end of the speech to punctuate the sentiment, but when it came to it her left buttock had gone numb and she didn't trust it to carry her with any dignity. So she sat back and buried the lower half of her face in the fleece, as Brown Owl Wendy began pledging to take herself on more spa breaks, 'for Ed'. The sun was fully risen now, and the eerie promise of the dawn replaced by the anticlimax of a grey January morning. Bryony could tell just by looking that everybody's breath smelled terrible.

Finally, they had all spoken except Ann. There was a certain amount of anticipatory shuffling as the group steeled itself for an emotional finale; people rearranging their legs so as to be better able to leap up and hug her, if needed.

'I think this is the year,' she began, eventually, 'that I will finally stop biting my nails.'

A polite pause followed, but it became apparent that was all they were getting. Ann took a final swig from her hip flask and belched, softly, as though calling their meeting to a close.

56

Unclear blue

Oddly, after being so insistent that Bryony must stop hiding from the truth, it was Kelly who didn't want to scour the house for hidden pregnancy tests 'like a fucked up Easter egg hunt'.

'Ann only stopped doing Easter egg hunts for the family about five years ago,' she told Bryony. 'Announced that she was going to save her energy "for future generations".'

'That tracks,' Bryony had said. 'It's fine. Even if we found one under an ancient stack of *Reader's Digests* or something, I don't think I'd trust it to be accurate.'

Kelly had agreed. 'We should leave it for now. Just relax and enjoy the rest of the night.'

'Absolutely. Let's worry about it tomorrow. I mean, in the morning. Later in the morning. Once the shops are open. Do chemist's open on New Year's Day?'

'Of course they do, they're not banks. And you can get pregnancy tests in Sainsbury's.'

'How about Aldi?'

'Sure,' Kelly had said, deadpan. 'They're called Unclear Blue.'

Bryony smirked. 'Vaguely Turquoise?'

'Third Response.'

They had both laughed. It was probably a good thing, noted Kelly, if she is going to be accompanying this woman to an abortion in the near-future, to have established some kind of rapport.

She hasn't told Leo about the test mix-up yet, because what would she say? 'Funny story?'

This is a shame because it is a funny story, or will be one day, and Leo is usually the first person she wants to take her funny stories to. Or was, before Ed died and his sense of humour vanished like his appetite.

It's been months now since she even told him about the tests, let alone waited for him to be there, to hold her hand while they filled the three-minute wait with nervous nonsense-talk, babbling like background actors in a play. This weather is muggy isn't it? I know. What did you have for lunch today? Oh nice. I saw a really big dog earlier. What breed? I don't know just a really big one. Oh nice.

The first rule of pregnancy test club is don't talk about the pregnancy test. Don't look at it, don't think about it, don't let it hear the roar of hope in your heart.

Besides, to fill him in on the whole farce feels like tempting fate, like reaching for the light switch when instead she could sit for a little longer, comfortably, in the dark. For as long as she doesn't know for *sure* that the positive test isn't hers then she inhabits a world in which she could be pregnant, more solidly than she has ever been possibly-pregnant before.

'It's Schrödinger's foetus,' Bryony had said, barking out a laugh that Kelly hadn't reciprocated, and not just because she didn't understand the joke.

She rests her cheek on Leo's chest now, on the sagging sofa bed that tends to roll them both together as though it is doing Ann's bidding. He is asleep, snoring softly into her hair. Kelly has never felt more awake in her life.

57

The only sane way

For perhaps the first time in her life after making a resolution, Bryony was resolute. Enough of this now. She had given three good months of her life to pretend-grieving Ed – over half the relationship! – so surely nobody could begrudge her drawing a line under it all and moving on. Surely.

Unfortunately this line was dependent on another line, still TBC, which in turn was dependent on making a break for the nearest shop as soon as Kelly deemed it a reasonable hour. She and Leo had gone back to bed when the group got in from the mound, leaving Bryony suspended in ignorance re: dependents. Marco had 'gone for a walk' with Mr Duggan Jr and Annie had – five points to Bryony – gone for her annual naked swim in a local lake with all the friends who should by rights have stopped her joining a pyramid scheme.

Everyone else had drifted off into the morning, presumably to their own homes or hungry cattle etcetera, and now she and Ann were the last men standing.

It dawned on Bryony that this was the first time she had ever been alone with Ann. She looked smaller and older without a whirl of activity around her, without the usual band of orbiting acolytes and assorted hangers-on. Smaller, older and sadder.

'Thank you for staying, love,' she said, clutching at Bryony's hand and squeezing it until she feared for her bones. 'It would have meant so much to him that you were here for his favourite time of year.'

It was hard not to picture Ed looking down now, thoroughly creeped out by the fact she was here for his favourite time of year. But Bryony only said 'of course' and squeezed Ann's hand back. Of course she was here. Where else would she be? Spending time with the Slingsbys had begun to feel more natural than spending time with her own friends; her own family; even her own thoughts.

'The trick is to start the clean-up now, while you're still a bit fuzzy – before the hangover hits.' Ann snapped on a pair of marigolds like a surgeon. 'It's the only sane way.'

Bryony was interested to see what constituted Ann's version of a clean-up. She was also conscious that if this was her last day in the house, the last day of the charade (new year's resolutions didn't begin until the second of January, everyone knew that), she was fast running out of time to solve the mystery of Ed's true feelings. She couldn't spend the rest of her life pretending to be a grieving girl-friend, but she also couldn't spend the rest of her life not knowing if she'd been a girlfriend at all.

'Let me help you,' she told Ann, grabbing a black plastic sack and beginning to shovel in miscellaneous party waste.

'Oh Bryony, what would I do without you?' Ann cupped a hand at the side of her face, and guilt throbbed in her still-raw stomach. 'Not these dear,' she added, fishing a handful of paper napkins out of the bin liner. 'If I smooth them out they could do for Easter.'

Bryony hummed a little tune, mindlessly, as they worked.

'That's nice,' said Ann. 'Is it Brahms?'

'Yes … yes, I think it is,' said Bryony, not wanting to admit it was the doctor's surgery hold music.

She opened a hallway cupboard in search of a broom or mop and yelped as an avalanche of boxes, bags and loose items all crashed down on her head. It was a confusing mix of things, almost all still in their packaging – candles and calendars and scarves and tea towels and ancient bath products with logos from several rebrands past. It seemed to have all been crammed onto the shelves like a hoarders' Tetris, waiting for an unwitting intruder to send the whole lot tumbling.

'Ignore all that!' said Ann, bustling up behind her and starting to shove everything back in again, quickly and with zero precision.

'It's okay,' Bryony told her, rubbing at the tender spot on her head where a bath bomb had landed with force. The air smelled of geranium, and chalk. 'What is all this stuff?'

'Present cupboard,' said Ann, still bundling.

'Oh, of course. I'm in awe – I always wish I was organized enough to buy gifts for people in advance instead of flapping around on the day in a panic and throwing too much money at Oliver Bonas.'

Ann looked mildly sheepish, an expression Bryony hadn't seen on her before.

'No dear, it's actually presents people have given *me*. All very kind of course, the kids are always far too generous even though I tell them I don't want anything at all – "don't waste your money on me!" I tell them, but they don't listen, always too extravagant, especially Ethy – such a generous boy, I remember once—'

'And you don't *use* the presents?' Bryony interrupted, fearing another Ethy the Angel story would tip her over the edge.

'Oh you know, it's not always my thing. Or it'll be one of these fancy brands with ingredients that don't agree with me, or I want to save it for a special occasion . . . or in all honesty Bryony, I can't always work out what it's *for*.'

Bryony's eye fell on a box of gold collagen eye masks that she'd bet came from Leo and Kelly.

'But I'm very grateful for it all, of course, nothing changes that.'

Ann said this last part loudly, as though someone might be listening.

'And you don't get rid of them? Or regift them?'

'No! Oh no.' Ann looked horrified. 'Never! I couldn't. I just pop them all in here, so they're safe. I expect you think I'm barmy.'

Bryony shook her head. 'Not at all,' she said. 'I completely understand.'

Because she did, in a way that didn't feel entirely comfortable – like judging someone's outfit across a room before realizing she is looking at her own reflection. Were she and Ann kindred spirits? And if so, then had Ed felt some kind of oedipal attraction to her? Had he hoped to package her up and deliver her to his mother for approval, the way he had once with a devoré scarf or a Sanctuary gift set?

'Do the rest of the family know about the cupboard?' she asked Ann.

Ann looked as though she'd never considered this. 'I suppose they do,' she said. 'But the gifts keep on coming, lovelier ones every year.'

'And you still don't use them?'

'No but I *keep* them,' said Ann, beginning to sound impatient. 'I keep them all in here.'

Bryony accepted this and left her hostess re-stacking her shelves. She moved on to the washing up instead, averting her eyes from a Brillo pad that looked like it might have scrubbed plates on the *Titanic*.

'Ann,' she began. 'Can I ask you something?'

'Of course you can Bryony,' said Ann. 'You can ask me anything!' She had a sudden vision of how sex talks with Ann must have gone, or possibly still did.

'Can I ask – what exactly did Ed–um–*Ethelred* – well, what did he tell you about me? Before he – well. I suppose I'm just curious. We hadn't been seeing each other all that long, and I must confess, I didn't quite realize he felt so . . . um.'

Ann smiled slyly. 'That would be breaking mother-child

confidentiality, dear. After all, I think Ethelred's feelings are his own private property, don't you? Even now.'

Bryony wanted to smash the wine glass she was drying against the wall.

'But,' Ann went on, teasingly, 'he was obviously head-over-heels. A mum knows these things. Still waters run deep and all that, and my lovely boy ran deeper than most.' She let out a little hiccup, the type that usually preceded a fresh bout of sobbing. Bryony sensed her window of opportunity slamming shut.

'But *how* did you know? Did he tell you that? With words?' She pushed. 'Did he tell you we were . . . in love?'

Ann blinked at her in momentary confusion. The wailing was imminent, she knew it, and this time it would be entirely Bryony's fault. She would be kicking off the new year by making a grieving mother cry. But then Ann let out an enormous belch instead, not unlike the MGM lion's roar, and suddenly everything was stable again.

'Yes ducks,' she said calmly. 'He told me, in words, that you were in love. Should he not have?'

Ann no longer looked small or old, but about ten feet tall and solid as marble. Bryony felt a small tremor in one of her own hands, and her eyelid began to twitch as her hangover threatened to break the surface.

'No! I mean, yes. Of course he should have. That's lovely to hear,' she replied meekly, then turned her attention back to the sink. She was startled to find that what she felt in that moment wasn't dismay, but relief.

'Actually I think I might have a little nap, if that's okay.'

'Of course pet, you go and get your head down.' Ann shooed her out. 'Take Ethy's room. I kept it clear for you.'

She held her breath on instinct when walking in. But instead of the swampy shrine to arrested development she had pictured, the room was tidy and clean – at least compared to the chaos downstairs – and appeared to have been redecorated at some point since the last Labour government.

There were a few duplicates she recognised from his London room; the same charcoal waffle bedding, the same drum lampshade and anonymous console table from Madedotcom. She found the idea of Ed buying two of every item, one for each of his 'homes', oddly moving.

Bryony hadn't intended to actually get into the bed, but now she was here and the need to sleep was tugging at her eyelids, it didn't seem such a terrible idea. Climbing beneath the covers (smell neutral, a relief), she made herself comfy, but before she could nod off she noticed something digging into her thigh. It was hard, papery, book-shaped.

She felt another surge of affection, thinking of the way she used to sleep with multiple paperbacks lining her bed; old Judy Blumes and copies of *The Babysitters Club* forming a comforting barricade between her body and the wall. Did Ed *read*, was Ed a reader?

She half recalled a few books on a shelf in his Acton bedroom – a Murakami and a couple of Iain Bankses? Maybe a Bill Bryson? – though it was hard to know if this was a truthful recollection, or if she'd just filled in the gaps from a stock image labelled 'bedroom, male'. She scanned her memory for conversations about literature and drew a blank, but that didn't prove much since nearly all her memories involving Ed were blank except the sex ones, which had grown more vivid as the weeks had gone by. Oh god, was it an erotic book? Was Ed the only millennial man in England taking his porn in print form?

But when she drew the item to the surface it turned out not to be erotica, or in fact a book at all, but rather a soft-covered notebook.

Bryony thumbed through a few pages covered in writing, and realized she'd never seen his handwriting before. It was odd how it somehow felt more intimate than seeing him naked.

Then she realized with a jolt that she was holding the very thing she'd been so sure couldn't exist. Ed's diary.

She dropped it back onto the mattress as though it might be booby-trapped. Bryony's childhood diaries had rarely made it beyond the second week of January, but she'd practised the tricks nonetheless; laying a single hair on top to catch out intruders – presumably those desperate to know about her romantic fixation on Buzz Lightyear, or exactly why Lindsey from school was such a b-word. And, later, the hours she'd spent scrawling mad pages through hot tears about Kath, who was often a c-word, leaving it lying around the house on purpose and then feeling wounded that Kath didn't care enough to violate her privacy.

Bryony pulled Ed's duvet around herself and gingerly picked it up again, appraising it as an object, feeling its weight in her hands. Holding it by the spine she flicked through a few more pages – but quickly, forcing her eyes to swim out of focus so that she couldn't read any of the words. She clocked a few bullet pointed sections, even a couple of doodles – did Ed *draw,* was Ed an *artist?* – but mostly solid text with dates at the top of the pages. She chose a page at random and paused long enough to check the date, placing her hand primly over the rest of the writing.

July this year. Or last year, rather. Right around the time they'd first met.

The idea of Ed keeping a diary as an adult man was perhaps the most unnerving of all the revelations so far. Combined with the lack of sleep, the sugary booze and god knows what hormones swirling around her system, it was making her shiver violently. Was it a trend, she wondered? Perhaps a billionaire had recommended it on a podcast. Were all the lads journalling now? But even silently, her scorn didn't sit right.

Because if these were Ed's innermost thoughts and feelings, his thoughts and feelings about *her* had to be among them, didn't they, or else obvious by omission. And even if they weren't, the very fact of the journal's existence had shifted the ground beneath her feet several places. Here it was, the Rosetta Stone of Ethelred Slingsby's heart.

There came a sudden knock at the door, and Kelly's voice hissed from the landing.

'Bryony, are you awake? Come on, it's time.'

Without thinking or even looking at her own hands, she shoved the diary into her bag and squinted into the little round shaving mirror, wiping uselessly at the residue of last night's eye makeup.

'Coming,' she whispered back.

58

Making peace

There is a moment, as they approach the car, where Kelly honestly thinks Bryony is going to climb into the back seat as though it's an Uber. Kelly supposes non-drivers in their mid-thirties must be allowed to exist, but they shouldn't be allowed to take the piss with it.

She looks pointedly at the passenger door. Bryony course corrects and gets in.

The Tesco Superstore is a fifteen-minute drive away, which they spend in silence. Not companionable silence, exactly, but business-like silence. The silence of two soldiers on their way from witnessing horrors to witness a few more.

At the entrance, Bryony gets distracted by a large pyramid of stollen on special offer and Kelly must steer her firmly towards the pharmacy aisle. It is very important to her that nothing derails this mission. Also, she hates marzipan.

Tests procured – two each, for safety, Bryony smirking up at them both in the little mirror above the self-checkout while Kelly refuses to make it A Moment – they make their way to the accessible bathroom of the Costa Coffee in the retail park next door. Nobody notices them slip in together, or if they do then they probably assume it's just some New Year's Eve hi jinx continuing long into the morning.

Once they're both inside, Kelly wonders why they felt the need to do this together, again.

'Because either way the wait for the other person would be horrific,' answers Bryony, although Kelly hadn't asked the question out loud. 'We started this together, we're finishing it together.'

She has noticed that girls like Bryony feel the need to make everything a bonding experience.

'Fine,' says Kelly. The odour of public toilet is mingling with the scent of burnt cheese and gingerbread syrup in a way that threatens to make her gag. 'But me first this time.'

Bryony doesn't argue, only gestures for her to take a seat with a hostessy flourish. When all four tests are complete – they each clutch their own this time, for the avoidance of doubt – Kelly sets a timer.

'You know it doesn't actually take three minutes, right?' says Bryony. 'Your result will have come up in the time it took me to do mine. You can look right now, I don't mind.'

Kelly isn't an idiot, she knows she can look. But the sooner she looks, the sooner Schrödinger's foetus is out of the box – or rather, firmly in Bryony's and not hers.

'I like to do things properly,' she says. 'Thoroughly.'

So they wait.

Because no one has updated the Costa playlist yet, Jona Lewie's 'Stop the Cavalry' creeps beneath the door, and the jolly trumpet refrain conspires to mock them. Bryony sings along with the *dub-a-dub-a-dubs* softly under her breath and Kelly tries not to picture her, swollen and haloed, draped in blue and riding on a donkey.

The minutes pass like hours. Sleeplessness finally catches up with Kelly and by the time the alarm goes she is in a near-vegetative state, reading and re-reading the laminated plea to please not flush paper towels, nappies or sanitary towels, until it has almost taken on the rhythm of poetry. She wonders who the hell is flushing nappies down toilets, and tries to picture the parenting scene in which such a crime might happen. Kelly never would, surely. Bryony might.

Bryony reaches over and turns off Kelly's bleating phone, nudges her into action.

'Three ... two ... one ...' she chants in merry parody.

Kelly guesses Bryony is so calm and cheerful now because has made peace with her choice. 'Making peace' is a theme Kelly has done battle with for a while; has listened to podcasts about it, read books and articles and long, desultory Instagram captions about it. Peace would be lovely but she has about as much of an idea of how to achieve it as the man in the trenches in the song, wishing to be home for Christmas.

Oh I say it's tough,
I have had enough

'Go!' orders Bryony, and they flip their tests over in unison.

Kelly stares at the little red crosses for several seconds, trying to remember what they mean, if not an emergency. Then the answer explodes in her heart.

59

Happy mug

'I'm not pregnaaaant!'

She screeched it with a funny intonation, gravelly and feral, as though the words had been lodged in her throat like a furball. Several early morning shoppers looked around in the car park to see where the noise came from. Then Bryony realized she was doing an impression of Rizzo at the end of *Grease*, yelling the good news at Kenickie from the Ferris wheel.

'Well, thank fuck for that,' said Marco down the phone, a little muffled. She wondered if he'd gone home without her, or if he was still with Mr Duggan Jr. If he was, news of her not-baby would probably be all over the village before she'd driven her flying Cadillac into the clouds.

'Not that you ever were, of course,' said Marco, and Bryony said no, obviously, the whole thing was always in his imagination.

But as she said it she felt the elation begin to leak out of her, like air from a pricked balloon. Because if she wasn't pregnant, then what was she? Dying? Bulimic for quiche? Fully insane?

Kelly emerged then from the Costa with a large hazelnut latte ('Decaf,' she said defensively) and bleeped the car unlocked. They both climbed in, both smiling, but past each other rather than *at* each other. On their newly divergent roads, the intimacy of the last twelve hours seemed to have been replaced by something more formal.

'Are you okay to drive?' asked Bryony.

'I'm pretty sure you're allowed to drive pregnant, last I heard,' said Kelly.

'I meant, do you need a minute? In case you feel, like, shaky or anything?'

Kelly shook her head and smiled again. 'I'm great! I feel fine. Haven't had a single symptom so far, that I've noticed. Maybe I'll be one of the lucky cows who doesn't get any.'

Bryony could believe this. Kelly would be the kind of woman who went to yoga throughout; who never farted or felt the urge to lick dirt off a potato.

'I bet you'll glow,' she told her.

'Don't be stupid,' said Kelly, though she looked a tiny bit pleased. 'Nobody glows.'

When they arrived back at Ann's house it looked smaller and stranger than it had before, like a set from a low-budget play. Steve was sitting on the wrought iron bench by the back door.

He was wearing tartan pyjama bottoms and his fisherman's sweater, and he was smoking, something Bryony hadn't been aware that he did. He gave a coy little salute as the two women approached, the rollie dangling from between his huge fingers like a theatrical prop.

'Don't make me give you a pamphlet, Steve,' said Kelly, in a playful way that caught Bryony off-guard. She hadn't noticed the two of them interact like that before.

'Just my one a year, Kel,' he replied, his tone casual but his cheeks starting to flush a little. 'I'm a man of moderation, you know that.'

Kelly laughed and disappeared into the house, presumably to find

Leo and share the happy news. Bryony was about to follow her in, but something – elation, liberation, the need to bathe her hangover in cool, clean air – held her back. She sat down next to Steve instead, squeezing herself into what turned out to be a smaller space than it looked. But he didn't seem to mind, wriggling in a token way to accommodate her hips against his.

'Sorry, I'll just . . .' he said, making to stub out his cigarette.

'No, no, don't,' she said. 'Not your one a year! Enjoy it, I don't mind.'

'Sure?' He grinned in thanks and took a self-conscious drag, looking vulnerable and semi-adolescent.

'Actually I get quite nostalgic about the smell of fag smoke,' she said to fill the silence. This was true, despite the cancer risk. 'You know, back in the pre-ban days, when you'd wake up after a night out reeking like a bonfire? Now everyone walks around in these vape clouds that smell like a tween's lipgloss collection, it's so unsexy.'

Steve chuckled as he exhaled. 'Can't be unsexy.'

'I'm just saying, I'd rather my hair stunk of fags than a candyfloss ELF Bar.'

'Noted.'

She laughed too and she wondered if her relief was palpable; if her presence was lighter somehow. A few hours ago she'd been a mess and he'd been, unbeknownst to Steve, an almost-not-quite-honorary-uncle. Now they were just two free, young people on a bench, on the first day of a brand-new year. Young-*ish*.

'How's the head?' he asked her.

'Oh, fine,' she said, wishing she'd snuck a look at her face in Kelly's vanity mirror. She wiped discreetly beneath her eyes, where mascara flakes had probably settled into the creases. 'I've had worse.'

'Ann's bacon sandwiches will fix anything you've got,' said Steve, jerking his head in the direction of the house.

'Is that so?'

'She burns it all to a crisp. The secret ingredient is carcinogens.'

'Noted,' she said.

But she made no move to get up. They sat quietly for a few seconds more, until Bryony asked, 'So, how are you going to make good on your resolution? What big risks are you going to take this year?'

Steve shrugged. 'I thought I might try 'nduja.' He pronounced it *undoodger*.

Bryony laughed. 'You're bullshitting me again.'

But Steve only looked confused and said, 'What? Why?', so she moved quickly on.

'Well, whatever you end up doing, I think it's a really good resolution. I bet you'll all make Ed so proud this year.'

It was such a benign statement, another cost-free platitude, but Steve seemed to appreciate it. 'Thanks Bryony,' he said, stubbing out his cigarette on the wall and then carefully pocketing the butt to throw away. It dawned on her that if she made good on her own resolution, this could be – *should* be – the last time she saw Steve again. Combined with her rapidly descending hangover, the thought made her sentimental and end-of-termish.

'Honestly,' she went on, 'I think it's lovely the way your friendship clearly meant so much to you both. I wish I'd got to know you sooner.'

'N'aw,' said Steve, putting a friendly arm around her shoulder. 'You too, pal.' Bryony nestled into it, Steve's size making her feel the thing that busty five foot eight women rarely get to feel – are rarely allowed to admit that they *want* to feel – which is dainty, precious, contained.

She shivered, making it seem as though she was grateful for his warmth when really a kind of latent teenage thrill was surging through her. She was young-ish, free and on a bench with a boy's arm around her. She wasn't pregnant with a dead guy's baby. She was dainty, precious, contained. In that moment, all other earthly obligations – council tax and booking her smear test and buying moth traps and the many outstanding messages that needed replying to – didn't exist, had floated away in a plume of fag smoke.

This had to be why, instead of pulling out of the hug after a normal duration and taking herself back inside, Bryony turned her face towards Steve's and did the thing, the trick stowed away in the back of her brain for at least two decades since she'd first learned it through repeated exposure to American teen shows. She glanced at his mouth.

And it worked, which was astonishing. Like discovering that one weird trick really could make you a millionaire.

Because now Steve's lips were on hers and for a second they were still but decisive. Now they were moving, tenderly, then hungrily, Bryony sliding her hand along his brushed cotton thigh. But as she did, she felt his lips clamp shut and his arm fall away, and when she opened her eyes, she found Steve's wide with panic.

'No. No, I . . .' was all he said before they heard the sudden clang of metal on metal and both looked up to see Emmett squinting at them from the end of the path, his arms full of newspapers. A scare-crow to startle the crows.

Steve was on his feet now, stammering good mornings and some-thing about Old Les Trindle driving into the fountain again. Bryony took her cue to disappear.

60

Call it a day

Back in the house, she felt sick with relief to find Marco sitting alone in the kitchen, fully dressed and polishing off a bacon sandwich. The fug of burnt fat hung in the air and he had a bucketful of coffee in one of those vast, nineties *Friends*-style mugs with a cartoon on the side that said 'Happy'.

'Here she is, Our Lady of the inaccurate conception!' he greeted her, mopping up some ketchup.

'Shall we go? Let's go,' she said briskly, not sitting down.

Marco swallowed. 'Annie was just saying something about a New Year's Day football game in the village, then everyone goes to the pub and—'

'Don't care! Sounds shit! Let's go please,' she yelped, shifting from foot to foot. She could still see Steve's silhouette through the frosted window by the door. Would he come in soon, or bury himself in a flowerbed to avoid her?

Marco frowned at her in confusion, then put down his crust and stood up. 'Fair enough. May I pee first, or are we making a hasty getaway with the fine china?'

'You can pee,' she told him. 'Make it quick.'

'Oh! You're not going are you?' cried Annie, appearing in the doorway in a candyfloss-pink onesie. 'You'll miss the new year's match, you have to stay for that!'

'Sorry Annie, we've got to head off,' she said. 'I've got plans with some friends back home.'

'Oh? But surely they'd understand if you were a bit late. Come on, you'll love it. Come for meee,' she wheedled.

'I'm really sorry, but honestly – we need to get going.' She could feel her resolve begin to crumble, and willed Marco to hurry up.

'I thought we could have a bit of a sales summit while we're at it, come up with a few personal and professional Lyfe goals for the new year?'

'Another time!'

Annie pouted. 'Come on, it was Ed's favo—'

'Ed's favourite?' interrupted Bryony. 'Was it really? Because so far Ed's favourite time of year has been Halloween, Bonfire Night, Christmas and New Year. What next, Maundy Thursday? The Battle of the Boyne? Was there any calendar occasion the man felt lukewarm about?'

Annie laughed, weakly, as if trying to figure out the joke. 'He was enthusiastic,' she said. 'You know Ed.'

'Actually I don't!' exploded Bryony. 'I barely did!'

'What?' Her smile contorted in confusion.

Bryony knew it was wholly unfair to be taking it out on poor Annie and yet the only kind of damage limitation she could think of right now was to cause further damage. To blow her own cover once and for all. The words began to rush to the surface in a way that felt curiously similar to retching; an involuntary expulsion of the truth.

'Look, I'm sorry, but the truth is we'd only been dating a few months, Annie. Actually no, not even dating – we were fucking, casually fucking! Just sex with bar snacks, that's all! I wasn't his loving partner, I wasn't his girlfriend, I never even saw him during business hours.'

Annie tried to interrupt, but now she'd started, the urge to purge was too great.

'I don't know his life story, his star sign, his blood type or his McDonalds order. I don't know what he actually did for a living! Something in marketing? Spreadsheets? Software? I wasn't listening! I'm sorry but I don't know what his childhood goldfish was called, I don't know what his favourite time of year was and I especially don't know why the hell he's been telling everyone we were some kind of couple when he never let *me* in on that information. But I *do* know I'm not pregnant with his baby and so I'm going to go back to London now and have a massive drink and maybe a rare steak and end this insanity now, if that's okay? I'm sorry,' she added again, reflexively, and steadied herself on the back of a chair.

Annie was silent for a moment, her eyes huge and horrified. Then she said, quietly, 'You're pregnant?'

'*No!!*' roared Bryony. She was surprised to find, via a mouthful of saltwater, that she was the one who was sobbing. 'I am not!'

'I think you'd better go home and get some sleep, Bryony,' said a voice, crisply, from behind her.

In the doorway stood Ann. She was wearing a strange array of leisurewear, presumably her attempt at a football kit, and a strange expression – less shocked or sad, more disgruntled. 'In fact let's all get some sleep, everyone's overtired and acting out.'

'But Mum, she said—' wailed Annie in a child's voice and her mother cut across her with practised force.

'Leave it, Antigone.'

It was impossible to know how much Ann had heard, but Bryony wasn't about to enquire. Marco handed her her coat – with pixie-like stealth he had somehow gathered their bags and belongings while she'd been screaming – and began steering her with a firm arm towards the door. Out of the corner of her eye she could see

Leo and Kelly appearing behind Ann, confusion wrought on two of the three faces.

'Ann, it's been a pleasure,' Marco called back over his shoulder as he ushered Bryony to the doorstep, past a mute Steve and a slowly advancing Emmett. 'Thank you for a lovely party – I'll be getting in touch for that roulade recipe! Happy new year, all.'

61

Resolution

Outside on the road, she drank in gulps of cool January air as though it were medicine, while Marco prodded at his phone.

'Did you know Uber doesn't work here?'

Bryony nodded. She dug around for a tissue with which to dab at the big snotty rivulets that were pooling in the creases of her neck.

'Do you have the number of a cab firm?'

'Good luck.'

Marco sighed. 'Then I guess it's a lovely day for a walk.'

It was barely lunchtime but the light already seemed to be fading, a glowering band of cloud advancing towards them across acres of sky. It felt fitting, given so much had already been started and finished since last night, to call it a day now. She thought longingly of bed – not just her own, but Ed's, half a mile behind her. The extra weight of his diary in her tote bag dragged at her shoulder, threatening to aggravate her neck problems, but the pain felt like the least she deserved in the circumstances.

'Well.' said Marco, as though it was a full sentence.

'I don't want to talk about it.'

'I wouldn't even know how,' said Marco, and they plodded on in silence for a while.

'I'm furious with you, by the way,' she said. 'For telling Kelly.'

'Quite right too, so you should be,' said Marco.

'I think I might just keep crying for a bit, if that's okay,' she said. 'I don't know why.'

Marco said this was fine by him.

62

Morning after

Ann hates the house to be quiet. She tells people it is all she wants –
'If only everyone would leave me *alone* so I could hear myself *think*
for one sodding second!' – but really she dreads the moments, and
there are more of them as the weeks pass, when the house empties
and she is left with only her thoughts for company.

It doesn't help that Emmett has barely spoken a full sentence since
about 2006, though this is why she married him. Ann needs to be
with someone who gives her space, to be her most expansive, and
silence to fill. Modern discourse is keen to stress that couples should
never have secrets, but Ann believes this to be wrong. She is grateful
that her second husband knows when to keep things to himself.

The start of the year is always hard for her. She suffers from
SAD, although personally she feels the issue is less about lack of
daylight and more about the abundance of night. There is simply
too much night for one person to take. So she fills hers with noise
and colour and mess and as many people as she can gather, willing
their energy to buoy her through the hours where she feels most
like she is drowning.

Ann's mother lost her husband at forty-three and made a flan for
dinner the same day. Her mother's mother lost two sons in the war

and reupholstered an armchair with their uniforms. Ann puts out bowls of crisps and busies herself sloshing Prosecco into plastic cups because it is part of a long matriarchal tradition and because she has no earthly clue how to let anyone look after her instead.

Once she has cleaned up the house, consoled her overgrown, over-tired children and sent everyone back to bed, she pulls a blanket around her and sits in the garden. Someone has been sick in the cabbages. This pleases her – the sign of a successful party. Ann hates cabbage: only keeps growing them to score points against her ex-husband, who used to say she killed everything she ever tried to nurture.

She's always seen a little drama as the sign of a successful party too. This is what she tells herself, as Bryony's words, still hot and painful, play on loop in her mind.

'*Just sex with bar snacks*'. If nothing else was true, the girl really was a poet.

Ann chews on each of her nails in turn, as she watches birds tussling around the feeder, glad that someone is still enjoying her hospitality. New Year's resolutions don't start until the second of January. Everyone knows that.

PART THREE

63

Acting is reacting

The symptoms arrive suddenly and violently, like an Evri delivery hurled at her in the night.

Kelly goes to bed feeling normal; she wakes up irritable and sore, stuffy-nosed and bitter-mouthed. Everything tastes wrong. Everything feels wrong. Everything smells revolting. Around her the world keeps on moving in a way that makes her bilious – and inside her, a tiny cluster of cells is doing the same.

'I think it must be some kind of stress reaction, to everything that's been going on,' she tells Leo, who barely registers that his wife is bent double on the carpet, trying to massage her own lumbar with a Babyliss Big Hair. He only frowns at her, as though trying to work out what goings-on she could be referring to. His grief is still too huge to see beyond – and yet there's no room for anyone else in it.

Back in their own house, things feel too clean, too quiet, too stiflingly calm. Kelly limps from room to room, seeing hazards and sharp corners and gags when she opens the fridge.

Ten days have passed since new year, and she still hasn't told Leo. It's strange, surely, that she didn't leap out of the car and straight into his arms, waving the positive test like a trophy? Kelly knows that deep down she is scared of his reaction, or lack of.

But she also knows that she is on borrowed time, so she concocts a plan – a stupid one, ridiculous really – to fake her confirmation test.

Far too long has passed now to casually announce the fact. She'd have to lie and pretend she'd only just done the test anyway, so what was a little more deception? Not *deception*. Optics management. She wants to scrub out the memory of the past few months and start a fresh page that they're both on together. Act two, scene one: the curtain rises on a bathroom.

She draws on all her dimly-remembered acting tuition, practising her expression in the mirror – shock, delight, joy tempered with recognition of the poignant circumstances – until she begins to feel like the Olivia Colman of pregnancy tests. She drinks a pint of Robinson's Fruit & Barley. She is ready.

'Leo? Honey?'

She mutes the TV then crouches between him and it, her hands on his knees, and tenderly kisses his forehead. He looks up.

'This pair's about to go to auction with a Toby jug they think is worth three hundred pounds, but it's actually only worth sixty,' he tells her.

'That's great!' she says, then, 'Babe, my period is twelve days late.'

'Mm? What's that?' He is still watching the TV beyond her shoulder.

'My period. Late. It hasn't come.'

Leo looks puzzled for a few seconds, as though trying to remember what these words mean. Then it clicks.

'Oh. *Oh.* Right.' His eyes widen and he looks at her properly now. 'Wow, okay.'

'I wanted to wait a little while to find out, in case it was a false alarm. I knew Christmas and new year would be a tough time, emotionally,' she lies. 'But do you think we should do a test, yeah?'

'Probably should,' he nods in agreement. His eyes flicker back towards the telly.

'... Now, maybe?' she perseveres, taking the Clear Blue Digital from her pocket. It seemed right to splash out for the occasion.

'Yes, sure! Wow,' he says again. 'Okay.'

Leo gathers himself and turns the TV off. They walk into the bathroom together, he busies himself straightening the towels while she does the deed, and they hug, the way they used to, only wordlessly this time, while their future is drawn up by the creeping liquid line behind the plastic case in its special spot on the side of the bathtub.

After three minutes, she reaches for the test and turns it over with ceremonial slowness, and they gasp and cry and laugh and hold each other some more, saying 'I can't believe it, I can't believe it, shit, wow, shit,' over and over. She worries they are both acting, in a way. Both watching themselves from above and striving to look and sound as convincing as they can. But then, thinks Kelly, isn't that what everyone is doing, really, all of the time?

In the end she's pretty pleased with her performance. Especially the face she pulls when Leo steps back, beaming, to say: 'You know the best thing? Ann will be *thrilled*.'

64

And, breathe

The weekend approached, for the first time in months, without any kind of summons from Ed's family. Bryony told herself she was excited to finally have some downtime.

'What is it this Saturday?' asked Marco. 'Late Diwali? Early Burns Night? The ceremonial disposal of Ann's empty Advent calendar?'

She shook her head. 'Nada.'

Marco whooped. 'The decree absolute! You must feel so free.'

'So free!' she echoed. 'Such a relief.'

And it was a relief, at first. To lie back and do nothing, and pretend nothing and be selfish. She luxuriated in the emptiness of her diary as well as her womb.

One day her phone buzzed – 'Hey! The tickets just went on sale for that pottery club night! I know you said you were interested, shall I book us a couple of places?' – which was the kind of message Bryony received on a semi-regular basis, usually with no memory of the pottery club night, circus skills workshop or bottomless slam poetry brunch, but no doubt she had said she was interested whenever it may have come up. What else were you supposed to say when people mentioned these things?

'Hey! Sounds great,' she began to type, then paused and deleted.

She remembered her new year's resolution and the urgency of that vow on the Little Buckton mound. Already it felt as though that passion belonged to a different, better, stronger person; Ed's souped-up fantasy version of herself. Amazing Girlfriend Bryony, with her mystery courses and altruistic pursuits, who was probably already proficient in pottery.

But then what was she going to do? Keep sleepwalking through her own life, sparing everyone's feelings until she was just Withered Husk Bryony with a trapeze injury and no backbone?

'Hey! Actually I'm not that bothered, sorry! Have fun though!'

She looked at it for a moment, then went back and took out the 'sorry'. Then all the exclamation marks. 'No' was a complete sentence, she'd read that somewhere. She sent the message quickly without re-reading, retching slightly.

'Ok no worries!' came the reply a few minutes later. 'Drinks soon though?'

As easy as that. Bryony enjoyed the giddy rush again, of having stuck her fingers in the socket of social disapproval and survived. And this time she hadn't made anyone cry.

'Sure!' she messaged back, luxuriating in the comfort of vague plans that might never happen. 'Let's.'

Pumped by this small success, she turned down several more invites and ignored the messages that rolled in wishing her a happy new year, enquiring about her Christmas, suggesting drinks or soft drinks or bracing walks across the marshes. Nobody seemed concerned by her falling off the social radar, but then this was to be expected in the first week of the year. In recent times it had become fashionable to eschew going out in January entirely. Her friend Dee called it 'Nopeuary' – the blanket turning down of all plans and all fun in favour of early nights, prestige television and simmering oneself in long baths like a human stew. It had all the traits of clinical depression but if you did it in designer loungewear, that made it fine.

The Slingsbys, however, operated in a different world, one where having a social life wasn't loaded with cultural significance and personal turmoil; you just went out and did stuff, all the time, easy as breathing. Hearing nothing from them at all was unmooring.

She spent Saturday doing her washing, watering her crisping houseplants and attacking her face with a hot flannel to turn a few barely-noticeable pimples into large, crusted sores. By the time evening rolled around with still no contact from any of the Northants contingent, unmoored had evolved into unsettled – unsettled and slightly hurt. It was not unlike the time the nameless man who used to reply 'sexy xoxo' to every single one of her Instagram stories stopped one day with no explanation.

'I think I've really upset them all,' she told Marco.

'Brian. Of course you've really upset them all,' he said. 'But look, you just told the truth. Only in the least sensitive way possible.'

'I feel awful.'

'You always feel awful.'

This remained true. As the rush of relief after New Year had faded, Bryony's symptoms had returned – only reconfigured a little this time; less queasy, more wheezy.

'Will you listen to me breathing?' she asked Marco.

'I'm busy,' he'd said. 'There are men on the internet who will pay you for that.'

With nothing better to do she spent the evening cruising breathwork videos on YouTube, watching animated spirograph shapes expand and contract, expand and contract in time with her ribcage.

The pain was back. Or rather, it was a slightly different pain in an entirely different place, but she recognised its character. It felt like the old pain in a wig.

She became obsessed with the pain, breathing more and more

deeply in order to note its characteristics – halfway between a stab and a throb? A stob? – until she started worrying more when it didn't appear than when it did. The pain was keeping her company now. The pain was her only friend.

She googled *pure oxygen therapy,* then *pure oxygen therapy near me,* checked her bank balance, then idly investigated OnlyFans to see if Marco might be right. She tried techniques to distract herself, jogging on the spot to see if the exertion would jolt her back into breathing normally. But this only left her bent double and panting raggedly into a paper bag, accidentally inhaling several historic croissant flakes.

Finally, she found herself picking at the sorest spot of all.

'Hi Ann, just wondered how you're doing? All well I hope, as well as can be expected. Did you decide any more about the school prize? Just let me know if you need anything! Xx'

No reply came.

65

Determinedly full of life

On Sunday, Bryony went with Marco to see his parents and not talk about cancer.

All afternoon they danced around it, smoothly and beautifully, gliding from topic to topic without setting off any of the trigger words: ill, well, treatment, future, prostate, hospital, death. Not being able to talk about death was useful in preventing her from talking about Ed too, although when she thought about it she realized that death had rarely entered the family conversation. Their conversations about Ed were always determinedly full of life.

In Marco's parents' small, neat living room they ate empanadas and KitKats and drank builders' tea and performed two hours of cheerful improv on the theme of 'everything's normal'. Marco regaled them all with stories from the vet's, which were always funny and made funnier by the continued pretence that he did not really like animals. Bryony told stories from the council, which were not particularly funny but gave them the chance to click their tongues at the dire state of public services in this country, which everyone enjoyed.

Marco's mum caught them up on everything that had been happening with the neighbours and on *The Archers*, somewhat interchangeably, and his dad leapt up every few minutes to show them something or other, as though keen to demonstrate that he still could.

Nobody got drunk or stoned or danced the Time Warp or swam naked in anything and that was fine.

'Thank you for coming,' Marco said, as they ate paninis on the train home.

'You don't need to thank me,' she told him. She was touched that he'd even asked her. 'I'm just glad I could come to support you.'

'Oh, that's sweet,' he said, 'but you didn't come to support me. We went to support you.'

'What?'

'Well you're clearly desperate for some kind of surrogate family – I just thought it might help if it was a less messy one.'

'Oi,' she grinned, teeth coated in molten cheese. 'Those are my fake in-laws you're talking about.'

Marco rolled his eyes. 'I am more of your husband than the Egg Man ever was.'

'I thought we weren't even outside friends?'

'Beyond the M25 doesn't count.'

She accepted this logic.

'How are you though? Seriously. After seeing your dad and everything?'

Marco opened his mouth to say something flippant and then appeared to think better of it.

'Actually I thought it would be harder, seeing him there. You know, in his little lounge, with his little puzzle books, his little world – like he should be out there, owning it, doing something grand and thrilling while he still has the chance. Jumping out of planes or trekking Machu Picchu, or buying a motorbike or what-ever. I was worried I'd snap and yell at him, "Go live your life, man! Life is short! Do it better!" and start trying to dress him up and take him to Electrowerkz, or something. But then I saw him there, perfectly content, and I thought . . . well.'

'Life is short?' she offered.

'Exactly. Do what makes you happy, Dad.'

'I wish anything made me as happy as your dad's puzzle books make him,' she said.

'Same,' Marco agreed, and they bumped the greasy ends of their sandwiches in a toast.

Ann replied to her text three days later. 'Thank You Bryony all fine hope u r too', followed by a string of emojis – prayer hands, a swan, a pouting cat and a toadstool. Then, nothing.

66

Ready, steady

Ann is thrilled. Kelly begins receiving folate-rich food parcels before the week is out.

'I told you we should wait until twelve weeks!' she wails at Leo. 'It's bad luck! We shouldn't be telling anyone, not this early – what if . . . ?'

But she can't bring herself to voice the worry, not with the shadow of death still cold on their backs. It's clear Leo just wanted to give his mother a gift she might actually approve of, for once. 'It was the first time she smiled in months, Kel,' he tells her. This isn't true – Ann had been positively beaming as she packed everybody off from the wake with Tupperwares of leftover paella – but she lets it go. Because it feels good to please Ann, she can't deny that.

She lets the food parcels go too, begging Leo to dispose of them before the smell hits her nostrils and she's submerged again beneath another great crashing wave of nausea.

'Morning sickness is mainly psychological,' a male GP at work once told her. 'It's just women panicking about being pregnant. But if they're really *ready* to be a mother, if the baby is really *wanted*, they feel fine!'

It was years ago but the words are haunting her now. Wasn't she ready for this? Wasn't all the fruitless shagging and folic acid and ovulation sticks and lying with her legs in the air and a cushion under her hips preparation enough? This baby is *so* wanted! The *most* wanted! Isn't it? No – she is trying to train herself not to call the baby 'it'. It sounds heartless and unmaternal, even in her own head. *They.* Aren't they?

Leo will walk past from time to time as she retches and groans over the bowl, and he will sweep the hair away from her temple and kiss it and mutter: 'I'm sorry.'

67

The other checklist

'Hi Bryony, how are you feeling today?'

It was always a pleasant surprise whenever a Talking Therapies referral came through – like winning a dusty bottle of bubble bath in a raffle you couldn't remember entering. But this time she seemed to have reached the top of the waiting list in record time. It felt fortuitous. Oddly so.

Bryony adjusted her laptop on its stack of cookbooks and squinted into the camera.

'Not amazing,' she said.

The therapist performing her assessment call was a middle-aged woman with owlish glasses and a blurred Zoom background, which to Bryony always seemed like a person might be concealing something sinister. Still, she looked more like Bryony's idea of a therapist than any of the previous lot, who had mostly been her age or younger, dressed like work experience and reading nervously from a sheet of disclaimers. There was an embroidered scarf around her shoulders. This was promising.

'I've been feeling pretty terrible, to tell you the truth,' she went on. 'Like my whole body is turning on me.'

'Aw, I'm sorry to hear that,' cooed the therapist, head tilted to one side. 'Well, you *look* great.'

At first Bryony thought she'd misheard, that the microphone must be glitching.

'I beg your pardon?'

'I said you look great,' the therapist repeated. 'Lovely skin!'

'Oh,' said Bryony. 'It's the lighting. I'm sitting in front of a window.'

'Nice hair too,' she said, as though perhaps she might be able to fix Bryony's brain with compliments alone. 'So shiny.'

'Um. Thank you, I washed it,' said Bryony, wishing she hadn't. Clearly she didn't look mad enough to be claiming therapy on NHS dollar. She rubbed at her eye makeup with the back of her hand.

'That's great,' said the therapist. 'Really good. So you're looking after yourself well?'

'I guess so,' Bryony told her. 'I mean, if anything I look after myself *too* well, that's the problem.'

'So you aren't finding it difficult to perform basic self-care? Making meals? Getting dressed, showering?'

'No,' she said, a little defensively, looking down to make sure all her buttons were in the right holes.

In fact her showers were usually protracted affairs, because she liked to perform a full-body inspection; probing at herself like a curious alien, checking her skin for moles and her breasts for lumps, pressing for so long that eventually every spot felt tender and telling. But then sometimes they were also very short – in, out, soap it all about – because she was scared of what she might find. It was the odd inconsistency of a high-functioning hypochondriac. Marco could never understand why she slavishly covered herself in Factor 50 come summer but never, ever flossed. Or why she took every supplement under the sun but didn't do anything that could reasonably be called 'exercise'. Why she had spent amounts running into the thousands on letting Ewa pummel her body but couldn't justify paying for a therapist to do the same for her brain.

'That's great,' said the free therapist. 'And are you having difficulty sleeping at all? Any loss of interest in the activities you normally enjoy?'

'I'm not depressed,' she told the therapist, and the therapist smiled the small, benign smile of therapists everywhere.

'And why do you say that?' she asked.

Bryony pictured the first day of therapy school. Classrooms of women in statement earrings and silk scarves, studying a marked-up diagram of a mouth. *Here to here, never ear to ear. Repeat.*

'No, I mean, I'm the other checklist,' explained Bryony, trying to save them both time. 'Anxiety. GAD, obviously – but more specifically, health anxiety. You know. Hypochondria.'

'Health anxiety' was the official term. Bryony returned to the page on the NHS website often, soothing herself with the knowledge that of all the diagnoses in the world that she couldn't claim, there was one she definitely could.

'So you think you might be ill a lot,' said the therapist.

'No, I *feel* like I'm ill,' Bryony clarified. 'All the time.'

'Do you feel ill now?' asked the therapist. She sounded as though she hoped to catch Bryony out.

'Yes,' said Bryony. 'I have a sinus headache.'

The therapist said she was sorry to hear that, then insisted on running through all the standard checklists anyway. Together they worked through them the way she had with many therapists, many times before. They recorded how often in the past two weeks she had felt nervous, anxious or on edge, had not been able to stop worrying, had trouble relaxing, had been so restless it was hard to sit still, had been irritable, or felt afraid, 'as if something awful might happen'. Several days, more than half the days, nearly every day, or constantly?

Bryony paused after each question, pretending to consider each answer truthfully while really trying to strike the perfect balance; not so bad it sounded hysterical, but just bad enough to make up for her nice hair. Negotiating the semantic difference between 'several', 'more than half' and 'nearly every' took so much energy that she felt exhausted by the time the therapist said,

'And what are you hoping to get out of CBT?'

Her heart sank.

'Ah,' she said. 'It's just – I've actually done quite a lot of CBT in the past and I've never found it really worked for me. All a bit too much like homework, you know? Which just stresses me out more. I was wondering if I might be able to try another . . . flavour.'

'Well Bryony, CBT is usually what we recommend for people as an initial starting point,' said the therapist, still smiling.

'Sure, but like I say, this isn't my initial starting point,' she told her. 'I've been through this system a few times– um, several times . . . before. So I thought if I could maybe skip up a level and try something else now, that would be great.'

The therapist smiled more broadly. 'I'm afraid that isn't usually what we would recommend for someone fitting your profile, on a general basis.'

'Right,' said Bryony. 'Sure. But is it something you *could* recommend for me, on this *specific* basis?'

The therapist's connection froze for a few seconds, or maybe the therapist did.

'I'm sorry Bryony,' she said after the pause, 'I think it will just have to be the CBT for now. Unless you'd rather be taken off the waitlist?'

'No, no!' said Bryony. 'That's fine, I'll take the CBT. Thank you so much.'

'You're welcome,' the therapist beamed. 'Well, that concludes our assessment – someone will be in touch soon to arrange your first session.'

'Thank you so much,' said Bryony again, as though she was accepting a giant cheque for a charity.

'My *pleasure*,' said the therapist.

'Take care,' said Bryony.

'You too,' said the therapist. 'Have a lovely evening.'

'You too!' said Bryony, and they beamed at each other for a few more painful seconds until the call screen disappeared.

68

The big ask

'So. Any thoughts on names?' asks Ann during the year's first Sunday Salon, dumping a heap of runny cauliflower cheese onto Kelly's plate without asking. Kelly watches in silent horror as the white sauce oozes into the gravy.

'A few!' says Leo. 'Haven't we Kel?'

'Yep, a couple we like for each,' smiles Kelly. She tries to sound enigmatic but naturally this is useless.

'Well? Aren't you going to tell us what they are?' demands Ann, proffering a pot of Colman's mustard as though this is a fair exchange.

'We thought it might be nice to keep it a surpri—' she begins, but Ann is still going.

'I always think it's nice to have people's opinions, isn't it? Gather a few ideas, get some feedback – you know, so you have an idea of how the names might serve them out in the real world.'

Kelly thinks this is rich from the woman who named her off-spring like a mutant British Museum exhibit, but doesn't have the strength to point this out. To her right, Galileo chuckles fondly.

'Trouble is, Mum, as soon as you start telling people, they ruin the names with their associations.'

'But associations can be good!' insists Ann, waving a charred carrot like a tiny flag. 'You could choose a name with *positive* associations. For everybody. You know, something really *meaningful.*' Her giant saucer eyes dart between the two of them, reddening a little. And the penny drops. Kelly doesn't know how she hadn't seen this coming, except that she has been walking through fog for the last few weeks.

'Let's just hope she's a girl, then she can be Ethel,' says Leo on the drive home, after they've pulled over for Kelly to hurl cauliflower cheese onto the hard shoulder.

'But I don't want a daughter called Ethel!' Kelly wails. 'It sounds like she'll come out of the womb with a tabard on and a fag in her hand.' Even her own late mother's name, Margaret, doesn't make the cut (too Tory).

Leo persists. 'Everyone is naming their kids like pensioners these days. I heard a two-year-old Doris in Leon the other day. Bloke at work called his baby Bernard. People love that shit.'

But not Kelly. She's had baby names percolating her whole life; rechristening her hypothetical future children at the start of every school year. Her choices have changed with fashion and with passing infatuations – Willow and Xander during her *Buffy* obsession, Coco and Marc during her outlet mall era – but in recent years, certain contenders have lodged themselves in her heart and she has held her breath when each birth announcement looms up on her feeds, begging the universe that her favourites wouldn't be taken. It seems incredible that she's made it this far, with babies shooting out of friends and acquaintances every which way for almost a decade, without anyone using her secret choices. It's miraculous. To abandon them now for a baby called Ethel? Fuck off.

'Ed, I could live with. Little Eddie. Maybe. But you know Ann—'

'She'd want it to be the whole hog,' agrees Leo. 'Couldn't call the kid Edward or Edmund, she'd see that as a bigger insult than not using it at all. Middle name?' he ventures.

Kelly tries it for size, mentally shoehorning 'Ethelred' into her favourite name, which has been balanced carefully for rhythm and cadence, heritage and modernity, conventionality and quirk. She winces.

'Of course the irony is, Ed would never want to burden the poor little sod with that name,' says Leo. 'He's probably up there right now, yelling, "Don't do it."'

He casts his eyes skyward for a moment and blinks hard with his own giant saucer eyes, swerving precariously close to a cyclist. Kelly covers his hand on the steering wheel with hers, wondering how her child can have become communal property while it's still inside her body, still only the size – according to the app which is charting its progress via the fruit bowl – of a zinfandel grape.

New topics for debate present themselves daily. Will they be gentle parents or rigid parents? Will they sleep train, or kowtow to their infant's every wail? Breast or bottle? Are dummies the devil? Will it be a natural birth or is Kelly Too Posh To Push?

Kelly is currently Too Sick To Think, but the combined force of her in-laws and the internet is determined to make her.

'It's just such a magical time!' cries Annie down the phone, because naturally Annie knows too now. 'How are you feeling, do you feel like a goddess?'

Annie knows, Susan knows, Ian from Budgens knows. None of Kelly's friends or family know yet because she is too superstitious to tell them, giving her the curious feeling that her baby exists only in Little Buckton and the surrounding villages. Everyone asks how she is feeling but they rarely leave space for an answer, preferring to fill the gap in for her.

Kelly does not feel like a goddess. She feels like shit and admits as much, and Annie prescribes seventy-two all-whole, nature-inspired minerals and adaptogens to help with that, and Kelly says thank you, Annie, goodbye Annie.

'Love you!' says Annie, who ends all her calls this way. 'Love to my future nibling!'

Kelly has never heard this term before and thinks it has something to do with sweetcorn, which makes her feel nauseous, and now sweetcorn is on the list of foods that are newly revolting to her.

But the most stomach-churning conversation so far comes when Leo, unloading the dishwasher one night, says, 'I've been thinking. Maybe we should move back.'

'Back where?' says Kelly.

'To Buckton,' says Leo. Leo never says the 'Little' part, feeling it too twee for his personal style.

'That isn't "back" for me, I've never lived there,' she says.

'It feels like you have though,' says Leo and she cannot deny this is true. 'Think about it, Kel. We'd have free childcare on tap, Ann would be falling over herself to help. Annie too. We could probably afford a massive house, the kids–' they are plural now, as though their baby-making potential has been proven and unlocked indefinitely '–can play outside like we used to, run though the fields and ride their bikes all over the place and we won't have to worry about them joining gangs. It'll be great.'

Kelly wants to point out that they'll have to worry about them drink-driving somebody's tractor aged thirteen instead, but she doesn't. She knows this isn't about Leo suddenly craving a return to rural idyll. He has always been vocal in his relief at living somewhere with public transport; ethnic diversity; Deliveroo. No, it's about needing to retreat to his family. It makes perfect, painful sense and she wonders how her heart can burst so fully with love for somebody even while she wants to throw a mug at his head.

This is marriage, she knows. Friend after friend has done it, made the big sacrifice for the familial dream machine. Their home, their career, their social life, their nail extensions. She's had a good run. Besides more Sundays around Ann's kitchen table than she would ideally like, theirs has so far been a relationship in which neither has really had to compromise much. But now, here it is. The big ask.

'Our lives are here, babe,' she tries, weakly. 'Our jobs are here.'

'I could work from home and commute down once or twice a week,' he says. 'Plenty of people do.'

'Well I couldn't,' she says. 'What about my job?'

He chuckles nervously.

'Kel.'

'What?'

She knows what, but she wants to hear him say it: that her job is dispensable. That if being a receptionist is her true calling then she can find any number of doctor's surgeries in Northamptonshire to do it in instead, probably nicer ones. She can't claim he's wrong.

And besides, they've had years here, in her hometown; it's only fair to take turns. Kelly can't deny the logic, but worse than that, she can't fight the sentiment. There is a gap around Ann's table, a tug of war going on in her husband's heart and a baby on the way that could help to repair all that. Kelly worries that if she were a better wife she'd be agreeing immediately, selflessly, unquestioningly. If she were a better wife maybe she'd have suggested it herself.

Instead, when Leo asks her that night what she's thinking, she says, 'I suppose I could live with Ethelred as a middle name. Maybe. If there were other middle names too.'

And Leo kisses her in the dark and says thank you, that's very generous.

69

Consequences

'Hiiiiiiii, is that Bryony?' the voice asked.

'Speaking?'

A few months ago unknown numbers had terrified her, but the Slingsbys and their freewheeling telephone habits had been a form of exposure therapy. Now she found she missed it. Not least because answering her phone at her desk and then taking it into one of the small, soundproofed meeting rooms had made her look more productive at work.

'Bryony, hiiiii! So great to finally speak to you. It's Maxine.'

Who was Maxine? She racked her brain for possible contenders among Ann's entourage. The pink-haired one who kept ferrets, was that Maxine? The woman who made her own yoghurt in an airing cupboard?

'Maxine, your Diamond Team Queen,' the voice supplied, a little tersely.

Shit. She made a sprint for a meeting room, closing the door firmly before the interns could hear anything.

'Maxine! Hi!'

'How *are* you, Bryony? I just wanted to check in and see if everything was okay.' There they were – the hushed inflection, the drawn-out syllables. Only synthetic this time, like compassion via ChatGPT.

Bryony steeled herself the way she did when charities called to follow up on her one-off donations.

'All fine thanks!' she told her. 'But I'm afraid I'm not involved in Gel Lyfe anymore. Thanks so much for checking in though, byeee.'

She hung up. Maxine immediately rang back.

'Hiiii Bryony, sorry we must have got cut off there! As I was saying—'

'Actually Maxine,' she interrupted, '*I* was just saying, unfortunately I'm not involved with Gel Lyfe anymore. Sorry! Take care.'

She hung up.

Maxine immediately rang back.

'As I was saying Bryony, we've noticed you seem to be having a bit of trouble getting off the starting blocks with your sales—'

'As *I* was saying Maxine, I'm afraid I won't be continuing my association with Gel Lyfe.' She adopted the cadence of a disgraced politician. 'It was an unfortunate mistake. I have quit the team and ask to be removed from your lists. Please consider this my, ah, official notice.'

Maxine laughed a tinkly laugh, and Bryony's jaw clenched.

'Bryony, my love, I'm afraid it doesn't work like that. You see, as Annie's downline you made a commitment to her, to sell all that product. And as my downline, she made a commitment to me. And I've made a commitment to *my* Team Queen, and we've *all* made a commitment to Tamara. That commitment to each other is the foundation of the Gel Lyfe community philosophy. It's all about women helping women.'

'Mm,' said Bryony. 'And that's all *great,* but the thing is I never actually signed up in the first place.'

'You mean Annie coerced you?' asked Maxine, faux-scandalized.

'Well, no. Not exactly. But I didn't want to upset her, she's been through a lot recently. I don't know if you're aware, but her brother—'

'Yes poor, *poor* Annie, I'm aware of her situation,' Maxine cut across her. 'We've covered it thoroughly in our Turning Trauma into Triumph workshop, she's been making amazing progress to reclaim that pain. But I think you're underselling your own ambition, Bryony. I mean, surely you wouldn't go into *business* with someone just to avoid upsetting them.'

Bryony bristled. 'It's not actually a *business* though, is it?' she said, hoping to prick the bubble of insanity around this whole conversation. 'It's a pyramid scheme.'

If she'd expected Maxine to gasp or weep at the phrase, she was disappointed. Her voice only became more honeyed, dripping patience and reason as she said, 'Sadly that's a common myth. But I can promise you Gel Lyfe is absolutely a business, Bryony. It's an independent empowerment franchise for female founders.'

'What are they founding?' she asked. 'I thought it was selling plant juice. Seventy-two all-whole, nature-inspired minerals.'

'Right, but it's about *more* than our amazing product – it's a springboard for women to build their own futures. We support single mothers, retired women, women who face barriers to traditional employment—'

'I mean, that's great, but—'

'So by quitting on your own journey, you're also holding Annie back from realizing her potential. Is that what you really want to do?'

'No of course I don't, but—'

'Great!' Maxine drew the word out in a manner not unlike Tony the Tiger. 'I'm glad to hear it Bryony because it would be such a shame to lose you at this stage. We need you! You're a vital member of Team Maxine.'

'I thought I was Team Annie?'

'That's the wonderful thing, we're all on each other's teams. We all champion each other's potential. You have *so much* potential Bryony, I can sense it right now, just reverberating down the phone! If you feel yourself slipping into a doubt ditch, if you need a bit more support to really get your business up and soaring, we can all help you with that. You only need to ask.'

Bryony felt increasingly like Alice trying to talk to the Duchess. Through the meeting room window she could see her line manager, Mercy, hovering near her empty desk with a laptop, looking murderous. Mercy was not known for living up to her name.

'Thank you Maxine. But honestly, I don't think the Gel Lyfe, er, life, is for me. I already have a job.'

'We all have jobs, Bryony! Most of our gelievers begin their journey as a side hustle, because it fits so well around their day jobs or childcare or other life commitments. But anyone can have a *job*. We're talking about an *empire*, being your own boss, building a future in which you only answer to *you*.'

'And to you, though? And Annie. And Tamara . . .'

'Women helping women!' bleated Maxine.

'And I don't want an empire! I never actually wanted to join a . . . to *start my own business*.'

'Well then WHY would you sign up?'

'That's a VERY good question, Maxine.'

There was a pause, in which both could hear the other panting slightly. Bryony leapt in before Maxine could rev up again.

'If it's okay with you I think I'll end my journey here. I've already paid for my gel, so I guess I'll just keep it and, ah, enjoy it myself.'

'I'm afraid that's not going to work Bryony.' The honey was suddenly spiked with vinegar. 'You don't own that product.'

'What? Yes I do. I can show you my bank statement.'

'That wasn't the purchase price, my love, it's only rented.'

'I'm sorry, what?' Bryony spluttered, and noticed she sounded briefly, unnervingly, like her father. 'How can I *rent* sachets of gel?'

'What you purchased was the right to the franchise, and the licence to *sell* gel. Until you shift the units and transfer those profits into the Team Queen well of fortune, the product is still owned by Gel Lyfe, not you. It was all in the terms and conditions, my love. Did you read the terms and conditions?'

'Obviously not!' wailed Bryony. 'Nobody reads terms and conditions!'

'Well you can, of course, buy the product outright if you'd prefer—'

'Yes. I'll just do that, thank you.'

'. . . for a one-time payment of twelve hundred pounds plus VAT.'

'You fucking what?'

Even as she screeched in horror, part of this felt inevitable. She thought of all the times she'd blithely ticked away her right to ignorance and wondered if this was the price of modern life; if maybe everyone, sooner or later, was going to be slapped with a twelve hundred pound penalty for their right to flit around the internet like an idiot.

'—but I do need to explain to you Bryony, that if you take that option, there will be consequences for Annie as your upline.'

'What kind of consequences?'

'Well, she'll lose her Team Queen fast-track status and drop back down to Flint level until she can recruit someone else to fill your space.'

'That isn't fair!' she protested. 'Annie shouldn't be punished for my decision, especially not with everything she's been through! And you might not be aware, but her brother was also my, ah, partner?'

She closed her eyes as she said it. This was the last time she'd use it, she vowed, absolutely the last.

But Maxine only said:

'All the more reason to turn that trauma into triumph, Bryony. Think about it. Why make poor Annie suffer more when you could both prosper instead? Women are too used to denying themselves everything, too scared to invest in our futures. Believe in yourself, Bryony! You can do this, I know you can.'

When Bryony didn't respond, she turned spiky once more. 'But if you do decide to quit, better to do it soon before the inactivity fees kick in. Let's chat once you've had time to consider, mmkay?'

Bryony hung up. Maxine did not ring back.

70

Treat yourself!

Seeing her father in Hackney felt like seeing a moose in the flamingo enclosure.

'I'm going to be in town,' was all he'd said by way of explanation, and Bryony had felt both grateful and furious that he'd felt the need to invent a pretence to spend time with her.

'This is a lively place,' he said, after the barista in bondage trousers brought their coffees. If she was honest, she enjoyed choosing the place he'd be least comfortable, somewhere he'd have to drink out of a handleless stoneware cup. It felt petty but important.

'Well, you need to get used to a cosmopolitan lifestyle. You'll have to start drinking coffee at midnight and eating raw steak with raw egg on it.'

Richard laughed heartily, as though teasing were their usual currency. But when it was clear he had failed to think of a pithy comeback, he just said, 'How's work?'

'It's fine. Busy. Catching up on a lot of stuff that got pushed back before Christmas.'

'Shouldn't you be there right now?'

She shook her head and smirked. 'I have a meeting.'

'Who's that with?'

She stared at him. 'Dad. You.'

'Oh. Oh, I see,' he chuckled gamely, then turned stern and added, 'I hope you don't take liberties, Bryony. Since Covid, they're having real trouble keeping bums on seats in offices, I've heard – people swanning in and out and looking after their kids while they're supposed to be working from home, sounds like a complete nightmare.'

'The prohibitive cost of childcare in this country is the real nightmare, I think you'll find,' she said, then cringed at the way conversations with her father turned her into a *Guardian* headline generator. 'But I don't take liberties,' she added, primly. 'I've actually been working very hard.'

'Well, we're wading through our own admin swamp at the moment with these visa applications,' he went on. 'Christ alive they like to make it complicated.'

'I think you'll find *Brexit* made it complicated,' she said, unable to swallow this point either. 'What did you think you were voting for, restrictions on movement for everyone except you?'

'I didn't vote for it, Bryony, we've been through this,' he said tersely.

'Kath did.'

'Kath is her own person, what she does in the polling booth is her business. It's neither here nor there.'

'Well it sounds like she's trying to be both here *and* there.'

'Yes, yes, very clever.'

Her father sipped his coffee and winced, although it wasn't clear at what.

'Look,' he said, 'I'm sorry if the news came as a shock to you. But people move abroad, Bryony. It isn't the act of personal betrayal you seem to think it is.'

He didn't use the words 'this isn't all about you, you know,' though he may as well have. Suddenly she felt twelve years old again, being told it wasn't all about her, or in fact at all about her, when the new woman was drafted in to fill their silences. The colossal weight of not-enoughness filled her chest and it was all she could do to croak out a sulky, 'I know it isn't.'

'Frankly I'd have thought you'd rather visit us in France than Orpington. France!'

'It's just France, Dad, it isn't Beverley Hills.'

'Would you rather we moved to Beverley Hills?'

'God no.'

'Well then. It isn't far, we purposely chose somewhere not too far away – we could have gone for Australia like Rod and Deirdre! And look, any time you want to come over, I will pay for your flights.'

He said this as though it was a deal-closer, the offer she couldn't possibly refuse.

'Thanks but I'd prefer to get the train,' she said. 'You know, for the planet.'

Her father's eyes bugged with the effort of not rolling them. 'Fine, suit yourself. I'll pay for your *train*. And have a pain au choc-olat and a nice bottle of red waiting for you, how's that?'

Bryony smiled in spite of herself, the thirty-four year old being bribed with treats. At least he was trying.

She fought the instinct to say yes please, thank you. Instead she said, 'Honestly Dad, if you want to pay for something, I'd rather you paid for therapy.'

Only when she heard herself say it did she realize how much sense it made. There was no universe in which she could bear to ask her father to bail her out of the Gel Lyfe debacle – but to bail her out of the worry pit she'd lived in since childhood? For that, absolutely, he could pay.

He laughed again, then was forced to rearrange his expression once he realized this wasn't more millennial satire. The t-word danced between them like an unwanted street performer, trying to make them both uncomfortable.

'Therapy? Is that . . . ah, something you're considering, then?' he asked, looking genuinely alarmed.

'It's something I'm *having*, Dad – I've been having it on and off for years, when I can. But there's a limit to what I can get on the NHS and I can't afford to go private. So if you really wanted to throw some money at me to make yourself feel better, you could fund that and maybe it would help me feel better too.'

'It's not about making myself feel better, Bryony, I don't know where this is coming from. I thought you were doing fine! With your job, and your social life and everything. I had no idea you were struggling, you know . . . *mentally*. You never mentioned it.'

Not for the first time, she boggled at the generational gulf. That she barely had a friend without a diagnosis, while to her father everyone was assumed sane until proven otherwise.

'I *am* doing fine,' she said, with exaggerated calm. 'Mostly I'm doing fine, but sometimes I'm doing terribly, and overall I could be doing a lot better if I had a bit of professional help to sort through some stuff rather than falling into the same holes again and again and again.' She exhaled slowly and tried to appeal to his business sensibilities. 'Think of it as an investment. In my wellbeing.'

'Well,' he said, slowly. 'Well, I suppose I can certainly consider it. If you really think it's necessary. But I should say, we've got an awful lot tied up in this house sale at the moment, and with interest rates what they are . . .'

'I do think it's necessary, Dad.'

'. . . and obviously I'd need to discuss it with Kath, she might think it's only fair if we offered Tim the same amount and then we'd be looking at twice the outlay . . .'

'I'm pretty sure Tim doesn't need any of your cash, Dad.'

'Well perhaps not, perhaps not – but it's about fairness isn't it, we have to treat you both equally. You're both our children.'

'But you are my only parent, Dad. You are the only person actually obliged to support me.'

This might have been the first time she'd ever said it out loud, though she'd thought it plenty, tucking it hastily away beneath some mental rug each time it reared up. Besides her ailing grandmother, his mother, who was ninety-two and actively unpleasant, her father was her entire blood family. Her whole safety net. And he was looking at her as though she were asking him for coins on the tube.

'I told you, we'll be giving you a nice chunk from the sale of the house, of course we will – it might even be enough for your own deposit, if you wanted, or I could help you look at one of those shared-ownership deals. It's just going to take a while to get everything sorted, you know, you might need to be patient while—'

'That isn't the point, it's not about *money*, Dad. I don't mean financial support, I mean *support*-support. I'm having to go out and cobble together my own family from bits of other people's.'

'Well of course Bryony, I'm always here for you. You know that.'

'Do I?' she said. 'Do I know that? You can't just say words, Dad, they actually have to mean something. If you're "always here" for me then why are you never fucking here, right here, for me? Soon you won't even be in the country for me.'

'It's only *France*, for pity's sake!' His face was turning purplish. She wondered what his blood pressure was these days, whether she needed to start worrying that her safety net was going to keel over on the golf course.

'You're in your mid-thirties, Bryony! I don't think it's unreasonable to assume you're self-sufficient by this point. If I'd known you were having . . . personal problems, perhaps things would have been different, but it's not like you ever call, not like you ever tell me anything.'

'Sorry, would you like me to phone every time I have a panic attack?' she asked.

'Are you having those?'

Richard looked genuinely concerned. He was probably imagining her hyperventilating, frothing at the mouth, causing a scene in a public precinct.

'Dad. Come on. I've had them since Mum died. I have spent a big chunk of the years since Mum died feeling like I'm dying, too.'

Bryony had always believed the first one of them to mention her mother lost the argument by default. But in this moment it felt like the strongest hand she had to play.

'Your funny turns, I know – but you've always had a healthy appetite for melodrama, Bryony.'

She bit down on her tongue in frustration and inhaled sharply through the pain. The blousy strains of Roxy Music's 'More Than This' could be heard above the coffee shop clatter.

'I have needed therapy, *proper therapy*, since Mum died,' she said slowly. 'So if it makes you feel better, backdate the payment twenty-four years. Or, why not, go and get some too. Treat yourself!'

He was quiet for a moment, wearing the same expression he used to wear at the end of their fights over curfews, over the way she spent her allowance, over what Kath considered 'appropriate' school shoes. The expression he wore when he knew he was bested.

Finally he said, 'I suppose they'll want to blame me for everything.'

She sighed. 'Is that what you're afraid of, that it's going to be one big, long Freudian dad-bash?'

He looked weary now, older and greyer amid his 'lively' surroundings. She felt a sudden urge to see him in France after all; to see her father happy and energetic, riding bikes through lavender fields with an ex-pat's chestnut tan.

'No, Bryony,' he said, quietly. 'I'm afraid I'd deserve it.'

71

Better to keep it off the carpet

Phlegmma Thompson and Dave the Grave appear to have formed an alliance. It's hard to say whether this is romantic or more a kind of workers' union, but they sit together now, muttering under their breath to each other between moans and coughs.

One day, Dave walks up to the counter and presents Kelly with a slip of paper bearing the sum total of the hours they have spent over the past year, either in the waiting room or on the phone to the surgery. He presents it like he is playing a trump card, mouth set in a line of grim performance, and even Kelly is shocked at the number.

'I'm very sorry,' she told him, and suggested they take it up with one of the managing partners. 'We are incredibly busy at the present time.'

'What present time?' he'd said. 'Tory Britain?'

'Yes,' Kelly had replied, and he had accepted this and gone to sit back down.

Life is different now that she's spending so much more time herself on the hard plastic chairs; now she is a patient being thanked for her patience too. Kelly always thought she had the inside track on the ailing NHS, but it's only now she's regularly pissing in a margarine tub because the midwife has run out of sample pots again, that she feels, viscerally, the service pulling apart at the seams.

After so many years as a robustly healthy person it has come as a cruel surprise, to feel this bad all the time. And even though there is no mystery illness in her case – turns out pregnancy is the blanket diagnosis to rule them all – she finds the condition is filled with smaller mysteries. What's that twinge? That itch? That taste? Is this a bad sign or a good one? Each day brings a new cause for concern, another urgent Google, until she finds herself identifying with Phlegmma and Dave and Alfred Itch Cock, Bryony, even, more than she ever thought possible.

It's hard not to see signs in everything, from her craving for salt and vinegar Chipsticks, to her newly orchestral farts; each one a tiny flare sent up by her future child. Suddenly, danger lurks around every corner – every hot bath a risk, every egg a vessel for salmonella, every man at the bus stop a potential psychopath who might push her under a moving car.

'Babe, it'll be fiiiine,' says Leo when she wakes in the middle of the night lying on her back, and screams. 'The midwife said it was okay until sixteen weeks. And the odds for these things are tiny anyway, you know that. They have to cover themselves.'

She knows it academically, but she does not feel it. Now she has precious cargo on board, the whole world seems to have been designed to trip her up.

Kelly begins feeling panicked every time someone wheezes their way up to the counter. Even the plastic screen doesn't feel like sufficient protection from the legions of lurgies that walk through the door daily. She starts wearing a mask behind the counter again, which doesn't raise an eyebrow among the patients but attracts comments and jibes from her colleagues on this sudden, fastidious turn.

One of the GPs asks if she has a cold sore; another assumes she has had a botched cosmeceutical treatment. She laughs along with them, but doesn't explain.

And all the time, Ann is calling.

Their relationship was never like this before she got pregnant, and it is hard to know whether the sea-change has come on account of Ann's future grandchild, her grief, or because Bryony encouraged this behaviour and left the floodgates open behind her. She calls to recommend radio programmes and TV documentaries about experimental child-rearing in Denmark. She calls to ask if Kelly is sleeping with a pillow between her knees, and if she's heard of something called an 'Aniball' because a neighbour has one she can lend ('It's been through the dishwasher!').

Today she is calling to offer her services as Kelly's doula.

'I know it must be so hard for you, ducks, without your own mum at the birth, so I wanted you to know that I'm more than happy to lend a hand. I'm qualified, you know – I took a course before Molly at The Stag and Barrow had her twins.'

Kelly tells her that she wouldn't have had her own mum at the birth even if she were alive, but Ann only laughs as though she is joking and tells her, 'You need someone who's seen it all before, Kelly. I wouldn't trust my son not to faint at the sight of a tearing perineum. And if you wanted to put an inflatable pool in our kitchen I can easily move the furniture out. Better to keep it off the carpet, you know – for an easier clean-up?'

Kelly tries to follow this train of thought back to its murky origin, but fails.

'Ann, I'll be having the baby here. In London. At a hospital.'

'Oh! Well I suppose if that's your preference, but I just thought you might be local by then and you know the maternity department at the General has a terrible rating, Susan's niece had a load of shocking trouble with a catheter – and we probably have more space for the pool than you would have, especially if you go for one of the mews cottages? Although I suppose you could put it in the garden, weather pending!'

'Ann, I'm not sure what you—'

'Gally told me you were thinking of moving back this way!'

The scary thing is she doesn't even know when these conversations happen. Sometimes she wonders if he sneaks out of bed after she's asleep, to debrief his mother.

'Oh. I mean, we *talked* about it, like, as a hypothetical – but obviously it wouldn't work right now, not with our jobs and stuff . . .'

The 'stuff' is Kelly's longtime aversion to farm smell and her need to live within five miles of a Space NK.

'But he could work from home! Just commute down once a week, plenty of them do it, especially since the pandemic.'

'Yes but *my* job, Ann. I can't do that from home.'

'Oh, well – you'll be on maternity leave! Plenty of time to find something else up here. In fact I could ask around, they might need someone in Billingham's.'

'The *butchers*?'

'I'm just brainstorming, Kelly! But we know you're not squeamish about blood and guts, that could work in your favour. Not like my delicate son.'

'No,' says Kelly, faintly.

'And it would make sense to do it sooner rather than later, lord knows you don't want to be moving with a newborn – although in fairness we did with Tigs, but then she was never any trouble . . .'

She says this as though it is a given that Kelly's baby will be trouble.

'How is Annie?' asks Kelly. This is the deflection tactic she has landed on over the years, whenever she wants to steer Ann out of a conversational cul-de-sac. Ask about one of her children. It occurs to her with a pang that her options in this respect have been recently halved.

'She's fine,' says Ann. 'It sounds like her business is really picking up, she's just bought a load more of the gel what-have-yous.'

'Oh?' says Kelly. 'So she's actually sold some, then?'

'Well I would assume so, Kelly,' Ann says, defensive. 'Anyway, it was very good of you and Gally to put in a bit more, she said having that bit extra to replenish her stocks has made all the difference. Something about reaching a special level? I don't pretend to understand it all, but apparently it's very impressive. We would have lent it ourselves of course, but it's looking like Twinkle might need a hip replacement and Emmett's cashed in all his premium bonds.'

Already exhausted by the conversation, it takes Kelly a moment to register what Ann has said.

'Sorry, we've lent her more money? Recently?'

'Oh I assumed you'd discussed it!'

'No,' said Kelly, plainly. 'We hadn't.'

'Well, you know the boys have always had a soft spot where their little sister is concerned. And Tiggy is very confident you'll see a return on your investment. Some people are making six figures, apparently!'

Kelly makes a noise. The foul taste in her mouth has returned.

'Besides,' adds Ann, 'he works so hard, I'm sure you'd never want to stop him spending his wages as he sees fit.'

And Kelly says sorry but she has to go now, because she thinks she might be sick. She only has limited time in which to end conversations this way, so she may as well make the most of it.

72

Fine, fine!

When Kelly's name came up on her phone, Bryony's first thought was that perhaps the doctors' surgery was firing her as a patient. Her second thought was that the Slingsby family were suing her for impersonating a loved one's loved one, and her third thought was that there was some kind of mistake with the tests and it was really she who was pregnant after all.

Before she could have a fourth thought, she answered.

'Hi! Ah, Kelly? How are you doing?'

'Oh, fine,' said Kelly, briskly. 'Fine, fine!'

'But how are you feeling? With, you know – the baby and everything?' Bryony was genuinely curious. A part of her still felt like Kelly was a kind of surrogate, taking on the physical burden that she had been spared.

Kelly laughed, hollowly. 'Oh I feel like shit on a plate, babe. But that's all part of the deal isn't it? Can't complain.'

Bryony wanted to tell her that she absolutely could complain, but Kelly had moved on.

'Look, could we get a coffee sometime soon? There's something I need to talk to you about.'

'Oh! Sure, that would be really . . . really, um—'

'Good. How's Saturday?'

It was hard to work out from her tone whether Bryony was in trouble or about to do her a favour. It didn't sound as though even Kelly quite knew. But curiosity pulled her back into the Slingsby orbit as it had so many times before.

'Sure, Saturday works for me!' she told her. 'Where? Can I come to you, make it easier?'

'Great. Wherever you like, just message me the details,' said Kelly, sounding more impatient than gracious. 'Not the cat place.'

Bryony debated the location for far too long. It was more comfortable than pondering the reason for the invite.

Kelly seemed like the kind of person who liked places with an arch of fake flowers around the doorway. But if this was a doomy coffee, if Bryony was about to be served legal papers for her part in the Great Ed Deception, she'd rather it didn't happen underneath a neon sign urging her to live, laugh, latte.

Eventually she settled on a quaint kind of patisserie shop, with no neon but old French soap adverts on the walls. On the walk over she rehearsed her boundary-setting, muttering 'Thank you but I'm busy,' under her breath like a mantra. She repeated it until the words slid together into a meaningless putter-putter noise, and she had to apply more lip balm.

Kelly didn't look like shit on a plate. She looked like the most glamorous person in the cafe on merit of being the only person not wearing Birkenstock clogs. But as she ordered a peppermint tea, refused a pastry and lowered herself into her seat with nervous precision, Bryony could see the spots along her jawline, the waxen pallor beneath her immaculate contour. It was a familiar energy. She looked hungover.

'How are you feeling?' she asked again, tearing into an almond croissant before Kelly's condition could infect her too.

'Oh yeah, fine! Fine,' Kelly insisted, suppressing a small belch behind a manicured hand. 'Can't complain! I mean, it could be worse. Apparently ten weeks is when your hormones peak? Loads of women start feeling better after this bit. Apparently. Some of them. I think I might be already.'

'Great!' Bryony smiled back. She sent up a silent prayer that Kelly wasn't one of those casual vomiters who thought nothing of doing it in public, into a bin or a carrier bag.

'You must both be so happy,' she said.

'Sure,' said Kelly, looking unsure. 'I mean, not *happy*-happy – obviously it's still a pretty weird time, what with Ed . . .'

'Of *course*, yes.' Bryony shifted her expression into her grieving girlfriend one. After a few weeks out of action, her facial muscles creaked.

'Lots of emotions flying around. What with the grief, and the hormones, and the family getting . . . well, involved . . .'

'Mm,' said Bryony. 'I can imagine.'

'I mean, obviously I *love* Ann . . .' said Kelly.

'Oh me too!' Bryony added quickly. 'She's brilliant, isn't she?'

'Totally,' agreed Kelly. 'So strong. Really inspirational to be honest.'

'Completely,' echoed Bryony.

The women paused and sipped their drinks. Kelly fiddled with her hair, and coughed queasily. Bryony flinched.

'You know you can complain though, yeah? It's okay not to be enjoying this part of the process.'

'Sure, I know,' says Kelly, 'But we were trying to get pregnant for a *while*. I don't want to sit around whinging when I'm supposed to be grateful, cherishing every second.'

'I think you're allowed not to cherish the seconds you spend with your head down the toilet,' said Bryony and Kelly smiled. 'You know that if men had to have babies they'd be churning them out on 3D printers by now and complaining that the buttons hurt their fingers.'

'Yeah. Maybe.'

'No, seriously.' Bryony could feel her eyes widening in earnest, it seeming suddenly important to give Kelly this reassurance, as a kind of gift. A thank-you, or an apology. 'Pregnancy hormones are *wild*; I read that some of them increase up to a thousand times. They say it's comparable with puberty. You know parts of your *brain* are actually changing shape?'

'Ha. I know,' said Kelly, weakly, although she didn't look as though she had known this, or was especially glad to.

'It's woefully under-researched,' Bryony went on. 'Like, they spend millions on curing erectile dysfunction but we barely know *anything*, still, about all the ways pregnancy fucks with your mind and body. But people expect women to just suck it up and float around being stoical and grateful, and *normal*, when actually you're going through this massive, gruelling experience with pieces of yourself being leached away at for months, and then you're going to be thrown into the other massive, gruelling experience of parent-hood before your body or brain have even recovered, if they ever truly recover – and then there's *birth*, which is basically still Medieval but glorified to such an extent that women feel like failures if they ask for pain relief, and it's . . . it's . . .'

Kelly had turned a shade of pale chartreuse, reminiscent of a hospital corridor.

'. . . it's . . . a lot,' finished Bryony, dumbly. 'Sorry, anyway, the point is: you're absolutely allowed to complain. To me, if you like. It seems like the least I can do.'

'Thanks, hun.' She mustered a smile. 'I appreciate it.'

There was a pause. Bryony chased croissant flakes around her plate with a dampened finger. Kelly took a series of delicate sips from a monogrammed water bottle.

Each table in the cafe was occupied by a different mum group. Bryony pictured them all warring like the gangs in *West Side Story*, pirouetting with their Bugaboos, hurling Lamaze toys like throwing stars. It was hard not to tune into snatches of their conversations, which pinballed from scars and stitches to shallow latches and cradle cap, to Netflix recommendations and nursery school waitlists and sleep consultants and the relative merits of something called a 'catchy'.

She wondered how she and Kelly, with her blow-dry and nail extensions, no visible bump yet, looked to those women. Did they symbolize something other? Something they remembered being, missed being, or were proud not to be anymore?

'So, what was it you wanted to—'

Kelly cut across her, looking relieved the small talk portion of their meeting was over.

'You need to get Annie out of this pyramid scheme.'

'I . . . what?'

'The pyramid scheme. You're getting Annie out of it,' she repeated.

'Multi-level marketing scheme,' corrected Bryony, uselessly.

'Whatever, you're getting her out of it,' said Kelly. Then she seemed to switch tack and try a softer approach. 'I *need* you to get her out of it. Please. She's borrowed a heap of money off Leo and we can't afford not to get it back.'

Despite all her hard work to reprogram, Bryony was annoyed to find her ego bending towards the request like a flower to the sun.

'I mean, I'll help if I can – but I don't quite see *how* I can, especially not after . . .' she trailed off, the memory of yelling 'casually fucking!' at Ed's bereaved sister crashing to the front of her brain like a lewd pop-up ad.

'Oh god no, she won't want to talk to you,' agreed Kelly, which was painful if fair. 'But she respects you – or, you know, she did. I need you to try because you're the only one who knows how this whole gel thing works. You have the inside track.'

Because you're the only one stupid enough to have joined, was the unspoken end to her sentence. Bryony grimaced inwardly.

'I only joined because I wanted to support Annie,' she insisted. It bothered her a great deal, she realized, if Kelly thought she was an idiot.

'I thought you'd joined because you felt so guilty after we saw you on that date,' said Kelly.

'Well, yes. That too.' She grimaced outwardly. 'So what do you need me to do? What's the plan?'

'I don't have one, babe,' Kelly sighed. 'I thought I did but . . . well, I dunno, it hasn't worked. And time is ticking. But I'm sure you can come up with something.'

'Oh. Right.'

Thank you but I'm busy thank you but I'm—

'You like a scheme, don't you Bryony? Big into the capers?'

Kelly was grinning but not malevolently, and for a moment it felt as though they were back on Ann's bathroom floor again. She accepted that if this was her comeuppance, it could be worse. She thought about the doctor's call, and the surprisingly quick therapy referral, and the calm, selfless offer of an abortion buddy. She thought about all the times she'd darkened Kelly's reception desk in the past.

busy but I'm thank you but—

'I'll see what I can do,' she told her. 'Leave it with me.'

73

A season, a reason
or a lifetime

As it turned out, 'leave it with me' was an easy thing to say but a far harder thing to follow through on.

Bryony had 'reached out' to Annie multiple times – texts, DMs, even several courageous phone calls – and received no answer. After leaving all the Gel Lyfe group chats in one fell swoop she was surprised to find she couldn't get back in without a personal invitation. The daily word salads from *Tamara xoxo* were as plentiful and bountiful as ever, but alongside pep talks on self-belief and 'letting the world see her power' she seemed to have been added to a new mailing list, this one specially for gelievers who had been marked as a flight risk. 'Don't be a doubter!' shrieked this morning's email. 'If you let negativity in, you let negativity WIN.'

On Instagram, Annie posted a photo of herself in a field, eyes closed and arms stretched wide, accompanied by a missive against the doubters, the haters, and so-called 'stifling people'.

Do not listen to the stifflers [sic]*, who only want to hold us back and keep us within their comfort zone because if we achieve our full potential then they might have to confront the fact they aren't living up to theirs and that scares them!!!*

That Bryony was a stiffler seemed obvious. She liked the post, to be defensive.

She checked her bank balance, and did a little more breathwork. When this failed to shift the feeling that an adult pig was sitting on her chest, she remembered Ewa's tension release exercise and tried biting down hard on a silicone cupcake case, which only made one of her incisors hurt.

That evening, Marco walked into the bathroom in his underwear to find her cleaning it. This was a disturbing first for them both.

'I thought you were scared to use bleach in case you accidentally inhaled it?' he said, swiftly pulling on a dressing gown.

'I read this article online, about how physical clutter in our surroundings can actually impact on our physical wellbeing – like, literally cause stress symptoms, which makes us feel overwhelmed, which in turn makes us less able to do basic self-care tasks like cleaning and tidying. It's a whole thing.' She returned to chipping limescale off the base of the tap.

'What have I told you about staying off Reddit?'

'It was *The Atlantic*! Anyway, I thought if I really get on top of the housework, it might help with my symptoms.'

She took a swig from a mug of Gel Lyfe. She'd carbonated it, semi-successfully, in an old Soda Stream.

'You didn't want to start with the mountain of cult juice instead?'

Bryony shook her head. 'Can't face it.'

'May I suggest something?' Marco asked, sitting down on the toilet lid with a heavy air of forbearance.

Bryony paused, a clump of drain hair in her hand like a class pet. 'You may.'

He cleared his throat. 'Perhaps you miss them?'

'Who?'

'Egg Man's family. The Eggs.'

'Oh. Them. I wouldn't have thought so.'

'Brian.'

She could tell he wanted to take her face in his hands but was put off by the drain hair. For a man who spent his days immersed in fur and animal fluids, Marco was oddly squeamish about human debris.

'Look, I'm not saying it wasn't fully insane, what you did, because it was.'

'I'm aware.'

'Completely batshit.'

'Yes, alright.'

'And part of me wants to tell you to leave that poor family alone, they've been through enough, do not darken their wonky doorway again——'

'Okay thank you!'

'But then I think, well. What is an evolved society if not the freedom to choose a surrogate mum when you need one? Drag queens have house mothers, public schoolboys have matron. Orphaned monkeys imprint on a bit of wire in a sock. Maybe you have Ann.'

'I don't have Ann! I didn't chose her to be anything,' she protested. 'It was simply a very sad and weird mistake, and it's over now.'

'Well, maybe the universe has chosen her for you,' he said. 'People come into your life for a season, a reason or a lifetime, and Susan sent me that on Facebook so I know it must be true.'

'*Ann's* Susan?'

Marco shrugged. 'Some of us haven't been so quick to sever ties, Bryony.'

74

Pregnant, actually

Kelly has forgotten all about Jenna McKenzie and her stool sample by the time she comes back to the surgery.

'Kels! You're still here!' she says, from behind Chanel sunglasses and a vast, monogrammed scarf. 'What's new?'

Feeling immediately defensive, Kelly blurts, 'I'm pregnant, actually.'

She hasn't told anyone yet. Plenty of people *know*, of course – an entire galaxy of Slingsby relations, Pete the Little Buckton postie, Susan's niece who knits mutant unicorn-mermaids and does 'very reasonable commissions' – but she has not told anyone, personally. It's still too early. She's still too scared. And if she's really honest, she doesn't want to tell anyone, because whoever she does tell first will not be her mother.

Still though, she could have found a worthier recipient than Jenna McKenzie.

'Oh my god congrats! I'm so happy for you! How are you feeling? You *look* GREAT,' she says, which Kelly is baffled by because she doesn't. Her skin is terrible, her hair lank. She assumes this means 'you look thin,' which can't be denied because she's living on oat-cakes and Smints.

'Thanks,' says Kelly, embarrassed to be fussed over when she has only done the thing that girls she went to school with have been doing for the past twenty years. Some of them have kids in secondary, now. Some of them have kids who can *drive*.

'Anyway, what are you here for?'

Jenna takes her shades off, as though only now realizing she had them on inside. Her eyes beneath are bare of makeup and her long, feathery lash extensions are crushed and wonky, like a bird's broken wing.

'It's my test results. The . . . ah, sample, you remember, that I brought in? I know it was ages ago they called me about it but for some reason I've only just got my shit together to actually book the appointment. Life's been manic!'

She laughs, although it isn't particularly funny, and as Kelly checks her in on the system she feels she ought to return the gushing, so she asks, 'How are your kids?'. Jenna looks confused and says she doesn't have any.

'Oh,' says Kelly. 'I assumed you did.' She didn't know she was allowed to describe life as 'manic' over the age of thirty-five without it including nursery pick-ups.

'No,' says Jenna, playing with the tassels on her giant scarf. 'Hopefully one day. Hasn't quite happened yet, for various reasons. But congratulations to you and your fit hubby though, that's so wonderful!'

Then Jenna sits down and looks at her phone until she is called for her appointment, and Kelly spends the rest of the day feeling awful. For various reasons.

75

Boundaries

As Valentine's Day approached Bryony found herself wondering what plans would be afoot in Little Buckton. Disco in the scout hut? Heart-shaped sausages in the butchers?

She never celebrated it – not since her early twenties, when an ex had told her, genuinely baffled at her upset to not receive anything, that he thought Valentine's Day was 'for children'. Culturally it was hard to know where we were now. The Clintons Industrial Complex had been so thoroughly denounced for so many years that it was more fashionable at this point to defend Valentine's Day and your right to commercialized romance, to go all in on hearts and teddies and red lace suspender belts, but Bryony wasn't sure. She'd lost track; maybe we'd flipped back to cynicism again.

The apps were, if anything, quieter than usual because nobody wanted to appear to be fishing for a Valentine. Nobody wanted to have the *'When are you free?'*, *'Thursday but would that be too weird lol'* exchange. And nobody wanted to endure whatever gimmick Alloi's marketing team came up with to encourage spawning, like research scientists playing Barry White to lab rats.

In the platonic realm, Bryony had received invites to two Galentine's dinners, a British Library lecture on 'What the

Romantic poets can teach us about self-love' and three different Nora Ephron screenings. She had turned them all down with her newfound superpower – *'No thanks!' 'Sorry I'm busy!' 'Not my bag, but enjoy!'* – shivering with adrenaline each time she hit 'send'.

It was thrilling until the day itself rolled round and she found herself with no plans except a lunchtime smear test.

'Not even dinner first?!' she quipped as the nurse winched open the speculum. 'Sorry, I bet I'm not the first person to say that.'

'Every single one today,' said the nurse.

It was a relief that there was no sign of Kelly in the surgery, as progress on getting Annie to quit Gel Lyfe remained stalled at 'Stage 1: get Annie to speak to me'. On her way back to work, she bumped into her friend Laura, who was carrying a vast bouquet of pink tea roses. Laura looked embarrassed about it.

'I told him to scale it back this year, but you know what Doug's like,' she said.

Bryony did know what Doug was like – he was like a man who earned a lot of money and wanted everyone to know it. She admired the flowers nonetheless, and they made small talk until Laura's expression turned grave and she said:

'So, are we . . . okay?'

Bryony flinched.

'Of course! Why wouldn't we be?'

'It's just – well, you were pretty curt with me about the pottery thing.'

Bryony silently despaired for a moment. Apparently society's delicate calibration couldn't handle her sudden vibe shift. She swallowed down the sorries that rose in her throat.

'Oh, it's a new thing I'm trying,' she explained. 'You know – setting more boundaries, getting better at saying no. It was my new year's resolution.'

'Right,' said Laura. 'Well, you might want to do it more gently. I was quite hurt.'

'I'm so sorry!' Bryony blurted out before she could stop herself. Was it possible that just being honest with everyone *wasn't* the path to inner peace and contentment?

'I thought you hated me or something.'

'Why would I hate you?' said Bryony.

'I don't know! I thought maybe because I called your hair "fun" that time?'

'Did you? I don't even remember that,' said Bryony. 'I promise, you didn't do anything at all. It was just the boundaries thing.'

'Okay phew!' Laura looked visibly relieved. 'Not that I want to disrespect your boundaries, obviously,' she caveated. 'But maybe you need to warn people about them before you, like, put them into place? So people don't get such a shock.'

Bryony considered this. She pictured a disclaimer like a road sign. *'Warning! Boundary ahead'*. She fiddled with her scrunchie and wondered if Laura was right about her hair.

'I feel like that would defeat the object?'

'Or maybe you could say no without being quite so blunt about it? You know, soften it up. Add a few exclamation marks.'

'Mm,' said Bryony. 'Maybe I just need more practice.'

Laura agreed that maybe she did.

The flat was empty that evening. Marco was working a locum shift at a 24-hour hospital 'because if I'm going to spend my Valentine's beneath a great slavering animal, I may as well get paid for it.' Bryony made dinner slowly, taking the time to caramelize onions and zest lemons and finely chop herbs, garnishing the whole thing as though she were hosting an elegant dinner for twelve. *Demand more for yourself!*

She poured a goblet of wine, running her fingers up and down the stem of the glass like a sensual woman in a film. As she ate, she listened to the *futzz futzz futzz* of club music coming from their downstairs neighbour, and reassured herself that alone or not, they were having a less romantic night than she was.

After resisting for a heroic amount of time, she gave in to the inevitable and picked up her phone.

Alloi was buzzing, a fresh slew of notifications in her inbox and a full carousel of faces 'online and looking for a chemical reaction – with you??'.

She swiped, demanding more for herself, drinking down each micro-hit of dopamine until her thumb started to ache. Five more, then bath and bed, she told herself in the manner of a weary parent. She had a novel to read, something critically acclaimed with words like 'searing' and 'urgent' on the cover. She had a clean-ish pair of pyjamas to slip into and the rest of the wine to finish. She had a five-step cleansing routine to perform. She had a life to live. Two more, then bed.

She could feel herself growing slack–jawed, repetition lulling her into a sleepy trance. She was at one with the sofa now, embedded. It was hard to tell where its padding ended and hers began.

Three more, then bed.

Bryony sat upright with a jolt as his face filled her screen, more tanned than she'd ever seen it, smiling affably at a bar somewhere in mainland Europe. Steve.

Seeing him on the app felt exposing, like walking in on him in the shower. His photos were sweet – a modest selection of selfies and holiday snaps, none of them, she was relieved to see, holding a freshly-caught fish. Ed appeared in one of them, a group shot featuring men all familiar to her now from various village/death events, and her stomach contorted as she recognised the same photo from his own profile. It would be rare for women to choose the same group shot. Usually in every photo there was a clear winner.

Just as she was trying to guess the location (her money was on the 19th annual Brigstock-stock), she noticed something else unnerving. Steve had liked her profile. Or in Alloi parlance, 'taken a shine' to her. A silver heart pulsed, coyly, in the corner of the screen.

Thanks to the app's shonky functionality, there was no immediate way to tell *when* he had liked her, so Bryony found herself sifting through two years' of inbox notifications, virtual flirtations and impotent DM-slides. It turned out numerous Steves had liked her in that time, their eager faces turning into a kind of Steve soup as she scrolled back through the months in search of . . . well, not *her* Steve. Ed's Steve.

Finally, she found it. April. Steve had liked her profile before she'd even met Ed and that felt somehow stranger than him hitting on his dead friend's ex.

Would he remember? Almost certainly not, nobody remembered the profiles they'd swiped on nearly a year ago. Had Ed shown him her photos, had he recognised her? And if so, had he kept it to himself, or had they laughed about it and bantered crudely about taking turns? She sensed it was the former.

It didn't *mean* anything, not in the frenzied trolley dash that was dating apps. She'd taken a shine to enough virtual men to light a football stadium. And yet seeing him here, a souvenir of Little Buckton, in between all the Uniqlo bum bags and topless mirror selfies, it was impossible not to see it as some kind of sign. Could he help her convince Annie to listen to her, at least? Steve had been her route in, her friendly concierge to the Slingsbys' world – it felt fitting that he might be her bridge back.

She felt fully awake, wired, even, as she hit the silver heart icon and tried to compose a message, any message that was not 'Fancy seeing you here!'

'Hey stranger!' *Ew. No.*

'Well, hello there!' *Absolutely not.*

'Hi Steve.' *Nauseating.*

Hours passed, tides turned, empires rose and fell. Eventually she drained the last of her wine, typed *'Fancy seeing you here!'*, hit send and crawled into bed.

76

Not like a date

Bryony woke to a furry mouth, a pounding head and a sinking feeling. Her message to Steve remained blessedly unread, but there was no way to guarantee he hadn't seen it. She couldn't explain why, but Steve didn't seem like the kind of guy who turned off email alerts.

'Sorry, the rest never sent!' she added. Oh, faithful friend. She wondered what people did before they could use that lie. *The answerphone ran out of tape. The post carriage was held up by highwaymen.*

'Sorry if this is weird, but I wondered if you wanted to have a drink sometime? Not like a date! Obviously. Just, I feel terrible about the way I left everything with Ann and the family – and I could use your help with something. If you have time.'

She sat on her hands for a full minute before wrenching them free to add, 'No worries if not!'

'hey stranger,' he messaged back ten minutes later. 'sure sounds good. i'm in town tonight if you're around?'

If Steve was harbouring a grudge after her new year's antics, he didn't show it. His greeting was as warm and earnest as ever, stumbling a little as he leapt to pull out a chair for her, splitting his crisp packet down the middle so they could share. It was a Friday night in Soho and the pub was heaving, body heat clouding the stained glass windows from within, while the overspill steamed them up with warm breath and vape emissions from the pavement.

He was wearing his familiar jumper, this time with jeans and boots, his hair shorter and a pair of tortoiseshell-rimmed glasses gifting his face new angles. Out of his usual context, he didn't look like an off-duty fisherman. Or rather, he did, but only in the way that 'off-duty fisherman' was a dominant aesthetic in many parts of London. It worked for him.

'Why are you on the app in London?' she asked him, shouting above the noise. 'Has Little Buckton run out of women who aren't cousins?'

He laughed and shouted back. 'Nah, I'm just down here a lot for work.'

'Building work?' She still didn't know what Steve did for a living, only that he owned a ladder. Her brain had added a pair of paint-splattered overalls in post-production.

'Ah, sort of,' he said. 'I'm a chartered surveyor. The firm's based out of Milton Keynes but a lot of our big clients these days are London projects so I'm having to come down more and more for site visits. We specialize in sustainable developments.'

'Right, of course.' She nodded as though she already knew this, hoping the surprise didn't register on her face. It was so tempting to stall for time, to ask him about his favourite parts of surveying and the most effective types of loft insulation – but if she started trying to treat this as a normal, friendly drink, Steve would be entirely justified in getting up and walking out. It was a miracle he was even here.

'So,' she said.

'So.' He sipped his pint and waited.

'I don't know how much you heard about–'

'Oh, I reckon it's safe to say all of it.'

'Right. Well then, firstly, I'm sorry. I'm really sorry. I made some very questionable decisions.'

Steve nodded, his expression neutral. 'I reckon that's accurate.'

Bryony grimaced. 'Look, I'm not excusing myself but I want you to know I honestly never intended to deceive anyone. I'm not a sociopath. It just felt kinder to keep up the charade, for a bit, than tell the truth and cause more pain when everyone was already hurting so much.'

She had read enough critiques of non-apologies on the internet to know how a legitimate one should go, and she knew she was being defensive. But as much as she longed to clear her conscience, she had a newfound commitment to the truth.

'I thought I'd just have tea with Ann, say some nice things about Ed and then sort of . . . melt away into the ether. But I could never find the right point to start melting. Everyone was so welcoming and the invites kept coming and – well, look, I've never been very good at saying no to people.'

'Yeah I picked up on that.'

'It's something I'm working on.'

'Well,' said Steve, after a beat. 'As long as it's been an opportunity for personal growth.'

The words felt wounding, but his mouth was twitching at the corners. She tried to direct her eyes elsewhere.

'Honestly Steve, I am so sorry. I really fucked up.'

There was another pause as he took a swig and beneath the table, Bryony dug her nails deep into the palm of her hand.

'For what it's worth,' said Steve, eventually, weighing each word as though in a witness box, 'I think it was quite a sweet thing that you did.'

'Really?'

'Yeah. I mean, batshit—'

'Yes, thank you.'

'. . . but sweet. It came from a good place, clearly.'

'It did!' She felt her shoulders drop and her lungs fill with the relief of being taken in good faith. 'But if I'm honest, it was more than that. I was confused. Why would Ed tell everyone we were a serious couple when we weren't? It made me think I was the deluded one, like we'd been soulmates the whole time and I just hadn't noticed.'

Steve's expression was hard to read. Her mind twitched towards Ed's diary, which was wrapped in two jumpers and buried in the bottom of her chest of drawers like contraband, wondering if it contained the words 'Carshalton Beeches' surrounded by little doodled hearts. She hadn't even told Marco it existed, much less that she had stolen it. At this point she wasn't sure if she was resisting reading it on moral grounds, or because her ego would prefer not to know the truth.

'That's a headfuck,' he said finally. 'Look Bryony, I wish I had answers for you. Ed was my best mate and I loved him, but it doesn't mean he didn't make a few questionable decisions too.'

'Like telling his friends and family he had a girlfriend when he didn't?'

'Like that, yeah.'

'"Smitten" was the word you used, I think?'

Steve was the one looking uncomfortable now. She could see the pull of posthumous loyalty behind his eyes, and she understood. Nobody wants to call their dead friend a big fat liar.

'I guess maybe a few details got a bit . . . what's the word – *embellished*, along the way? Thing is Bryony, I can't really remember now how much I heard from him directly, one-on-one, and how much was him talking about you in front of his family, or other people talking about you, the whole village whisper network. You know what it's like.'

'I do know what it's like. I've had the whole village whisper network phoning me up to chat. But Steve,' she pressed a little harder, why not, 'you said it was the happiest you'd ever seen him. With me. Or was that pure coincidence?'

Steve shook his head.

'He *was* happy, those last few months, I swear. Ann likes to talk shit about his life in London but every Friday when he got back to Buckton he had this sort of . . . *glow* about him, like he'd been on holiday.'

This image of Ed was so at odds with the way London had made her feel recently – the grey-skinned, sweaty-backed, overpriced grind of it all – that she couldn't help but feel tender towards him. The big fat liar.

Steve turned sheepish.

'But if we're being completely honest Bryony, I suppose there was also an element of . . . y'know.'

'What?'

'Well. It's just the kind of thing you say, isn't it? To be nice.'

'Aha!' she shouted, a little too keenly. 'You see!'

He smiled to show the irony wasn't lost on him. 'Also – look, I didn't want to mention this because it seemed unfair to drag her into it, but . . . well, Ed had an ex. A real one, back in Buckton. They were pretty serious for a while a few years ago, but then she broke up with him and his mum never really got over it. I'm not sure Ed did either to be honest, but it was Ann that took it hardest – never forgave her, started blanking her mum in the corner shop, all of it. Couldn't believe anyone would do that to her poor Ethy.'

'Hang on,' said Bryony, remembering the woman at the funeral. 'Does she have long red hair?'

'That's her,' said Steve. 'Isobel. Ann calls her Jezebel.'

Bryony winced, wondering if she'd been similarly rechristened.

'Anyway, here's my theory, right? I wouldn't be surprised if Ed was just exaggerating about you and him to please Ann. To reassure her he would . . . you know. Find love again. Ed was a family guy, a generous guy. He liked to keep people happy.'

She laughed hollowly. 'I guess we did have something in common then. But lying to his whole family – lying to you! It just feels very . . . I don't know, childish.'

Steve nodded, looking thoughtful. 'I s'pose when you think about it, childhood never really ends does it? Not in some ways. We're always still somebody's child. And Ann is a pretty hard character to say no to.'

'You don't say.'

She sensed an opportunity to shift the blame, but Steve wouldn't hear a word against Ann.

'I've known her a long time,' he said. 'My whole life, actually. She doesn't get everything right but she's as decent as they come. Was always there for me, growing up. I had a few problems at home – not always the best relationship with my folks, let's say – and she made her place like a second home for me – even when Ed wasn't there. Walk in when I liked, stay for dinner, sleep over, no questions asked.'

Bryony remembered with a pang Steve's story about the extra Gold bars in Ed's lunchbox. She'd found it hard to separate the memory of Ed from the lure of his family, but perhaps that was a common hazard when he was alive, too. The curse of the charismatic parent.

'But all those parties, when her son had literally just died. Don't you think it's odd? I worry she isn't okay.'

'Bryony.' Steve held her gaze for a moment, as if to make sure she was paying attention. 'Of course she isn't okay.'

The simplicity of the statement felt cool against her burning conscience. It was a relief to hear it put so plainly. Nobody was okay.

'She isn't doing it to be the centre of attention,' he went on, firmly but not unkindly. 'It's the opposite. All the feeding people and looking after everyone all the time – that's her thing, isn't it? Means she can pretend she hasn't noticed that really, everyone is there to look after her.'

Bryony stared at him. She thought about the hot mugs of tea in her hands, the cardigans round her shoulders. The physical weight of Ann's affection, at once warm and soft and stifling.

'You're very wise, Steve, do you know that?'

She expected him to shrug off the compliment with some *aw shucks* mumbling, but instead he nodded and said, 'I have my moments.'

'I suppose I got a bit addicted to it. All the being looked after, I mean. Ed never really knew this about me, but I can be a bit of a hypochondriac. In fact I've been in a massive spiral these past few months, thinking I was – well . . .'

'Dying?' he supplied.

'Yeah. Well, or pregnant. But mostly dying. I know it sounds ridiculous. I think stress manifests itself in a very physical way for me? I just feel really quite ill, really quite a lot of the time.'

He listened quietly as she explained – about the symptoms, the pain, the panic, the endless quest for cures – and Bryony found herself eager to hear what he would say. Steve might be an unlikely sage but no less suitable than the guy she'd once paid to clear her sinuses in a shipping container next to a microbrewery. He listened, and nodded, and looked sympathetic, and she hoped for something else beautiful and profound.

Eventually he said, 'Out of interest, have you tried not drinking?'

She squeaked in outrage.

'Sorry, you think I'm an alcoholic?' she said, her voice ringing out on the third syllable like struck glass. Steve made to reply, but she cut across him. 'You've only ever seen me at parties, pubs – New Year's Eve, for Christ's sake, you can't judge me on the booziest night of the year. I barely even drink usually, I swear. Besides, like you said, we all have our coping mechanisms! Ann throws parties, I drink at them.'

She had forgotten, in her indignation, that she hadn't really been grieving Ed and that Steve knew this. Graciously he didn't point it out.

'I'm not judging, Bryony, I only mention it because I know booze can mess around with your body. And your brain. It can make you feel like shit in a lot of weird ways beyond a hangover. I dunno. Might be worth a go, cutting down? Just to see.'

She stopped spluttering and took a defensive slug of her wine, which was too big and made her start spluttering again. Steve poured her some water.

'Look, I'm not saying you don't have a point. I know alcohol is a poison that the body must work twice as hard to eliminate, yada yada – but it's not that simple is it? Drinking is woven into the fabric of our society. It's part of how we live, how we socialize, how we celebrate. How we grieve. And women get judged so much more harshly for it than men do. I've rarely seen you without a pint in your hand, come to think of it.'

Steve smiled ruefully and said, 'Non-alcs.'

But Bryony was in full swing now. 'People don't *let* you not drink, it becomes the only thing they want to talk about and then it becomes the only thing *you* want to talk about and honestly I don't know if it's even healthy to cut things out entirely, you know, like it can make you fixate on the thing and end up bingeing and I have so few vices as it is that . . .' She paused. 'Sorry, what did you say?'

He raised his glass. 'Non-alcoholic beer. It's really come on in recent years, you can get decent IPAs and everything. Even outside of London, believe it or not.'

He maintained eye contact with her as he drained it down to the dregs, then wiped a little foamy residue off his beard with the back of his hand.

'You don't drink?' she said.

'Not anymore,' he told her. 'It didn't agree with me. Mentally. I went through a rough patch a few years back and realized the booze wasn't doing me any favours. Plus I saw what it did to a few of the other guys I knew; the fights, the wrecked relationships, the totalled cars. I can't say I don't miss it. I've craved it these past few months if I'm honest, but Bryony, I know I'd have been a bigger mess with it than without it. And Ed was always really sound about it. Used to buy us zero percenters for the football like it was no big deal at all. Such a good guy.'

Bryony absorbed all this slowly, nodding as her mind scrambled to reconfigure its picture of Steve. The wise sage fantasy was looking less absurd by the minute. She had a sudden visual of him barefoot in harem pants, placing hot stones on her naked back.

'You didn't think I stayed sober all those nights just to drive you to the station?'

'No!' she lied. 'Obviously not.'

Steve smirked.

'Thank you for telling me all that,' she said. 'I mean, I'm not saying I think drinking is the source of all my problems, but it's something to think about. And, you know, good for you.'

He shrugged. 'Yeah, well. We have to look after ourselves. Nobody else is going to do it for us.'

'Except Ann,' said Bryony, and when Steve laughed she felt a warmth inside her that wasn't anything to do with the wine.

They sat for a while, squatting on their little stools around the sticky table, the way she had with Ed so many times. No, not 'so many' times. Five. Precisely five times.

Looking around the room, she could see at least four other couples bearing all the hallmarks of the early app date. The bowed heads and coyly clunking knees, the self-conscious hair-tucking and 'good listener' faces.

'So.' She turned back to Steve's good listener face. 'Can I get you another one? Push the boat out with a nought-point-five percenter?'

He hesitated and she immediately regretted the joke. Maybe the nought point five percenters were still considered booze.

'Actually, I'm afraid I've got to head,' he said. 'I'm going to a gig.'

'Oh, sure! Don't worry.' Of course she was a bolt-on plan, not Steve's entire evening. He probably had a real date after this. 'Are you meeting people? What's the gig?'

She wondered why it was that when Steve said 'gig' it sounded normal, but when she said it, she sounded like a dowager aunt.

'No, I was going to go on my own.' He said it unselfconsciously, without embarrassment or pride. 'It's this singer – Indira Moss?'

Bryony hadn't heard of her, and resisted the urge to pretend that she had. She and Marco were a Radio 2 household aspiring to be a 6 Music household, but every time they tried 6 Music it seemed to be nothing but a series of middle-aged northern men talking about The Fall.

'Ed got me into her actually, used to play her in the car when we went away places. Beautiful voice. We used to take the piss because he usually only ever listened to Snow Patrol and the *Kill Bill* soundtrack, but then he discovered her on some forum and became a proper fanboy, bought her limited-run EPs and everything. I saw she was doing something tonight and I was down anyway so I booked it last-minute. I'll probably cry like a twat through the whole thing but I thought it might be a nice thing to do. Cathartic.'

She started to say how lovely, such a nice idea, she'd leave him to it – but then Steve said, 'Look, it's probably not sold out if you wanted to come? I don't know if it would be your bag, but—'

'I'd love to,' Bryony said immediately. She didn't know if it was wanting to experience this Ed Slingsby deep-cut for her notes, not wanting to go home and eat ramen alone in bed, or not feeling ready to leave Steve's presence that made her so sure.

77

Communion

On the way to the venue, they walked past the queue for Sheifale. It was already noticeably shorter than it had been on that Friday night in October, London's cauliflower-fanciers all having moved onto pastures new. Bryony almost pointed it out to Steve, told him that was where she'd been standing when they'd spoken for the first time – but she caught herself and thought better of it. That call had probably been one of the hardest of his life. None of this was anecdote to him.

She had assumed the gig would be in some sweaty basement bar or room above a pub, so it was a surprise when Steve led her to a private members' club in a townhouse just off Soho Square. It was an even greater surprise when they were directed through the warren of the building, all low lighting, floral wallpaper and velvet upholstery, into an ancient stone chapel, like a secret pearl, that the rest of the house had been built around.

It smelled like every church Bryony had ever been into – of old wood and warm spices, with actual pews and stained-glass windows uplit to look like a cult meeting or a Madonna video. She cooed her appreciation. Steve didn't try to pretend he was in the habit of taking women to secret private members chapel gigs. He merely grinned and said, 'Nice innit? I didn't know it would be like this.'

He asked if she wanted a drink and, despite a hankering for a eucharistic red wine, she said no.

Then Indira Moss appeared – a tiny woman with a cloud of soft dark curls and a guitar strapped across her body like armour. The crowd fell silent.

Without any welcome spiel, she stepped up to the microphone and began making a noise like morning birdsong. High and fluted, her voice flew up into the eaves and seemed to expand like sunrise to fill the gloom of the chapel. Bryony closed her eyes in the darkness and felt, from nowhere logical, a cool, fresh breeze dance across her cheek.

Steve shifted in the pew next to her. His thigh pressed against hers in a way that was barely perceptible, and she held her breath until the swooping, soaring chorus gave way to gravelly verse. The music felt like springtime. She saw it in colours, each note a wash of pink and yellow and green that seemed to surround her, engulf her, cushion her gently and carry her far, far away to another place.

Only when rowdy applause broke out around her did she realize she had been, briefly, asleep. It felt like her first real sleep in months.

'Alright?' Steve whispered to her in the darkness, as the singer tuned up for the next song.

'Yes!' she told him, hastily scratching off the crust of dribble that had formed by her mouth. 'Wonderful. She's wonderful.'

'Thought you'd like it,' he said. 'Ethel had taste, right?'

Yes, she admitted without trying to make a joke of it. Ethel had taste.

Afterwards they walked in the direction of the tube, dazed in the way of people after a religious experience. Bryony had started gushing about the gig as soon as it had finished, but she'd stopped once it became clear that Steve could only manage to say, 'Yep' and 'I know', and 'Glad you liked it.' Instead they walked in comfortable silence, weaving through the drama and debris of a thousand different Friday nights. Finally she said, 'I really do wish I'd known Ed better, you know.'

'Yep,' he said. 'I know.'

'I'm not saying I think I would have been in love with him. Honestly, if we were destined for each other I'm pretty sure I would have picked up on it while he was alive. But he had so much more going on than I ever knew about and I'm genuinely sad we never found a way to cut to the chase, share a bit more of ourselves. Actually get something off the ground.' She grasped for a metaphor, feeling poetic after the music. 'It was like we got stuck in the departure lounge, eating stale paninis and staring at a WHSmith.'

Steve chuckled softly. 'Don't beat yourself up Bryony. I've had plenty of – whatever you want to call them – *situationships* . . .'

He said the word the way one might order a sandwich in a foreign language. She wondered if he'd learned it from a magazine cover or from a former participant.

'. . . that never went anywhere. And maybe they'd say that was my fault but actually, I don't think it was anyone's fault. Like, maybe we could try harder – but there's a reason we don't, isn't there? Because it's knackering. It's really tiring to put your whole self out there, again and again, spilling your guts out to random people off the internet, knowing there's a high chance you'll get your heart mangled and have to do it all over again anyway. So, I think it's fair enough we go onto autopilot. Go through the motions. Conserve our energy.'

'You're very—'

'Wise,' said Steve. 'I know. You mentioned.'

They had arrived at the tube station now and they turned to face each other, illuminated by the orange glow of a takeaway noodle kiosk.

'Well, thank you for a really lovely night,' she said. 'I feel very . . .
at peace. If that isn't a weird thing to say.'

She felt nothing was too weird to say to Steve now, as though his
largeness and gentleness could absorb any amount of her neuroses.

'You're welcome,' he said. 'Thanks for coming with me. It's good
to see you.'

'You too. And you'll talk to Annie for me?'

'I'll talk to Annie. Leave it with me.'

And of all the people in the world she could be leaving things
with, Steve felt the safest. She went in for a hug goodbye and was relieved when he reciprocated, wrapping his arms around her in a way
that felt like forgiveness, safe hands firm on either side of her waist.
With Indira's music still chiming in her ears, it felt near-miraculous
to be ending the evening so far from the mess it began in.

The hug went on for a beat too long, and then another. Steve
wasn't a long-hugger by nature, but even so, Bryony left what felt
like an abundantly cautious margin of error before she pulled back,
tipping her head up towards his, meeting his eyes just before she
closed hers, lips parted in anticipation.

She felt the evening chill whistle past them for a second before
Steve leapt away, shaking his head as though trying to exorcise a
horrible image.

'No. No, I'm sorry Bryony, I can't do that, I'm sorry mate. No.
I'd better go.'

And then he did go, striding off in a direction that she wasn't
even sure was towards his hotel. The 'mate', oddly, was the part that
stung like a slapped cheek in the wind.

Bryony carried her mortification down the stairs and onto the tube,
where she sat splayed beneath its weight like it was a fallen piano.

She avoided eye contact with her fellow passengers in case they
could smell it on her, the stench of hot shame, like burning hair. She

dug around in her bag and tried to numb the memory by applying too much Carmex.

At Finsbury Park, a group of drunk students in baggy jeans got on, blasting music from a phone. It was always unnerving, hearing youth listening to the songs she considered belonged to her generation. But of course this was exactly how her parents must have felt about her listening to Roxy Music.

Bryony burrowed deeper into her coat and smacked her minty lips, tasting bitter irony as 'Freed from Desire' rang out through the carriage.

78

Can't complain!

Kelly's prenatal yoga teacher likes to tell them to focus on how *large* they can get, how much *space* they can take up.

'Forget staying small! You should be trying to occupy as much of the world as you possibly can, mamas,' she says, as they wheeze their way into downward dog and try to direct light and energy to their perineums.

She likes this idea, in theory. All the women chuckle along with it in sisterly solidarity, while sneaking glances in the studio mirrors to see how their own silhouette measures up against everyone else's. Kelly watches them, their swollen forms like a fun house mirror, imagining how she will look in two months' time, three months, *five*, willing her brain to feel excited about none of her clothes fitting and her nipples turning to beef carpaccio.

The class begins, as always, by going around the group for each attendee to share how far along in their journey they are, and how they've been feeling.

'Feeling good!' says a cross-legged redhead in blush-pink Lululemon.

'Feeling great!' counters a lean woman with intricate box braids.

'Can't complain!' says a woman who limped in on crutches. Everyone gives some variation of the same. One person admits to an 'occasional twinge of heartburn' and receives sympathetic tsks and a recommendation for apple cider vinegar.

Finally, it is Kelly's turn. 'Feeling pretty good!' she says, smoothly taking her cue. 'I mean, still nauseous some days. Most days to be honest. And tired from the leg cramps at night. And all the endless peeing.' The rest of the group titter politely in recognition. Kelly goes on.

'And I'm finding I'm getting out of breath when I walk, or, like ... talk? Which feels soon, considering I'm barely showing yet? And I have a blocked nose all the time and sometimes it bleeds when I blow it. Oh and I'm anaemic but the iron supplements made me so constipated that I stopped taking them and then I fainted in Oliver Bonas and broke a table lamp.'

The instructor's head is tilted to one side and nodding. At each new symptom or ailment she either says 'aw' or clucks her tongue, alternating between the two until she begins to sound like a beatbox accompaniment.

'Um, and I've had the occasional twinge of heartburn too. More than occasional, actually – it feels like my whole stomach's coming up in my throat if I eat anything with more flavour than toast – and there's still a gross taste in my mouth, kind of bitter but also sweet? All the sites say it should have gone away by now but it hasn't. And all I want to eat is crisps but then the crisps taste disgusting.'

The instructor is mute now, still nodding, eyes wide and a fixed grin on her face. Kelly senses she may be losing the floor.

'Um, quite a few headaches. My boobs sometimes hurt so much I have to warm them under the hand dryer in the loos at work. So that's been interesting. And a bit of the standard stuff – brain fog, swollen ankles, back ache. But y'know, otherwise – all fine! Feeling pretty good,' she finishes, brightly. 'Can't complain.'

'Great!' says the teacher, looking relieved. The class begins.

*

Kelly thinks a lot about those slime aliens from the nineties, which were hot property at school. In fact, she had a cottage industry swapping them for lunch money. Everybody swore blind they could procreate under the right conditions. She feels like one of those jelly aliens now – a lot of the time. Squirming in her own hype, waiting and hoping for the miracle to appear and impress everybody in the playground; to prove she wasn't making it up all along.

Aside from the scan – which was wonderful and terrifying in equal measure; squealing at each flicker of a tiny hand or foot, panicking each time the technician fell quiet for thirty seconds – progress has been annoyingly subtle. Incremental. Like the wind, or God, she finds it is mostly not the force itself that is visible, only the devastation wreaked by the great storm inside her. The trousers that don't zip up anymore. The blood spat out in the sink. The angry red fault lines that creep up the yoga women's bellies like cracked ground during an earthquake.

And she knows she should feel grateful. She's meant to be lit up from within by her gratitude, or at least faking it better for the friends and colleagues who grab at her belly each day. But the guilt is there, always, thrumming within, every time she sees the abandoned Co-Q10 supplements in the bathroom cabinet, the pantyliners and piss sticks, the paraphernalia of that whole other life she was living only a few months ago. Kelly always thought it would feel like a continuation of the same journey, but instead it feels as though she's crossed over to join the other side in battle.

Thump goes the guilt against her abdomen walls. *Thump. Thump. You don't deserve this if you're not going to enjoy it.*

Leo is doing his best to help her enjoy it. He buys her bouquets of crisps like bunches of flowers, switches to decaf in solidarity, rubs her back across the nightly barricade of her maternity pillow. He applauds the farts, which are now minute-long overtures with key changes and great, trumpeting crescendos. Having once been the kind of woman who wouldn't poo while her husband was in the house, she marvels at how far they have come.

In fact, she finds she *wants* Leo to witness it all. The grislier, the better. She wants him to know about mucus plugs and haemorrhoids, to watch *One Born Every Minute* without hiding behind a pillow. Part of her hopes she does grow enormous, taking up half the flat and never deflating afterwards. She wants to become a monument to her own physical sacrifice. She wants him to call her a 'rockstar', a 'lioness' in gushing Facebook posts. She wants the stupefied admiration and adoration she had seen across the faces of friends' partners and celebrity dads on talk show sofas. That expression, somewhere between haunted and humbled, of one who has looked directly into the hellmouth and cut the cord afterwards.

'My wife,' she has pictured him saying in the pub, shaking his head like an astronaut trying to describe how it feels to look at the earth from the moon, 'was just ... amazing.'

'The baby is a grapefruit today,' she tells him one morning, after a dream about trying to shove a Furby up his penis, which cannot be coincidental.

'Is that why you're so sour?' he asks. He is only joking, but she cries, because she always cries these days – and every time she curses her tear ducts for the act of treason.

Things she has cried at in recent days include, a tube advert for a banking app, losing the end of a roll of Sellotape, a pigeon cooing forlornly in a tree and the quiet beauty of a watermelon seed. When Leo brought home sushi for his dinner the other night she cried at that too, as though an old friend had blanked her in the street.

'Is this still about lending Annie the money?' he asks and Kelly, still crying, says no, she's over that now.

In reality she is sending Bryony new messages every few days.

'Any progress?'

'Sorry, not yet! I'm on it! Hope you're not feeling too shit today? Or this hour, at least? x'

It's funny, that Monica Munchausen should turn out to be her pregnancy confidante. The only person giving her the space to fill with her whines.

Bryony sends her a link to an article, then a podcast, then a scientific journal. *'Thought you might find this interesting! x'* she messages each time, and Kelly does find them interesting, and comforting and horrifying in equal measure.

She learns that her baby's cells are crossing her placenta all the time, taking up residence in her body, and that even after she gives birth there will be microscopic pieces of her child left inside her for decades, maybe forever – a living biological bond. None of this is mentioned on the pregnancy apps, which are mostly concerned with not eating too much tuna.

Kelly finds herself thinking, not unhappily, of the tiny specks of herself that were buried with her mother. She thinks of Ann, carrying Ed around within her like a living mausoleum and wonders if it would bring her comfort to know it too.

As for Leo, she forgives him for the comment, the sushi, the tears. He falls to his knees and wraps his arms around her waist, pressing his ear to her belly as though listening for the roar of the sea.

79

Irrelevant if dead

Bryony was having lunch with Noor at a place in a railway arch, famed for serving comically huge sandwiches in surroundings so grim they were frequently raided by confused police. The tables were planks of chipboard perched on naked scaffolding, the seats empty oil drums. The smell of car paint from the neighbouring garages drifted in, making her feel slightly high, as they attempted conversation through sloppy mouthfuls of brisket and slaw.

When Noor had messaged, Bryony had almost said no but wavered. The novelty of Nopeuary was wearing thin now, and clearing out her social life seemed to have had fewer benefits for her brain than her bank balance.

She could have a lunch, she decided. Lunch would be great.

'So what are you working on at the moment?' she asked, chasing a drip up her chin with a corner of sodden focaccia.

Noor's eyes flashed with pleasure as she replied. 'Actually I shouldn't say, it's a pretty juicy one. The paper had a tip-off and I've been working on it for months, putting all the pieces together – just struggling to find the last case study I need before we go to print, and if anyone scooped it . . .'

There was no way Noor wasn't going to tell her. Noor had a

thirst for gossip that was at once both at odds and entirely compatible with her chosen career. But Bryony played along, wheedling,
'Pleeeease,' as Noor checked over her shoulders for spies lurking in
the scaffolding.

'It's about that pyramid scheme, Gel Lyfe – you know the one all
the huns from school do? Where you sell the drink that tastes like
old vase water.'

Bryony worked her way through a fibrous piece of beef. 'Rings
a bell,' she said finally, when she'd swallowed. 'So, what, are you
exposing it as a scam?

'Nah, everyone knows it's a scam,' said Noor. 'Only actual idiots
are still doing it, it's famously impossible to make any money.'

Bryony laughed at the idiots.

Noor went on, 'We're exposing it because somebody *died*.'

Bryony inhaled sharply and a chunk of dill pickle lodged itself
neatly in her windpipe. She felt it – almost heard it – fly into place
with a percussive *thwup*.

It took several seconds to realize that she was choking. Actually,
truly choking, choking the way people did in films, choking in the
same way an actor in a first aid video would choke – eyes bugging,
mouth tunnelled like a surprised fish, hands pounding the table in
panic.

Her first thought was *'oh, this is what not being able to breathe feels
like!'*. Having thought herself close to dying so many times in her
life, it was striking how different a true near-death experience felt.
Strangely calm. Oddly clear. Her second thought was that if she was
going to die right here, right now, she didn't care what Marco did
with her sex toys but only hoped he had the good sense to hide all
her Gel Lyfe.

By now Noor had registered her distress and snapped into action,
yelling 'oh my god oh my god, help! Someone!', which was nice but
lacked the attention to detail one might desire in an investigative

reporter. Bryony was just evaluating the benefits (not dying) versus potential organ damage of jamming her torso hard into a piece of scaffolding (irrelevant if dead), when she felt a strong pair of arms around her waist.

It had been a few years since a strange man had last embraced her from behind, and she had to fight the instinct to clobber him while he balled his fists below her ribcage and executed a perfect Heimlich manoeuvre. The pickle piece left her throat with a blessed squelch and skidded across the table to rest against Noor's San Pellegrino. Bryony gagged in relief, and vomited a small mass of cabbage onto the floor.

For a second she stayed bent over, panting, coughing, drinking in oxygen and wondering how she'd never noticed before how delicious it was, how sweet. Instinctively, without seeing who they belonged to, she reached for the arms and pulled them back towards herself in a grateful hug. Had her nose not been streaming with mayonnaise she might have kissed them.

'Oh my god! Oh my god!' Noor was still yelling. Another restaurant stranger had stepped in to hug her too.

Finally Bryony straightened up and dabbed at her face before turning around to greet her hero.

Her hero looked alarmed, if not downright annoyed, to recognize the woman who had poured soup down his sweatshirt two months earlier.

'Oh,' said the man. 'It's you.'

Was it possible to regret saving someone's life? He definitely looked as though he might, especially as it turned out the regurgitated cabbage hadn't only ended up on the floor but also on his shoes. The sheer force of filmic coincidence almost bent her double again.

'Thank you so, *so* much,' Bryony began stammering, but he waved her off modestly with the same strong, lightly tanned arms that had saved her.

'Please,' she said, 'Let me buy you lunch! As a thank you?'

'It's fine,' said the man. 'That's really unnecessary. I'm a para-medic, it's all in a day's work.' He helped himself to a handful of napkins from their table and began to walk away.

'But I still owe you for the soup!' she cried while Noor and her emotional support stranger looked on, confused.

'Honestly,' he said, as firmly as the last time. 'Thank you, but my wife and I were just leaving.'

True enough, there was a woman standing a few feet away, with the proud and quietly possessive expression of a person married to a hero with lightly tanned forearms.

'Enjoy the rest of your lunch,' he said, then as a final kindness, 'take care.'

This was the trouble with Marco's deathbed paradox, Bryony realized as he walked away. You could hold out for option B, but there was no guarantee your soulmate hadn't already settled for someone else.

She tried a grounding exercise she'd seen in one of Annie's TikToks, focusing not on how her body felt but on how the environment *around* her body felt – the solid concrete beneath her feet, the warmth on her skin, the scented air in her nostrils and the throb of mortality in her throat. She was alive, and she still had half a sand-wich left, and in that moment both felt precious beyond measure.

'Are you okay? Fuck,' said Noor.

'I'm okay,' she told her, and it was astonishing to realize that was true.

She sat back down.

'Where were we? Gel Lyfe killed someone?'

'Well, kind of,' said Noor. 'They had a long-term condition and needed meds to regulate it but became convinced that drinking the gel stuff was going to cure them instead. So they came off the meds and started taking it three times a day and within a few months they were dead. So awful.'

'Awful,' Bryony echoed. 'But I guess there are always going to be wackos in any of these things, right? Can Gel Lyfe actually be held responsible?'

'That's the thing,' said Noor. She took a delicate bite of her sandwich and chewed with exaggerated care. 'It seems her group leader – they call it "Team Queen", hilarious – told her to do it. There's speculation that the founder was urging lots of the sellers to swap Gel Lyfe in for their usual medication. She wanted miracle cure stories to boost their profile.'

'Wild,' said Bryony, faintly.

'Anyway, it's all going to blow up but only if I can find another firsthand source – I have plenty of ex-sellers but my editor's obsessed with getting someone who's still *in* the scheme, which is the hardest thing because naturally nobody wants to dish any dirt in case Tamsin Fucklethwaite takes a hit out on them or whatever.'

'Naturally,' said Bryony, aware of the whirring sensation in her brain. 'Are you paying? For the interviews, I mean – is there a fee?'

'I mean, not usually – not with the state of the industry these days. It's not the nineties. I basically have to beg them to pay *me*.'

Noor was obsessed with the idea of the nineties as a golden age of splashy commissions, boozy lunches and being flown to St Barts to try on a Swatch. Bryony wondered if the nineties were full of journalists bemoaning the fact it wasn't the seventies anymore.

'But they probably would, if it was the only way to get someone to speak,' she said. 'Why?'

'Well.' Bryony nibbled at the remains of her sandwich. Oddly she felt hungrier after her brush with death than before. Perhaps it was the adrenaline, or her newfound appetite for life. She chewed slowly, congratulating herself on getting back on the horse so soon.

When she finally swallowed, she told Noor, 'I think I might have an amazing business opportunity for you.'

80

Instinct

———————————

The bonding happens suddenly and takes her by surprise.

Kelly didn't realize separation anxiety could kick in while the baby was still inside her, but she finds herself resenting time spent with other people, time spent at work, time spent anywhere loud and distracting, because she only wants to be at home, lying down, focused on the butterfly-soft flutter that could be gas – but isn't. It seems astonishing, this private daily performance that happens only for her. How rude to miss even a second.

She is at work, resenting it, when the mole woman returns. Her baby is in tow – a sweet little thing with a snub nose and a shock of dark hair, coiffed upwards like Elvis. It has a ribbon of drool hanging from the corner of its mouth and the remains of something orange and crusty down the front of its dungarees.

The baby looks up at Kelly and grins, bearing two tiny white pegs, and although it must be the fifteenth baby to pass through the waiting room today (it is Wednesday), Kelly finds herself entranced. She greets it like an adult, as though they are the only two people in the room.

'Hello.'

'Hello,' says its mother, giving her name and date of birth. 'I'm sorry I'm late, will the doctor still see me? I would have called, it's just . . . one of those days.'

'What's your name?' Kelly asks the baby. The baby keeps grinning.

'I just gave it to you,' says the woman, and Kelly realizes her baby voice needs practice. She only has five months to get it right.

'Sorry,' says Kelly. 'I was miles away.' She sticks her tongue out at the baby and it giggles obligingly. 'How do you get anything done with this charmer to distract you all day?'

'I don't,' the woman says and Kelly laughs, and although the exchange is banal, she feels a spark of something like belonging.

'I should have had this thing on my shoulder looked at ages ago,' the woman goes on. 'Years ago probably. I kept saying I'd get round to it and then I had him and fffpooww . . .' she mimes a bomb exploding, rolling her head back at the imaginary impact. 'This was literally the first spare minute I've had to get on the phone and make an appointment.'

Kelly nods sympathetically, feeling inwardly triumphant.

'I'm pregnant,' she tells the woman by way of reward.

Apparently she can't stop telling the patients now – and the hazardous waste guy, the cashier in Pret. It isn't that passing the twelve-week mark has made her less nervous, more that she needs to keep telling people in order to make sure it stays real.

The woman congratulates her and asks how far along she is. Kelly tells her and the woman asks how she is feeling. Kelly is about to give the stock response ('Over the worst, can't complain! So excited!'), but just then Phlegmma Thompson makes her presence known with a loud chorus of hacking, which startles the baby, who then starts wailing and needs to be soothed with an elaborate routine of bouncing, rocking and shushing.

Kelly watches, studying each move as if she might be asked to repeat the performance in an audition. The way she bobs and sways, one confident hand cupping the tiny head, kissing it on the off-beat, until Kelly feels she herself is ready to rest her cheek against the woman's chest and take a nap. When the baby is docile and smiling again, a spitty thumb lolling in its mouth, the mother looks up and asks Kelly again how she is feeling.

'Honestly?' she replies. 'Shit-scared. I don't know how to do that.' She gestures at the infant and mimics the swaying and rocking routine. The mother laughs.

'Nobody does,' she says. 'It's all improv. You just sense what they need and make it up as you go along.'

Kelly smiles and thanks her, but inside she's doubtful. Because there is Leo, and all her futile attempts over the past few months to help him, reach him, rouse him from his grief. If she can't intuit her own husband's needs, then how can she expect to do any better with a baby? She pictures Ann and her scattergun style of nurturing, showering them all liberally with love in the hope some of it will stick. Her own mother had been more precise with her efforts, rationing hugs and compliments so that their value increased – supplying only the most practical care. If she'd been around now, Kelly knows, she'd have been yelling 'Can't complain!' even while she was holding her hair back for her.

The thought of being parent to an adult child one day is so overwhelming it makes her woozy. She looks again at the baby, focusing on its component parts: the smooth cheeks, the shrimpy fingers, the puff of downy hair. She takes in each individually, then together, watching until she can almost feel the warmth and weight of him against her own chest. Somewhere in the seabed of her stomach, the butterfly wings stir again.

'Good luck! You'll love it, I promise,' says the mole woman as she wheels the pram through the double doors for her appointment. Kelly crosses her fingers beneath the counter, the way she does for only her very favourite handful of patients, hoping that it is a benign scabby Bran Flake and nothing more.

81

Vindicating, at least

'So, Bryony. What brings you here?'

This therapist, Lisa, wasn't wearing an embroidered scarf or statement glasses. In fact she was no-frills, in jeans and a sweat-shirt with a bare face and hair claw, as though taking the bins out. Bryony had purposely chosen one of the less expensive therapists that her research had thrown up – but now she worried she'd gone off-brand, bought herself the psychiatric equivalent of Mallibo Fizztastic.

'Well, two things really.' She knew GPs hated it when you tried to cram two different problems into one appointment and hoped they didn't have the same rule here. 'If that's allowed.'

Lisa laughed, softly. 'Yes, that's allowed.'

'Well, number one is that I spent three months pretending to have been in love with the dead guy I was having casual sex with.'

She saw Lisa's nostrils flare in alarm.

'*Before* he died. I was having sex with him *before* he died. Then I found out his friends and family all thought we were a serious couple, so I pretended that we were. It seemed polite.'

'For three months?'

She nodded. 'Thereabouts. I spoke at the funeral, went to a

million events and joined a multi-level marketing scheme – to make his sister happy. And I considered keeping a phantom pregnancy.'

'To be polite?'

'Yes.'

Lisa wrote this down.

'And the second thing?'

Bryony wondered if she should have led with the second thing.

'I have health anxiety. I think I'm ill, or dying, a lot. All the time.'

'I see,' said Lisa. 'Do you feel ill now?'

'Yes,' said Bryony. 'I'm lightheaded. And my neck hurts.'

Lisa said she was sorry to hear that. She offered her a biscuit from a packet in her desk drawer – custard creams – in case sugar might help with the lightheadedness. Bryony thought this unlikely, but took one anyway.

'Tell me a little about your family history,' said Lisa, as they both ate, brushing crumbs from their fronts.

'Of anxiety?'

'Well, yes – or anything else?'

This seemed like a lazy move, going straight for the family can of worms without dancing around it a bit first. Bryony would have preferred to make her work for this revelation, but she was conscious they were already ten minutes into the session and it was important to squeeze every drop of value out of it, lest her father change his mind before the next one.

'My mum died when I was ten,' Bryony told her. 'She'd been ill for a long time. On and off. My whole life, really, as far back as I can remember.'

'I see,' said Lisa. 'I'm sorry, that must have been incredibly hard.'

Bryony nodded. 'It was.'

'And did you worry about your health back then, when you were a child?'

'No,' said Bryony, feeling the answer was almost too obvious to need saying. 'I worried about hers.'

Lisa wrote something down. Bryony thought about the times she'd paused her beauty potion production to mix up 'cures' for her mother instead. The recipes had been remarkably similar – oats, avocado, bits of grass, Ribena – delivered on a tray like breakfast in bed and administered by the eager chemist to the grateful patient, who never got up to wash them off afterwards, but had happily fallen asleep with the gunk on her arms, chest and face. Her thoughts shifted unexpectedly to Ann and wondering how many toxic mother's day breakfasts she must have endured in her time; how many flaking macaroni necklaces she must have worn.

'So now you worry about your own health because you're afraid of dying, the way she did,' said Lisa. 'Would you say that's accurate?'

Bryony thought about it. She tried to picture death often enough, a normal amount, but always drew a literal blank – just a nothingness where the static crackle and hum of somethingness usually was. After her brush with mortality at lunch with Noor, she had expected death to haunt her thoughts, but in fact the opposite had happened: she'd felt energized. Vital. For a few days, she had whistled in the office, kicked children's footballs back to them in the park, replied to everyone in her inbox. She had made this appointment.

'Not exactly,' she told Lisa. 'It's more like a fear of the logistics.'

'The physical process of death, you mean?'

'No – more like the inconvenience of it? Like, what if I've made plans with people and then I can't go.'

'Because you're dead?'

'Yes.'

'Well,' said Lisa, after a pause. 'I should think that would be a valid excuse.'

Bryony nodded. 'I mean, if anything, death would be better than just being ill because nobody could question it, could they? It's the ultimate get-out. People have to believe you.'

'You don't think people believe you when you're ill?' asked Lisa.

She considered this. 'Sometimes they do. But a lot of the time I worry I just look flaky, like I've let everyone down for no good reason? Although to be fair, people love having plans cancelled so sometimes I feel equally bad if I actually go. It's pretty complicated.'

'Is that what you mean by logistics?'

'Yeah,' said Bryony. 'Like, when I'm worrying I have cancer or kidney failure or DVT or something, I think it's not so much fear of actually *having* it — it's more a fear of ruining everything. It's that sense of, "oh god, I can't have kidney failure now, I have tickets to that thing on Tuesday."'

'And you don't want to let everyone down?'

'On Tuesday. Yeah.'

'Because you fear they would dislike you if you did?'

'Because I just need everyone to have a nice time. Does that make sense?'

Lisa nodded, and said that it did make sense, which Bryony supposed was part of her job no matter how absurd the statement. She fell silent then, leaving such a long pause that Bryony had the urge to scat.

'And what makes you think you're responsible for everyone having a nice time?' asked Lisa, eventually.

'Well, somebody has to be.'

'You feel other people are shirking their responsibilities, in that regard?' said Lisa.

'Not *shirking*,' said Bryony. 'Just — well, *deprioritizing*, maybe.'

'By prioritizing their own happiness instead of other people's, you mean?'

'Well, it sounds bad when you put it like that. It's not like I don't want other people to be happy, I just wish I didn't feel like it's my fault if they aren't.'

'It does sound like a lot of responsibility,' said Lisa.

'Yes,' said Bryony, and then it was her turn to go quiet. The air conditioning hummed. Outside, builders clanked and swore. She listened to her left nostril, whistling slightly, as she breathed. It was hard to say if it was the biscuits or something in Lisa's overall manner, but she felt a childlike urge to bare her soul, holding up her darkest thoughts to be inspected and kissed better.

Finally, she said, 'Sometimes I wonder if, while I'm worrying all the time about illness, I'm also actually craving it. For the relief.'

Lisa arched an eyebrow and made a noise like '*huh*', an interested noise. She didn't seem to care about staying neutral or unshockable and Bryony liked her better for it.

'You think you want something to be wrong with you?'

'No! I mean, not really,' said Bryony. 'But, like – do you ever fantasize about having some mild-to-moderate illness, or maybe an injury, for example a broken leg or something, that would be incapacitating but only temporarily? So you know you'll be fine and get better, and you don't feel too awful, but at the same time you can't really go anywhere or do anything for, ideally, about six weeks? You'd just get to lie around in a nest of soft fabrics, watching TV and eating snacks and you can't work or do anything productive on doctor's orders? All you're *clinically allowed* to do is rest. And maybe take a gentle stroll around the block for a little fresh air.'

'I suppose I can understand the appeal of that,' said Lisa, looking as though she absolutely understood the appeal of that. There was a photograph of two small children on her desk. 'And is this scenario something you think about a lot?'

'Well, I did,' said Bryony. 'But the pandemic killed it.'

'I see. Because you experienced a period of enforced isolation, and you realized it wasn't such a luxury after all?'

'No,' said Bryony. 'Because of Zoom.'

'Zoom?'

'Video meetings. Remote working. These days even if I had a broken leg I wouldn't get to stay off work for weeks, would I? I'd just have to do it from home.'

'I suppose that's true,' said Lisa. 'I hadn't considered that.'

'Also,' Bryony went on, keen to purge fully now she'd started, 'a boy I went to school with – man, I should say – has some kind of mysterious chronic fatigue condition and it's been going on for years. He genuinely can't work, or go out, or do anything except watch TV and occasionally go for a walk if he feels up to it. And every time I see one of his Instagram updates, looking so happy because he made it round the corner to Spar and smelled a flower or something, I feel like the very worst person in the world.'

She whispered this last part and Lisa lowered her voice to a respectful hush.

'You feel like the worst person in the world for wanting to be ill?'

'Like I said, I don't *want* to be ill,' Bryony insisted.

'Of course, my mistake,' said Lisa.

'I suppose it would feel vindicating, at least? Because it would prove that it wasn't all in my head. And everyone who said, "it's fine, you're just being dramatic" would be wrong.'

'So you'd rather be ill and right, than well and wrong?' said Lisa.

Bryony considered this. She thought about the odd, anticlimactic shame that always descended when she was leaving the hospital after an A&E stint, with a furry tongue from a vending machine dinner and a crick in her neck from trying to nap in a series of hard plastic chairs. She thought about the way she felt every time a blood test or scan came back normal, so unremarkable, they didn't even phone her to say. Like a child with an imaginary friend who the grown-ups refused to see.

'I'd rather be well and right,' she told Lisa. 'But you can't have everything.'

Lisa smiled a little and wrote something down.

'Well,' she said, 'I think we've done some really good work here today Bryony.'

'Thank you so much,' said Bryony, although the 'we' felt audacious. She had done all the work and had simply told Lisa everything she already knew about herself anyway. She hadn't even cried. If you didn't cry during your first proper therapy session, did that mean there was something wrong with the therapy, or with you?

'Is there anything else you'd like to ask before we wrap up?' said Lisa.

'No, no, that's all good,' she replied.

'Great!' Lisa was opening a large day planner on her desk and picking up a biro.

'Actually . . .' Bryony forced herself to speak. 'Ah. Well, it's just – I guess I'm wondering how I *stop* feeling all these things?'

Lisa laughed softly. 'Well, that's the million dollar question! But realizing all this about yourself is an excellent start, Bryony.'

'Oh. Great. Thank you.'

'And I'd like to set you some homework before our next session.'

Bryony prepared to nod in recognition at one of the usual assignments – listing her safety behaviours, keeping a symptom journal with a percentage rating (out of a hundred, how strongly do you believe you're going to die?) – like the excellent student she was.

'I'd like you to make an effort this week to observe your people-pleasing habits. Look at your interactions with people and note down all the ways in which you're acting to keep them happy at the expense of your own needs.'

'People-pleasing?' repeated Bryony. 'I thought we were talking about health anxiety.'

'It seems the two are connected, don't you think?' asked Lisa. 'After experiencing so much insecurity in your early years, your worry around your physical health seems to be strongly linked to your worry around everyone else's happiness – a desire to optimize situations beyond your control. A sort of emotional perfectionism, if you like.'

Bryony felt bad for writing her off as an Aldi counsellor. This was beginning to feel like more premium service.

Still, she was compelled to be honest.

'Look, I know it's a hot term right now and everything, but I feel like pleasing people is broadly a good thing? I mean, what's the alternative? Imagine the world if we were all just running around saying what we thought and doing what we wanted all the time. Carnage.'

Lisa laughed, not softly this time but a proper, belly-deep bark.

'Ha! Well, it's a fair point but I think most people would agree there's a balance to be struck. And pleasing people in the short term isn't necessarily always the same as doing what's best for your relationship with them in the long term.'

Marco's words rang in her ears. *You're being nice. Not kind. They aren't the same thing.*

'Will you do that for me?' Lisa went on. 'Write down every time you agree to something you don't really want to do. Even just tiny things – the language you use, the small decisions you make each day to keep other people happy. You don't need to change any behaviours yet, just note them down.'

And Bryony agreed, although she didn't really want to.

82

The enemy of potential

Steve had gone silent, which was unsurprising, but he stayed true to his word. A few days later, Annie called her.

'Annie! Hi!' Bryony answered an octave too high in panic and struggled to lower her voice without sounding strange. 'How are you?'

'I'm only calling because Steve asked me to.' The cartoon mouse voice was surprisingly cutting when angry. 'What do you want?'

'I want to see you, if you'll meet me. I have something I need to tell you about. Business-related,' she added, hurriedly. 'Nothing to do with Ed, I promise.'

When had her life become nothing but a series of awkward confrontations? This incessant having of chats, like living in a scripted reality show – she didn't care for it.

Annie sighed. 'You'll need to come up here. I'm really busy preparing for the birthday memorial.'

Bryony felt a pang of guilt at having forgotten this was happening, then briefly hurt to hear that they were carrying on without her. She wondered what they had called the prize in the end, and who had designed the trophy, if Ann had bought a giant hat and whether Susan would video the whole thing on her iPad. It would be wholly inappropriate to turn up and sit in the back row like the ghost at the feast, and yet she found she wanted to, quite badly.

Not to mention the task of returning Ed's diary, which was still in her bottom drawer and provoked such a visceral shame response every time she saw it, that she had simply stopped wearing jumpers. Bryony had almost completely decided not to read it, now. She was fairly certain she probably wouldn't. But getting the diary out of her flat and back to his family, somehow, was the only way she could make sure.

'I'll come up, of course. That's absolutely fine,' she told Annie, and hoped to god that Terry the Taxi would be free.

They met in a surprisingly nice cafe on the high street. Despite her many trips to the village, Bryony realized, she'd only ever really been to Ann's house and the pub. A Little Buckton where you could get an oat flat white and a cardamom bun jarred considerably with the Little Buckton of her mind and she was forced to swallow some prejudice along with her coffee.

Annie arrived looking exhausted. Her eyes were tinted pink, her skin ashen and dry in a way Team Queen Maxine would surely never approve of. She went to hug hello, as if on autopilot, then caught herself halfway through and turned rigid in Bryony's arms.

'It's really good to see you,' she said, pulling out a chair.

'Yeah, well,' said Annie, sitting down with a thump and crossing her arms. This felt like taking a sullen niece out for a treat. She pressed on.

'I know I said I wanted to talk about business, and I do. But obviously I want to start by saying, again, how very sorry I am for all the confusion.'

'Confusion, is that what you're calling it?'

Bryony swallowed. 'Lies. I'm so sorry, I should never have let you all believe Ed and I were something we weren't. It's a problem I have. I'm a chronic people-pleaser. Recently diagnosed.'

Annie snorted. 'Is that a joke?'

'I mean, maybe our most recent encounter wasn't that . . . pleasing. But the whole charade, the reason I went through with it all and let you carry on believing Ed and I were really a couple – I know it was stupid, but I honestly did it for good reasons, Annie. I wanted to make everyone happy.'

'Ed had just died, Bryony. We were never going to be happy.'

Annie's words echoed Steve's. It dawned on Bryony that her biggest mistake had been thinking she could make any kind of dent in their pain.

'No, of course – but you know what I mean. Happ*ier*. Or . . . or not sadder than you already were, at least. It would have felt so cruel to kick poor Ed when he was . . . ah, down. As it were. And I know I should have told the truth at some point along the road, but, well, I guess I missed the exit. And the longer it went on, the harder it was to . . . find the turn-off.'

The longer this driving analogy went on, the harder it was to find the turn-off. Did she think this was the only way to appeal to rural people? The language of cars?

'And if I'm really honest—'

'Yes,' interrupted Annie. 'Be really honest! I dare you.'

Bryony took a deep breath. 'If I'm really honest, I was enjoying being a part of your family. It was nice to feel included. You know, looked after. Special. I don't get a whole lot of that with my own family. Ann is . . . well, she's a very powerful maternal figure.'

'Alright, that's enough. Your mum died so you fancied mine, I get it.'

Annie didn't sound wholly unsympathetic, but nor did she sound surprised.

Bryony thought about what Steve had said, and she could feel it – the many years of waifs and strays wandering into the Slingsby fold and being showered in love and snacks. The need for Ann's children to compete for her affection; with skits and prizes and performances, by conjuring up a business, or a baby, or a girlfriend. She wasn't special at all, and that was the point.

'I'm sorry. It was weird and wrong and counter-productive and I know I should have just told the truth.'

She said this with an upward inflection – the *truuuth* – because in all honesty Bryony still couldn't see how that would have been better. Quicker, admittedly. Cheaper, definitely. But better?

'Yes,' said Annie, sternly. 'You should have. Did you know dishonesty is actually toxic? It triggers a stress response in the body. It raises your heart rate and your blood pressure, sends all these negative hormones whizzing around your bloodstream – I've read about it. It's like Tamara says, it's just so important to live your truth.'

Bryony chose to file this information away to be examined later. She returned to the task at hand.

'Well, if you really want me to be honest, Annie, we need to have a word about Gel Lyfe.'

This would have had a more dramatic impact, she realized, if she'd pre-loaded Noor's notes on her phone before she got there. As it was, Annie had to sit waiting, brow furrowed in pre-emptive displeasure, while Bryony searched through her emails, opened up the attachment, and finally slid her phone across the table.

Annie took it and began to scroll.

Bryony held her breath, poised for the moment of epiphany, ready to hush away the shame and horror that would descend the moment Annie realized she'd been had.

'I know all that,' said Annie, calmly handing her back the phone.

'But . . . what? All of it?'

'We get a weekly bulletin of all the stifling speak to avoid. Did you never check your join-inbox? I told you it was important to stay up-to-date with—'

'You know all this and you're still selling the stuff?' Bryony cut across her. She had never checked her join-inbox.

'I said I *know* about it, not that it's *true*. People are always trying to attack Tamara. They hate to see a strong woman empowering other women to be self-sufficient.'

'Right,' said Bryony, feeling newly liberated by this honesty pact. 'Only it's not really self-sufficiency, is it? You're relying on selling that stuff to your friends and family. You're borrowing money off Leo and Kelly.'

'All businesses have start-up costs, Bryony. Gel Lyfe's joining fee is like, five hundred percent cheaper than founding the average company, that's why it's such a savvy investment. And once I break even and move up to Peridot Level, I'll be making so much that I can pay them back with interest. Everyone wins! A rising tide gathers no moss!'

She said it breathlessly, as though it wasn't the first time she had made this speech. Bryony changed tack.

'Did you see what the article said about the side effects? The stomach cramps and nausea? The fainting?'

'Adaptogens are powerful,' shrugged Annie. 'It takes the body a while to adjust and eliminate the toxins, so obviously there can be short-term—'

'Liver damage?' said Bryony. 'Kidney failure?'

'There were never proven links,' squeaked Annie. 'There are always going to be rare cases where something doesn't agree with—'

'At least six hundred people?'

Annie pressed her mouth into a firm line and for a second she looked exactly like her mother.

'So maybe the gel isn't perfect,' she said. 'Yet! All iconic businesspeople have to deal with failure, that's part of the

process – failure is just a stepping stone on the path to success.'
Bryony opened her mouth to argue but Annie powered on.
'Anyway, that isn't really the point. Gel Lyfe is about so much
more than the product. It's a whole philosophy. It's a *community*.
We all support each other and cheer each other on to overcome
those failures. We're shaking up traditional patriarchal power
structures. It's women helping—'

'Women, I know,' said Bryony. She held her gaze steady for a
moment, the way Steve had when he wanted to make her understand. 'Annie. It's women helping one woman get very, very rich.
It's exploitation.'

Annie glared back at her, defiance flashing amber in her eyes.
'Nobody said that about Steve Jobs, did they? When men become
millionaires, everyone calls it visionary.'

Bryony was fairly sure people *had* said it about Steve Jobs, but
instead she said, 'Annie, I get it. I do. I know it's a seductive idea, but
the maths doesn't work. You saw the article. To make a six-figure
salary you would need *eight hundred thousand* downlines. Does that
sound realistic to you?'

'Realistic is the enemy of potential,' said Annie, though she
sounded less convinced now.

Bryony kept going. It was a rush not dissimilar to defeating a boss
on the platform games of yore – watching Annie's resolve flicker
and grow weak with each new blow she dealt in rapid succession.
Biff! Logic. *Kapow!* Reason.

'Ninety-three percent of gelievers never make any money, Annie.
Most of them lose money. The odds are always going to be stacked
against you.'

Thwap!

Annie stammered wordlessly as Bryony served her final blow –
'By participating in the whole thing, you're not helping women,
you're just scamming more of them out of their money in the same

way you've been scammed. And maybe damaging their kidneys in the process.'

Ker-blam!

She sat back in her seat and took a long, triumphant swig of cold coffee foam.

Annie burst into tears.

'I just ... *hegghhh* ...'

Oh shit.

'I only wanted to ... *heggh* ... I was trying ... *heggh.*'

For a chronic people-pleaser, it must be said she was remarkably skilled at making this poor woman cry.

'It's just been so h– h– hard.'

Bryony fumbled for napkins to mop up the deluge, wondering if it might be better all round for everybody if she simply got up and ran for the hills.

'Annie, I'm so sorry, I didn't mean to—'

'I know you think I'm a fucking idiot,' she wailed.

'I don't, Annie! Not at all, I think you're inspiring!'

'I'm not inspiring, I'm a massive fucking failure. I've barely sold anything! I've been buying my own stock just to make my monthly targets, Bryony, it's embarrassing.'

'No, Annie, it's a pyramid scheme. You saw it in Noor's notes, that's the whole point – they're designed so you end up funnelling more and more of your own money in to make up the shortfall. They don't care if no actual customers ever buy that shit, they don't care if it sits in your bedroom gathering dust forever, as long as you keep pouring money into their coffers. Sorry, their *well of fortune.*'

She tried as best she could to keep the mockery out of her voice. After all, there was gel gathering dust in her bedroom too. Only less so, on account of how much she had drunk.

'It's okay for you,' said Annie, between shuddering gulps. 'You have a great career. I've done so many jobs and I've tried so many times to get my life together and nothing's ever stuck, I don't know what's wrong with me. Everyone thinks I'm this waster, stupid Annie just drifting around, always earning peanuts and getting bored and quitting to chase the next idiotic dream. I know everybody thinks that.'

Bryony saw then that the odds already *were* stacked against Annie, or at least Annie felt they were. There was nothing quite as humbling as hearing that your own scant achievements were the stick someone else used to beat themselves with.

It threw up a feeling she'd had often herself – that your thirties were like the deciding moments of a horse race. Where once you'd all run as a pack, the winners changing moment by moment, there came a point where certain people started pulling out in front, gathering pace until it was all you could do to keep trotting straight in a cloud of their dust.

'And all your qualifications and your talents – I don't have any of that, okay?'

She remembered that her scant achievements had been embellished by Ed, and wondered if now was the time to come clean, or—

'I was never trying to scam anybody, I just wanted to catch up a bit! I wanted to think positive for once. You know, believe that maybe amazing things could still happen for me.'

'I get it,' said Bryony, and she did. It was nice, sometimes, to be an optimist about things.

She leaned across the table and rubbed Annie's wrist. 'Listen, it's okay. The reason I wanted to see you is that I have a way for you to get out. Noor – that's the journalist who found out all that stuff – she's looking for another case study, ideally someone still in the scheme. If you're up for talking to her, her newspaper will pay you enough of a fee to cover all the exit costs. We'd both be able to leave Gel Lyfe without you losing anything.'

Annie sniffed a little and said nothing.

'Anything financial, I mean,' added Bryony, because of course Annie would still be losing plenty. Dignity, community, hope. She had read enough about sunk cost economics to understand why it was often harder to quit a pyramid scheme than it was to keep on throwing money in the hole. What's the price of a dream?

'Think about it. I know it's incredibly hard when you've poured so much time and energy and, er, *potential* into it, but sharing your story now would be a far braver act than anything Tamara can preach about. You'll be helping a load of other people discover the truth and get out before they lose more.'

'Will you be getting anything?' asked Annie, finally.

'Me?'

'Are you getting a fee?'

'No,' Bryony shook her head. 'I'll lose what I put into the starter kit, plus the buy-out fee, but that's fine. No more than I deserve. And hey, I'll be set for adaptogens for the next five years.'

Annie laughed a little and finished shredding a napkin into a pile of confetti. 'Okay,' she said, in the small voice of the defeated. 'I'll talk to them. Only if they change my name though.'

'You can use mine if you like, I don't mind,' said Bryony. It would be her final act of penance.

'I'd rather not,' said Annie, 'but thanks.'

83

A rich, full life

Back on the village high street, Bryony felt deeply self-conscious; the wicked witch strolling back into Oz. She scanned passers-by for familiar faces and dirty glances, imagined mutterings from the mums doing judo pick-up outside the church hall. Nobody seemed perturbed by her presence, or to have even noticed it, but it must be only a matter of time before one of the Brixworth Sixworth rounded a corner and pushed her into the duck pond.

She turned to Annie to say goodbye. One hand was inside her tote bag clutching the flat, tissue-wrapped parcel that she had not yet found the right moment to hand over. Bryony steeled herself. Their talk seemed to have healed the breach, however crudely, and this was only going to blow it back open.

'Annie, there's one more—'

'Are you coming, then?' Annie asked, breezily.

'Coming where?'

'To Ann's.'

Bryony wondered if this were the final test and if she were about to fail. Would a hidden camera crew leap out from the shrubbery, lead by Marco with a microphone? Was there an invisible electric fence? A restraining order?

'I really don't think that's the best idea. I can't imagine your mum wants to see me, of all people. I'd hate to trigger anything for her, especially today, before . . .' She trailed off, hands growing clammy on the tissue paper.

Annie only blinked at her and said, 'You're quite self-involved, aren't you, Bryony?'

She didn't say it viciously, just matter-of-factly, as though noticing a birthmark. Bryony stammered for a response, but in the end could only laugh.

'I'm working on it,' she said.

'I told Ann I was meeting you, and she said to bring you back afterwards. It's all hands on deck before tomorrow – and you have hands.'

Bryony let go of the diary and pulled her hands out of her bag. She waved them to confirm that yes, she did.

At the Slingsbys they were met with familiar chaos.

Assembled neighbours and family members filled the kitchen and the hallway beyond, some carrying armfuls of flowers, balloons and craft materials, others drinking tea with a leisurely air. Two half-eaten pieces of burnt toast were abandoned on the kitchen counter in a valley of crumbs, along with an open bottle of milk and a mountain of half-peeled potatoes. In the sink, several paintbrushes were soaking alongside what looked like a pan of burnt cheese.

Ann was nowhere to be seen, and nor – she sent up a silent prayer of thanks – was Steve. A couple of people looked up as she and Annie appeared at the door, but no collective hush of horror swept through the room at the sight of Bryony. Nobody shouted, or threw things. She gave a feeble wave to no one in particular and tried to walk into the room with purpose.

Framed photos of Ed filled every available surface. They varied in size in an assortment of frames, suggesting half the residents of

Little Buckton had turfed out their own family to lend them for the occasion. There was Ed as a gap-toothed boy, a rangy teen, a beaming, apple-cheeked baby. Ed on his travels, Ed at the football, Ed in a crisp shirt and lanyard on some kind of company away day. Ed delivering his speech at – presumably – Kelly and Leo's wedding, in a French navy waistcoat that brought out his eyes. Bryony took them all in as though they were an art exhibit, moving slowly, pausing to give each one the respect it deserved.

There was a single photo of him from her era, taken at a day festival on August bank holiday weekend, which she knew because he had arrived to meet her late that night, smelling of cut grass and burnt onions. The next morning she'd laughed at his tan lines, the tender lobster of his arms and neck making it look as though he was wearing a milky-white t-shirt.

'Are you familiar with SPF?' she had said, half scornful, half teasing, and Ed had protested – he'd worn some, he swore, but he must have sweated it off and she'd asked what factor and he'd said twenty and she'd squeaked in camp disapproval.

'You need to look after yourself better,' she had told him and Ed had grinned and said, 'Why? Do you worry about me?'

Bryony had scoffed, swatted at his sunburn and said absolutely not. And when he'd laughed and pulled her back down on top of her almost-clean sheets, she'd felt yesterday's sun still hot on his skin.

'Bryony!'

Susan's voice crashed through the memory and she felt her cheeks flame. 'Hold this will you?' With no further warning, Susan handed her Twinkle, who snorted in displeasure. 'She keeps walking through the mosaic.'

Susan disappeared back into the hallway before Bryony could explain her presence. She staggered a little under the weight of old dog, grateful for a furry shield to hide behind.

'This all looks wonderful,' she told Annie, and Annie nodded in agreement.

'Yeah, Ann's outdone herself. We wanted this to be a proper celebration, you know? Not serious and miserable like the funeral.'

Bryony thought back to the funeral, at which a man in a football strip had read a passage from *The Beano* and said, 'Absolutely. Lovely plan.'

'Glad you approve, Bryony!' came Ann's voice from somewhere behind her. Bryony jumped, Twinkle leaping out of her arms and making a bid for freedom. 'Come here, ducks.'

Ann hugged her as tightly as she ever had, and it didn't feel like forgiveness so much as a consolation prize. Until then, she hadn't considered the possibility that Ann might see her as the victim in all this, pining for a love that had never existed.

Eventually she slapped Bryony on the shoulder, then pulled away to examine her.

'You look well,' Ann concluded. 'Fuller around the face.'

Bryony spent the next couple of hours 'mucking in' as best she could – folding programmes, blowing up balloons, arranging daffodils in vases, hovering behind people saying, 'Can I help at all?' without finding out how she might do so. There was no special attention paid to her, which was a relief, and nobody seemed to question her presence either, which was a bigger one. Annie's words – 'You're quite self-involved, aren't you, Bryony?' – played on a loop in her head. It seemed as useful a mantra as any.

The weather had taken a golden turn and after a while the helpers spilled out into the garden, shrugging off jumpers and gilets, admiring Ann's crocuses and lifting their faces to the sun. Bryony did the same and the unfamiliar warmth on her cheeks felt like a spa treatment.

'I've never known a winter as long as that one,' said Lynn, and everyone *mmmm*-ed in agreement.

'Aslan is on the move,' intoned Old Les Trindle.

Mercifully there was still no Steve. Kelly and Leo arrived just after the bulk of the preparations had been done, bearing fish and chips and ultrasound photos, which prompted a frenzy of cooing and vinegar-dousing. She took Kelly aside to tell her the deed was done.

'Thank fuck for that,' muttered Kelly. 'And she's really out of it? Will she lose all the money?'

'The newspaper are going to cover her exit costs, in exchange for going on the record,' Bryony told her. 'Apparently it's next to impossible to get these things actually shut down, but I think Annie's seen the light – and the exposé ought to draw a line under it. Just keep an eye on her, yeah? Don't let her fall into anything else.'

'Yeah,' said Kelly, her flawless forehead furrowed in concern. 'Fair enough. I never wanted her to be humiliated, I just didn't understand why we were all enabling her instead of telling her the truth. It seemed cruel.'

Bryony was compelled to agree. Then Kelly hugged her and the force caused Bryony to stumble a little in surprise. She hoped she didn't still smell of Twinkle.

'Thanks hun,' Kelly said. 'I know you probably think I'm pathetic, that I couldn't help her myself . . . I just . . . well, families are weird aren't they?'

'Bizarre,' she agreed.

'How are you feeling, by the way?' asked Kelly.

Bryony was surprised to find the answer wasn't readily at hand. She paused and performed a quick body scan, but found nothing. On the battleground, a ceasefire had been called.

'Uh, fine? I think? Nothing to report right now.'

'Good,' said Kelly.

'I'm having therapy,' she offered, because she felt that of all people, Kelly should know.

'Well, thank the lord,' said Kelly, grinning.

'Anyway, shouldn't I be asking you how you're feeling?'

'Oh, still shite,' replied Kelly. 'I want to put my head down right now on one of those battered haddocks and sleep for the next five months. But it's fine, it's only temporary.'

'Exactly,' said Bryony. 'This too shall pass. It'll be worth it.'

'It will,' said Kelly and Bryony followed her gaze to where Leo was proudly holding the little black and white photo up next to one of Ed's, debating the traits of the Slingsby nose with Brown Owl Wendy.

She looked more sentimental than Bryony had seen her before, as she added, 'And I swear to God, that fucker is doing every single nappy change to repay me.'

Most of the helpers beat a hasty retreat once the food was finished and Bryony came out of the downstairs loo to find that everyone except the family had gone. She could hear Annie and Leo sharing stories about Ed in the living room – 'And the way he believed gherkins in McDonalds burgers were sliced frog until he was, like, twelve!' – so she quietly gathered her coat and bag and prepared to slip away through the kitchen. It felt like the classiest thing to do, in the circumstances. An Irish exit, or a French exit, or whichever term was least offensive.

'Are you leaving us, Bryony?'

It was Ann, wearing marigolds and too-big Crocs, coming in from feeding batter scraps to the chickens.

'Yes, I think I ought to be going,' said Bryony. 'But it's been lovely to see you all again. Thank you for having me.'

'Bryony,' Ann said, 'I've told you about that phrase. Anyway,' she added, her expression shifting a little, 'from what I understand it's us that's been had.'

She said the words lightly, but they cut deep. Bryony took a long, shaky breath before beginning the third in her apology trilogy. The one it felt most important to get right.

'I'm so sorry, Ann.'

She resisted the urge to bluster and gush, to get defensive or dilute the sentiment with self-flagellation.

'Of course you are, pet.'

'I hope you know there was nothing malicious in it. I simply had no idea how to tell you that Ed and I weren't ... like that. Or at least, not as far as I realized.'

Ann flapped a hand at her in a vague way that might have meant anything. She sat down and gestured for Bryony to do the same. From under a pile of leaflets and newspapers, Ann uncarthed a box of Matchmakers and took one, then pushed them towards her. They both sat, dragging on little chocolate sticks as though they were cigarettes.

Eventually she said, 'Do you know the hardest part of being a parent, Bryony? It isn't all the things you have to do for them. It's all things you *can't* do for them.'

Irrationally this brought to mind not her own mother, or even her father, but her Victorian grandfather, Marco, and his loving exasperation from the sidelines.

'I remember the first time Ethy went off to cubs camp, he couldn't tie his shoelaces. And he was so scared the other boys would tease him, or the leader would tell him off for holding everyone up – you know what a considerate boy he was—'

This was a verbal tic Ann couldn't seem to drop, even now she knew the truth. Bryony was relieved to be able to smile fondly and say with all honesty that yes, she did know what a considerate boy he was. A pleasant human male.

'Anyway, it became this whole drama. And we practised and we practised and we learned the bunny-ears method and we made up rhymes to help him remember, but despite all my best efforts, by the time the day came round he still couldn't do it. So I waved him off on that coach with my heart in my throat, Bryony, hoping he'd somehow figure it out. Wishing I could just tuck myself into his bag and pop out every morning to tie them for him.'

Bryony nodded, privately wondering why he couldn't have had velcro. Maybe it was something to do with Northampton's shoe-making tradition.

'Anyway, the first night he rang home and he was *so* excited to tell me—'

'He'd learned to tie them?'

'No,' said Ann. 'He'd realized if he just loosened the laces and trod the backs down a bit he could slide his trainers on and off without undoing them. That was Ethy – always a problem-solver. But he was a lateral thinker, Bryony. Loved to find a workaround.'

'That makes sense,' said Bryony, although the moral of this tale made very little sense to her.

'And it turned out I'd been so fixated on those bloody shoelaces when I should have been sorting out his bedwetting. He came home two days early because he'd pissed through to his mattress. *Anyway*, the point is, all I ever wanted for my boy was to find love and be happy. And so Ethy – well, I suppose he found a way to give me that.' Ann's eyes bugged with meaning as she added, 'Laterally.'

And then it did make sense, of a kind. To Ann's mind, Ed hadn't lied about their relationship so much as given his mother another gift she would cherish but never use. Call it a generous interpretation or a maternal blind spot, but she would rather think of him trussing up the truth to please her than being emotionally stunted or deficient in some way.

And Steve had been right. Of course Steve had been right. We're always somebody's child.

'So you don't think he was actually in love with me?' She had to ask it.

'Oh Bryony, I have no idea. If *you* don't know, then I'm not sure any of us ever will.'

She thought of the diary, which was now safely tucked into a pile on a shelf in the hallway cupboard, between a David Hockney desk calendar and an adult colouring book. Not a perfect solution, but it did have a kind of poetry to it. She felt proud of having respected Ed's privacy, even while she suspected the main reason she hadn't read it was because she would rather hold on to the possibility of having been loved. On both scores, it seemed nicer not to know for sure.

She must have looked crestfallen, because Ann clutched her by the hand and added, 'But he certainly thought you were worthy of telling us all about, anyway! All your achievements, your volunteering, all those wonderful hobbies. You have a rich, full life Bryony.'

By rights she supposed she should correct this narrative too. But then, what was the harm? She had come to love the version of herself reflected in Ed's mythology. Even if she didn't have the rich, full life of legend, she had a rich, full life by most people's standards and there was nothing to stop her adding a few hobbies into the mix. She wondered when Laura's pottery club night was next on.

'Well,' she said, squeezing Ann's hand back. 'That's a comforting thought.'

'And you're sure you won't stay for tomorrow?'

'No,' said Bryony. 'I don't think I will. But thank you. I know it'll be beautiful.'

84

Brave and stupid and gorgeous

In the middle of the night, wide awake on Ann's sofa bed while Leo snores beside her, Kelly is struck by a craving for white toast with a slice of cold cheese on top.

'Craving' isn't the right word, though, because 'craving' implies desire, whereas what she feels is more like a medical necessity. She is consumed by the need to consume white toast with a slice of cold cheese on top. If she doesn't have white toast with a slice of cold cheese on top right now, she might ... die?

Shuffling into the kitchen, she is surprised to find her mother-in-law, who she thought had gone to bed hours ago, sitting in her dressing gown at the table. She is popping bubble wrap, the way other people might knit or do a crossword. Ann looks up as she walks in and smiles, as though they have a pre-arranged meeting.

'Hello ducks. Can't sleep?'

Kelly shakes her head. She wants to explain about the toast and cheese emergency, but she knows Ann will insist on making it for her and she will make it wrong, lavishly buttering the bread and putting it under the grill and sullying it with Lea & Perrins or something – and to her tyrannical diva stomach, this would be worse than not eating it at all.

'Sleep when you're pregnant is both a curse and a con,' announces Ann, cheerfully. 'Nobody tells you that. You're so tired, and it's all "sleep now, while you can!", but nobody bloody warns you that your brain and your legs and your bladder have other ideas. My ex-husband used to find me weeding the garden at four a.m. Got worried I was licking soil off the potatoes. Which I was, from time to time, but really it was just the only way to stop the mind spiders, you know. And we didn't know about toxoplasmosis then,' she says. Kelly adds this to her mental list of terrifying words to Google later. Ann passes her a sheet of bubbles and they sit for a while, popping together.

'So what is it tonight?' asks Ann, after a few minutes.

'Oh, nothing,' says Kelly. 'Just normal stuff. Hoping the baby's okay. Thinking about all the things that can go wrong.'

She ends the sentence there, although there are any number of ways to complete it. Things that can go wrong with the pregnancy, with the birth, with her marriage. Things that can go wrong in the near future, the distant future, the world at large. Things that could go wrong for the child, even after she is gone, on a burning planet where bodies fail and bullies win and free-flying wasps fill the sky. Worries that might be quieted, even just for a few minutes, by a piece of white toast with a slice of cold cheese on top. Kelly looks longingly towards the fridge.

'I've never known you be a worrier, Kelly.'

Kelly hasn't known herself to be a worrier either, not before the trying began. She hasn't known herself to lie awake at night turning over doomy possibilities in her mind, or to Google things like toxoplasmosis. She is seemingly a stranger now, growing around another stranger, and this matryoshka doll of unknowns is what feels so disorienting. She expected to be responsible for one new person, but nobody said anything about two.

'Whatever it is, spit it out,' says Ann, without looking at her. 'Give it a good airing. You know me, I'm unshockable.'

Kelly does know Ann. She is about to deflect some more, but then something inside her softens and relents, and something else rises to the challenge. If Ann wants honesty, she can have honesty.

'It's not just being pregnant,' she tells her. 'Although that is a headfuck, I can't lie. I guess I was so focused on wanting it to happen that I wasn't really prepared for what it would be like if it did.'

Ann nods. 'Well Kelly, I can't say I identify completely – as you know, I barely had to take my socks off near my ex-husband and I was immediately up the duff—'

Regrettably, Kelly does know this. Ann's fertility is the stuff of family legend.

'But it's everything that comes afterwards,' she interrupts, feeling that her window for vulnerability is rapidly closing. 'Having to look after it, follow all the rules and the advice and buy the right stuff and do the right stuff and keep it safe every single day, it just feels impossible. Sometimes I'm scared – well, convinced to be honest with you – that the baby will . . . er.'

Only as she approaches the end of the sentence does the hazard sign flash up in her mind. *Crass and tactless, turn back!*

She stalls.

'Die?' finishes Ann.

'Yes,' whispers Kelly.

Ann hoots with laughter, loudly but not unkindly. 'Oh Kelly, love! Everyone thinks they're going to accidentally kill their baby.'

'Do they?'

'Of course they do! Totally normal. In fact, it's the people who *don't* worry about accidentally killing their baby who want to worry. As long as you have a modicum of terror at all times, you'll be grand.'

Kelly nods, gratefully. 'Noted.'

'Besides, everyone fucks it up, that's part of the process. I once left Antigone in the loos at BHS and didn't even notice until they announced it over the tannoy. Ethy singed his eyebrows off during my crêpes Suzette phase. Gally got dropped on his head, for God's sake! Multiple times! They're far more resilient than you think. But more to the point, so are *you*.'

Then Ann cups her face, a gesture Kelly has seen her enact on her children hundreds of times but has never received herself before.

'Listen to me, pet. I know this is hard. I know it's a thousand times harder than you imagined it would be and you haven't even started yet.'

Kelly opens her mouth to protest – not *a thousand times*, that seems excessive, she's honestly fine – but shuts it again when she sees Ann's expression. To stop Ann mid-pep talk is to mess with the natural order of the universe, she knows that much. She closes her eyes and feels that sincerity warming her cheeks like the sun.

'I know you feel guilty for wasting even a minute of it. I know you don't want to admit you feel like shit when anyone with eyes can *see* you feel like shit . . .'

Kelly tries not to take this personally. Her neck is beginning to ache in Ann's grip and she needs to pee again.

'. . . but I'm telling you right now, Kelly, feeling guilty is the only true waste of time in this life. Look, I could be tearing myself apart right now thinking about every time I yelled at my Ethy, every time I suspended his pocket money or sent him out to play in the rain because I wanted half an hour to myself, or nagged him about getting a girlfriend, or told him he was being a blithering prick. But I'm not because sometimes he *was* being a blithering prick, and that's the truth of it. And I wouldn't have had him any other way.'

Ann's voice cracks and Kelly pictures her brother-in-law – the proud, sweet, earnest uncle he would have made. Does the baby need water, or a jumper?

'I read a thing about the placenta,' she begins, wanting to say something comforting and reaching for the closest thing she can think of. 'Apparently scientists have found that our cells—'

But Ann interrupts her. 'Parenting isn't science, Kelly! It's *art*. It's messy and inexact and there are no right answers, only gut feeling and ego. The world doesn't need any more of us and still we keep on having a go anyway, trying to make these little people that are better versions of ourselves. And feeling shit now is only the start of it. Because whoever's in there, my blessed grandchild—'

Ann doesn't grab Kelly's stomach but hovers her hands over it, as though warming them in front of a fire. '. . . well, I guarantee, Kelly, they're going to break your heart and your favourite vase and obliterate your pelvic floor. There will be times when you will wonder why you did it at all, when you could have just left yourself intact and had a perfectly lovely life. There will be moments when you feel convinced the entire concept of parenthood is a con and you will want to *riot* in the *street* over it, yelling "who can I sue??"'

Kelly is holding her breath now, as well as her bladder. She prays that Ann has a 'but'.

'*But*, it's all the mess and the pain and the heartbreak that makes every bit in between so beautiful and so goddamn human. We just can't resist! Having children is like putting your heart in a rocket and sending it to space, just to feel it soar. It's a brave and stupid and gorgeous thing to do and I promise you won't regret a single minute of it.'

Finally Ann removes her hands, but only to wipe away the tears Kelly hadn't noticed she was crying.

'Now,' she says, 'are you hungry?'

'Yes,' says Kelly.

She tells Ann about the toast and Ann makes it for her, and she insists on buttering the bread and grating the cheese and sticking the whole lot under the grill until it is a pile of molten yellow lava. And when she serves it to Kelly, it isn't what she was craving at all. But it turns out to be exactly what she needs.

85

Why is it you?

Bryony sat on the train home, her cheek against the window, a book she was pretending to read in her lap.

Just then a large wasp appeared, buzzing laconically against the window right next to her head. It was squat and muscular-looking, apparently unaware it was the beginning of March or else willing to fight anyone who pointed it out. She heard Steve then, the way he'd said it in that first call. *Fucking climate change.*

Without thinking twice (although she did look around quickly to see if anyone else was watching), Bryony lifted the paperback in a salute to Ed and squashed the wasp, hearing and feeling the crunch as its sturdy body gave way between cardboard and glass. An alarming streak of purple blood, like thick Ribena, appeared against the window and across the back cover of her book. She was immediately horrified, mopping up the crime scene with a napkin and some antibacterial gel.

She googled: 'is it ok to kill wasps'.

'Wasps are being wiped out as quickly as bees – and their disappearance will be just as disastrous,' shouted a *Guardian* headline. Bryony sighed.

*

She got off the train with the weekend hordes, all bound for a big night in London. Letting herself be swept along in a sea of hen sashes and pre-theatre gin tins. It felt too sad to go straight home, against the direction of the tide. So she walked instead towards town, thinking about what she might have been doing tonight before the Great Friend Edit. Perhaps it wasn't too late to see if Agnes was up to something she could tag along to, or if Blod wanted to get a drink. She'd even take a panel talk.

She had stopped looking up at the evening sky and started peering at her phone when she walked smack into a man's chest, hitting her nose hard enough to leave her eyes watering.

'Fuck!' yelled Bryony. 'I'm so sorry!'

'Watch yourself!' yelled the chest's owner and when she looked up, it was Steve.

'Fuck!!' she yelled again.

Then, 'Why is it you?', which made no sense, but seemed correct in the moment. She could feel the brief warmth of him on her forehead.

'What are you doing here?'

'On my way back home, aren't I?' He gestured towards the station, a holdall swinging against his back. 'It's a nice night, so I thought I'd get off and walk for a bit. I hate the tube.'

That Steve would hate the tube was unsurprising – the tube was awful, Bryony knew, it was just that millions of Londoners had learned to go somewhere else, mentally, for a portion of every day of their lives.

'Have you been down for work again?' she asked, trying to check that the wetness seeping from her nose wasn't blood. It was throbbing quite badly. Was it broken? Was this karmic retribution for the wasp?

Steve nodded. 'Actually I'm renting Ethel's old room.'

'In Acton?'

'Hammersmith.'

'Sure.'

'Just for a month or two, until this job's done,' he said. 'Wasn't strictly necessary but I fancied a change of scene. You know, get out of my comfort zone.'

She grinned in approval.

'I thought it might be nice to retrace his footsteps a bit too, I dunno,' added Steve. 'Maybe that's weird and morbid.'

'No,' said Bryony, 'I don't think that's weird, or morbid. I think it's really nice. I'm sure Ed would like to think of you living there.'

Whether she'd in any way earned the right to make proclamations on what Ed would or wouldn't like, she wasn't sure, but Steve seemed to allow it. Bryony pictured the anonymous grey box of a room and wondered if it looked any different under Steve's jurisdiction. She tried not to picture the bed, or Ed watching over it like a winged pervert.

'Hang on though, it's Saturday,' she said. 'I thought the room was a Monday to Friday arrangement?'

'Yeah, it is. I stayed at someone else's last night,' Steve shrugged, sounding strenuously casual. But there was a smile playing at the corners of his mouth. So! He was on the apps. She already knew this, she reminded herself. He was enjoying the apps! Good for Steve.

'Oh, right,' she said, and realized she was grinning in spite of a few other feelings unfurling themselves in her gut. 'I see. Good for you.'

Another man might have looked pleased with himself, or embarrassed for Bryony, but Steve didn't. He didn't look embarrassed for himself either – just matter-of-fact. He had kissed Bryony two months ago, and had sex with someone else last night and the sky was blue and the tube was horrible and that was simply the way things were. This open-palmed honesty prompted a response in Bryony that she would later identify, with Lisa, as arousal. Honesty was her new kink.

Steve grinned back and said, 'Yeah, well. When a tourist . . .'

'Oh, totally,' she replied quickly. 'Got to take in the sights!'

He did have the manners to blush then, though she sensed more at her joke than the situation.

'Nobody who knew Ed, this time,' he added. 'Seemed simpler.'

'Mm,' she agreed. 'Sensible.'

'Look, Bryony,' said Steve, and although she had known the 'look, Bryony' was coming, it was no less horrifying when it arrived.

'I wanted to say, after you – after we . . . well, both times . . .'

Lalalala! she wanted to shout, ramming her fingers into her ears. *Shutupshutupshutup.* Hearing Steve reference the kiss, or the non-kiss, the hasty flee from both – all of that would be worse, far worse, than living through all of it again. For a moment she felt convinced that if he even said the word 'kiss' she would burst into flames on Euston Road and trigger some kind of terrorist response procedure.

'Oh god, don't apologise!' she bleated, trying to craft a verbal fire blanket. 'It was stupid, I was very drunk – you were absolutely right to leg it.'

'No you weren't,' he said.

'What?'

'You weren't drunk.'

'Oh. No. Yes, you're right, I wasn't,' she said, remembering. 'But still, it was a mistake, and inappropriate, and so disrespectful to Ed, and it shouldn't have happened the first time, and I *definitely* shouldn't have tried to make it happen again, and I'm . . . I'm sorry.'

Steve waited patiently for her to run out of steam, then said, 'I was going to say, I'm sorry for legging it like I did. It was seriously rude. And disrespectful to you, actually.'

'Oh,' she said, considering this. 'Yeah, I suppose it was. Thank you.'

'I just – I panicked,' said Steve. 'The whole night, the gig, I wasn't sure if you were actually into it, or if you were just being nice.'

'I wouldn't have gone if I wasn't into it,' said Bryony, and Steve studied her from beneath a raised eyebrow and said, 'Wouldn't you?'

'Fine, maybe I would have done,' she conceded. 'But I wouldn't have tried to kiss you, would I?'

She marvelled at her own maturity, saying the word. No flames burst. No sirens sounded.

'True,' said Steve. 'But by that point I'd convinced myself it was off the cards and that it was for the best. And the music, talking so much about Ed – I kind of felt like he was there with us, you know? So then when you . . . well, it really threw me for a loop and I panicked. I'm sorry, I tend to get a bit in my own head about things.'

'Then what about New Year's Day? You didn't even know about the whole girlfriend charade at that point. I did, but you didn't.'

'Yeah, very fucked up,' said Steve, simply. 'Fucked up of *me*. I've spent the past few months feeling like the worst person in the world. But hey, it's not like there are exactly rules for this situation.' He coloured and smiled a little. 'And I *did* like you first. If an app like counts for anything.'

She smiled too. 'Technically you "took a shine to" me first.'

'Right,' he nodded, grinning.

'Although that was before you discovered I'm a fraud and a lunatic with a borderline drinking problem.'

Mercifully, Steve laughed. Then he looked coy again and said, 'But Bryony – you never liked me back.'

She cringed at how juvenile the conversation sounded. But perhaps it was appropriate, given that contemporary dating had reduced finding love to a rudimentary platform game. Scoring points, levelling up, collecting interested parties like golden mushrooms. Losing interest and quitting halfway through because dinner is ready. She cast her mind back to Steve's Alloi profile and it was hard to say now why Ed had made it through level one when Steve hadn't. Steve's photos weren't any more or less attractive, although of course now they were all filtered through familiarity. His answers all read differently now too, their gaps in charisma coloured in by knowledge of the man behind them. A pleasant, human male.

'No,' she replied, honestly. 'I'm afraid I'm very shallow on the apps.'

Steve seemed to accept this as her failing, not his. Or maybe it was Big Dating's failing and they were both entirely blameless.

'So,' she said. 'I guess you're going back for the memorial?'

He nodded, then looked down at her bag and asked, not without alarm, 'Are you too?'

Bryony shook her head. 'I think I'll leave it for the people that really knew Ed. Don't want to be weird about it. Besides, I've spent enough on West Midlands Trains for a lifetime.'

'They don't make a railcard for fake widows?' asked Steve.

'Shockingly not.'

'Discrimination,' he said and she laughed.

'Well, look,' he said, and she didn't mind this 'look' as much. 'I'd better head for my train, I've only got six minutes. But I'm really glad we bumped into each other, Bryony. Literally.'

He rubbed the spot on his chest where her face had made contact, and she realized her nose had stopped throbbing. It probably wasn't broken, she decided.

'Me too,' she said. 'It's very weird that we did. Like something from a romcom with a lazy screenwriter.'

'I'll take your word for it,' said Steve. 'I only really watch action films.'

As she was wrestling with the urge to write him off for this transgression, Steve went in for a hug. His arms enveloped Bryony whole and, rather than patting her shoulder or rubbing her back or anything else friendly and mortifying, he simply held her for a while, perfectly still. She pressed her cheek gladly into his sweatshirt.

It became clear at some point during the hug that there was to be no kissing today. But knowing this only made her want to linger there for longer, breathing in salt and earth and detergent – not, she realized in relief, the same one Ed (or Ann) had used. Eventually it seemed polite to pull away and as she did so Steve ducked his head and landed a kiss somewhere between her cheek, ear and neck. It burned there like a dropped ember.

'Promise me you're not going to be a stranger, yeah?' he said, squeezing her hand as he stepped away.

'I promise,' she said. 'And Steve?'

He turned back, his timing curiously on point for a man who never watched romcoms.

'Wish Ed happy birthday for me,' she said.

86

It's always been like that

After she watched him disappear into the crowd around the station, Bryony took her phone out – stepping safely into a shop doorway this time – and called Marco.

'Why are you phoning me? You never phone, you're scared of phoning. Who died?'

'I'm allowed to phone you,' she said, indignant.

'BRYONY FOR FUCK'S SAKE, WHO HAS DIED?'

'Nobody,' she said hurriedly, hearing the real panic in his voice. She tried to sound soothing. 'Nobody has died. That I know of. I promise, everything is fine.'

'Okay,' breathed Marco. 'Okay. Then what do you want?'

'I want to know if you're busy tonight.'

'Yes,' said Marco. 'I saw your blue dot was in Northamptonshire. I was going spend some quality time in the bathroom and list out your room on AirBnB.'

'But it's Saturday. It's a nice evening, feels like spring is actually coming. Do you want to get drinks?'

'Brian, we never get drinks.'

'Well, I'm asking you to,' she said, patiently. 'Marco, will you go for a drink with me?'

*

They met at a pub halfway between town and home, somewhere she'd never been before but he regarded as one of his favourites. It was on a back street in the no-man's-land where Islington turns into Haringey – a narrow, one-room Victorian place with original tiling and an elderly honky-tonk duo playing in a corner.

'Who do you come here with?' she asked. 'I love it.'

'People,' said Marco, vaguely. 'Don't go bringing dates here, okay? I won't have you ruining it.'

She promised she wouldn't, then told him about Steve. The kiss, the non-kiss, the question mark of a relationship that now existed firmly in a holding pen of lingering hugs. If a part of her was hoping Marco might say, 'I knew it! I knew from the moment I saw him that you two were destined to be together,' she was to be disappointed. Marco merely sucked air through his teeth and said, 'Well, *that's* messy.'

'So messy.'

He took a long slug of wine, clearly relishing his own restraint, before adding, 'But hey, life is short.'

'Does that mean: life is short, he might be my soulmate,' she asked, 'or: life is short, why not bone the dead guy's best friend?'

'I don't know, you tell me,' he said. 'Is Steve The One?'

'Oh, I wouldn't have thought so,' said Bryony.

'Probably not,' he agreed.

They sipped and they sat, watching the patrons at the bar shuffling and swaying in time to the double bass. A few looked as though they threatened to start dancing. Bryony wondered if she and Marco might dance, too, in a while; put their phones away and drag each other up on their feet, holding hands and relishing in the ordinary strangeness of enjoying each other's company outside their own kitchen. It might be nice.

'By the way,' she said. 'Does my nose look broken?'

'No.' Marco replied without looking. 'It's always been like that.'

Bryony accepted this and raised her glass. 'A toast, to Ed. Happy birthday for tomorrow.'

'Happy birthday, Egg Man,' said Marco. 'A remarkable man, after all.'

Epilogue

In the end, it is a girl.

Kelly goes into labour ten days early, while she is at work and Leo is at a company away day in Margate, wearing a Hawaiian shirt and limboing under a bamboo cane to demonstrate good leadership. He had been hesitant about going, but Kelly had shooed him out the door that morning.

'For fuck's sake, go! What else are you going to do, sit under my desk all day massaging my feet?' she had said, knowing full well that he would if she asked. And because that old, superstitious part of her believed that the further away she sent her husband, the more likely the baby was to appear. So, he goes and an hour later so do her waters, the biblical gush that the antenatal class had promised only happened in films.

After she calls him, feeling as though she is reading from a script – *Woman in labour (agitated)* – she calls Ann, barely noticing she is doing so until her mother-in-law answers the phone on the second ring, yelling, 'IS IT TIME?'

Somehow Ann manages to make it down from Northamptonshire in half the time it takes Leo to get back from Kent, leading Kelly to wonder if she has been camped out at a local hotel. She charges in with her sleeves rolled up and looks disappointed to find Kelly fully clothed and watching *Selling Sunset,* rather than naked in the bathtub, lowing like a dairy cow. She looks even more disappointed when her son arrives to assume his role of birth partner and he does not faint, not even once, not even hours later when his daughter's perfect meatball of a head bursts forth, jellied and screaming.

Between contractions Kelly finds herself telling everyone about her job, which is strange and quite out of character. The man on the front desk of the delivery ward, the hospital porter, the midwives – especially the midwives, whose brisk, no-frills, 'I've seen it all before!' attitude she finds deeply comforting – for some reason it becomes very important to her in those moments, those vanishing snatches of time where she can still do a passable impression of herself, that they know what she does for a living. She wants them to know that she has absorbed the public's pain and spittle and fury, has mopped their blood off a laminated poster, looked at their rashes and comforted their wives. She needs the staff to know that she is, even in her minor supporting role, one of them.

'You must be hard as nails,' says the woman with a blue-gloved hand inside her, checking for centimetres dilated (four). 'I couldn't do it.'

Though her doula services are not required, Ann does find a use for herself, as both bouncer and official head of comms, fielding enquiries from half of Little Buckton and advocating fiercely for Kelly when a zealous midwife tries to persuade her that she does not want an epidural.

'You're almost there! You're so strong, Kelly, I know you can do this! Your body knows what to do! You can do this on your own!' she trills. Kelly whimpers and sobs in submission and Ann snaps.

'My daughter is strong enough to know her own mind!' she roars, and even in the locked jaws of her pain, Kelly notices she's omitted the 'in-law' and feels touched. 'There are no trophies for suffering! *Give her the drugs.*'

They do, and the relief is exquisite. Her legs become lead and time becomes treacle and 'almost there' turns into hours. Hours of letting the waves crash over her and outside the sun rises and it seems absurd to know that soon people will be getting up and going to work as though everything is normal, when nothing will ever be normal again. Every time she looks at Leo, it is all over his face, the stupefied admiration and adoration she wanted, though after a while even this gets annoying and she sends him to the vending machine for a break from being adored.

When he comes back bearing crisps, his wife has gone and in her place is an animal with a bit between its teeth and a brave new world between its legs and she is no longer beneath the waves but riding them, screaming, to shore. And finally there is another small woman roaring in the room and Kelly wonders how she could ever have thought any other voice mattered.

They name her, not Ethel, but Margot Ann Slingsby.

'Why would you give her such a dull middle name? It's beyond me,' says Ann, stately on the only chair in the hospital room, her arms full of swaddled infant.

'We like it,' says Kelly. 'I think plain names are making a comeback.'

When they're all home and suitably medicated and Ann can hold back the tide of visitors no longer, in they roll. Annie, sobbing before she is even through the door, bearing news of her new coaching course and confirming with joy that Margot has her uncle's eyes. Kelly's father and brother, both moist-eyed and croaking with the effort of keeping their feelings in check, taking it all out on Leo's shoulder instead. Bryony and Steve, who make an enthusiastic show of pretending to have bumped into each other on the doorstep.

Susan, Susan's Bob, Cousin Chloe, Chloe's Bob, Fake Auntie Merle and assorted other chorus members are marched in for their allotted hour of cooing, then firmly kicked out again. For two – three? – days Kelly sits, sore and dazed and delighted and lets the chaos soothe her like white noise.

'How do you feel?' the visitors ask, when they remember to. She tells them, 'Well!', although her definition of the word has changed and its meaning stretched beyond comprehension. Is she well? She feels flayed. She has a beating heart in her arms and a mattress in her knickers. Still, food tastes like food again, which is the second-best gift of all.

Then, on day five, just as the sleeplessness and hormonal come-down are compounding in spectacular fashion, Ann leaves. She slips away with minimal fanfare, leaving a pair of breast pads in the freezer and several inedible meals in the fridge.

'It takes a village,' quips Leo. He hands his wife the mono-grammed water bottle he has refilled for the eighth time that day. Then, with a pleased flourish, he places an old fashioned in a crystal tumbler on the coffee table.

'Drink that,' he says, 'then you can have this.'

So Kelly drinks while the baby does, obedient, letting the water flood her desiccated insides, relishing the sweet medicinal burn of the booze. She strokes the downy cheek and pleads with her daughter to open wider, wider, latch better, drink more. Is she still hungry? Warm enough? Too warm? Was that a cough?

Sometimes Kelly can still feel the baby's kick inside her, which the midwives explain away as retracting muscles but she thinks is something else entirely. The tug of a rope, now as long as the world.

As Margot sleeps, she watches the rise and fall of the perfect dumpling form against her chest. Is she well? Kelly breathes her in, deeply, then exhales.

Acknowledgements

I'd like to begin with some health advice: don't write a book and have a baby in the same year, it's a terrible idea. But if you must, you'd better hope you have a team behind you as patient and brilliant as mine.

It is such a nice thing, to find an editor whose notes make me smile rather than sulk for three days. Thank you to the magnificent Molly Crawford, for knowing what this book needed better than I did, and for handling my neuroses as skilfully as my manuscript.

To my wonderful agent, Jemima Forrester, and all at David Higham Associates. Thank you for filling me with ideas (and halloumi) every time I think there are no words left. I'm so lucky to have you in my corner.

Thank you to Jessica Barratt, Sarah Jeffcoate and Sara-Jade Virtue for your infectious passion and enthusiasm, and to Maddie Allen, Naomi Burt, Heather Hogan, Mina Asaam and all at Simon & Schuster for your hard work spreading the book around like a (nice) seasonal flu. Thanks to Nia Bragg for your thoughtful copy-edit, Paul Simpson for your proofread and for letting me keep all my most self-indulgent jokes. Thank you Pip Watkins and Eva Bee for creating this delicious vitamin-C shot of a cover.

Gratitude as always to my wonderful parents and my extended network of Bravos, Brennans, Cliftons and beyond, for being endlessly supportive − verging on, but never quite tipping into,

Ann-like behaviour. Tom and Dan, I promise the next book won't have a dead brother in it.

I'm so grateful to every single healthcare professional who has looked after this Monica Munchausen, especially during the last couple of years when I've been particularly demanding. Protect the NHS. Don't vote Tory.

This book owes a great debt to Lucy Jones and her masterful work in *Matrescence*. Lucy, I hope you don't mind that a few traces of its DNA are retained here. Thanks also to Margaret Cabourn-Smith's brilliant *Crushed* podcast, for inspiring Bryony's retro compatibility test.

Ewa's biting therapy is not a real thing, I made it up. Please don't try it at home.

To my beloved friends, I cannot stress this enough: you are all Marcos, not Maireads. I'm sorry I'm so bad at texting back. Please don't stop asking me to brunch.

I would have been a mad, milky husk of a human this past year (more so) without the Walthamstow Bump & Baby class of '22. Thanks guys, for filling those long days with laughter. I can only hope Kelly gets as lucky with her mum group as I did.

I'm fortunate to have so many great and generous writers in my life and DMs. In particular – Daisy Buchanan, Amy Jones, Clare Finney, Lucy Vine, Jessica Pan, Justin Myers, Caroline O'Donoghue, Kate Weston, Eva Rice, Becca Caddy, Helena Hamilton, Holly Bourne and others I've doubtless forgotten. Thanks for all the motivation, inspiration and pep talks.

Matt, forever my first reader. Thank you for propping me up, physically and metaphorically. Life is short. You can drink all the protein shakes you like, babe.

Finally, to Cora, our magic bean. Thank you for making everything brighter, louder, messier and a hundred times more fun. I blamed you for handing this book in late, several times – I hope that's okay.

About the author

Lauren Bravo is an author, journalist and lifelong hypochondriac who has written about fashion, popular culture, food and feminism for titles including *Grazia*, *Stylist*, *Vogue* and *Sunday Times Style*. Her debut novel, *Preloved*, was named one of *Red*'s best books of 2023. She lives in London with her husband and daughter.